"James writes smart, taut, high-octane thrillers. But be warned—his books are not for the timid. The endings blow me away every time."
—Mitch Galin, producer of Stephen King's *The Stand* and Frank Herbert's *Dune*

PRAISE FOR THE NOVELS OF STEVEN JAMES

Checkmate

"High tension all the way. James writes with precision and incisiveness. Fast, sharp, and believable. Put it at the top of your list."
—John Lutz, Edgar Award–winning author of *Single White Female* and *Frenzy*

"Steven James pens another fast-paced thriller chock-full of great characters, head-snapping plot twists, impeccable research, and a truly fun ride. Highly recommended. Not to be missed."
—D. P. Lyle, award-winning author of the Dub Walker and Samantha Cody thriller series

The King

"His tightly woven, adrenaline-laced plots leave readers breathless."
—The Suspense Zone

"Steven James offers yet another slam-dunk in the Bowers Files series!"
—*Suspense Magazine*

"Highly engaging with consuming tension and solid storytelling."
—TitleTrakk.com

continued . . .

"If you love edgy, intense, on-the-edge-of-horrifying coupled with great writing, then click and order this one now."   —Novel Reviews

Opening Moves

"A mesmerizing read. From the first chapter, it sets its hook deep and drags you through a darkly gripping story with relentless power. My conclusion: I need to read more of Steven James."

—Michael Connelly, *New York Times* bestselling author of *The Burning Room*

"Steven James has created a fast-moving thriller with psychological depth and gripping action. *Opening Moves* is a smart, taut, intense novel of suspense that reads like a cross between Michael Connelly and Thomas Harris . . . a blisteringly fast and riveting read."

—Mark Greaney, *New York Times* bestselling author of *Dead Eye*

"[A] high-octane thriller."   —*Suspense Magazine*

The Bishop

"The novel moves swiftly, with punchy dialogue but gruesome scenes. Readers must be ready to stomach the darkest side of humanity and get into the minds of serial killers to enjoy this master storyteller at the peak of his game."   —*Publishers Weekly*

"This novel is fresh and exciting."   —*Booklist*

"Absolutely brilliant."

—Jeff Buick, bestselling author of *One Child*

"Steven James locks you in a thrill ride with no brakes. He sets the new standard in suspense writing."

—*Suspense Magazine*

THE BOWERS FILES

EVERY CROOKED PATH

THE BOWERS FILES

STEVEN JAMES

A SIGNET SELECT BOOK

SIGNET SELECT
Published by New American Library,
an imprint of Penguin Random House LLC
375 Hudson Street, New York, New York 10014

This book is an original publication of New American Library.

First Printing, December 2015

ISBN 978-0-451-46735-5

Printed in the United States of America
10 9 8 7 6 5 4 3 2 1

Penguin
Random
House

To the National Center for Missing & Exploited Children

"Society prepares the crime: the criminal commits it."

—Found in a fortune cookie next to two smiley faces

Author's Note

Dear readers,

This is a work of fiction, and yet, in a very real sense, it also tells the truth about our world today. While the characters and situations in this story are made up, the nature of the crimes is not.

Online predators are real.

As a parent, I found this book particularly difficult to write, since it involved research into crimes against children. However, because of the impact of this issue on modern culture, I felt it was an important story for me to tell—perhaps my most important one so far.

Finding out what's really out there lurking online was a wake-up call to me. Rather than describe any exploitative images in this book, I chose to show the reactions of the characters to seeing them. I'll trust your imagination to fill in the rest.

During my research, I came across an organization called the National Center for Missing & Exploited Children. It's dedicated to rescuing children and catching those who target them. NCMEC is a nonprofit organization that depends on private donations, so please consider supporting their work. For more information, go to www.missingkids.com.

Together we can make a difference in protecting the next generation from those who would steal their innocence from them.

—Steven James
Autumn 2015

PART I

Masks

1

I clicked on my Mini Maglite as I slit the police tape criss-crossing the apartment's front door, swung it open, and stepped into the darkened living room.

Jodie and I would reseal the door after I was done in here.

I pocketed my automatic knife.

The NYPD's Crime Scene Unit had finished up this morning so the scene had been processed, but I put on a pair of latex gloves just in case I did find anything.

At thirty-four years old, I'd been with the Bureau for eight years, after leaving the Milwaukee Police Department, and I'd worked with evidence recovery teams and analysts from all around the country. The CSU here in New York City was sharp, so I wasn't necessarily looking for forensic evidence they might have missed; I doubted I would find any of that. I was here to look at context.

Though this would normally have been an NYPD case, because of my work with the joint task force, the

Bureau was involved. Assistant Director-in-Charge DeYoung had asked me to take a look around.

I'd been consulting on another investigation earlier today, so this was my first time at the actual scene, which worked out well since it was the same time of day as when the crime occurred. Similarity brings perspective. I'd taught that at the FBI Academy. Now was my chance to put it into practice.

Almost exactly twenty-four hours ago, the man who rented this apartment was stabbed to death in the room just past the kitchen.

Orienting myself to the lighting, the sounds, in this location at the time of day of the crime was crucial. It's always about the intersection of an offender being in a specific place at a specific time. Start there. Motives you can try to decipher later—if you venture in that direction at all. Most investigators go about things completely backward.

My partner, Special Agent Jodie Fleming, would be up in a few minutes. She was on the phone down by the car talking over a personal matter with Dell, the woman she was living with. Their relationship had hit a rough spot lately—actually, things had been going downhill for a while and I wasn't sure they were going to weather this storm.

The lights had been off in the apartment when the responding officers arrived, so, to get a better understanding of how the room had looked at the time of the crime, I kept them off as I closed the door, swept the flashlight beam before me, and studied the room.

Well-worn, mismatched furniture. A couch. An easy chair. Two floor lamps. The glass end table was still over-turned from the struggle. A wide-screen television looked out across the room from its mount on a swiveling arm on the wall. From studying the files, I knew that the win-

dows on the south side of the room overlooked a park—
even though it wasn't visible from where I stood.

The television was angled so that the screen was visible
from the reclining chair, rather than the couch that lay
perpendicular to it.

Two remote controls sat on the arm of the recliner. I
checked them—one matched the VCR player, one the
DVD player. A wireless keyboard for surfing on the TV's
Internet browser rested nearby on the footstool. The
television remote lay tossed haphazardly out of reach on
the couch.

Clicking off my flashlight, I noted how the residual
light from the city found its way into the room through
the windows.

The struggle that started in here had ended in the
master bedroom.

My specialty wasn't blood spatter analysis, but I'd looked
over the initial reports, and now, Maglite on again, I could
picture the struggle playing out.

At a crime scene, blood can tell the story.

The progression of the attack, the location and responses of the individuals involved—did they duck? Try to
run? Fight back? If there was a struggle, the blood spatter
could show who struck first, where he was standing, where
and how quickly he moved while he was trying to escape.
It was a study in microcosm of geospatial interactions.

And *that* was my specialty.

I watched the tale unfold.

According to what we'd been able to piece together,
the offender had accessed the apartment through the front
door, apparently, based on the tool marks, picking the
lock. The victim, a forty-two-year-old African-American
man named Jamaal Stewart, had been seated in the recliner
facing the television.

At some point the intruder must have startled him, because the blood spatter indicated that Jamaal was most likely rising from the chair when his arm was sliced.

Low-energy stains are created simply by the force of gravity and are circular. Impact spatter is more distinctive and happens when blood forcefully impacts a surface, so perhaps, from someone swinging his cut arm. The void patterns, that is, the absence of blood spatter where you would expect it, showed where the offender was standing during the struggle.

When studying blood spatter that's not just a gravity drop, you analyze the length and width, and take into account the concentration of the blood in the different parts of the spatter to identify the point of origin.

For an unknown reason, Jamaal fled to the master bedroom rather than the front door.

I studied the droplets, following them down the hall. Based on the size, shape, and directionality of the spatter, he was moving rapidly.

Since he had defensive wounds, we knew he'd struggled with his attacker. The orientation of the capillary and arterial bleeding showed that the fatal stab wound was to the right side of the neck, which might have indicated a left-handed assailant, or a right-handed one, depending on how he—or she—held the knife.

Jamaal bled out sprawled facedown on the covers of his neatly made bed.

Often, evidence isn't so much finding what is present, but what isn't present that should be—like the voids in the blood spatter. Emptiness where you wouldn't expect it speaks to you.

The CSU found a computer cord in the apartment, but no laptop. There was a cell phone charger here, but no cell phone. Also there were two Xbox controllers but no console and a VHS player and a DVD player, but no videocassettes or DVDs.

By all appearances, someone had taken all of Jamaal's computers and recorded media storage devices. When we followed up to see if the computer, phone, or gaming system had remote location services turned on, none of them showed up.

If our premise was correct that the intruder was looking for something, I wondered if he'd found it.

And of course, what it was.

A neighbor had heard the struggle, called 911, and two NYPD officers responded, only to find that Mr. Stewart was already deceased. There was no sign of his attacker.

I checked the bedroom, under the bed, in the closet, but didn't find anything noteworthy.

The French doors opened to a balcony four meters long and two meters wide that overlooked Manhattan.

I snapped the flashlight off, pocketed it, and then stepped outside. Twelve stories up. Directly below me, at the entrance to a dance club, twenty-two people stood on the sidewalk, waiting to be admitted inside.

A storm earlier in the evening had left the smell of damp concrete lingering in the air, a musty scent of summer rain.

A few horns honked in the distance. Someone flagged down a taxi at the end of the block. Nothing out of the ordinary.

I was thinking of the missing electronics and recorded media, the location of the remotes, the television screen's angle, the fact that the unit was off when the responding officers got here.

Off.

But—

I heard footsteps behind me in the bedroom.

"Hey, Jodie, I'm out here."

No, the television was off. So—

Jodie didn't respond. The footsteps came closer.

And it wasn't her gait.

Because it wasn't Jodie.

2

The man came at me lightning fast, swiping the blade across my left forearm. My shirtsleeve offered little protection and the knife left a streak of red behind.

I threw my other hand up to grab his wrist and disarm him, but he knew how to block the move and easily knocked my hand away. I pivoted backward to keep him from driving the blade into my chest. When I turned, it drew him with me, onto the balcony.

Four inches taller than me, six foot seven. A beast.

There wasn't much room out here for a fight.

He held the Bowie knife military-style, with the blade angled back parallel to his wrist. A lot harder to disarm. This man knew what he was doing. He'd been trained.

I was not going to fare well.

It didn't scare me.

Motivated me, though.

I would have gone for my gun, but I needed both hands to stop him from slicing me open. I tried to sweep his leg, but it was like trying to knock a tree trunk out of the way.

Normally, I could hold my own in a fight, but this guy was better than I was and I wasn't going to be able to keep him at bay for long.

Get some distance. Shoot him if you need to.

I head-butted him, slamming my forehead brutally against his nose.

It took him by surprise and he staggered back two paces. Before he could come at me again, I whipped out my gun and leveled it at his chest.

"Federal agent. Drop the knife."

Immediately, he stopped. He stood his ground but didn't come at me. "You're a federal agent?"

"FBI. Now get rid of the knife or I will put you down."

He took a step backward and tossed the blade over the railing of the balcony. I just hoped it wouldn't hit anyone on the sidewalk below us.

"Hands up," I said. "Get on your knees."

He didn't comply. "Do you have the file?"

"What?"

"You said you're with the Bureau. Did you find it? Do you have the file?"

I wasn't thrilled about the idea of trying to cuff this guy by myself. I had a feeling that he would be able to get my gun from me and overpower me before I could stop him even if he was lying facedown when I approached him. But now that he'd gotten rid of his knife, I wasn't about to shoot him either.

Jodie was on her way. Once she got here we could take him down. Until then we were in a bit of a standoff.

"What file?" I asked.

"Aurora's birthday."

I was aware that my sleeve was soaked with blood from my injured arm, but I didn't feel any pain—adrenaline will do that to you.

But the adrenaline would go away.

The pain would come.

He didn't kneel, didn't look afraid, and I didn't know

if he had another weapon. Seemed likely to me that he would be packing, though.

Keeping my gun on him, I tugged out my phone, speed-dialed Jodie, and told her to call NYPD for backup and to get up here ASAP. Then I slid my phone into my pocket. "If you make a move, if you come at me, I'm going to put you down."

"I understand." Then, "It wasn't on the computer or the phone."

"What wasn't?"

"The file."

"Aurora's birthday."

"Yes."

"Were you here last night?" I asked. "Did you kill Jamaal Stewart?"

"They won't let this happen." He eased back half a step.

"Stay where you are. Who? Who won't let this happen?"

He took another step. He was at the railing.

"Do not move!"

"They know things. They can find out things. It'll never stop."

He glanced down at the street, then looked in my direction again.

"Don't even think about it," I said.

There are people down there.

He's not the only one in danger here. They are too.

"You can't stop me," he said.

"I'll do whatever's necessary to protect those people down there. Now get on your knees."

Slowly, he turned away from me, perhaps guessing that I wasn't going to shoot him in the back.

You can't let him jump, Pat.

"Step away from the railing!"

Thoughts raced through my mind, thoughts of the people outside the club twelve stories below us, of what might happen if this man did throw himself over the edge.

I shouted again for him to stop, but he just lifted one leg to the railing to climb over it.

I considered his state of mind, the danger he posed to those people—

He tossed the knife. He might not be armed.

You can't kill him.

But he's posing an immediate threat to innocent life.

I stared down the barrel.

Made my decision.

Avoid the femur.

Fired.

The leg that was supporting his weight buckled and he collapsed onto the balcony.

"Do not move." I took a step forward.

"You're not sending me to prison." In obvious pain, he grimaced as he pushed himself to his feet. "I'm not going to prison. I'm dead already."

"We can protect you."

He scoffed. "Like you protected Ted?"

I had no idea who he was talking about. "That wasn't our fault." I was making this up as I went along. "We're trying to get to the bottom of that. You can help us. Now just—"

Jodie called my name from the other room.

"Out here!" I hollered.

"You have no idea how far this goes," he said to me, "what they're going to do if . . ." His voice trailed off.

"Tell me."

But instead of replying, he made the sign of the cross

in front of his chest and then, in one swift and desperate motion, grabbed the railing and heaved himself over it and disappeared from sight.

I rushed forward and got there while he was still in the air on his way down.

He didn't cry out. He didn't scream. He just fell silently toward the sidewalk, where he collided with the ground within a meter of one of the women waiting outside the club.

The sound of impact followed, rising through the night, a thick, sickening thud.

Then the screams of the people in front of the club began.

And they didn't stop.

3

"Jodie, I'm heading down." I was back in the bedroom and she had turned on the light. "I want you to stay up here, make sure no one else comes in, and get the CSU over here."

"First of all." She indicated my bloody sleeve. "Are you okay?" Though her father was Caucasian, her mother was Persian and Jodie shared her dark hair and rich-toned skin. Small-framed but tough. I'd seen her take down guys my size.

"It's fine." Using my left sock, I wrapped the wound and tied it off to create a rudimentary dressing to quiet the bleeding. "Listen, the TV was off when the officers arrived. The chair was angled toward it, the DVD remote next to it."

"So, he was watching TV," she surmised.

"But the remote for that was out of reach."

She caught on. "Who turned off the television?"

"Right." We walked into the living room. "Also"—I pointed—"that wireless keyboard is for surfing through the TV's cable Internet connection."

"Prints?"

"Possibly."

I went to the television. "The jumper told me the file

wasn't on the computer or the phone. All the DVDs and videocassettes were taken. So there might be . . ." The television was directed toward the chair. I angled the arm it was attached to over to the other side so I could access the back of it.

Oh yes.

"Right there." I directed her attention to two USB input devices inserted into the data ports on the back of the unit. "One has the same insignia as the keyboard. That's probably its wireless input. But the other one—"

"Is a flash drive."

"It sure looks like it. We need to find out if there's a file on it called 'Aurora's birthday.' It might hold the key to figuring out who murdered Stewart, and why this guy tonight just killed himself. He warned me about the people who are behind this. Whoever they are, it sounds like they do not play nicely with others, so tell the computer forensics guys to be careful."

On the way to the elevator I texted Christie Ellis, the woman I was seeing.

Earlier, I'd canceled dinner with her tonight, then later, canceled drinks afterward as well, all because of my work. I'd told her I would swing by her place on my way home, but it didn't look like that was going to happen now either.

She texted back almost immediately that she was still open to me coming by, just to let her know.

I replied that I would be in touch.

By the time I arrived at the front of the building, nearly everyone in the crowd had their cell phones out and was filming the rather grisly scene. I wondered how many times it'd already been uploaded to YouTube or tweeted.

I drew out my creds and held them up as I approached the body. "FBI. Everybody stand back."

The man had landed on his back and the posterior of
his skull was crushed. One of his legs was bent profusely
to the side. The end of a fractured bone punctured his
pants leg.

I heard sirens.

NYPD.

Based on the extent of this man's injuries, I didn't
think there was any chance that he was still alive, but
perhaps for my sake, perhaps for the crowd's, I gently
placed two fingers on his throat to check for a pulse.

Nothing.

The woman who'd been closest to the jumper when
he hit the sidewalk was sitting on the curb nearby. Blood,
along with gray matter from the dead man's brain, had
splattered onto the hem of her skirt. She wasn't shaking.
Wasn't crying. She just sat staring blankly across the
street. Shock.

"Ma'am?" I said. "Are you injured?"

She didn't move.

I knelt beside her. "Are you hurt, ma'am?"

This time she shook her head. "No."

I visually assessed her but saw no injuries. "You're going to be alright," I said, though I wasn't sure that was
going to be the case, not after having this happen to her.
A body crashing to the pavement within arm's reach of
you? That's the stuff of nightmares. Not everybody
would be able to shake off something that traumatic.

Rising, I returned to the body and inspected his pockets.

No phone. No wallet. No ID.

But there was a folded-up envelope labeled OPEN ONLY
IN THE CASE OF MY DEATH.

Whether he'd been planning to take his life or afraid
someone might take it from him, I didn't know.

Using my knife as a letter opener, I cut along the edge of the envelope and removed the single sheet of paper inside.

Dear Billy,

I'm sorry it came to this, but it's the only thing I know to do. Whatever you want to believe about me, whatever anyone says, you need to know that I never did the things she's claiming I did. I'm sorry I let you down.

—Randy

Okay, a clue, but also another mystery—who was Billy?

At least the names in the note might help us identify the jumper.

In his pockets I found some loose change, a subway MetroCard, and a single key. Earlier, I'd seen the key to the apartment we'd just been in, and this one didn't match it.

Well, we would run his prints and DNA. If he was in the system, we would identify him. At least we had a first name to work with. The rather crudely drawn tattoo of a shamrock on the back of his right hand might help if we could find a studio that had done it for someone named "Randy."

I stood and eyed the crowd, took note of posture, stance, body language, but no one was acting in a suspicious or aggressive manner. They were still filming and now a number of them directed their phones at me.

Assistant Director DeYoung had told us not to instruct people to put their phones away when we're at a scene, since it ended up manifesting resentment toward the Bureau, especially after the people invariably wouldn't listen and would eventually post those videos of us telling them to turn off their phones anyway. "People will wonder, 'What are they trying to hide?'" DeYoung had explained. "Or, 'What don't they want me to see?'"

The problem was getting worse year by year. It bothered me when people treated death like a spectator sport. From what I'd seen in the past, these videos would be watched by tens of thousands of people, especially if the media picked up any of them or, for whatever reason, they went viral. Then you could be talking about hundreds of thousands of views. Or more.

All to satisfy the macabre curiosity of the masses.

No, we really haven't come all that far since the days of the Colosseum.

An NYPD cruiser arrived.

I explained who I was, briefed the officers, and mentioned that, based on the jumper's comments to me, he was a person of interest for the homicide the night before.

One of the officers went to string up some police tape. The other said to me, "So you really think this is our doer from last night?"

Doer, perp, UNSUB, I'm not a fan of any of those terms. "It's possible, but let's not get ahead of ourselves."

He noted the shamrock tattoo. "That's an Aryan Brotherhood symbol. Prison tats? An ex-con?"

"He might just be Irish. And I'm guessing he's never been to prison."

"Why's that?"

"On the balcony he said to me, 'You're not sending me to prison,' rather than 'you're not sending me *back* to prison.' I've never known anyone who's been locked up who would have phrased it like he did. You serve time, you don't want to be sent *back*. It's how you'd typically put it."

"Good point." He was looking at the makeshift bandage on my left forearm. "You alright?"

"I'm alright."

I stared at the body.

I'm guessing that most people who take their own life don't think about what has to happen afterward, about what their choice is going to require other people to do.

Someone will have to clean up the mess, replace the carpet, paint over the bloodstain, remove the empty bottle of pills from your rigid, clinging hand, or, in this case, wash off the sidewalk.

It was so tragic.

Cleaning up the dead is a messy business.

And there was no reason this man needed to die tonight.

An ambulance rolled to a stop near the edge of the police tape.

I directed one paramedic to assist the woman who was seated on the curb, the one who'd been so close to where the jumper impacted the ground.

The other EMT snipped off the sleeve of my shirt, cleaned the laceration on my arm, and tried to convince me that I needed stitches. I avoid those whenever possible since needles are part of the deal. I've never had an affinity for those things.

Facing a psychotic killer on the street, yeah, I'm good with that.

Facing a grinning nurse with a needle, not so much.

It took some convincing, but she finally gave in and agreed to just bandage it up.

While she worked on that, I dictated my incident report into my phone. The latest voice-recognition software was accurate enough to cut down almost by half the amount of time we spent on filling out paperwork, and you weren't going to find me complaining about that.

In the morning I could review the report, proofread it, and then submit it to DeYoung before heading to the Field Office.

Eventually, another ambulance rolled in, loaded up the body, and left for the morgue at Presbyterian Central Hospital. One by one, the people filming things dispersed, busily posting, texting, and tweeting what had just happened.

After I was done with my dictation, I called Christie to tell her that I'd see her tomorrow, but she explained that she had chicken Parmesan waiting. "I'll warm it up when you get here. Come on over, it'd be nice to see you."

I'd missed dinner earlier and it was nearly ten thirty. "You're sure it's not too late?"

"I'm certain."

"Alright, I'll get there as soon as I can."

After the Crime Scene Unit left with the USB drive and remote-control devices along with the items I'd found on the victim's body, I took off for Christie's place.

4

"Hey, you," I said.

I stepped into her fourth-story apartment and closed the door behind me.

Her gaze went immediately to the snipped-off shirt-sleeve and my bandaged arm. "How many?"

"How many?"

"Stitches."

"I just had the paramedic bandage it."

"Is it serious?"

"No."

"How did it happen?"

"A knife." I gave her a kiss. "Don't worry. I'm fine."

She said nothing.

The two-bedroom, cramped, and ridiculously over-priced apartment had a typical New York City floor plan: a breakfast nook opened up to the living room, which led to a hallway past the single bathroom to a pair of bedrooms. That was it. Yet, as modest as this place was, her rent devoured nearly forty percent of her monthly salary. Space is definitely at a premium in a city of 8.5 million people.

In order to make ends meet, a lot of FBI agents live in New Jersey and commute ninety minutes each way just to get by.

With my joint work with the NYPD and the requirement to be on-site for so many cases, it was necessary for me to live in the city and have a vehicle—even though battling New York City traffic was not by any means my favorite pastime. Though the royalties from the two criminology books I'd written were relatively meager, they helped. Without them I wasn't sure how I could afford to live here on what I currently made.

Christie preferred not using the breakfast counter, so she had a small table pushed up behind the couch on the edge of the living room.

Two candles flickered on it—one orchid, one lavender. By the amount of wax flow, I could tell they hadn't been burning for long. Two dishes, two wineglasses, and her finest silverware waited on either side of them. Most people save their best dinnerware for special occasions. Not Christie. "You never know what's coming your way," she told me once. "This might be the most special day of your life and you just haven't found that out yet. Why not celebrate proactively?"

Celebrating proactively.

Not a bad life philosophy.

A Tupperware container with chicken Parmesan sat beside the candles. "It got cold earlier," she said. "I didn't want to reheat it until you got here."

"Did you eat?"

"Just dessert."

This woman always ate dessert first.

A quirk I'd come to love.

And emulate whenever possible.

Her blond hair shimmered in the golden candlelight. She was a few months older than me, but could have passed for five years younger.

Never married, Christie had gotten pregnant in college, opted to keep her baby, and eventually dropped out of school to raise her daughter. I didn't know the story about Tessa's father, why he'd never been in the picture, or how Christie and Tessa ended up in New York City from rural Minnesota. It seemed like a sensitive topic and I figured she would share the details when she was ready.

These days, she worked at a small design firm developing logos, identity packages, and marketing campaigns for start-up tech companies. She made enough to live on, but I knew things were tight.

She took the chicken to the microwave. "This'll only take a minute."

I set down my computer bag and took a sip of the wine she'd poured for me.

I was as clueless when it came to grapes as she was when it came to coffee beans, so I had no idea what kind of wine this was—except that it was sweet and light and fruity, and right now it hit the spot.

She placed the food in the microwave and punched the reheat button.

"I would have been here earlier if I could," I said.

"I know."

"Things got a little crazy."

"I understand."

The dated microwave hummed somewhat chunkily in the background.

"Would you like a slice of Key lime pie?" she asked. "It's vegan, but it's good."

"Two slices would make my arm feel better."

"Really."

"Mm-hmm."

"And how is that?"

"A little-known fact: Key lime is famous for its healing properties in treating knife wounds."

She raised an eyebrow at me. "If it's a little-known fact, how is it also famous?"

"Good point."

"We'll go with one piece to start." She took a sip of her wine. "I heard a new one today."

"Tongue twister?"

"It's a tough one: 'Irish wristwatch.' Five times fast. Go."

I tried and it wasn't pretty, but it did bring a smile to her face. "Your turn."

"I've had practice." She tried. Nailed it.

The day we met she'd told me a tongue twister and she'd been trying them out on me ever since.

The microwave dinged but she didn't take out the chicken.

"And do you know why I wanted to see you tonight?" she asked.

"Because I'm irresistible?"

"Besides that."

"Adorable?"

"Do you remember when we first met, Mr. Adorable?"

"Of course."

A slight smile. "What day of the week was it?"

"Ah. A Wednesday."

"Uh-huh. Good. And what brought us together?"

"That storm. It was very serendipitous."

"I would call it providential."

"A spring rain."

"And you let me share your umbrella with you. Such a gentleman."

"As I recall, you were pretty taken with me at first."

"Oh, really? Is that how you remember it?"

"Yup. *Very* taken."

"And what makes you think that?"

"Your eyes. The way you looked at me."

"My eyes?"

I did my best imitation of her.

"I seriously hope I didn't look like that."

"Well, something along those lines. I might not be remembering it exactly."

"Why is that?"

"I might have been a little distracted by seeing such a gorgeous woman coming in from the rain."

"Good answer. And how long did we stand under that umbrella?"

"I don't really remember. It's all a blur after that."

"After what?"

"After I looked into those eyes."

"Two for two."

"And then when we went out for coffee, you told me your first tongue twister."

"And that was?"

"Cryptic stripped script crypt."

She nodded. "Very good."

"And so that's it, then—why you wanted to see me this evening. We met seven weeks ago tonight."

"And we went on our first official date one week later."

"A double anniversary."

"So it is."

"Well, you oughta get a kiss for each one," I offered generously.

"Is that so?"

I took her in my arms to pay up.

And sort of wished it was a triple one.

At last she stepped back, brought the pie out of the fridge, and said, "Okay, I need to just go ahead and say this: I know you can't tell me the details about what happened and I'm not going to press you, but the bloodstain coming through that bandage worries me. If you can't tell me, I get that. But it's . . . it's hard not knowing how it happened, besides that it was a knife."

I was quiet, unsure how to respond.

She knew I couldn't share the specifics of my cases with her, but I usually told her as much as I could to allay her concern. Figuring out where to draw that line was always a challenge.

"So." She dished some pie onto a plate, laid a fork beside it, and handed it to me. "At least tell me this much: am I going to hear about what happened when I turn on the news in the morning?"

"You might," I said, then added, "Yes. You will."

I felt caught between the desire to let her into my life and the need to keep her out of my work. How do you draw someone close while at the same time keeping her at arm's length? It's not easy and I hadn't done so well with it over the years—at least the drawing-someone-close part.

Christie divided the chicken Parmesan onto two plates, and we returned to the table.

After evaluating things, I finally explained what I could. "A man took his own life. I tried to stop him, to save him, but I couldn't. It appears to be linked to a homicide last night."

"And he had a knife?"

"Yes. We struggled. He cut me."

"Is it deep?"

"I've had deeper."

"Okay."

"Listen." I reached across the table and took her hand. "I'm fine. And I'm here now. I'm putting all that aside."

"I'm going to hold you to that, alright?"

"Alright."

Christie was a woman of deep faith and before we began our entirely-too-late-to-be-good-for-you dinner, while still holding my hand, she closed her eyes and said a prayer of thanks for the food and for my safety. Then she asked God to comfort the friends and family of the man who'd died. "Let them see a bigger plan at work, find hope even in grief, and love, somehow, despite their sorrow. Amen."

"Amen."

I wasn't sure where I stood when it came to matters of faith and religion. I knew there was evil in our world, no question about that. I'd seen too much of it over the years to doubt that, but I needed people like Christie to remind me that there was good here too.

Work this job long enough and you'll start to believe in sin—whatever label you want to give it. Grace, forgiveness, redemption, those are harder to find. Christie said to me one time, "When you look at the world as it is, how can you not be racked with grief? But when you look closer, how can you not be overwhelmed with awe?"

I was still working on the awe part.

I started with dessert, and while we ate, I tried to keep my promise to her, tried to leave my work behind, to make that difficult and yet necessary switch from professional life to personal life, but it didn't go as well as I'd hoped.

Questions about the scene, about Randy—if that really was his name—about the note, all pecked away at my attention.

Christie was concluding telling me about her day when

Tessa emerged from her room, staring at her phone, texting someone as she walked to the fridge. She glanced up just long enough to nod a greeting in my direction.

"Hey, Tessa."

"Hey."

Fifteen years old. Independent. A loner. Her obsidian hair swished idly across her shoulders when she turned her head to look at us. Black eyeliner, black fingernail polish, and sometimes, although not tonight, black lipstick to match it. She was as ambiguous about school as she was fiercely intelligent, and I had the sense that she was searching for a place to belong, but at the same time couldn't care less what people thought of her. A bit of a paradox.

She slid a slice of pie onto a plate, hesitated, then dumped the last two remaining pieces on top of it. I didn't think Christie noticed. Then Tessa dug a fork out of the drawer and without another word, texting with one hand now, took the pie with her back to her room.

"You're going to put that plate in the dishwasher when you're done with it, right?" Christie called after her.

"Uh-huh," Tessa replied noncommittally.

"Uh-huh," Christie said to me with a small smile, then mouthed, *We'll see*.

When I first moved to NYC, I was surprised by how late in the summer school stayed in session here. Even though it was mid-June now, Tessa still had one more week of classes. When I was growing up, I lived for the summertime and I would have hated being in school in June.

Christie and I talked for a few more minutes, but finished the meal in relative silence.

"I should probably be heading home," I said.

"It's late, Pat. Stay here. Get some sleep."

I knew her well enough to realize that this wasn't a sexual invitation. As rooted as she was in her faith, Christie had strong convictions about the sanctity of marriage and, although I had a dresser drawer set aside here for the nights when I did stay over, every time I'd spent the night so far it'd been on the couch.

Often, with my work schedule, the only chance we had to see each other was late at night, and since I lived across town it made sense to just stay over when we did manage to get together. I respected her views, but I had to admit I looked forward to the day when I would graduate from the couch.

I had my laptop with me, everything I would need for tomorrow morning, and I couldn't think of any good reason to go back to my place at this time of night just to sleep in my own bed.

"Okay. Thanks. I think I will stay."

After we'd deposited the dishes in the dishwasher, she gently cradled my wounded arm in her hand. "So you're sure you're okay?"

"I'm good."

Then she took my hand in both of hers, and the warmth of her touch reminded me that she was alive, that I was alive, here in this moment, here on this day.

Such an obvious fact, so self-evident, but one that we don't often pause to consider.

Today *is* a special occasion.

Every day we're alive is.

Earlier tonight, the man's skin had still been warm when I placed my fingers against his neck to check for a pulse.

Lifeless, but still warm.

It would have cooled by now, though.

It doesn't take long.

It's a mystery to me: We live, we die. It all happens in the blink of an eye, in the grand scheme of things.

If there really is a grand scheme to things.

I drew Christie into my arms and after we'd said good night with a kiss that I was glad Tessa didn't interrupt, Christie left for her bedroom and I got situated on the couch.

Tessa never returned with her pie plate and fork, but I did hear Christie down the hall informing her that I was staying over so that she wouldn't be surprised to find me here in the morning.

In lieu of turning on the air conditioner, I left the living room window open. Outside, the familiar sounds of my city kept me company.

The rain had started again and it was drizzling and dripping in a lonely, pitter-splatter-drop pattern onto and then off of the windowsill.

I tried to sleep, but the words of the man who'd leapt off that balcony kept cycling through my head: *"You have no idea how far this goes, what they're going to do if . . ."*

He'd stopped as soon as I told him I was a federal agent.

So, who did he think you were before that?

Who's Aurora and what's this file concerning her birthday?

Hopefully, tomorrow would bring some answers with it.

When I closed my eyes, I saw him again in midair, falling away from me through the night, almost gracefully, in a reverse swan dive that stopped abruptly at the pavement.

And I heard the sound of impact.

Heard it again and again.

There'd been that pause between him hitting the concrete and me hearing the crunch of impact, but then the screams of the bystanders came pretty much right away.

That was my lullaby when I closed my eyes.

The sound of a body hitting the ground and the screams that followed in its wake.

So much can change in the blink of an eye.

5

Francis Edlemore was in charge of changing the posters.

He didn't work full-time at it, no, there was no need for that, but it was a positive contribution he could make to St. Stephen's Research Hospital, a positive contribution he could make to the community, and he was thankful for the chance to do it.

The cardboard tube he carried contained eleven rolled-up posters of Gracie and one final one of Derek; it was his that Francis would be putting up in the subway terminal over on the northeast wall along the side of the tracks.

The hospital had provided him with Derek's poster—a smiling ten-year-old boy with a type of terminal brain cancer Francis couldn't pronounce, along with the words "You can make Derek's dreams come true." It included the toll-free number and the website that people could use to contact St. Stephen's to donate money toward their ongoing cancer research.

Francis didn't know the boy's specific prognosis or how long he was expected to live, but he did know it was unlikely that his dreams would ever come true. He'd been in to visit him five times and Derek wasn't getting any better.

The hospital's community volunteer coordinator, Mrs. Durkin, didn't explicitly state the reason why they needed to change the posters from Gracie's. No one liked to talk about it. Instead she'd just announced to Francis that they had "a new development campaign beginning." Then she smiled in a way that was meant to fend off any questions he might have had. "I'll need you to put up twelve new posters."

"How's the research going?"

"We're making steady progress. Plugging right along, but there's still more work to do. Always more work to do. Can you take care of the posters tonight?"

"We're replacing Gracie's?"

"You know how these things go."

She didn't need to explain the reason why the campaign featuring Gracie, a girl who'd just turned eleven a few months ago, had ended.

Francis knew that it was the same reason Derek's campaign would end in a few months, or maybe, if things went well for him, next year sometime. It usually happened about once a year, putting up the new posters. Once, though, Francis had been called on to replace the posters after only two weeks.

That time was the hardest.

Francis was twenty-eight years old, single, and sometimes he wondered if he would be single forever. But, since he didn't have too many friends or pastimes and no family obligations, he had the time to help with projects like this. It was one of the advantages of living alone.

Though his job at the International Child Safety Consortium kept him busy during the day, he had his evenings free.

A train must have just arrived, because a clump of people was coming his way up the steps as he descended into the tunnel that led beneath the streets of the city. Pedestrians in New York City have learned to keep their gazes to themselves when they pass others. So now, tonight, no one looked at him.

It was so different from growing up in east Texas, where people smiled and waved at strangers and thought it rude and presumptuous if you didn't at least nod to them when you passed them on the street.

He swiped his MetroCard and stepped through the turnstile.

Just like cattle on the ranch. One animal at a time. Patience. Patience. Patience. Wait your turn. One by one through the turnstile. Be polite and obedient on your way to the slaughter.

What does that even mean, Francis? Animals don't know what it's like to be polite. They only know what it's like to exist, to eat, to breed, to bleed, to die.

It's just that they're oblivious, though. That's what I meant.

Use "oblivious," then. Use the right word, Francis.

I will. Next time, I will.

He had to tilt the cardboard tube upright to maneuver it through the turnstile.

The under-the-city reek of the subway tunnel met him: oil or grease or something from the trains, along with the vague ever-present stench of garbage that most New Yorkers get used to, but visitors notice right away.

It's a little bit like when you have bad breath but you don't notice it. Other people's breath? Sure. Yes. No problem there. But not your own. Why not? Well, your brain gets used to it and shuts it out, stops noticing it.

Brains are good at that—at shutting out the disagreeable truths of life so we don't have to continually face them. Things like the stench of the city. The faces of the homeless. The sad eyes of strangers passing by, keeping their gazes to themselves as they do.

But Francis tried to notice things both big and small, had been ever since the accident when he was eleven.

Even after all these years he remembered what it was like to wake up in that hospital bed and find out that he had been dead.

He'd coded, as they called it, then been resuscitated. Fractured ribs. Bruises and contusions. And he'd lost his spleen, which left him susceptible to infection.

His little brother and his uncle had not been so lucky to be brought back.

You never get two chances at the moments that come your way. And you don't know how many more you're gonna have.

He came to the poster of Gracie, set down the tube, unlocked the hinged Plexiglas covering that protected her from vandals and graffiti artists, and swung it to the side.

The girl had playful, slightly mischievous eyes. She was sitting on a hospital bed, holding a stuffed lion cub. The caption above her head was different than Derek's: YOUR COMPASSION CAN CHANGE A LIFE FOREVER.

Each development campaign had its own slogan.

And its own child.

Mascot.

No. It's not a mascot. It's a child!

Francis had visited Gracie twice in the hospital and had made balloon animals for her.

Even though he was still learning how to do it and wasn't very good, she hadn't seemed to mind and kept the misshapen dog there in her room even after the air had leaked out and the balloon sat limp and wrinkled and distorted on the windowsill overlooking the city.

It was still there when they took her body out of the

room. Francis had noticed it in the trash can when he
went to see her and found the bed empty, found that he
had come in two hours too late.

He'd taken it home as a reminder of their visits.

Now it sat in the windowsill of his apartment.

After he was done replacing Gracie's poster with Derek's,
he rolled up her poster, slid it into the tube with the others, and then fastened the Plexiglas cover back in place.

There were no rules about what he was supposed to
do with the old posters after he'd taken them down.

"Where should I put the other ones?" he'd asked the
man who'd been in charge of the volunteers seven years
ago when he first started helping with the posters.

"They're paper, right?" He was poring over a pile of
forms strewn across his desk. "You can recycle them,
maybe?"

But to Francis, there was something about depositing
the posters into a recycling bin that didn't feel right. For
some reason he felt like doing that would have disgraced
the children. So, from the beginning, he'd taken the old
posters home, back to his apartment.

Now, as he rode the 7 train to Junction Boulevard, he
thought about how late it already was and if he should
really go online when he got home.

He wasn't sure he would do it, even when the train
stopped and he left, carrying the cardboard tube, and
walked the three blocks to his place.

Even then he wasn't sure.

Inside his apartment, Francis popped open the tube,
removed the posters of Gracie, laid eleven of them on the
stack of other posters near the window, then, taking the
remaining one with him, he picked up four pushpins and
walked to the living room wall.

There was just enough room for Gracie between Kevin and the window.

After pinning the poster up there, he stepped back and looked at the wall.

At the children.

Twelve of them.

Mascots.

No! Children!

He was running out of room. He would need to start using the hallway unless St. Stephen's found a cure soon.

At the far end of the room his laptop was waiting on his desk.

Go online. She's usually on at this time of night. You could chat, just for a few minutes. It wouldn't hurt anything just to chat.

He stared at his computer.

You're not harming anyone, Francis. She said she was eighteen. Dr. Perrior told you it would be good for you to meet people your own age.

But that's not my age. I'm ten years older than her.

But your dad was twelve years older than your mom when they got married.

I know, but he was forty-four and she was thirty-two. It's different when you're that age.

Well, anyway, you're just chatting online. It's not like you're ever going to meet her.

He didn't want to chance using his real name, not with his career and how things would look if it leaked out what he was doing here, so he used the screen name Jared4life73 and made sure the browser was set to private browsing.

Clicking to graciousgirl4's Krazle page, he sent her a message: "U still up? It's me."

Why would it matter if people found out? You're not sending or receiving obscene material. It's just a friendship.

But it just wouldn't look good. It wouldn't reflect well on the ICSC.

He got ready for bed, but the voices didn't leave him alone. They kept arguing with each other, arguing, arguing, arguing about whether or not he should be chatting with graciousgirl4.

When he returned to the computer he found that she'd replied, "Yah. Couldn't sleep. Whatcha doin?"

After a moment's hesitation he picked up where he'd left off, chatting with the girl who'd told him that she was eighteen, but, based on the subjects she said she was studying in school, he wondered if she might be just a little bit younger.

6

Thursday, June 14

I rose before dawn and slipped quietly into Christie's room to get my running clothes. She stirred slightly in her sleep, but I did my best not to disturb her.

After changing into shorts and a T-shirt, I headed outside.

The air was sharp and surprisingly brisk for a June morning, but it felt good. Invigorating.

They say this is the city that never sleeps, but it certainly does doze at times, and just before sunrise is one of them. A few other runners were out, but for the most part the sidewalks were empty.

Though I'd been here for a couple of years now, I still considered myself a newcomer to New York City.

It was the only major city I'd ever encountered where the terms "downtown" and "uptown" were antonyms rather than synonyms.

It was terribly confusing to me at first when people spoke about taking a subway downtown or uptown, and only when I found myself at the wrong side of the line did I realize they weren't talking about the same thing, but were actually talking about heading in opposite directions.

Today it took a couple of miles before I started to really loosen up and get into my stride. At six-minute-
thirty-second miles, I figured I had just enough time for
my eight-mile loop.

Last night's events rotated through my mind and
seemed to bring up even more questions about the homicide the evening before. Did the USB flash drive contain
anything relevant to the investigation? Would the remote
control units contain any identifiable prints? If the jumper
was Stewart's killer, why did he choose to take his own
life? And who was the guy, Ted, whom he'd told me we
hadn't been able to protect?

In New York City, with few alleys or dumpsters, people put their garbage out along the curbs at night to get
picked up the next morning. If you get up early enough
to run, it'll still be there lining the sidewalks.

Today, as I passed a small deli, one of the bags of garbage twitched.

Though it startled me at first, it wasn't the first time
I'd seen that happen and I knew what it was: something
inside that bag was alive.

A couple of years ago when I first moved here, I'd seen
a garbage bag like this one quiver and it'd shocked me so
much that I'd lurched to the side and wrenched my ankle
on the curb.

I'd just gotten back from teaching a weeklong course
in Johannesburg, South Africa, on geospatial investigative
techniques, and we'd visited a few orphanages on the
morning before my flight home.

Both orphanages had signs asking mothers not to
leave their babies in the nearby fields ("velds") or the
garbage piles, but instead to set the child in a bin there
outside the orphanage and to ring the bell so a caregiver
from inside would know there was a child waiting and

come to take it in, or "fetch it," as they say in South Africa.

Yes, they actually had to politely request that new mothers not commit infanticide by leaving their babies in garbage dumps to die.

This is our world.

And so, that day when I first saw a black bag shiver on the streets of this city, I thought I knew what was inside it and my fingers were shaking as I tore open the thin skin of plastic.

But there wasn't a baby in there.

Instead a thick-bodied rat stared up at me, bared its teeth, but then, when I didn't come closer, it lost interest in me and went back to rooting through the food scraps someone had discarded.

They say there are twice as many rats as there are people in this city. Who knows? I just know that at night they get into the garbage bags and animate them, a bit like insect activity does inside corpses.

The body seems to shiver, and at first, despite its bloated appearance, you catch yourself thinking that the person is alive. You see that slight movement of the skin and it's enough to throw you off, enough to make you think that, despite the smell, you might have made it in time.

But then, when you get closer, you realize what's really happening.

The skin is moving in those tremors and ripples because of the maggots and worms squirming just beneath it.

So those were the things I thought of as I ran alongside the garbage bags of the magnificent city opening its eyes around me: rats and corpses and babies left to die.

*   *   *

By the time I'd made my circuit and was on my way back
to Christie's apartment, the morning was already warm-
ing up, and a wide-open, cloudless summer sky was beginning to unfurl above me, flower petal blue.

When I came through the door, the aroma made it
clear that Christie had put on some coffee.

A sweet, nutty smell. Unmistakably Peruvian.

Actually, I only had twelve possibilities to choose from,
so it wasn't too hard to nail it. I'd brought her some of
my favorite roasts for the times when I was over here.

Grown at nearly two thousand meters above sea level,
with a gentle, medium body and a mellow sweetness, Peruvian is perfect for a breakfast or morning coffee.

Christie popped her head out of the bedroom. "How
was your run?"

I was still thinking of that quivering bag of trash. "It
woke me up even more than I anticipated."

"And your arm?"

"I hardly noticed it."

"There's some first aid tape and bandages beneath the
sink in the bathroom."

"Thanks."

She asked how I'd slept, and after I told her fine, she
informed me that Tessa was in the bathroom getting
ready.

With just that one shower here, we needed to tag-
team it, so after grabbing some coffee and adding a little
honey and creamer, I took a seat at the breakfast nook,
logged in to the Federal Digital Database on my laptop,
and proofread the transcription of my report from last
night.

I filled in a few details, and then submitted it to Peter
DeYoung, the Assistant Director who was in charge of
the joint task force I worked with.

The report was definitely going to raise some eye-brows, especially the part about me shooting the man in the leg in order to protect the lives of the people below us.

Could prove interesting.

As I was finishing up my coffee, Tessa left the bath-room wearing the pajama pants and oversize T-shirt she liked to lounge around the house in, and retreated down the hall to her bedroom to get dressed for school.

I showered, replaced the dressing on my arm, and threw on some clothes. Christie slipped into the bath-room after me to finish putting on her makeup.

Tessa was at the breakfast nook when I returned to the kitchen for some food.

Now she had on a black long-sleeve T-shirt with the somewhat disturbing logo of one of her favorite bands, House of Blood, splayed in full color across the front. Despite the fact that it was summer, she'd chosen a ma-roon skirt over black leggings.

As a vegan, she zealously avoided all animal by-products, and now took a bite of her soy-milk-soaked granola.

"So, I found a link to a news story this morning," she said.

"What story was that?"

"It had to do with what happened in the apartment building in Manhattan last night. The guy who jumped. You were there, weren't you?"

I couldn't imagine that the Bureau would have re-leased my name already. "What makes you say that?"

"I heard you and Mom talking last night. You said you were with a guy when he died, that you weren't able to stop him. I figured it was the same deal. Then, with the videos people uploaded, well . . ."

"Yes," I admitted. "It was me."

She took another bite. "So, why'd he jump?"

"I don't know, not for sure. He seemed afraid, but even with that, any time you try to decipher someone's motives, it's a guessing game and you can never be sure you're right."

She looked at me curiously. "Why would you say that? Cops are always trying to find out people's motives. It's, like, the first thing they look for."

"True—all too often that is the case, but it shouldn't be."

"What do you mean?"

"It's simply not possible to climb into someone else's head and determine with any degree of certainty the motive behind his actions. All of us are influenced by a myriad of factors—some conscious, some unconscious—even when we perform the simplest of tasks. Take your outfit for example. Why'd you choose it? Maybe to express yourself, or to fit in, or because you thought it would look cool, or—"

"To rebel against my mom, or my other clothes are dirty or whatever. Okay, yeah, I get it. And how could you be sure which one it was if you tried to guess?"

"Right. We might have half a dozen different motives all present at the same time. So who's to say what someone else's motive was, especially in something as psychologically complex and traumatic as murder?"

"Or suicide."

"Well, it's still murder. It's just that you aren't around to stand trial for it."

"Huh, yeah. I never thought of it quite like that." She contemplated things for a moment. "So, why are they always looking for motives, then?" But before I could respond, she answered her own question. "Probably 'cause it makes us feel safer, right?"

"Safer?"

"I mean, if you can boil everything down to one specific reason, put a name to it, categorize it, you know—jealousy, revenge, a thrill kill, whatever—it's easier to accept it. It's the senseless crimes that scare us the most. That's why, when there's a school shooting and the kid kills himself when it's over, they're all, 'What was his motive?' and they search through his social media posts and stuff like that to see if he was bullied, or whatever. We want to pin a reason to it or else we get terrified anyone else might do the same thing. Including us."

"I think you might be onto something there."

I finished eating and was rinsing out my bowl when she said, "I heard they don't call 'em successful anymore."

"Successful?"

"Suicides. They call 'em *completed* because to say it was *successful* seems to be putting a positive spin on things and it might be triggering for someone." She spooned out the final bite of her cereal. "So, what was it like, though?"

"What was what like?"

"Being there when the guy murdered himself. When he jumped."

It was hard, I thought.

"It was sad," I said.

"How many times have you been there when someone's died?"

I didn't reply right away. "Too many."

She accepted that and silently cleared the table, then checked her text messages as she went to grab her backpack for school.

Christie came into the room twisting her left earring in. "What was all that about, with Tessa? Successful *suicides?*"

"Last night she heard me telling you about the jumper. She was asking about motives, about how many people I've seen die."

"I'm not so sure I'm thrilled to hear that."

"She's just an inquisitive girl. You know her better than I do, but I don't think it's anything to worry about."

"I suppose." But she didn't sound entirely convinced. "So, will I see you tonight? Carve out some time? There's something I'd like to talk about."

"Everything okay?"

"Don't worry." She gave me a quick kiss. "It's not you. There are just some things I need you to help me sort through."

"We'll have to see how things go today, but I think I should be able to come over."

"Let me know."

"You sure you don't want to talk about it now?"

"Later, when we have more time."

Then we all took off: Christie for work, Tessa for school, and I left for the FBI Field Office to start trying to untangle what'd happened last night and what it might have to do with the homicide in that same apartment the evening before.

++++

Maybe it was force of habit, maybe it was just prudence, but before walking out the door, Francis deleted last night's chat and double-checked to make sure his Internet browser's history was cleared.

You shouldn't be doing this, Francis. Not someone in your position. Not someone who knows the things you know. Promise me you're not going to chat with her again tonight.

He was about to argue with himself, but realized that this time the voice was right.

"I promise," he said aloud, then closed his eyes and repeated it as if it were an incantation that would come true if he said it often enough. "I promise. I promise. I promise."

He walked to the subway station, but he didn't head to the ICSC building.

Before going to work today, he had a session with Dr. Perrior.

His supervisor, Claire Nolan, had given him a few hours off to see the psychologist.

She was good about that sort of thing, and it made sense that she would be, considering what Francis did for a living.

7

Jodie was waiting for me in the lobby, holding two cups of coffee from Blessed Nirvana Roasters. She handed one to me, and even though I'd already had some java at Christie's, since this was from Blessed Nirvana I figured I could force myself to have another cup.

Besides, I wouldn't have wanted it to go to waste.

The lengths I go to sometimes.

Here on this corner, two federal buildings lie across the street from each other: 290 Broadway and 26 Federal Plaza. The Bureau has offices in both of them, and depending on the department or unit you're working with, you might be going back and forth between them all day.

A shining example of government efficiency at work.

Jodie wore the same outfit as yesterday. There were bags under her bloodshot eyes and it looked like she'd tried to cover them with makeup, which she didn't usually use. It hadn't worked.

She must have noticed me noticing her. "Spent the night at a hotel," she explained. "Dell kicked me out."

"Jodie, I'm sorry."

"I should have seen it coming. Things have been going downhill for a while." She sighed. "There's this guy from work she's been spending a lot of time with. Apparently, I'm not as interesting as he is. Said she's exploring her horizons, reexamining her sexual identity. Is it me, Pat? Or is it this job?"

"This job makes it hard for anyone who's trying to be in a serious relationship."

There was no doubt about that.

Jodie had been with Dell for six months, but had told me once that she'd never made it past two years with anyone. So maybe it *was* her. Hard to say. Probably both factored in there to some degree.

"Listen," I said, "if you need a place to stay, you could crash at my apartment. I can always move over to Christie's for a week or two until you get things sorted out. I'm sure it wouldn't be a big deal."

"I just might take you up on that. I'll let you know."

After passing through security, we crossed the lobby to the elevator bay, our footsteps echoing through the nearly vacant hallway.

"I checked the online case file just before you got here," she said.

"Any word on the jumper's identity?"

"No. Nothing on AFIS."

Well, if his prints weren't in the Automated Fingerprint Identification System, he'd never been arrested, let alone convicted. After all, you're printed when you're arrested for a crime, not when you're convicted of it.

Officially, you might be considered by the courts to be innocent until proven guilty, but while you're in police custody it's the opposite—you're treated as if you were guilty until you're proven innocent.

The system is skewed like that.

She went on, "We should have DNA results back sometime this morning."

Though the Bureau had been experimenting with a new device that could do a DNA analysis in ninety minutes, it was still in beta, and because of the backlog of more than five hundred thousand DNA kits nationwide that were waiting to be tested, even current cases didn't always make it to the front of the queue right away.

We entered the empty elevator.

"Did you submit your report yet?" she asked.

"I sent it in before I left Christie's place."

"Okay, so let's run through it, see how you do."

"How I do?"

"I'll be DeYoung. You be you."

I pressed the button for the tenth floor. "Alright, I'm game."

The doors closed.

She cleared her throat in a surprisingly good imitation of the Assistant Director. "So, Pat." Her voice was gruff, yet somehow ingratiating and avuncular, just like DeYoung's. "I read that report of yours. Glad you're okay, glad about that, but I see you didn't follow protocol here."

I'd never heard her imitate him before. "Have you been practicing?"

"Stay in character, Pat."

"Oh. Right." I regrouped and answered as if she were DeYoung, "I was trying to protect innocent bystanders on the street."

"Yes, yes, so you shot our John Doe? Do you have any idea on how this is going to play in the court of public opinion?"

"No, sir. I wasn't thinking of that."

"Not good, Pat. *Not good*. Could give the Bureau a

black eye. Now, I'm not saying you did the wrong thing. But I'm not saying you did the right one either."

"What are you saying?"

"That the OPR is going to have to take a close look at this. A close look indeed."

That much was true: the Office of Professional Responsibility would undoubtedly be poring over this closely.

She switched back to Jodie mode. "I'm sure you'll be fine. You'll have to let me know how it goes when you speak with him."

"I will. And I'll let you know how close you were— but it sounds like you've got him pegged."

The elevator doors parted and we passed the nine doorways between the elevator bay and my office.

There was a note waiting for me on my desk.

"DeYoung?" Jodie asked as I picked it up.

"He wants to see me right away." Though Jodie and I were partners, I was the senior agent and she typically looked to me for direction. "Listen, while I'm in there I'd like you to check on something. Our guy from last night mentioned that we weren't able to protect someone named Ted. I want to know who this Ted is."

"Where do you want me to start?"

"Look into people who've died or been killed while in custody—NYPD or federal protection. He said 'you' after I told him I was a federal agent, so start with the Bureau, then move to the witness protection program. The jumper signed his note 'Randy.' See if that helps, if any known associates come up."

"I don't have clearance for that, not with the DOJ."

"Talk to Harrington. He owes me one."

"Alright. Good luck in there with DeYoung."

"Thanks."

I finished the coffee and tried to bank the cup off the wall and into the trash can by the door on my way out, but I missed and it splatted some dark drops onto the wall and dribbled more onto the floor.

"Don't quit your day job."

"I'll keep that in mind."

8

Assistant Director DeYoung and a Hispanic woman I didn't recognize were waiting for me in the Louis J. Freeh Conference Room, named after the FBI's Director back in the nineties.

DeYoung had been with the Bureau for twenty-seven years, most of it seated behind a desk, and it showed around his waistline.

The woman beside him was in her fifties, wore a navy blazer and skirt, and had dark-rimmed reading glasses. Stern lines radiated out around her eyes.

DeYoung introduced her as Maria Aguirre. "She's from OPR. Legal."

An Office of Professional Responsibility lawyer.

Well, that didn't take long.

As we shook hands I noticed the scent of cigarette smoke on her. She asked, "Is this the arm?"

"Excuse me?"

"Your report noted that you sustained a knife wound during the confrontation with the subject and that one of the paramedics had to treat you. Is this the arm that was injured?"

"No. It was the left one."

"I hope it heals promptly."

"Thank you. I'm sure it'll be fine."

"You have to be careful out there."

That seemed like an odd thing to say.

"Yes. You do."

We took our seats at the conference room table, DeYoung struggling a bit to fit in between the table and the wall behind him.

To get things started, he cleared his throat in a way that was remarkably similar to Jodie's imitation. Then he mentioned offhandedly that he looked forward to reading my report.

I'd anticipated that he would have read what I sent in before passing it on to legal, so his words surprised me. Maybe this was some new policy that I wasn't aware of.

"Alright, Pat," he said, "as you know, any instance in which an agent discharges his firearm while on duty requires an incident review by the Office of Professional Responsibility."

"Yes." I'd been through this routine before, although normally the wheels didn't turn this fast.

"We just need to make sure that this whole incident doesn't give the Bureau a black eye."

Amazing—Jodie had anticipated he would say.

Ms. Aguirre pulled out a laptop and plopped a formidable stack of file folders from her briefcase onto the table.

"I think it might be best if I spoke with Agent Bowers alone," she said to DeYoung.

"Oh." By his demeanor I could tell he was caught off guard by that. "Well, yes. Certainly." With a bit of effort he extricated himself from the chair. "So . . . I'll just leave you two to it, then."

"Thank you."

Alright.

Here we go.

She opened the top folder.

I wasn't surprised that she'd read my report already, but her pile of papers contained far more material than a printout would have required, more even than she would've been able to skim through this morning.

Was she reading up on you already? Before last night?

Hmm.

I wasn't sure what to make of that. Although I couldn't think of why she might have been researching me, it seemed like a legitimate possibility.

"Forgive me for not being more familiar with your personnel file," she said, "but I'm new to the Field Office here. Just transferred in from L.A."

Most OPR lawyers were based at Headquarters in Washington, D.C., but L.A. was also large enough to have some on staff.

"It looks like they put you right to work." I gestured toward the file folders.

"Yes. It looks like they did."

"How has the transition been?"

"Taxing."

Okay.

She paged through her notes. "I must say, you have an impressive work history here at the Bureau, Agent Bowers."

"Thank you."

"You've been quite busy, I see: a master's degree in criminology and law studies from Marquette, a PhD in environmental criminology from Simon Fraser University. And two books to your credit?"

"One grew out of my dissertation on geospatial investigation."

"Yes, of course. But it's no less an accomplishment."

She peered at me over the top of her glasses. "And you teach courses at the Academy as well?"

"I fly down every few months, teach short-term and interim seminars."

"How do you pull it off?"

"Pull it off?"

"How do you do it all? How do you fit everything in?"

"I'm a bit thin in the hobby department."

"I see." Back to the papers. "And this isn't the first time you've been under an OPR review."

Well, no one's perfect.

It wasn't really a question, so I waited her out and finally she continued. "It looks like you have a habit of making judgment calls in the field that don't always line up with protocol."

"Protocol doesn't always line up with what happens in the field."

She set down the papers and turned her attention to her laptop screen, then repositioned her glasses. "I should tell you that I haven't signed off on your report yet."

"Okay."

"I wanted to verify a few things first."

"Alright."

"Can you walk me through what happened last night on that balcony?"

"It's all there in my report."

"Yes, but if you could just recount it for me verbally. If you don't mind."

"Are there any specific questions you have, or were there some details that were unclear? It might save us both some time if I could address those first."

My suggestion had no effect on her. "In your own words. Please."

I thought, *The report you have is already in my own*

words but didn't want to sound dismissive of her concerns, so I kept that to myself and just went ahead and summarized the encounter with the suspect, detailing the events that led up to him jumping from the balcony.

As I spoke, she glanced back and forth from me to the printed report and then to the laptop screen as if she were verifying one account against the other, even though there weren't going to be any discrepancies if the papers were simply a printout of the online report. And my memory wasn't too bad. I was pretty sure my verbal account lined up almost verbatim with my written one.

When I finished, she consulted the papers one last time. "So, he was coming at you with the knife when you fired, correct?"

"I'm sorry?"

"Coming at you. After you identified yourself as a federal agent and asked him to put up his hands, he failed to comply, and you fired as he threatened your life with the knife he was carrying."

She was putting words into my mouth and I didn't like it.

"I shot him in the leg to stop him from jumping. If I was afraid for my life I wouldn't have aimed at his leg. He'd already gotten rid of his knife. Just like it says right there in the report."

"Agent Fleming only arrived after the altercation and the shot, correct?"

"Correct."

Ms. Aguirre closed the folder and leaned back in her chair, steepling her fingers in front of her. "There were no eyewitnesses up there in the apartment."

"No, there were not."

"The man who attacked you had illegally accessed a restricted-access crime scene and he wounded you while apparently trying to take your life. As far as I'm concerned, there's no need to drag you through an OPR review. What purpose would it serve? A review of that nature would be time-consuming."

"Yes, it would."

"I'm sure we would both prefer not having to distract ourselves from the work we already have on our plates. After all, the man did have a knife. He was armed."

"Yes. When he attacked me, he was."

While I was working as a homicide detective in Milwaukee, there was one instance in which my partner had used deadly force to stop a man who'd murdered at least two children after he molested them. There was some confusion about whether or not Sergeant Walker had believed my life was in danger when he squeezed the trigger. I thought of that now, of how the investigation had ended at that point.

The district attorney had been satisfied.

Justice had been served.

Everyone was glad the killer was dead.

After what that man had done to those little girls, he deserved to die. Actually, in my mind, he deserved worse than that. There are times when death doesn't seem like punishment enough, and when you start talking about sexually molesting and slaughtering children—well, that pretty much tops my list.

"Obviously," I said to Ms. Aguirre, "I would prefer that there be no disciplinary action."

She nodded as if we'd come to some sort of an unstated agreement. "As would I."

"But I'm not going to change what's in that report."

She looked past me toward the west wall. "Agent Bowers, I've seen a lot of good agents come and go over the years. You seem like the kind of public servant we're going to want around working for the Bureau for a long time."

"I appreciate you saying that."

"We have only the matter of the timing of the shot to determine."

"It's been determined. Just like it says in the report."

She held up the paper. "Are you absolutely certain you have no corrections or clarifications that you need to make to this?"

"Nothing pops to mind."

"Kindly close the door on your way out."

I stood. "Have a good day, Ms. Aguirre."

"I plan to, Agent Bowers."

9

Jodie looked up from her computer when I entered. "Well, how did it go?"

"I may be looking at an official reprimand."

"Well, you've been down that road before. At least you know the ropes."

"That is true." I took a seat. "So, did you find out anything?"

"You know how you wanted me to look into people named Ted who've died in custody or while under police protection?"

"Yes."

"Well, your friend at the DOJ was quite helpful. Turns out there's a guy, Theodore Wooford, who was caught in a sting operation last month in D.C. that was set up to catch sexual predators—you know, people who target underage teens online and arrange to meet with the intent to have sex."

"Sure."

"Well, when they took him in, they found records of lewd chats he'd had with minors, as well as a few images of child pornography on his computer. He tried to cut a deal and offered to help them infiltrate an online group he called the Final Territory. In exchange, he wanted to be placed on probation but serve no prison time. And since he hadn't distributed any images, just downloaded them, they were considering a plea deal."

"What is that?" I asked. "The Final Territory?"

"Well, it wasn't on anyone's radar screen. Wooford claimed they traded in child porn. Sort of a twenty-first-century incarnation of the Wonderland Club."

Although I didn't know all the details, I did know that the Wonderland Club was an online, closed community of pedophiles on Tor, or the Dark Web, as it was sometimes called. To get into the Wonderland Club, you needed to upload ten thousand images of child pornography to their server. That was the membership requirement.

At the time, back in the late nineties, it was the biggest international child pornography bust in history. Most of the people arrested when law enforcement moved in weren't just distributing sexually explicit images of children but were also involved in child molestation, often involving their own children.

I wasn't sure how many people were caught and convicted, but I did remember hearing that at least twelve suspects had committed suicide before their cases went to trial.

"You said the DOJ was considering cutting the deal." I leaned forward. "What happened?"

"Wooford hanged himself the next day in his cell before he could give them any specific details regarding the group."

"He hanged himself? With what?"

"Tore his pants into strips of cloth," she said, "tied them together into a makeshift rope."

"Tearing your pants up into strips isn't easy."

"And that's a lot of work for someone who's trying to cop a plea deal and possibly get probation."

"Yes, it is."

"And you're gonna love this: guess what he had in his possession when he was arrested?"

"What's that?"

"A key. A single key."

"Just like our jumper."

"Yes."

"Interesting. And do we know if they match? If they're the same cut?"

"Harrington is going to send the key up here, but I compared the digital photos and they sure look the same."

"Good. So, besides the keys, did you find any other connection between Wooford and Stewart, or with the jumper last night?"

She shook her head. "That's next on my list."

We set to work.

She examined Wooford's known associates, pulling up DMV photos from the Federal Digital Database to run facial recognition to try to match any of them to the man I'd encountered last evening.

I called Harrington to have him send me everything he had on the Final Territory. There were a few hoops to jump through, but he promised he'd get the information to me as soon as possible.

After a few minutes, I received an email from DeYoung asking me to meet him at one o'clock. I guessed it would be for a follow-up from my talk with Ms. Aguirre. By then, he would certainly have had time to read my report.

Well, at least I had a few hours to make some progress on this thing before getting my reprimand.

10

"How have you been doing this week, Francis?"

"Good."

"The meds are helping, then?"

"I guess. The sessions help too."

"I'm glad to hear that."

Even though Francis had been here to see Dr. Perrior a dozen times, for some reason today he found himself wondering how long his psychologist had been in the business.

He looked like he was in his mid-sixties.

So maybe forty years, decades at least, if he got into this right out of college. That's a long time to sit and listen to people share their—

"And work?" Dr. Perrior scribbled something on his notepad. "How has that been?"

"Well . . ." Of course work came up. It always came up. In truth, that was why he was here. "You know."

"Tell me about it. About how things are going."

"There's some new software we're using that's supposed to make it easier to filter out more of the images."

A brown dove settled onto the outside of the windowsill. It strutted back and forth for a moment, then cocked its head as if it were listening in on their conversation.

The air conditioner rattled in the window beside it, working far too hard for the amount of mildly cool air it was spitting out.

"How has that worked out?" Dr. Perrior asked.

Francis was distracted by the inquisitive bird. "I'm sorry?"

"The software. How's that been going?"

"It doesn't take out the human factor completely, but it does help sort pixel patterns and hash values, makes it so that you don't have to keep seeing the same images over and over. So it's better that way." The dove shuffled to the side and fluttered off toward the roof of a nearby building, and Francis redirected his attention at his psychologist. "We still need to verify things."

"You still need to look at the pictures."

"And the videos. Yes."

"And that's been difficult?"

A pause. "I saw some bad things this week."

"Pictures?"

"A video."

"One that disturbed you."

"I think it would have disturbed just about anyone."

"Would you like to tell me about it?"

"I don't think so. I don't want it in my head anymore."

"We've talked about this before, Francis. I know it's hard, but keeping these things to yourself can be detrimental in the long run. Sometimes talking them through can serve as a pressure valve, a psychological escape hatch if you will, to let off some of the intense feelings involved in your job. It's one of the reasons for these sessions."

"I know."

"What you do is important, Francis. It protects a lot of people. It helps a lot of children."

Go ahead, tell him. It'll help.

"The footage had a baby in it. A baby boy. About, maybe, six months old. They did things to him."

"Did you report it?"

"Yes, right away, to the FBI. And I entered the hash values in to our database."

The organization Francis worked for, the International Child Safety Consortium, focused its efforts on trying to stop child pornography, child molestation, and human trafficking across international borders.

Though the ICSC had support from dozens of governments and law enforcement agencies around the globe, it was a privately funded organization. Their annual child safety summit and donor development event was less than a week away, so things at work were crazy and even more stressful than usual, especially as they geared up to try to recruit more countries to join the consortium.

"So you're doing your job," Dr. Perrior said.

Francis found himself wringing his hands and laid them on his thighs. He stared at them for a moment, watching to see if he could make them be still, make them stop shaking.

You're calm. You can be calm. It's safe here. You can be honest.

An escape valve.

His hands weren't moving anymore.

So that was good.

"Yes. I'm doing my job."

Tell him about the chats.

No!

She's too young.

No. She's old enough. She told you she was.

But what if—

Dr. Perrior's eyes flicked up to the clock that he kept

prominently on the wall beside a fake Monet painting of a woman with a parasol, and Francis glanced up as well and noticed that they only had a few minutes left in the session.

Time had flown by and he hadn't even brought up the most important thing yet.

You need to tell him.

I will, just be patient.

"And what about the other issue we talked about last week?" the psychologist asked. "Have you been engaging in any more chats?"

"Yes. But just with girls over eighteen. I've been careful."

"You mean women?"

"Women?"

"Women over eighteen. Girls would be under eighteen."

"Right. Women."

Okay, say it.

"Dr. Perrior, there's a line and it's like I can see it there."

"A line?"

"Right in front of me."

"And it's one that you don't want to cross," his doctor said.

"Right."

Not even in my thoughts.

Tell him. Not even in your thoughts—

"Who put it there?"

Distracted. Too distracted.

"What?"

"The line—who drew it in front of you? Society? Your conscience?"

"It's just wrong to look at girls that way."

"In a sexual way."

"Yes, but not if they're over eighteen, right? I mean, then it's okay, isn't it?"

"Well, that is the age of consent. That's when our society has determined that young women and men can legally engage in consensual sexual relationships."

"But for other cultures it's different, isn't it? I mean, around the world, and throughout history? It used to be lower in the past—it used to be okay for men my age to be with teenagers—I read that. And what about teens under eighteen being together with other teens? That happens all the time, doesn't it?"

Rather than address those questions directly, Dr. Perrior said, "You mentioned a line in front of you. What steps are you taking to keep yourself from crossing it?"

"I'm trying to get enough sleep, like you told me to. And I'm exercising—I started walking around my neighborhood every other day—and taking the meds, and I stopped drinking: you said drinking can make it worse."

"It lowers a person's inhibitions. Yes."

"Right. And filtering software. I use it on my phone, my computer, everywhere."

"And how close have you come to crossing over it? The line, I mean."

Pretty close.

You crossed it already.

No! She said she's eighteen.

But how can you be sure? You can never be sure.

Unless you were to meet her.

"Francis?"

Dr. Perrior looked concerned and Francis didn't want him to think that there was something wrong with him, so he said, "I heard somebody on a news show say that people who think those things, who're tempted that way, are sick. Then this one cop came on and he said they're just bad people."

"What things?"

"Being with girls—or boys—who aren't eighteen yet. But it's things I have to deal with in my job. I've never done anything though. So are those people sick or bad?"

"What do you think?"

I think I'm a bad person. And I think I'm weak.

Don't tell him that!

Too weak to keep saying no. Too weak to—

"I don't know," Francis said.

"Do your chats ever become romantic or sexual in nature? The ones with the women?"

A pause. "Sometimes."

"Have you ever tried to meet one of the people you've chatted with online?"

"No. I would never do that. I'm not a bad person."

"Would that make you a bad person? If you met one of the women you chat with?"

I'm already a bad person just for thinking these things.

"Normal people aren't tempted like this, though. I mean, you can't look at the things I have to look at every day and then have it not affect you, right?"

"I'd be worried if it didn't affect you. Francis, you need to know that everybody thinks things they're not proud of sometimes. It's part of human nature. No one is perfect. All of us are tempted by things we know are wrong. We all have dark desires. Part of being healthy—mentally healthy—is accepting that about yourself."

"Accepting that I have dark desires."

"Yes. As all of us do. But not acting on them."

"Not crossing the line."

"Correct."

"Do you have dark desires too, Dr. Perrior?"

A slight laugh. "You didn't come in here today so I could tell you about my problems. We're here to help you work through the pressures of the job you have to do."

"I know, but I was just curious about it, if you did too. Have dark desires."

He knew that Dr. Perrior worked with the NYPD sometimes, especially on crimes that involved children, but he didn't know what the doctor was thinking in those times, if he'd ever had bad thoughts.

"As I said," Dr. Perrior replied, "we all do and, as you pointed out, it's only natural that someone in your position would have these sorts of questions and struggles. But it sounds like you're doing what you need to in order to deal with them in a healthy way." He checked the clock again, then closed his notebook. "I'm afraid it looks like our time is up for today. But I'll see you next week, alright? And in the meantime, I'd like you to keep journaling your feelings."

"That's something I needed to tell you. This is the last session they're paying for."

"Your insurance company?"

"Yes."

"And will the ICSC cover the visits?"

Francis shook his head. "They give us time off for the sessions. I mean, they pay us to come, but we need to cover the sessions ourselves. I guess since different doctors charge different amounts. They're just trying to be fair."

"Of course. So you'll be handling the cost yourself, is that what you're saying?"

"I can't afford to. Not if I have to pay for them."

"I'm afraid I'm not in a position to be able to see clients pro bono."

"I was wondering if we could work something out.

Or, I mean, maybe if I paid cash, you could . . . Maybe you could give me some sort of . . ."

"How about this, Francis: let me recommend a doctor to you who's getting started. She's looking for new clients. She has less overhead than I do and might have more flexibility in her fee structure. Why don't you contact her? I'll write you a referral and—"

"I really think it'd be better if I could keep seeing you."

Dr. Perrior jotted a phone number down. "I'll tell you what: try your insurance company one more time. Meanwhile, give Dr. Tignini a call. See how it works with her and if we need to, we can revisit things then."

As Francis left, he heard the voices in his head again.

You didn't tell him everything, Francis.

I can't tell him everything! If I did, he would think I'm dirty, that I'm a pervert, that I'm going to do something bad or hurt someone. But I'm not. I can say no. Dr. Perrior talked about self-control. I can control myself.

What about the chats? What about those?

They're with a woman. She said she's a woman.

You need help, Francis.

I'm getting help. There's nothing else I can do.

Maybe you should quit your job.

No, I need the money and I'm good at what I do. I help a lot of people, just like Dr. Perrior said.

The questions twisted and tightened around themselves, making it so that he didn't know what to do, like a net that was spread before him and there was no avoiding it.

A line he couldn't cross.

And a net he couldn't avoid.

He decided he would ask his supervisor, Claire Nolan,

if the ICSC could cover the cost of the sessions. It wouldn't hurt to ask.

And Dr. Perrior was right: he should try his insurance company one more time too. He could at least give it a try. The worst thing they could do was say no.

But what then? What if they do say no?

We'll see. We'll just see.

He left for the International Child Safety Consortium's offices.

Yes, he would talk with Claire. Things would work out.

And he would be able to see Dr. Perrior again next week. Just like he had for the last three months. It was all going to work out okay.

11

The DNA came back without a match. So, whoever our John Doe was, if he really was named Randy as the note in his pocket indicated, he wasn't in the system. No one fitting his description had been reported missing. And despite the robust nationwide media attention, no one had shown up to claim his body.

Jodie wasn't able to pin any DMV photos to him either.

Evidently, Wooford, Stewart, and Randy were somehow linked together, so I had Stewart's key ring brought up from evidence to see if any of the keys matched the one I'd found on Randy's body.

One of them did.

I wasn't sure where that left us, but it was something to work with.

Three dead guys each who had the same type of key.

We just needed to figure out what those keys opened.

We'd put out word online, but so far no tattoo studios had come forward to identify anyone named Randy who'd gotten a shamrock tattoo. An officer was calling studios in the city to follow up.

I decided to release the contents of the note I'd found on the body to the press. Normally, I wasn't excited about working with the media, but in this case it seemed like a logical step. Maybe Billy, whoever he was, would see it and come forward.

We knew how the man died—he fell twelve stories onto concrete—but we didn't know what led him to jump. We also needed to find out if there were any drugs or alcohol in his system. So I verified that there was going to be an autopsy—it was scheduled for tomorrow morning.

We sent out some NYPD officers to interview Stewart's friends, family members, work associates, and neighbors to see if they could identify our jumper.

Jodie and I worked through lunch—sandwiches from the cafeteria—and a few minutes before one o'clock, I left to meet with Assistant Director DeYoung.

He was leaving his office as I approached it.

DeYoung cleared his throat heartily and gestured for me to join him. "Walk with me, Pat. Something came up. I need to brief Media Relations ahead of the press conference."

We started down the hall.

"So we still don't know the jumper's identity?" he asked me.

"No, sir. Not yet. But we have a few things we're looking into. So you'll be releasing the contents of the note?"

"I'm not convinced it's the right call at this point, but I trust your judgment." Then he pivoted the conversation. "I understand the meeting with Ms. Aguirre went well earlier?"

"We talked things through. Yes."

"Good, good, good. I'm glad to hear that. She tells me everything is in order. I'll look forward to reading her final report."

"You haven't read it yet?"

He rubbed his forehead melodramatically. "Been a hectic day. A *hectic day.*"

"Is that what you wanted to talk with me about? The incident last night?"

"Actually, I'm assigning you to work with Detective Cavanaugh. I think your expertise will be beneficial to an investigation he's heading up."

"I already have the Stewart homicide and the suicide last night on my plate."

"This might be related to them. That's one of the things I need you to help sort out."

We rounded the corner. "So, Detective Cavanaugh," I said. "Is this Tobin Cavanaugh?"

"You know him?"

"I've heard his name, never worked with him. He's with the Special Victims Unit?"

"Yes. Nearly nine years with the Vice Enforcement Sexual Exploitation of Children Unit. Recently transferred to SVU."

The Exploitation of Children Unit investigated cases of child pornography, while the SVU focused on crimes involving rape, sexual assault and the molestation of children. The two units worked closely together and it wasn't uncommon for detectives to switch from one to the other.

I wondered about the Final Territory connection. Maybe with his background, Cavanaugh had run into it before and would be able to help shed some light on all this.

Often that's how these things work: you start to uncover folds of one case and they lead you to the folds of another.

"The origami of death," my mentor, Dr. Calvin Werjonic, used to say. "Our job is to see the final shape by studying the creases before any more people die."

"You mentioned that Cavanaugh's work might be re-lated to what happened last night," I said to DeYoung. "What makes you say that?"

"I'll have to let him fill you in. Time. I'm too pressed for time right now."

"Is he here?"

"He's at NYPD headquarters leading a briefing in their cyber crime center. They're analyzing the flash drive from the apartment. I told him you'd be right over."

12

Francis spent his days looking at the things most people would prefer to pretend weren't really happening in the world.

Now, as he sat in front of his computer in his cubicle, he kept an eye out for Claire to leave her office so he could talk to her about having the consortium pay for his counseling.

A little while ago, he'd called his insurance company but had been put on hold for so long he'd finally hung up, deciding he would try again this afternoon during his coffee break.

Most people knew that child pornography was out there on the web, but search engines were getting better at weeding it out and at posting warnings about it, and it was retreating into the deeper cracks and crevices of the Internet, so it was more difficult to stumble across accidentally.

But it was still there, and if you knew where to look, you could find it. Especially on the Dark Web, or Tor, where two percent of the sites involve child porn, but receive eighty-three percent of the traffic. A chilling statistic that spoke volumes to the real reason people went on Tor.

When Francis started at this job eight years ago, the images were less violent and easier to stomach.

But those didn't seem to satisfy today's consumers of child porn, and every year the pictures and videos became more and more deviant and hard-core.

Basically, his job was simple.

After law enforcement agencies, search engines, and individuals reported images and videos that were suspected of being child pornography, Francis entered them into a giant searchable database.

Every photo and video file has a unique digital signature known as a hash value. Those values allow you to track and identify files.

In 2002, in the Ashcroft v. Free Speech Coalition case, the Supreme Court had ruled that child pornography was criminal only if it contained images depicting actual children. So cartoons and computer generated images didn't officially count.

That meant that it was vital, whenever possible, to identify the children who were being molested so their molesters could be prosecuted and the images taken down.

To try fooling law enforcement, child pornographers would insert random images into the videos or embed the videos inside a text document so that the pixel pattern was different.

But Francis was good at his job. He knew the tricks and how to get past them.

He even knew ways of back-tracing emails and chats to specific IP addresses, and had learned how pornographers could turn on and turn off another person's webcam without the person knowing. That way they could film them during their chats.

He'd never done it, of course, but part of his job required knowing ways around the law so he could help law enforcement officers find those who were breaking it.

Francis was responsible for four things: screening, identifying, cataloging, reporting. It was easy to remember by using the acronym "SICR." All he had to do was keep in mind that there was no one *sicker* than the people who were filming these things and he could stay focused on the core elements of his job.

Simple.

The acronym wasn't as necessary for him now as it had been back when he was getting started, but he would sometimes still use it to remind himself of his responsibilities, just so he wouldn't get distracted.

The ICSC was creating a registry of all known child pornography so they could search servers in real time and help law enforcement identify when IP addresses were distributing or downloading illicit material. Since 2002, ICSC's computers had screened over a hundred million images from North America. It was the most comprehensive single-country database in the world.

Combining the databases of the eighty-four other participating countries brought the total of the ICSC's image database to more than seven hundred million unique files that had been identified as child porn or as exploitative of children: one image or video of a child being molested for every ten people on the planet.

Of course, it would be impossible for a human being to search through or organize hundreds of millions of photos and videos, so Francis used advanced software to sort and compare the hash values and pixel patterns. He informed law enforcement agencies in different countries when a child's image came up so that, if possible, he or she could be identified, located, and protected.

Over the years he'd helped to save three hundred and forty-one children, at least that he knew about, from molestation, and he'd assisted law enforcement in identifying twice that many people who were trafficking in violent child pornography.

The numbers were something tangible, something real.

Those six hundred seventy-eight men and women had over four hundred thousand images of child pornography among them, and with average sentences of fourteen years, they were serving, collectively, nearly ten thousand years in prison.

It was something specific he could look at to remind himself that he really was helping to make a difference: getting child molesters off the street for nearly ten thousand years. Even if he died today, he'd done something good with his life.

He brought those things back to mind when his job wore on him, when the images got to him.

His position wasn't entirely unique in the tech community. There were staff members at Yahoo, Google, Bing, Krazle, Facebook, Twitter, every major website, file-sharing site, or search engine, who also had to view child pornography for a living.

They would spend their days looking at the most vile and heart-wrenching acts against children ever filmed, report them, block the users or take down the sites, report the images to the ICSC and law enforcement, and then clock out at the end of the day and go home and do their best to act like everything was normal and okay in the world.

Most of them received no counseling, no stipend for counseling, no time off for counseling.

This is what the Internet has spawned.

Or more accurately, what human nature has spawned through the Internet.

No one could look at those things hour after hour, day after day, and not be affected by them.

Most people quit within a couple of months. Some turned to drinking or drugs, or slipped into depression, or committed suicide at nearly fifteen times the national rate.

At least the ICSC paid for their staff's time when they went to see counselors.

It proved that they cared for their employees.

Francis had heard that they usually tried to hire women for these positions, but because of a discrimination lawsuit before his time, they'd had to give that up. He'd been hired soon after that.

He'd been doing this almost ten times longer than the next most experienced analyst at the ICSC.

When Claire didn't appear, Francis finally left his cubicle and, somewhat hesitantly, tapped on her door.

"Yes?" she called.

He eased it open and peered into her office.

"You can come in, Francis."

He took two small steps.

A few months ago she'd gone to a conference and come back encouraging everyone to call her by her first name from then on. "I want this office to be one of openness, of familiarity, of transparency," she'd said. "I don't want you to look at me as your boss, but rather as your work associate." Then she gave a double thumbs-up. "As your friend."

This sort of thing happened a lot after conferences. It

didn't always stick, but Claire typically did come back with a whole handful of new management ideas.

Francis was still getting used to it. He still wanted to call her Mrs. Nolan.

An imposing painting of the ICSC's president, Alejandro Gomez, stared at him from above her shoulder. Francis always found it a bit intimidating.

Mr. Gomez spent most of his time with world leaders at the U.N., or with major donors. The donor banquet next week was his brainchild, and Francis hadn't seen him around the ICSC offices hardly at all in the last few weeks as his meetings picked up.

"What can I do for you, Francis?" Claire asked.

"How are you?"

"Very well. And you?"

"I've been seeing Dr. Perrior."

"Yes, and how is it going?"

"Good. Um, that's the thing. My insurance, it's not going to cover the visits anymore."

"I'm sorry to hear that."

"Is there any way you could, I mean that the ICSC, could pay for the sessions?"

"As per our company policy, we can give you paid leave for the time you spend in counseling, but as you know, with the disparity in what different therapists charge, we have to be fair."

"I know."

"So if we paid for yours, we'd have to pay for everyone else's too, wouldn't we?"

"Yes. I guess."

"So perhaps you can find another counselor?"

"Dr. Perrior recommended someone."

"Well, good. That's good, then." She smiled and lifted

her hands in a slightly celebratory manner. "Problem solved."

"Okay."

"Will there be anything else?"

"No. Thank you, Mrs. Nolan."

"Claire."

"Thank you, Claire."

13

I arrived in the New York Police Department's CCS, or Cyber Command Suite—a public-relations-sensitive term that the police commissioner came up with to describe the room.

A *suite*?

Really?

Yeah, there was a term guaranteed to strike fear in the hearts of criminals everywhere.

Although not as glitzy and slick as Hollywood might have portrayed it, the main workspace of the CCS did look a bit like it came from the set of a movie: Dim lights. No windows. Arrays of computers. Monitors covering the walls. Servers stacked in the corner for easy access for the technicians.

The room was almost empty when I entered, but one analyst pointed to a briefing room and put her finger to her lips to indicate for me to be quiet as I entered.

The door was open. I slipped in the back.

Never a fan of briefings, I was just glad I didn't have to sit through this one from the start.

I recognized Detective Cavanaugh right away from some internal memos I'd seen in the past. He was standing up front between a projection screen and a white-board speaking to the officers.

Caucasian. Medium height. Mid- to late forties. He had a narrow face that might have appeared haggard on someone else, but gave him a look of calculated intensity. I got the immediate impression that he was a man who was serious about his work, focused, and driven.

Well, if that was the case, we were going to get along just fine.

Trying not to disturb anyone, I found a folding chair leaning against the back wall, but the legs didn't have those little rubber knobs on them and scraped noisily on the floor as I positioned it. Most of the people in the room turned to look.

"Sorry."

I sat beside Agent Aldéric Descartes, another joint task force member.

When Cavanaugh went on, I couldn't tell if he was perturbed by the interruption or not. "As I was saying, keep in mind that these guys know how children think. They might spend weeks or months grooming the child so they can initiate a sexual encounter."

I thought of a guy whom a friend of mine had put away, a pedophile named Hal Lloyd. As a computer expert he'd consulted with the Bureau's Cyber Division before he was arrested. He knew how to hide his tracks and was only caught when he made the mistake of trying to groom the daughter of a city commissioner for sex.

Cavanaugh typed at his laptop's keyboard, and a video appeared on the projection screen. It showed children swinging, laughing, and chasing each other around a playground. Light, airy, uplifting instrumental woodwind music played in the background.

He paused the footage. "This is a training video for groomers. Our unit pulled it off YouTube yesterday."

Although people had already been paying attention, now the room went stone silent.

No one moved.

"By the time it came to our attention, it'd already been viewed more than fifteen thousand times. It keeps popping up again on other sites, we keep taking it down. As you know, once it's out there, it's out there. There's no bringing it back. This video is targeted more at hebephiles than pedophiles."

From my work over the years, I knew that a pedophile is someone who has a sexual interest in prepubescent children. A hebephile is sexually attracted to young adolescents, usually between ages eleven and fourteen.

Cavanaugh tapped the spacebar to restart the video.

A woman's voice came on: *"In the past, child lovers had to hide in the shadows. We were isolated, ostracized, persecuted. Today, through technology, we have the ability to support one another in our pursuits. We have community. We have the resources to help establish and promote long-term, committed intergenerational relationships."*

Cavanaugh stopped it again. "Note the phrasing, the spin, the word choice: 'child lovers' and 'long-term, committed intergenerational relationships.' The web provides accessibility, anonymity, community, and plenty of social reinforcement for deviant behavior. In the past if you were interested in molesting children, you had to pretty much go it alone since it was so hard to find social support and justification for your activity. Not anymore. Now there are dozens of sites out there dedicated to helping you get away with it, as well as videos, like this one, on how to avoid prosecution, on what you can and cannot say in chats to skirt around the variances in state laws, and ways to claim entrapment if you are caught."

In a twisted and tragic way, the Internet was a child pornographer's dream come true. It removed geographic, societal, cultural, jurisdictional, and psychological barriers and offered sites that provided supportive, facilitative communities. Throw in powerful sexual addictions, the anonymity Cavanaugh had just mentioned, and 24/7 access, and you've created a potent mix.

He started the video once more and, as the narrator spoke, footage appeared of children at recess filmed through the metal fence surrounding their elementary school, then went to a little girl walking through a mall holding her mother's hand, and half a dozen young teenagers playing volleyball on a sandy beach near the ocean.

"In North America, children ages ten to twelve are ideal. Younger children are easier to encourage to engage in a romance, but are more likely to tell their parents that something strange or 'scary' has happened.

"Also, children in those preteen years are still, for the most part, trusting, looking for affirmation, and less likely to tell their friends about the relationship. As you know, we have to protect children from feeling guilty or dirty or shameful, but also from shying away from us, so we need to do whatever's necessary to protect the privacy of the relationships.

"Some children are best convinced through promises, others through gifts, others through enhanced persuasion—although this is only in the service of continuing the romance. In time you'll learn to read the children in your life and find the best ways to help them keep things confidential."

It infuriated me to hear the way the narrator was phrasing things: "continuing the romance" and keeping children from "shying away" and using "enhanced per-suasion," pretending that the situation was meant to pro-tect the child, when that was precisely who it was harming.

"Appeal to what they want most. For girls it's often an emotional connection rather than a physical one. Most girls desire affirmation. They want to be told that they're special, that they're pretty. Gifts work wonders—stuffed animals, jewelry, flowers, love notes. It's helpful to use things that will act as constant reminders of you."

As the voice-over continued, the video showed more laughing, happy children and I wondered what their par-ents would do if they found out what video their kids were appearing in.

Then the narrator described what to say to younger children: *"Try, 'This is our secret. We can't tell anyone what happened. You do know how to keep a secret, don't you?' Again, you must know your child, her needs, her wants, her desires. It comes with experience, with spending time with them."*

As the video played, Cavanaugh interjected, "Every second, more than thirty thousand people are watching porn online, and twenty percent of that involves children. If you count how many people are sexting, the number might be double that."

"And now enhanced persuasion. This is a last resort, but sometimes it becomes necessary in order to keep the relation-ship intact. 'It's your fault that this happened. I wouldn't have done anything if you didn't wear those kinds of clothes.' Or, 'You're dirty now. You've done things you shouldn't have. If you tell what happened, everybody is going to find out. You'll be in trouble and no one will like you anymore,' or, 'If you tell anyone, I'm going to have to hurt your pet kitty. You love her, don't you? You wouldn't want anything

to happen to her, would you?' Of course you would never harm the child's pet, that's only said to protect the integrity of the relationship."

The video showed a group of young teens standing around watching a soccer game. They looked maybe thirteen or fourteen years old.

Clearly, they had no idea they were being filmed.

"When chatting with teenagers, emphasize how you share something special with them. For example, 'I've never felt this way about anyone before. You can feel it too, can't you? I know it sounds a little weird to say it, but there's a chemistry, right?' 'I can be honest with you like I can't be honest with anyone else.' Bring up things that you have in common, study the music that they like and comment on it, then write, 'I just like how we can share stuff that's important to us, stuff that matters, you know?' "

I thought of Tessa, of how I would feel if she were ever targeted in this way. Even though I wasn't her dad, not related to her in any way, I found myself feeling protective of her.

"The age issue will inevitably come up, and when it does, remind the child that all throughout history it was common for older men—and women—to have loving relationships with boys and girls. Still today, in some countries, the age of consent is as low as nine years old. In two countries, there are no age of consent laws at all."

Cavanaugh pressed the spacebar and added, "Recently, a number of lawsuits have been brought by hebephiles who claim that since movie theaters, amusement parks, restaurants, and so on all charge an adult fare for children over twelve, our courts should officially recognize them as adults in the matter of consent laws as well."

"You're kidding me," an officer near the front exclaimed disgustedly.

"Not at all. The adult/child sex advocates argue that if society as a whole regards those over twelve years old as adults, why shouldn't we allow them to make adult decisions about what they do with their bodies?"

He looked at the screen, seemed lost in thought for a moment, then said, "That's probably enough for right now. I don't know about you, but I can only take so much of this. I'll make the rest available for you to watch and we'll discuss it during Monday's briefing."

He gave them the encrypted link to the grooming training video on the Federal Digital Database, took some time to hand out specific assignments related to current cases, and then dismissed his team.

Agent Descartes and Chip Hinchcliffe, the officer who'd been shocked by the mention of the lawsuit, walked past me, talking about finding the perverts who did this sort of thing.

I waited for the room to clear, and then, as Tobin unplugged his computer from the projector, I went up to introduce myself.

14

"I'm Patrick Bowers." I extended my hand. "Assistant Director DeYoung sent me over."

"Tobin Cavanaugh." He shook my hand. A steely grip. "So you're the guy I keep hearing about."

"I might be."

"The FBI agent who refuses to look for means, motive, and opportunity." Before I could ask where he'd heard that, he said, "Grapevine."

I wasn't sure we were getting off on the right foot here or not.

"I just don't start with those three things. I believe the key is in understanding the context of a crime—patterns, choices, cues. What decision led this criminal to this location at this time? What cues did he take from his victim and his environment to decide that this was an opportune time to commit the offense? Understanding these factors leads to an understanding of means, motive, and opportunity, but the reverse isn't true. You don't start with the conclusion and then try to make the facts fit. You start with the facts and follow wherever they lead you."

Cavanaugh gathered his things. "And geospatial patterns? Talk me through that. I haven't had a chance yet to read your books."

I couldn't tell if he was throwing me an attitude or just being direct.

I decided to give him the benefit of the doubt.

"First, we need to establish which cases are linked. Offenders don't act randomly or choose the locations of crimes randomly. Just like all of us, they have intentions in their travel routes— often to save time and money— and certain places and times hold significance to them. The relationships of the locations to each other show us movement patterns of the offender and reveal sites that he feels comfortable enough in to commit his crimes undisturbed. So, in a series of offenses, the relationship of the timing, location, and progression of the crimes gives us important data regarding the offender's understanding of, and familiarity with, the region."

Cavanaugh looked deep in thought.

Glancing around, I found a dry erase marker and turned to the whiteboard, then drew half a dozen circles as I spoke.

"Most crimes occur at the locations where offenders spend the majority of their time—we refer to them as activity nodes—or along the pathways between these places. However, it's not just proportionate to the amount of time they spend there, but related to how safe and confident they feel there."

I labeled the circles work, home, store, friend's house, park, and restaurant, then drew a web of interconnected lines, delineating travel routes.

"The decision-making process is shaped by environmental cues as offenders evaluate, among other factors, risk versus potential payoff, the availability of and desirability of targets in that specific place at that specific time and so on."

Cavanaugh watched me intently. Whether it was an inquisitive or judgmental gaze, I wasn't sure.

"So, after establishing which crimes are linked," he said, "what then?"

"If possible, I visit the scenes and view entrance and exit routes, study the lighting, the geospatial relationships, site usage patterns, and traffic flow in the surrounding areas. I'm looking for clues as to why the killer chose this location—Seclusion? Convenience? Expediency?"

"And the chronological and temporal aspects of the case—when did things happen and in what order."

"Yes. Then, taking cognitive mapping research into consideration, I work backward trying to identify the most likely home base for the offender to try and help us cut back on the time and resources it takes to complete the investigation. That's it in a nutshell."

"And you wrote two books on that?"

"Well, I went a little more in-depth."

"I see."

I still couldn't read him, so I said, "DeYoung told me that you wanted my help with a case, seeing if it might be linked to the two deaths at Brilington Towers over the last few nights?"

"I hear you shot the guy."

"Detective Cavanaugh, I—"

"Tobin."

"Tobin. What can you tell me about the case you're working on? How can I help you here?"

"We're looking at a series of missing children that we think might be linked to what happened at that apartment in Manhattan."

"Go on."

"Let's head to the computer forensics lab. They're looking over the USB flash drive right now. I'll explain on the way."

15

As we left the suite, Tobin said, "We're looking at four nonfamily abductions since the first of the year that we think might be linked. You may have heard of them: Maggie Rivers, age eleven; Andre Martin, age ten; D'Nesh Mujeeb Agarwai, nine; and LeAnne Cordett, four."

"Yes. Maggie was taken from a mall, Andre from a state park in New Jersey, D'Nesh when he was on his way home from school, and LeAnne from a day care center at a church."

That last one was when her teacher was helping another child in the lavatory. When they came out, LeAnne was gone. It was incredibly audacious to abduct a child under those circumstances, but it wasn't the first time I'd heard of something like that happening. Day care center abductions happen at least once a year somewhere in the U.S.

Tobin looked at me quizzically. "Did DeYoung fill you in?"

"No."

"How do you know those details?"

"I follow the news."

"And you just happened to remember all that off the top of your head?"

"Yes."

He blinked. "Okay."

"And all four are still missing—correct?"

"That's right."

"But these children all disappeared under remarkably different circumstances. What makes you think the abductions might be related to each other or to the deaths this week at the Brilington Towers?"

"Jamaal Stewart ran a website on real estate investment techniques. All of the children's parents subscribed to his weekly email newsletter."

Okay.

I didn't believe in coincidences. And even if I did, I couldn't imagine that this was one staring at me right now.

"How did you come across that?"

"I dig into things."

"We should have Cyber analyze that mailing list."

"Done. I have some officers cross-checking the names against other missing children or known sex offenders."

Yeah. I could get used to working with this guy.

I liked him already.

We arrived at the computer forensics lab and one of the technicians, a young officer who looked barely old enough to drive, told us, "Well, as you know, one of the USB devices was just for the wireless keyboard. There was nothing for us there. I've been working on the other one, the flash drive. Whoever set it up did not want the contents to be made public. Not at all."

"Were you able to pull anything off it?" Tobin inquired.

"It was programmed to reformat itself if it was inserted into a device that wasn't prefigured to accept it. So that wasn't good. Thank God we were able to identify that before there was a complete wipe. We're seeing if we can recover any data from it. It's going to take some digging, but I'm reasonably confident we'll be able to figure out at least some of what was on there."

"Did you try the TV?" I asked.

"Excuse me?"

"The one in Stewart's apartment. The flash drive was in the television's USB port when I found it, so doesn't it make sense to start there? The television would have likely been set up to accept the drive. If you reinsert it—"

The light went on. "We should be able to view the files—especially if they are video or audio files."

"Then just download them. Yes."

"Nice."

"Okay, get to it." Tobin did not sound thrilled that they didn't have anything for us yet.

As we left for his desk, I asked if he'd ever heard of the Final Territory or of Ted Wooford.

"Not Wooford, no, but I have heard of the Final Territory. Just rumors mostly, nothing solid. I always took it as sort of an urban legend in the field."

"What have you heard?"

"Live molestation on webcams. Other members send in requests while they watch. I've heard conjecture that it's located in Denmark, where the laws are a lot more lax—but who knows. It could be based here in the States. Was Wooford a part of this?"

"It looks like it, yes. But he's dead—apparent suicide."

"Apparent?"

"The timing and circumstances make it a little suspect. What about 'Aurora's birthday?' Have you heard of that?"

He shook his head. "What is it?"

"The jumper from last night mentioned it. It's a file he

was looking for. He told me it wasn't on the computer or the phone, asked if we'd found it."

"We can contact the ICSC, see if they have a record of it."

I'd heard of the International Child Safety Consortium but hadn't worked with them before.

When we reached Tobin's office, he put in a call to the ICSC and spoke with someone named Claire Nolan. While he was on the line, I phoned Jodie to touch base. She told me the press release had gone out with the suicide note's contents.

"DeYoung released a photo of it," she told me.

I found that a little curious. "Not just the contents?"

"He thought having the handwriting out there might help. Oh, and I'm going to analyze Stewart's mailing list to see if anyone on it is named Randy, Billy, or Ted, or any variant of those names."

"Good call."

After Tobin and I were both off the phone, I spent some time reviewing to him what I knew about the homicides on Tuesday night and what had happened last night at the apartment complex.

Then he read through the case files while I studied his notes on the missing children and began to input the locations we knew about into the algorithms I use to analyze the aggregate data to develop a preliminary geographic profile.

16

At two o'clock, Francis tried his insurance company again and this time he was at least able to reach a real person who pointed him to an online form that he could fill out to resubmit the request for them to cover his psychologist visits. "But," the woman said frankly, "they almost never reverse their decisions. I wouldn't bother unless there's a lawsuit or something."

Discouraged, Francis left the ICSC just like he did every day for his afternoon coffee at the Mystorium, an independent coffeehouse and used bookstore that specialized in crime books, thrillers, and mysteries.

As Dr. Perrior had told him once, "Habits can center a person. Habits can help him stay balanced when life seems to be spinning out of control."

So this was a habit he had developed to help himself stay balanced.

Every day.

Two o'clock.

The Mystorium.

If you were looking for the latest self-help book, you'd best go somewhere else, but if you were in the market for a first-edition signed copy of an Elmore Leonard or P. D. James novel, it would make sense to try the Mystorium first.

When Francis entered, a studious-looking woman who was typing on her laptop at a corner table near the Jeffery Deaver novels looked his way, then, embarrassed, quickly directed her attention back to the computer screen.

Red hair. Pretty. Looked a little like Scully from the early days of *The X-Files*. She was about Francis's age. He'd seen her in here before, had even almost talked to her once.

The barista, a college student named Rebekah Brown who liked to wear big loopy earrings and always changed the store's music to Muse or Arctic Monkeys when her boss wasn't looking, knew Francis by name and smiled as he approached.

"How are you today, Mr. Edlemore?"

"I'm good. How are you, Rebekah?"

"Excellent." She gave him a sly smile. "I think you have an admirer."

"An admirer?"

She put one hand up to hide the other hand, then pointed through her blocking hand in the direction of the woman. "She's had her eye out for you." Rebekah spoke in a whisper just loud enough for Francis to hear. "Yesterday too. You should talk to her."

"Oh, she couldn't have been waiting for me."

"Oh, I think she was."

"Are you sure?"

"Pretty sure."

"How do you know?"

"I'm a girl. Trust me."

"Woman."

"What?"

"You're a woman. You're over eighteen."

"Oh. Right, well, just trust me here. Go talk to her."

"I don't know."

"Go, on. Just say hi."

"I'll just take the coffee for today." He handed her his credit card and his nearly full frequent coffee buyer punch card. "The mild. Small. Thank you."

"Mr. Edlemore," Rebekah sighed. "What am I going to do with you?"

She ran the purchase.

Punched his card.

Poured him his drink.

"I guess I'll see you tomorrow, then," she said.

"I'll see you tomorrow, Rebekah." She nodded once more toward the woman in the corner, but he just did his best to smile and told her, "Maybe some other time."

However, as he left, he did glance in the woman's direction and almost, almost, almost took a detour past her table to pretend to look at some books on a nearby shelf, but then his nervousness overwhelmed his initiative and he went out the main door instead.

On the way back to the ICSC, he tried the number Dr. Perrior had given him for Dr. Tignini, but it went to voicemail.

He left a message for her to call him.

As soon as possible.

A message from Claire that the NYPD was looking for some information was waiting for him when he got back to his desk. "Detective Cavanaugh would like to speak with you about something called the Final Territory."

++++

While Tobin took a call from someone at the ICSC, I got word from Jodie that a man who'd seen the photo of Randy's note on the Internet believed it was his brother's handwriting.

Apparently, they hadn't been in touch for a couple of

years, but the guy lived in Brooklyn and was on his way
to the morgue now to see if he could identify the body.

"I'll head over there," I said to her. "If it is his brother,
I want to talk with him as soon as possible."

I hung up just after Tobin did.

"What do we know?" he asked me.

I summarized what Jodie had told me.

He pulled out his car keys. "I'll drive."

"What did the ICSC tell you?"

"They're looking into it. I spoke with a guy named
Francis Edlemore. I've worked with him before. Kind of
an odd cat, but he's been there for a while and he knows
what he's doing. He's going to see what he can pull up."

The two of us left in his car for Presbyterian Central
Hospital.

17

On the drive over, I learned that the man we were going to meet, Billy McReynolds, was a blogger and syndicated talk show radio host, leaned conservative, and had garnered a huge social media following since he got started three years ago. One of his fans had seen the note, made a connection since Billy would sometimes tell stories about growing up with his brother, Randy, and tweeted the link to him.

We met him in the hospital's first-floor lobby.

Billy wasn't as tall as his brother, but the family resemblance was there. His experience as a professional speaker was clear in his deep, resonant radio-voice. But even that didn't cover the nervousness and unease that came through from him being here now to identify his brother's body.

The medical examiner, a slightly standoffish French woman in her early fifties, led the three of us into the autopsy room.

I don't like morgues.

Most of the time they smell overly sanitized and look all too spotless and shiny with their stainless steel counters and sterile exam tables and polished dissection tools.

The floors are almost always vigorously mopped and

have no sign of blood or bodily fluids, but the drain on the floor in the middle of the room speaks volumes as to what really goes on in here.

Of course if you're here during an autopsy, the floor looks a lot different.

Smells different too.

Dr. Coutre went to the freezer. "Are you ready?" she asked Billy. "Or do you need a minute?"

"I'm ready, but I haven't seen my brother in over two years. I'm not sure I can identify him, especially if he's . . . I mean . . . I heard he fell pretty far."

"We'll give it a shot, okay?"

"Yeah," he managed to say.

Tobin stood stoically beside me. He was watching Billy rather than the doctor, perhaps to gauge his reaction. It was a good idea. I did the same.

Dr. Coutre unlatched the door to the freezer and swung it open, and a puff of chilled air followed as she pulled out the gurney containing the corpse. The body was covered with an unblemished white sheet. No stains. No blood. Not a spot. Nothing to signify how violent an end this man had met.

"Ready?" She respectfully waited for Billy to nod before drawing the sheet back to reveal the man's head.

Eyes closed. Grayish skin.

The autopsy was scheduled for tomorrow, so at least they hadn't cut into him yet.

Last night when I felt for this man's pulse, he at least looked alive. Now he had a claylike appearance that was troubling on a gut level, especially when you realized you were going to look just like that one day as well.

Billy cringed and swallowed hard.

"Is this your brother?" Tobin asked him.

"I . . . I think so. I'm not sure."

When people are dead, they look strikingly different than they do when they're alive, so I wasn't too surprised about his uncertainty.

Billy went on, "He had a tattoo on the back of his right hand. A shamrock. I would recognize that. It's pretty distinctive."

I recalled the tattoo and nodded for Dr. Coutre to go ahead. She slid enough of the sheet back to reveal the corpse's tattooed hand.

"That's him," Billy said softly. "That's Randy. Cover him up."

"Do you want a few minutes alone?" Dr. Coutre asked him.

"Yeah. I guess so. Thanks."

We retreated to the lobby and about five minutes later Billy joined us and Dr. Coutre went back into the autopsy room to take care of the body.

"Mr. McReynolds," I said, "I know this isn't an ideal time, but I need to ask you a few questions about your brother."

"Alright." He took a deep breath to calm himself. "Yes, go ahead."

"You mentioned that you haven't seen him in two years. Do you know where he's been in the meantime?"

He shook his head. "I lost touch with him. The last I heard he was in West Virginia. Beckley."

As a rock climber, I'd heard of Beckley. It's a climbing and rafting destination since it's so close to the stunning New River Gorge, but I'd never been there myself.

Tobin said, "You recognized his handwriting from the note that was found on his body?"

A nod. "One of my listeners sent me a link to it. Then when I read it, it made sense."

"How's that? How did it make sense?"

"What it said about the accusations, about letting me down."

"What accusations were those?"

"I'm not sure I should say. I mean, they were just . . . Nothing was ever proven."

"You can help us save time if you just tell us what they were."

"I don't know. I mean, some woman said he sexually assaulted her—date rape—when they were seniors in high school. He always denied it. I don't know, maybe that's what led him to do this."

"Which woman? Do you have a name?"

"No. Beth, I think . . . I'm not sure. It was a while ago."

I unpocketed my phone, logged in to the Federal Digital Database, scrolled to the DMV photo of Jamaal Stewart from the case files, and showed it to Billy. "Do you recognize this man?"

"No."

After swiping the photo to the side, I found one of Ted Wooford. "What about him?"

"No. I don't know how I can help you. I wasn't close to my brother. Now, please. I think I need to go."

"The Final Territory," I said, "does that mean anything to you?"

"Uh-uh. What is it?"

I debated how much to tell him and decided on a vague answer. "An Internet group we're wondering if your brother had any ties to."

"No, I don't know about it."

"What's Randy's full name?" Tobin asked him. "What else can you tell us about him?"

"It's Randy—not Randall—he was always adamant about that. And Quentin, that's his middle name. Like I said, the last I heard he was living in West Virginia. That's all I know, honestly. We had a falling-out. It happens—I wish it didn't, but it did. I should go. Really."

"Just one last thing." I put my phone away. I'd had a falling-out with my brother too. It's not easy when it happens. "When I met Randy, he seemed worried that some people might be after him. Can you think of anyone who might have wanted to harm your brother? Any enemies he had?"

Billy ran an uneasy hand through his short-cropped hair. "He was a good guy. Served in Iraq as a Marine. I don't know about anything like that. I can't think of why anyone would want to hurt him."

"He was a Marine?"

"Yes. Listen, if there's anything else you need, you can call me. I just need a little time to let all this sink in." He gave me his business card.

We thanked him for his time, told him we were sorry for his loss, and then, while Tobin checked his texts, Billy met up with a woman who looked a bit older and might have been a friend or another relative and they left together. I looked for Randy's military record on the Federal Digital Database on my cell. His name was listed, but his prints didn't come up.

His heavily redacted file was marked as confidential and only the most rudimentary information was available, including his name, rank, and service number.

When I showed my phone's screen to Tobin he said, "The plot thickens."

"Yes, it does."

My friend Ralph Hawkins currently worked with the Bureau's National Center for the Analysis of Violent Crime. However, before joining the Bureau he'd been an Army Ranger and I figured if anyone had the contacts to help us uncover more about McReynolds's past, it was him.

I put a call through to him.

My number must have come up on his phone because before I could even greet him he said, "Pat. Good to hear from you. What's up?"

I gave him the rundown, then said, "Randy's brother mentioned he was a Marine and I found only a very basic service record. Most of it has been sealed. I'm wondering if he might've been special ops?"

"Maybe. Let me make some calls, see what I can come up with."

Tobin and I ordered a couple slices of pizza for dinner at a storefront restaurant across the street from the hospital.

In New York City they heat the slices up for you after you order them, and while we waited for the food, I ran Randy Quentin McReynolds's name and found that indeed a man by that name had rented a place in Beckley, West Virginia. The last utilities paid by him were in January.

Tobin was busy at his phone as well. "No credit cards for Randy, no phone records. Nothing after the first of the year. The guy becomes a ghost for six months, then he shows up here afraid for his life."

"Well," I said, "at least it gives us a place to start. Let's contact the landlord in Beckley, see what he can tell us."

++++

Lily Keating took the subway back to the apartment she shared with two other women who were also in their early twenties.

The audition had not gone well.

The director wanted people with experience, and the

only way to get experience was to act—but the only way to act was to have experience so you could get the part in the first place. How did you break into a closed loop like that?

She wasn't sure, but ever since finishing college last year, she'd been trying to.

And failing.

So she'd taken up other ways of earning money to pay off her college debts.

Tonight she would go to work, pretending, acting, playing a role on the streets, one that, back when she was growing up, she'd never dreamed she would have to play.

18

Our efforts to reach the landlord came up empty and, by the time we'd picked our way through traffic back to the Field Office, it was already almost five thirty.

We convened in my office with Jodie, who offhandedly remarked that she wasn't in any hurry to get going and could hang around and work for a while if we were game.

Hearing her say that made me think again of her plight of being kicked out of Dell's place and of my offer to let her stay in my apartment until she could get back on her feet. Now, however, I realized I hadn't spoken with Christie to clear things with her.

Stepping into the hall, I called her, and after a quick hello, I said, "Hey, I need to tell you, Jodie and Dell are going through a rough spot—Dell told her to leave. She might need a place to stay for a while. I offered her my apartment. I was thinking I could crash at your place for a few nights while she looks for somewhere to stay. I'm not trying to invite myself over, but—"

"No, of course that would be fine. How's she holding up?"

I recalled her bloodshot eyes from this morning. "I don't think it's going to be easy on her if they're not able to patch things up. Dell means a lot to her."

"I'm sorry. I'm here if she needs someone to talk to."

"I'll let her know."

"By the way, I'm glad you called. I know we were going to try and get together to talk, but something came up with Tessa. I'll need to postpone that until tomorrow."

"Things okay?"

"I think so. Just some mother/daughter stuff we're going to need to talk through. Would you be staying over here tonight, do you think?"

"Let me talk to Jodie. I'll text you."

When I returned to the office, Jodie told me she was fine for this evening. "I never checked out of the hotel earlier today. My things are still there. I wasn't sure where I was going to go tonight."

"Save your money tomorrow. My place is available."

"Okay, we'll see."

I told her about Christie's offer to talk if she needed to.

To keep Tobin in the loop, she gave him a quick summary of what we were talking about while I texted Christie that I would be staying at my apartment tonight. Then the three of us worked for another hour and a half, searching through more folds in the cases on our plates, trying to find the true shape of what we were looking at.

The origami of the case.

Still a mystery.

Eventually, with a yawn, Jodie announced that she should probably be taking off. "Attention span is officially at zero. I need some sleep."

After she left, Tobin and I researched things for another half hour or so, then he asked if I wanted to grab a beer before calling it a day. Since I'd gotten my run in this morning and I had no other plans for the evening, I agreed. "Sure, why not? You have a place in mind?"

"Mally's Pub and Toffee Shop."

"Wait—did you say pub and *toffee* shop?"

"I know, it sounds crazy, but it's great. Lots of local brews on tap and freshly made toffee. You can't go wrong either way."

"You want me to drive?"

"It's on my way home." He gave me the address. "I'll meet you there."

++++

Lily Keating watched evening tilt across the city, the skyscrapers' long, narrow shadows stretching over the streets, all leaning simultaneously in the opposite direction from the setting sun.

With casting calls during the day, she needed to work nights. But as she reminded herself all the time, this was only temporary, a stepping stone. She'd heard someone say once, "Wishes are dreams without feet." So this was her way of giving feet to her dreams.

Thursdays were typically a bit slow, so she liked to be at her corner by nine in case she could pick up any early clients.

Lily had heard somewhere that girls wear makeup to look old and women wear makeup to look young. She found herself caught somewhere in the middle, but chose to shoot for the looking-younger route.

She went into the bathroom and put on the kind of makeup that served her best with the men she met at night.

19

The sweet smell of fresh toffee saturated the air, rich and smooth and inviting. It reminded me of walking into the kitchen when I was young and smelling my mom's freshly baked chocolate chip cookies.

Warm and gooey.

Only this place served beer too.

It was, admittedly, an odd combination, but also appealing, on a number of levels.

When I saw that they had Sixpoint's Gorilla Warfare, which is a craft beer made with beans from Gorilla Coffee in Brooklyn, I immediately went with that. Tobin ordered a Galia Melon Sour Sweet from Big Alice Brewing, then we found a booth in the back of the place where no one would be able to walk up behind us or startle us.

Watchful vigilance. Something you pick up early on in law enforcement.

If Christie were here, she would've ordered dessert first, but we decided to go with the toffee after we'd finished our beers.

Music throbbed through the restaurant. I recognized the voice—Johnny Cash—but not the song. As I took a sip of my beer, the scent of toffee baking in the kitchen mixed with the smell of the lager in a way that was unusual, but, with the coffee flavoring coming through, very inviting.

"How is it?" Tobin asked.

"Even better than I expected. Yours?"

He tried his beer. "Not bad at all."

We worked on our drinks as we discussed the case for a few minutes, then he said, "So, what's your story, Pat? Wife? Kids? Anything?"

"No kids. Never married. I am seeing someone, though."

"Serious?"

"Maybe. I hope so."

"That's good." He took a sip. "So, how'd you end up doing this for a living? What got you started?"

His questions took me back to when I was sixteen. That year, an eleven-year-old girl went missing from my hometown. I was the one who ended up finding her, dead, in a tree house on the edge of a marsh just outside of the city limits. Later we learned that she'd been sexually molested before she was killed.

It'd affected me, no doubt about that. But was that what led me into this life?

It was hard to know.

Still, that was what came to mind.

Tobin watched me quietly, waiting for a reply.

"Honestly, I'm not sure what got me interested in the first place, but what keeps me going is the belief that what we do makes a difference."

"You have to, right?"

"I have to?"

"Believe it makes a difference."

"Yeah. I think we do."

"My sergeant, back when I was a rookie, he used to say, 'Without hope, the only thing that keeps you going is either momentum or fear.'"

He paused to let that sink in, then elaborated, "I always took that to mean that as soon as you stop believing things can get better, you'll lose your motivation. So, instead, maybe you keep plugging forward because that's just what you do. You go to work. You come home. You spend a little time with the people you love. Maybe you watch TV or read a novel, whatever, then you go to bed. On the weekends you do your best to get out and hit a few golf balls around, or you spend some time at the beach house or the cabin, and then you do it all over again."

"Momentum."

"Right." He nodded. "So it's either that or you keep going because you're afraid of stopping and what that would mean: pausing long enough to look at the darkness that lies before you and the infinitesimally small and insignificant role you play in the sprawling script of the universe."

His words were striking, poetic, and I wondered if he'd read them somewhere or if he was just making them up on the spot, but he didn't specify and I didn't ask.

"What about you?" I said. "What's your story?"

"Divorced. I had a daughter; she was taken when she was five. Killed. A jogger found her body two years later."

"Tobin . . ." Words failed me. "I'm sorry. Man, I can't even imagine what that would be like, having to go through that."

"Yeah, it was hell. For a long time I thought it was the not knowing that was the hardest. There were days when I found myself thinking, 'Even if she's dead, okay, I just want to know, I just need to know the truth.' It seemed like it was closure, some sort of closure, that I wanted."

"But it wasn't?"

"No. I mean, of course I wanted a happy ending, to find her safe and sound—I wanted that more than anything in the world—but as time went by I realized that it probably wasn't going to play out like that. Eventually, you start to forget what your life was like beforehand. And when you're honest, you're a little frightened of what things would be like if they were different."

I was a little confused. "You mean, if she were alive and back with you?"

"Or dead. The uncertainty becomes a place to retreat to, almost like solid ground when life becomes unmanageable. It's hard to really put into words, and I suppose it's impossible for people who've never been through it to understand, but vacillating between hope and despair just takes too much of a toll on everyone involved."

I knew the stats, knew about the devastating toll that losing a child can have on a marriage. He'd mentioned he was divorced, but he still wore his wedding ring and now I found myself glancing at it.

He noticed. "Yeah. We were still together when it happened. Misty kept telling me that she knew Adrienne was alive, that a mother knows those things. And honestly, at first it helped. It did. It was almost like she had enough hope and faith for both of us. But then, as time wore on, it drove something between us. Her belief, my doubt— there wasn't room for them both. I knew too much about these kinds of cases and about what guys who take little girls do to them. I stopped believing Adrienne would be alright, and maybe that's what happened to Misty too, in the end. I don't know."

He let out a slow breath, then told me about the depression his wife had spiraled into, her suicide attempts, the razor blades and the blood in the bathtub and the stay in the psychiatric hospital. And he told me about how she left him and about her final suicide attempt two weeks after the paperwork for their divorce went through.

Completed, not successful.

Tessa was right: "successful" was not the right term to use when you were referring to someone's suicide.

"But the thing is," Tobin said, "Adrienne had been alive all that time. Misty had been right. All those months when she was struggling with depression before she finally took her own life, our daughter was alive. When they found her body, even though she'd been gone for two years, the forensic anthropologists confirmed that she'd been dead for less than six months."

He drained his beer and then stared at the glass as if it might somehow hold some answers to the tragic riddle of his past. But, finding none, he slid it aside and looked out across the pub instead.

I realized I hadn't had any of my beer since he'd started his story, and now I found that I wasn't in the mood to finish it.

Hearing what he'd been through, I understood his somewhat severe countenance. He was a survivor, a battered warrior of a man who'd been through a parent's worst nightmare and come out the other side, scarred in places most of us don't even know exist.

But maybe he hadn't really emerged from the other side yet.

Maybe he was still trying to claw his way back to a normal life.

Johnny Cash sang on. Another track on the playlist. The dark, gritty mood of Cash's voice seemed appropriate as the sound track for Tobin's story.

"You know," he said, "for those two years I prayed for Adrienne every day, but only when it was over, only after that man finally found her body, did I wish she'd died right away. We discovered evidence of severe physical and sexual abuse. Patrick, if I'd known what she was going to have to endure, if I'd known that she was going to have to suffer like that, I would have killed her myself the night she was taken to protect her from having to experience what she did in those eighteen months before she was strangled and dumped naked in that park."

I had no idea what to say.

Not being a dad, I found it impossible to imagine what it would be like to be in his shoes, yet when I thought of the things that might have happened to Adrienne while she was held captive, I at least understood how Tobin could come to the point of saying that.

"So, anyway . . ." He brushed his hand across the table as if he were trying to erase something. "That was all six years ago—I mean, when they actually found her body. You try to move on, you know? You try to put the pain behind you." He fingered his wedding band. "It's not easy, though."

"Did they ever find the person who did it?"

"No. We never did."

Sometimes I think that in this job we know too much, that there are some things that would be best left unknown.

I read once that the Japanese filmmaker Akira Kurosawa said, "To be an artist means never to avert your eyes."

I think it's true of people in law enforcement as well.

We must never avert our eyes.

Yes, there are some things people aren't meant to see. In this job we see those things. We're forced to look at them, to look past them, to see who is behind them and to recognize that they are human just like us.

The victims are.

The offenders are too.

All, so desperately, extravagantly, wickedly human.

Just like us.

We settled our bill and walked into the night. A slight breeze was feeling its way through the city streets, but it was too hot to be refreshing. It just felt corrosive on my skin.

"So I'll see you in the morning, Pat."

"Yeah. You okay?"

"I am. I just haven't spoken about all that in a long time. It's tough to walk back through those memories. It was tougher than I thought it would be."

Only when I was on my way home did I realize I'd forgotten to buy any toffee for Christie and Tessa, but I didn't want to be reminded of Tobin's story, so I didn't go back to the pub where he'd told it to me.

Instead I just aimed my car toward my apartment and thought of how, if Adrienne had never been taken, she would be just a couple of years younger than Tessa.

They might've become friends, might have complained about their parents together or gone to the movies or talked about boys or snuck out for a smoke or let each other in on their dreams or done whatever it was teenage girls did these days.

It might have turned out like that.

If Adrienne hadn't been taken.

Hadn't been killed.

But she had been.

I wondered how long Tobin had looked for his daughter's killer. I imagined that if I were in his shoes I would have been obsessed with the search, and just knowing what I did about him, I assumed he would have been too, for a long time.

And since I didn't believe in coincidences, I didn't believe that the daughter of a detective who worked cases involving sex crimes against children was just randomly abducted.

Unlikely things happen every day, so it was possible, yes, but I couldn't shake the thought that his family was targeted for a reason.

20

Francis had worked late at the ICSC, but hadn't found anything specifically related to the Final Territory. He'd located a few references to FT—which might have stood for Final Territory or just about anything else—and a video that had four simple, white, mime-style masks sitting on a couch, but there were no children in that video and because of that it hadn't shown up on most of the searches.

If there really was a site called the Final Territory, it was as well hidden on the web as anything he'd ever looked into before.

He would call the detective in the morning, tell him what little he knew.

Now he was at his apartment, and though he wanted to do all he could to help the NYPD, he didn't have his image-filtering software here and he didn't want to chance encountering illegal images while searching for the Final Territory or going on Tor on his personal computer.

He tried watching a little TV, but his computer in the corner of the room kept drawing his attention.

Things had started small, just a faint, barely discernible voice that whispered to him, *What would it be like?*

At first he was able to quiet the voice, to still it, to make it go away.

But he hadn't been able to make it go away for good.

And there it was: that line he didn't want to cross.

That net he couldn't seem to avoid.

What would it be like? Think about it, Francis.

No! Stop it! I'm a good person, I—

No, you're not. What about the things you've been tempted to do? The things you've considered. Remember? Remember what you—

No! I would never do something like that. I can say no. I can resist. It takes self-control, like Dr. Perrior was talking about, and I'm a self-controlled person. They gave me this job because they know I can handle it. Not everybody could, but I can. They trust me!

He needed to clear his head.

Maybe exercise would help.

He slipped out of his apartment to go for a walk.

++++

Interior decorating has never been my thing, and the walls of my one-bedroom apartment were empty except for a few photos of my friends and me rock climbing in Yosemite and a painting that I'd bought at an art exhibit from an ex-con who was trying to get on his feet after being released from prison.

It wasn't very good, but it pictured a V of geese flying over a northern marsh and it reminded me of growing up near Horicon Marsh, a thirty-mile-square wildlife refuge in Wisconsin, where millions of Canada geese stop by every autumn on their southern migration.

That was where I found the body in the tree house, right on the edge of that marsh.

Normally, the painting reminded me of my childhood

home. Now, because of the connection to the dead girl, it made me think of Tobin's devastating story.

I used to wonder what it would be like for parents who lost a child, what it would be like to come home one day and find that your son or daughter was gone. Just like that. No explanation, no clues, nothing, just missing. Or maybe, one moment she was right there, right behind you at the store, or the park, or the beach, and now she wasn't.

You turn around and everything has changed.

Everything is different.

Forever.

Having heard Tobin share about Adrienne and Misty tonight, I'd at least gotten a glimpse at the pain parents go through when their child is killed.

I tried not to think about that as I put my things away.

I hardly spent any time here in my apartment. If I wasn't at the Field Office or at a crime scene somewhere, I was usually at a coffee shop, at Christie's place, or slipping in a workout at the Hangout, my favorite local climbing gym.

As I'd told the OPR lawyer, Ms. Aguirre, I was a little thin in the hobby department.

Bookshelves covered one bedroom wall, but they couldn't hold all my books, so there were three precarious stacks of criminology textbooks beside my bed. I had a Metolius hangboard for doing pull-ups in the living room. I got my news online and didn't have much time or interest in television and I just never got around to buying one after I moved in here.

Actually, come to think of it, I didn't have one before that either.

No easy chairs. No love seat.

The only furniture in the living room was a stout table

and two somewhat wobbly wooden chairs I'd picked up cheap from an estate sale. I ate and worked there at that table, often at the same time.

Retiring to my bedroom, I called Christie and told her good night. Then I sat in bed with my back against the wall, flipped open my laptop, and went to Jamaal Stewart's site to read through the real estate investment material the parents of those missing children subscribed to.

++++

The charcoal Mercedes-Benz SLK 55AMG crawled to a stop on Lily Keating's street corner and she sashayed up to it, making the most of every step.

She knew her cars.

Came with the gig.

And this one spoke of impeccable taste.

By the time she got to the driver's door, the guy had lowered his window. She leaned close. "Looking for a little companionship?"

She might have said, "Looking for a good time?" or "Do you want someone to party with?" but she'd learned to gauge these things based on appearances and someone driving a car in this price range would likely be more open to her services if she offered him "companionship."

Semantics.

It's all about semantics.

He didn't answer, but rather let his gaze travel down her neck, pause at her chest, and then move slowly back up to her face. There was a time when men looking at her that way had bothered her. Not anymore. Now she was used to it, expected it.

Finally, he said, "May I ask how old you are?"

"How young do you want me to be?"

She was careful how she phrased that.

Semantics.

"You could pass for sixteen."

"Sixteen it is, then."

Shifting his attention forward, he stared out the windshield for a moment as if he were debating things, then scratched absently at his chin and motioned toward the passenger door. "Climb in."

She told him how much she usually got for her services and he didn't argue or try to negotiate. "That'll be fine."

In truth, her rates were adjustable. She was an entrepreneur and looked at her fee structure kind of like airlines' fare pricing—there were peak hours and peak seasons when the prices would go up, and of course you could always pay for first-class service if you wanted to.

Tonight, being a Thursday, was not exactly a peak night.

Usually, she was good at reading how much a guy would be willing to spend, taking into account his car, his clothes, and how nervous he seemed to be. Now, however, based on how quickly he agreed to what she quoted him, she wondered if maybe she'd way undershot things.

She waited in the seat beside him as he let the car idle.

Sometimes men would talk dirty as soon as she was alone in the car with them—sometimes they wanted her to, other times they would promise her how much she was going to enjoy things—which seemed a bit ironic to her, almost as if they'd forgotten what kind of transaction this was.

"What's your name?" he asked her.

"Lily."

"Okay."

She could tell he didn't believe her and for some reason tonight she felt like she wanted him to. Shooting for a teenager's word choice and speaking rhythm, she said, "It is. It's actually my real name. Some girls make up the names they use, you know? But I didn't have to. I got a cool name right off the bat. My dad always brought my mom a flower whenever he saw her for their first twelve dates. Every date, another flower. That's it. She loves flowers. That's why she named me Lily."

"I see."

Lily knew how these things worked, so she didn't ask for his name, but instead said, "What would you like me to call you?"

"Shane will be fine."

"Okay, Shane."

A pause. "I'm a little new at this."

She almost said, "Well, sweetie, I'm not," but then remembered he liked the idea of her being young, so she opted for "Me too" instead, and said it as naively and innocently as possible.

He still didn't pull away from the curb, which might've meant that he was going to change his mind.

"Lily, as long as we're being forthright with each other, that's not my real name; Shane, I mean."

"That's fine." She put her hand on his knee. "There's a place I know. It's close."

"I had somewhere in mind."

"Is it far? Because I'll need to get back to—"

"It's not far." He put his hand on hers and it seemed to her like a gentle and familiar gesture, as if he were used to her being by his side, as if they were a couple rather than complete strangers.

"I'll make it worth your time." He pulled away from the curb. "I promise."

21

He took her to an upscale apartment building on the Upper West Side, and when they drove up to the valet parking attendant she knew that she'd definitely asked too little for her services tonight.

Wait, for her *companionship*.

Well, maybe she could throw in some extras.

A few added amenities.

First class.

After dropping off the car, Shane took Lily's arm in the crook of his own and led her toward the building's front door.

"So, how long have you lived here?" she asked as they ascended the steps.

"Actually, it's a friend's place. I just come here sometimes when I'm on business."

He opened the door for her.

"Thank you, Shane."

"My pleasure."

"So business brought you to the city?"

"In a sense."

At first she thought he said *innocence*, but then she realized what he'd really said.

He showed a key card to a disinterested doorman, who nodded them toward the elevator.

Once the doors had closed, Shane inserted the card into the penthouse-level access slot. It was accepted and he tapped the button, then pocketed the key card.

She laid her hand lightly on his shoulder.

He faced her, then slid aside a strand of her hair that had draped across her face. "You'd look good in a ponytail."

"I do," she said.

A slight pause. "I may want you to stay longer than we first discussed."

"I'm sure we can work something out."

The elevator doors opened on the twenty-fourth floor, and he led her down the exquisitely decorated hallway to room 2406.

He opened the door and gestured for her to enter.

Typically, Lily tried to take careful note of her surroundings and this place had a rustic and yet somehow sophisticated look, with two-toned trim and wainscoting that matched the handmade cherry furniture. The walls tended toward an eggshell white that accentuated the simple and distinctive forms and lines of the furniture.

The place was breathtaking in its simplicity and elegance.

"What do you think?" he asked.

"I think I could be persuaded to stay all night. If you want me to."

He was quiet for a moment. "Drink?"

"Whatever you're having. Seriously, this place is amazing."

"I'll let the owner know you said so."

She trailed a finger along the wall and took everything in. He put some music on. A flute player.

"What is this?"

"Ian Anderson. It's his seven-minute-and-ten-second flute solo in Tampa. July thirty-first. 1976."

"Who's Ian Anderson?"

"Have you ever heard of Jethro Tull?"

"Of course," she said, but hoped he wouldn't ask her too much about the group, since she only recognized the name but didn't know anything about them. She glided to the bedroom door. "I'm not super familiar with their music, though."

"Ian merged the sound of a modern minstrel with 1960s and seventies rock and roll. He once heard Eric Clapton play the guitar and was intimidated, thinking that he would never be that good. He wanted to be the best in the world at something. He opted for the flute. Some people say he achieved that goal."

She peered into the darkened bedroom.

Flipped on the lights.

A tripod stood in the corner with a video camera aimed directly at the bed.

She was well aware that with cameras as small and discreet as they were these days, a good number of the men she was with probably did record themselves with her somehow, but she'd never seen anything as blatant as this.

A camera on a tripod?

For real?

"No filming, Shane. That's not how these things work."

Silence from the other room.

"Shane?" She turned and he seemed to appear out of nowhere, startling her.

"Your drink." He held out a shot glass to her.

She accepted it. "I was saying, you can't film us."

"I'll pay you extra."

Well, then.

Amenities.

First class?

She threw out a number, an outrageous number, and without any debate he opened the dresser drawer and dug out a roll of Franklins.

"I get paid up front."

"Of course."

She watched him peel them off and lay them out, one at a time, on the bed.

He reached the number she'd quoted and kept going.

"That's more than I said."

"I might have some special requests."

A quiver of uneasiness scampered through her. That little alarm went off in her head, that "something's not right here" alarm that had served her well twice in the past when her clients were starting to get rough and she'd needed to use the pepper spray she kept in her purse.

Just find out what he has in mind. Don't commit to anything yet.

"What kind of requests?" she asked.

"Nothing too discomfiting."

He walked to the camera and turned it on.

"You're not so new at this after all, are you?" she said.

"I guess you're onto me." Then, "Well?"

"You still haven't told me what you have in mind."

He went into the closet and pulled out a cheerleader outfit and laid it on the bed.

"You want me to wear that?"

"I told you that you could pass for sixteen. I think it'll look good on you."

Well, that wasn't so bad. She'd been asked to do a lot kinkier stuff than dress up like a cheerleader.

She glanced at the camera, then at the money, then back at him.

"I accept your offer, Shane." She downed her drink and began to unbutton her shirt to change clothes, but he gestured toward the bathroom. "If you don't mind."

"Ooookay." She slid the money into her purse, collected the cheerleader outfit, and went into the bathroom. She didn't have a hair scrunchie with her, but she did have a decorative hair clip. She pulled her hair back. Pinned it in place.

Pigtails would have made her look even younger. Some men were into that, but she had the sense that it might insult Shane if she went that far. Besides, she didn't have bands to hold the braids and he'd requested the ponytail, so that's what she went with.

She laced on the athletic shoes he had for her. They were a little big, but she could make do.

She didn't figure she would have to wear them for long.

When she'd finished, she returned to the bedroom and found him seated on the bed, still clothed. He looked up from his phone where he'd been texting someone. She set her purse on the dresser.

"Well?" She twirled flirtatiously. "How do I look?"

"Serviceable."

"What did you just say?"

He reached behind him and picked up a plain white mask, then slipped it on.

Okay, well, whatever people were into.

Then he came at her as the video camera just a few feet away captured everything.

PART II

Ashes

22

Friday, June 15

After half an hour of push-ups and max sets of pull-ups on the hangboard—which were hampered by the injury in my arm where Randy McReynolds had cut me—I drove to work and arrived at just after seven to get an early start on the day.

I liked the office at this time. Quiet. Still. No distractions.

Last night I'd fallen asleep reading Stewart's investment advice on his site. I'd picked up a lot about the importance of how to find the right fixer-upper, but hadn't learned anything that seemed relevant to the case.

Now, settling in at my desk, I checked the online case files to see if anything had been added since last night.

The computer forensics team had gone back to Stewart's apartment, somehow wired up a computer to the television, and they were able to download the data from the flash drive. From what I could tell, they were going to be analyzing it this morning and would likely have some preliminary results sometime later today.

I hoped so. I was anxious to know if it had a file named "Aurora's birthday."

Yesterday, Harrington, my friend at the DOJ, had

agreed to send up Wooford's key by courier. We were expecting it this morning and would be able to compare it to the ones found on McReynolds and Stewart to determine if all three were a match.

I laid out a plan for the day.

(1) Figure out what those keys opened.

(2) Learn what Randy Quentin McReynolds had been up to since he left his West Virginia apartment in January.

(3) Work with Tobin to analyze the case files from the four missing children and see if the geoprofile overlapped with the known activity nodes and travel routes for either Stewart or Wooford.

Randy McReynolds's autopsy was scheduled for this morning. Hopefully, that would clear up the question of whether or not he had any drugs in his system when he leapt from that balcony.

I found an email from Harrington in my in-box.

He wrote that he'd passed along the search for the Final Territory to the Department of Homeland Security. "Last I heard the Child Exploitation Investigations Unit from their Cyber Crimes Center was looking into it."

Homeland often works closely with the Bureau and local law enforcement in joint investigations, so I emailed the agent in charge of Wooford's case, requesting him to give me a call.

At the bottom of Harrington's email, he'd included a link to a cache of Ted Wooford's chat logs. Clicking on it, I pulled up a chat that had begun a few months before he was arrested.

It was obvious by Wooford's and the girl's choice of screen names that they were both being sexually provocative and flirty. They used a popular social networking site called Krazle. It was also clear that they weren't using any kind of autocorrect function on their keyboards.

(Tuesday, March 20th. All Times Are EST.)

mrpleasuregiver56ga (8:05:14 PM):	love ur profile pic. hot!!
yngnrdyblond (8:05:20 PM):	relally? u think im pretty?
mrplcsuregiver56ga (8:05:30 PM):	um yah
yngnrdyblond (8:05:37 PM):	aww
yngnrdyblond (8:05:45 PM):	what'r u doin?
mrpleasuregiver56ga (8:06:02 PM):	hangin out
yngnrdyblond (8:06:08 PM):	cool
mrpleasuregiver56ga (8:06:012 PM):	u?
yngnrdyblond (8:06:16 PM):	chatting!
mrpleasuregiver56ga (8:06:20 PM):	lol
mrpleasuregiver56ga (8:06:32 PM):	so how old r u?
yngnrdyblond (8:06:36 PM):	13/f
yngnrdyblond (8:06:39 PM):	u?
mrpleasuregiver56ga (8:07:01 PM):	a litle older
yngnrdyblond (8:07:12 PM):	how old?
mrpleasuregiver56ga (8:07:20 PM):	34 m
mrpleasuregiver56ga (8:07:24 PM):	is that wierd?
yngnrdyblond (8:07:34 PM):	what?
mrpleasuregiver56ga (8:08:01 PM):	that im that much older than u?
yngnrdyblond (8:08:18 PM):	no i don know not if ur nice 2 me
mrpleasuregiver56ga (8:08:40 PM):	im nice but u can emet some sick peoole on the internet u know?u hear about it all the time
yngnrdyblond (8:08:59 PM):	yah
mrpleasuregiver56ga (8:09:06 PM):	im not like that. i just liek chating
yngnrdyblond (8:09:21 PM):	kewl
mrplesuregiver56ga (8:09:42 PM):	cool cus some girls don like it
yngnrdyblond (8:09:49 PM):	i don mind

Often, online predators lie about their age at first, and
then slowly reveal that they're older than they first claimed
to be. Wooford, however, just laid it out there right at
the start that he was twenty-one years older than she
was.

And she didn't even hesitate, which, taking into account her screen name, made me wonder if this might be
the very thing she was looking for.

I scrolled down. They chatted about the TV shows
they liked and then shared a series of links to prank and
epic fail videos on YouTube.

Over the next two days yngnrdyblond complained
about some of her classmates being mean to her and
Wooford sympathized about how hard it is to deal with
other kids sometimes, and how important it is to say no
to peer pressure and not to lash out at them.

Then he played the role of helpful mentor, telling her
to stay in school and to stay away from drugs.

Even though I didn't specialize in cases like this, I'd
seen this type of thing before. These tactics are seemingly
innocuous ways that sexual predators use when grooming
their targets in order to build their trust and to justify, in
their own minds, their behavior: *I was just trying to help.
I wasn't doing anything wrong.*

The next day things turned the corner, quickly becoming intimate and deeply personal.

mrplesuregiver56ga (10:16:35 PM):	i really like chatin wih u
yngnrdyblond (10:16:41 PM):	me 2.
mrplesuregiver56ga (10:16:51 PM):	thx
mrplesuregiver56ga (10:17:03 PM):	u live with ur parent?s
yngnrdyblond (10:17:12 PM):	jst my mom thdy got divorced
mrplesuregiver56ga (10:17:18 PM):	sorry

yngnrdyblond (10:17:25 PM):   no its kewl he was a jerk anywau

mrplesuregiver56ga (10:17:29 PM):   o

yngnrdyblond (10:17:35 PM):   he used to do stuff 2 me

mrplesuregiver56ga (10:17:45 PM):   what stuf?

yngnrdyblond (10:17:56 PM):   make me touch him

yngnrdyblond (10:18:01 PM):   then when i didnt hed hidt me

mrplesuregiver56ga (10:18:05 PM):   hard?

yngnrdyblond (10:18:08 PM):   yah.

mrplesuregiver56ga (10:18:12 PM):   did you like it?

yngnrdyblond (10:18:18 PM):   no!! course not. it hurt!

mrplesuregiver56ga (10:18:25 PM):   yah

mrplesuregiver56ga (10:18:37 PM):   did he make u go all the way?

yngnrdyblond (10:18:45 PM):   no!

mrplesuregiver56ga (10:18:52 PM):   that sucks. i mean that he hit u

yngnrdyblond (10:19:08 PM):   no kding

mrplesuregiver56ga (10:19:15 PM):   im glag hes not with u anymroe thne

yngnrdyblond (10:19:24 PM):   mc to

I scanned the chats over the next couple of weeks.

Slowly, systematically, Wooford delved deeper into the topics of the girl's sexual interest and experience. One night he asked her what her bra size was and if she had a webcam and could film herself, but she told him no, that it was broken.

At that point you'd think most girls would've closed the account or blocked his user name, but by then he had her convinced that he cared about her and wanted what was best for her, that he was her friend, that he wouldn't hurt her.

He had her hooked.

They kept chatting.

Then, on Friday, May 11, he started getting specific, working toward setting up a time to actually meet with her with the intent of having sex.

mrplesuregiver56ga (11:39:34 PM):	what r u wearing?
yngnrdyblond (11:39:41 PM):	shorts and a t-dhirt
yngnrdyblond (11:39:44 PM):	shirt!
mrplesuregiver56ga (11:39:50 PM):	ha!!
mrplesuregiver56ga (11:39:59 PM):	can u change for me?
yngnrdyblond (11:40:05 PM):	change?
mrplesuregiver56ga (11:40:12 PM):	change cloths
yngnrdyblond (11:40:16 PM):	riht not?!
yngnrdyblond (11:40:18 PM):	now?
mrplesuregiver56ga (11:40:26 PM):	yah
yngnrdyblond (11:40:34 PM):	jest a minut
mrplesuregiver56ga (11:40:52 PM):	u there?
mrplesuregiver56ga (11:41:21 PM):	hello?
yngnrdyblond (11:41:35 PM):	k im back.
mrplesuregiver56ga (11:41:39 PM):	did u change?
yngnrdyblond (11:41:45 PM):	uhhuh
mrplesuregiver56ga (11:41:48 PM):	into a skirt?
yngnrdyblond (11:41:53 PM):	panties.
mrplesuregiver56ga (11:41:59 PM):	that all?
yngnrdyblond (11:42:06 PM):	yah
mrplesuregiver56ga (11:42:15 PM):	oh man. thats hot. y r u doing this 2 me?
mrplesuregiver56ga (11:42:22 PM):	when can i c u?
yngnrdyblond (11:42:27 PM):	whenever
mrplesuregiver56ga (11:42:33 PM):	i don't know. i don wanna get in troubl
mrplesuregiver56ga (11:42:40 PM):	u need to be carful who u meet onine

yngnrdyblond (11:42:42 PM):	cna i trust u?
mrplesuregiver56ga (11:42:49 PM):	of coure.
yngnrdyblond (11:42:53 PM):	i like u
mrplesuregiver56ga (11:42:56 PM).	me tooo!!
yngnrdyblond (11:43:00 PM):	my momz gon this weekend
mrplesuregiver56ga (11:43:14 PM):	what does she do?
yngnrdyblond (11:43:20 PM):	management stuff. i don't know.
mrplesuregiver56ga (11:43:24 PM):	managmetn stuf?
yngnrdyblond (11:43:33 PM):	like teaching seminars on how to b someone's boss.s hes' goin to atlanta.
mrplesuregiver56ga (11:43:40 PM):	u home alone?
yngnrdyblond (11:43:42 PM):	yah
mrplesuregiver56ga (11:43:45 PM):	all weekend?
yngnrdyblond (11:43:53 PM):	well firday nite. she trusts me. i just lock the door. whatever. u knw.
mrplesuregiver56ga (11:43:56 PM):	k
mrplesuregiver56ga (11:44:01 PM):	so were do u live?
yngnrdyblond (11:44:10 PM):	dc
yngnrdyblond (11:44:15 PM):	u?
mrplesuregiver56ga (11:44:20 PM):	close by.
mrplesuregiver56ga (11:44:23 PM):	i wanna c u.
yngnrdyblond (11:44:26 PM):	me to
mrplesuregiver56ga (11:45:33 PM):	we cud hang out
yngnrdyblond (11:45:38 PM):	thatd be kewl
mrplesuregiver56ga (11:45:44 PM):	i mane watcha movie or somehing what kind of movies do u like?
yngnrdyblond (11:46:01 PM):	comedy
yngnrdyblond (11:46:04 PM):	romance ;)

mrplesuregiver56ga (11:46:09 PM):   we cud wath something
                                     then whatver u want
mrplesuregiver56ga (11:46:13 PM):   i cud hold u. would you
                                     like that?
yngnrdyblond (11:46:15 PM):   yah
mrplesuregiver56ga (11:46:22 PM):   do u like to kiss?
yngnrdyblond (11:46:26 PM):   lol of cours!
mrplesuregiver56ga (11:46:31 PM):   i wnana kis u. hold u.
yngnrdyblond (11:46:34 PM):   aww.
yngnrdyblond (11:46:36 PM):   protect me?
mrplesuregiver56ga (11:46:43 PM):   from what?
yngnrdyblond (11:46:50 PM):   i dunno
yngnrdyblond (11:46:53 PM):   i just wanna feel safe
mrplesuregiver56ga (11:47:01 PM):   u can feel safe with me.
yngnrdyblond (11:47:04 PM):   ok
mrplesuregiver56ga (11:47:15 PM):   do u have condoms?
yngnrdyblond (11:47:20 PM):   no
mrplesuregiver56ga (11:47:26 PM):   i can bring some
mrplesuregiver56ga (11:47:31 PM):   if u want
mrplesuregiver56ga (11:47:39 PM):   i maean we don't have to
yngnrdyblond (11:47:42 PM):   no
yngnrdyblond (11:47:45 PM):   that'd be kewl.
mrplesuregiver56ga (11:47:54 PM):   u sure?
yngnrdyblond (11:47:59 PM):   yah.
mrplesuregiver56ga (11:48:10 PM):   u ever done it before?
yngnrdyblond (11:48:19 PM):   no
mrplesuregiver56ga (11:48:22 PM):   realy?
yngnrdyblond (11:48:30 PM):   im not that kind of girl
yngnrdyblond (11:48:34 PM):   to sleep around or what-
                                     ever
mrplesuregiver56ga (11:48:40 PM):   i didnt mwan it like that.
yngnrdyblond (11:48:43 PM):   i kno
mrplesuregiver56ga (11:48:51 PM):   so id be ur first time?
yngnrdyblond (11:48:56 PM):   uhhuh

yngnrdyblond (11:49:00 PM):	is that ok??
mrplesuregiver56ga (11:49:09 PM):	id like to be ur first
mrplesuregiver56ga (11:49:12 PM):	like that very much
yngnrdyblond (11:49:21 PM):	ud be gentle,right?
mrplesuregiver56ga (11:49:26 PM):	of course.
yngnrdyblond (11:49:33 PM):	tell me abot it
mrplesuregiver56ga (11:49:39 PM):	wed hug and kiss a lot first
yngnrdyblond (11:49:48 PM):	i kno that
yngnrdyblond (11:49:50 PM):	then?
mrplesuregiver56ga (11:49:59 PM):	id take u. make u mine.
yngnrdyblond (11:50:08 PM):	does it hurt?
mrplesuregiver56ga (11:50:15 PM):	maybe a litle but then it felels good. and ill ake it feel real good
yngnrdyblond (11:50:17 PM):	kewl
mrplesuregiver56ga (11:50:21 PM):	ill teach u everythhing
yngnrdyblond (11:50:24 PM):	when can i c u?!
mrplesuregiver56ga (11:50:30 PM):	dunno. soon.
yngnrdyblond (11:50:35 PM):	this weekend??
mrplesuregiver56ga (11:50:39 PM):	youll be by yourself Friday nite?
yngnrdyblond (11:50:52 PM):	she leaves at lile four or something tor the airport
mrplesuregiver56ga (11:51:01 PM):	i haveto work til five
yngnrdyblond (11:51:04 PM):	k
mrplesuregiver56ga (11:51:11 PM):	but i cud come over then. at tnigth
yngnrdyblond (11:51:15 PM):	kewl bring someting
mrplesuregiver56ga (11:51:18 PM):	what?
yngnrdyblond (11:51:24 PM):	dunno a rurprise.
mrplesuregiver56ga (11:51:29 PM):	what do u like?
yngnrdyblond (11:51:32 PM):	chocolate!

yngnrdyblond (11:51:34 PM):	kisses :)
mrplesuregiver56ga (11:51:39 PM):	sure ok
yngnrdyblond (11:51:42 PM):	i cant wait to c u

But then Wooford seemed to lose his nerve. He backed off from pressuring to meet at her house and tried to set up something close by instead.

mrplesuregiver56ga (11:51:56 PM):	we should maybe meet at a park aor soemting
yngnrdyblond (11:51:57 PM):	why?
mrplesuregiver56ga (11:52:11 PM):	cuae were there are other people so you can trust me
yngnrdyblond (11:52:20 PM):	but i can trust u right?
mrplesuregiver56ga (11:52:23 PM):	yees1
yngnrdyblond (11:52:25 PM):	kewl
yngnrdyblond (11:52:31 PM):	cus u wouldnt hurt me right?
mrplesuregiver56ga (11:52:41 PM):	i wounld neer do anything to hurt yuo!!
mrplesuregiver56ga (11:52:44 PM):	i ll protect u
mrplesuregiver56ga (11:52:47 PM):	take care of u
yngnrdyblond (11:52:52 PM):	awesoem
mrplesuregiver56ga (11:53:00 PM):	we have comething u knw?
yngnrdyblond (11:53:04 PM):	yah.
mrplesuregiver56ga (11:53:11 PM):	so can u go toa park?
yngnrdyblond (11:53:14 PM):	no bike
yngnrdyblond (11:53:18 PM):	and it stoo far to walk
yngnrdyblond (11:53:20 PM):	like 2 miels
mrplesuregiver56ga (11:53:26 PM):	i cud pick u up or some-thing
yngnrdyblond (11:53:30 PM):	i dunno

mrplesuregiver56ga (11:53:35 PM):	i have a motorcycle
yngnrdyblond (11:53:41 PM):	thats kewl
yngnrdyblond (11:53:46 PM):	my mom tol me i need to be creful
mrplesuregiver56ga (11:53:54 PM):	with meeting guys?
yngnrdyblond (11:53:58 PM):	yah.
yngnrdyblond (11:54:03 PM):	did u mean it?
mrplesuregiver56ga (11:54:08 PM):	wat?
yngnrdyblond (11:54:12 PM):	what you said b4
yngnrdyblond (11:54:15 PM):	the stuff about caring for me
mrplesuregiver56ga (11:54:21 PM):	of coruse
yngnrdyblond (11:54:28 PM):	cus it maee me feel safe
mrplesuregiver56ga (11:54:32 PM):	good.
mrplesuregiver56ga (11:54:38 PM):	btw u should prolly delete this chat
yngnrdyblond (11:54:41 PM):	y?
mrplesuregiver56ga (11:54:45 PM):	case someone sees it
mrplesuregiver56ga (11:54:50 PM):	i don want u to get in troubel
yngnrdyblond (11:54:56 PM):	o
yngnrdyblond (11:54:59 PM):	y wod i get In trouble?
mrplesuregiver56ga (11:55:05 PM):	cus i'm older ya kno
mrplesuregiver56ga (11:55:09 PM):	some places its illegal
yngnrdyblond (11:55:12 PM):	y?
mrplesuregiver56ga (11:55:19 PM):	i don kno maybe they don trust odler guys
mrplesuregiver56ga (11:55:26 PM):	but im not like that.

The grooming techniques were clear in his responses threading their way all through these chats—enticing her to trust him, promising that he would never harm her, vowing to protect her, and assuring her that he would only go as far as she was comfortable with.

I wished more kids knew the approaches these guys used so they'd be able to identify when they were being targeted. And I wished more parents were aware of what's really going on in some of these chat rooms and with their kids' online activity so they could put a stop to this stuff before it was too late.

The chat continued rather innocently for a few minutes, then cycled back to the age issue one last time.

mrplesuregiver56ga (11:58:44 PM):	i could get in trouble for this.
yngnrdyblond (11:58:51 PM):	why?
mrplesuregiver56ga (11:58:55 PM):	cus your age. ur not a cop r u?
yngnrdyblond (11:58:58 PM):	lol no!!
mrplesuregiver56ga (11:59:07 PM):	cool. just wanted to make sure
yngnrdyblond (11:59:12 PM):	r u a cop?
mrplesuregiver56ga (11:59:17 PM):	no way
yngnrdyblond (11:59:25 PM):	didn't think so
mrplesuregiver56ga (11:59:30 PM):	so il be there around 7
yngnrdyblond (11:59:34 PM):	cant wait 2 c u
yngnrdyblond (11:59:38 PM):	and for my chocolate
mrplesuregiver56ga (11:59:44 PM):	me too c u soon

From looking over the next few chats and reviewing Wooford's file, I discovered that he had indeed driven to her house that night, but had changed his mind at the last minute and gone past it without stopping to go in.

Later, when the girl's mom found this chat on her daughter's computer, she reported it to the police.

So that brought up the obvious question: why didn't they just arrest Wooford then?

And the answer: because there was no proof that he

was the one who'd been sitting at the keyboard at the time when the chats were taking place. He could have (and would've almost certainly been advised to do so by his lawyer) argued that it wasn't him, even though the chats were occurring at his IP address. To get a conviction, we have to place the person alone at home when illegal material is being downloaded or transmitted.

Timing and location.

It's always about timing and location.

So instead, the police had put together a sting operation that ended up nabbing Wooford when he set up a meeting with another "thirteen-year-old girl," who was really an undercover officer.

Still, I hated to think what would have happened if there really was a young teen girl home alone when he showed up with his condoms and candy.

At first he argued entrapment, but that would never have stood up in court. He would've had to demonstrate that there was a pattern of law enforcement coming after him for a long time without any evidence. These chats were evidence, they were not entrapment.

Then he told them about the Final Territory and tried to cut his deal.

But before anything could be finalized, he was killed—either by himself or, possibly, by someone else.

Harrington also sent me a link to the security camera footage of the inside of the detention facility where Wooford had been held when he died, and now I reviewed the video.

There was a convenient eight-minute gap in the footage that occurred about an hour before the rounds when they found him dead in his cell.

It was ruled a suicide and no relatives came forward to dispute the medical examiner's finding. Case closed.

I was sorting through all that when Jodie came in through the door.

Glancing at my computer, I saw that it was almost nine o'clock.

She looked like she'd barely slept at all, but before I could say anything, she held up a hand. "I know, I know. I look like crap."

"Crap wasn't exactly the word I was thinking of," I said lightly, "but that'll work."

She gave me a faint smile.

"Jodie, like I mentioned, my apartment is available— but I'm not going to keep bringing it up. You do what you have to do, just know that you have a place if you need one."

I expected her to decline the offer again, but instead she said, "I think I could use it, actually. I was hoping to stay with a friend for a couple days, but that fell through. So, if I'm not imposing . . ."

"Not at all. I cleared everything with Christie. Come over after work tonight. I'll give you a key, get you settled."

"Dell told me she wants my stuff out of her apartment by the end of the weekend—this is all happening way too fast." She shook her head in exasperation. "I just can't believe how quickly things can fall apart."

Yes.

All in the blink of an eye.

She turned her head to the side, but not before I noticed the tear she was trying to hide.

"I'll be right back." She edged into the hallway again. "My contact's coming out."

"Sure."

Then she slipped off to compose herself and I texted Christie to give her a call to encourage her.

*   *   *

When Jodie returned, we consigned personal matters to the backseat and worked for an hour searching again for Randy Quentin McReynolds's electronic trail since January.

When he'd confronted me in that Brilington Towers apartment, he didn't dress or smell like someone who'd been living on the streets for six months.

In our world, it's pretty tough to drop off the grid for that long unless you're homeless, so I assumed there would be traces of his movement—credit card usage, traffic violations, online activity, cell phone records, something—but we kept coming up short, even though we had his full name and Social Security and driver's license numbers.

"And," Jodie said reflectively, "there's an even bigger question than *how* he managed to slip off everyone's radar screen."

"What's that?"

"*Why* he did."

"Ah, now it sounds like you're plumbing for motives, Agent Fleming. That's not my wheelhouse. I'll leave those up to you."

"Come on, Pat. Don't you ever ask why?"

"And why would I do that?"

"Ha." She leaned back and folded her arms. "So, what's next?"

"Well, if we don't have a record of McReynolds's travel patterns, maybe we can look into those of Stewart and Wooford. There's obviously some sort of link between the three men, so if we can't discover what McReynolds was doing since he left West Virginia, maybe we can see if either of the other two guys ever visited him there."

She guessed where I was going with this: "Gas and meal receipts in Beckley, West Virginia, or anywhere nearby."

"Yes. And phone records, GPS data from their cars, if it's available."

My cell vibrated: a text from Tobin that a family emergency had come up and he wasn't going to be able to come in this morning: "It has to do with my mother. I'll call later to explain. Also, Francis Edlemore found something he wants to show us." He ended the message by leaving me the ICSC's number.

I phoned Edlemore to set up a meeting. Eleven forty-five worked for him and gave me just enough time to get over there.

"Okay," I said to Jodie. "I'll swing by the ICSC while you keep things rolling here."

After replying to Tobin that I hoped his family situation got resolved and to take whatever time he needed to deal with it—that Jodie and I had things under control here—I wrapped some things up with her and then left for the International Child Safety Consortium offices.

23

Lily woke up unfocused, bleary, confused.

She rubbed her eyes and looked around, trying to emerge from the fuzzy, half-sleep world that was tempting her to just retreat into it and dream some more, dream her way into forever.

A narrow window that was formed with thick frosted blocks of glass let in enough diffuse light for her to see. About twenty feet away, wooden steps led up to a door that she could just barely make out from where she was.

Beneath her, a thin, tattered mattress on a dirt floor.

Cement block walls.

Cool, stale, dusty air.

A cellar.

She was in a cellar.

There were gardening tools, piles of boxes, old toys, and discarded chairs in the middle of the room.

She was still dressed in the cheerleader outfit, but her purse was gone. So was her phone. Her money. Everything.

Lily pushed herself to her feet, rubbed her throbbing head, and started toward the stairs, but a sturdy chain that was padlocked around her left ankle stopped her abruptly.

The other end of it was bolted to the wall.

No, no, no, this was not happening.

She tugged desperately at the chain, but there was no way it was coming off her leg or off the cement blocks it was fastened to. The padlock had a keyhole, and even though she knew the key couldn't possibly be there nearby, she scoured the ground and the mattress searching for it.

Nothing.

"Hey!" she screamed. "Let me out of here!"

Her cries were met with a coarse echo, and then a thick, spreading silence.

What happened last night? How did you end up here?

"Shane!"

She remembered having a drink, changing clothes, finding him seated on the bed, hearing him say that she looked "serviceable."

A word that had seemed like both an insult and a threat.

Serviceable for what?

Then he'd put on that white mask and come at her.

He filmed you.

Yes.

She remembered that.

The camera.

The tripod.

But how did you get here?

Did you pass out? Did he drug you?

She yanked futilely at the chain. "I swear to God you better let me out of here!"

Yes, he must have. He must have drugged you.

She tried her best to remember what happened after he approached her, but her memories were fragmented, like glass shards, like the ones in the kaleidoscope she'd found in her grandfather's basement when she was a kid—you stared into a tube, then turned it. There were mirrors in there and when you spun it, the crystalline pieces of glass tipped around them, reflecting ever-changing, unique symmetrical shapes.

She thought of that now, her memory hopscotching back through time.

Fragments of glass.

Her memories.

Shifting, changing, and now reflecting back to her images that were both real and not quite real at the same time: being in the apartment, riding in that Benz again . . . For how long? An hour? All night? She had no idea.

Then descending those steps . . .

No one knows you're missing. No one will be looking for you.

Some of the working girls had people who would check in with them each day, just a text or a quick call, just to confirm that they were alright.

The program had been started by an inner-city ministry that handed out free prepaid cell phone cards to prostitutes in an effort to help cut down on violence, since women in that profession were over a hundred times more likely to be murdered than other women were—the people from the ministry had told them that statistic, had made a lot out of it.

But Lily had never looked at this as her profession. No. She wasn't a prostitute, she was an actress, and since she wasn't going to be doing this for the long term or anything, she hadn't been worried.

She'd thought the cell program was overkill and unnecessary, and she hadn't gotten involved.

And now here you are. What is wrong with you! It's your

fault. You should have been more careful. No one will know you're missing.

Her pulse raced and her breath came in quick, shallow gasps.

Over a hundred times more likely.

Over a hundred times.

Gasping, gasping breaths.

The doorman at the condo had seen her enter. Yes, he could identify her, he could place her there with the guy who called himself Shane.

Maybe the cops will talk to him?

But why would they? Why would anyone be looking for you at all?

What about her two roommates? No. Their schedules didn't mesh with hers and she was gone so much that they barely saw each other anyway. And they weren't the kind of people to get involved with anything dealing with the police, even if it was out of concern for someone else. Yeah, that was probably not going to happen, at least not for a while.

As hard as Lily tried, she couldn't remember how she'd gotten back to the coupe.

She jerked at the chain until the skin on her palms and around her ankle was raw.

She called out for help until she started to lose her voice.

The echo and the subsequent silence were all she heard in reply. There wasn't even the sound of movement in the house above her.

You knew something wasn't right, remember? You were nervous about things last night. You had that feeling, that intuition. Why didn't you listen? You should have listened. Why didn't you? Why didn't you use the pepper spray!

She squeezed her eyes shut and let out the loudest scream she had so far.

The sound echoed hollow and stiff around her like a living thing that was looking for a place to go, and then finally settled resignedly into the dirt at her feet.

++++

Francis felt guilty about his recent chats with graciousgirl4. Last night after his walk he'd almost asked her if she would be willing to meet him, but he'd been terrified of doing so and had signed off before working up the nerve.

To get ready for his meeting with the FBI agent, he followed up by searching for more files that had masks in them. He found none, but he was distracted and kept eyeing the clock, not just to be ready for the agent when he arrived, but also to count down the hours until his afternoon coffee break when he could see if that red-haired woman was at the Mystorium waiting for him.

Maybe at least there would be one good thing about today.

Maybe, if nothing else, there would be that.

24

As I parked beside the International Child Safety Consortium building, I received a text from Jodie that the courier from D.C. had delivered Wooford's key to the NYPD's forensics techs. They confirmed that it was indeed identical to the ones found on Stewart and McReynolds.

So those folds of the case lined up, but the bigger question still loomed: what did those keys open?

The obvious answer was a door to an apartment, a house, a condo, or maybe a business establishment, but I tried thinking outside the box. Though certain types of keys would normally look different, what about a suitcase? A bank deposit box? A gym locker? A post office box? Maybe a storage unit somewhere? All legitimate possibilities.

Jodie also mentioned that she was able to track down Randy's landlord in Beckley. He told her that Randy had indeed lived there but had left no forwarding address or contact information when he moved out. He had no idea where Randy might have gone.

I entered the ICSC lobby, and after I'd identified myself, a friendly receptionist with a frizzy 1980s haircut pointed me in the direction of Francis Edlemore's cubicle.

He was a demure, somewhat frail-looking man in his late twenties.

"Mr. Edlemore, I'm Agent Bowers. We spoke on the phone. Detective Cavanaugh told me that you had some information to share that might be beneficial to our investigation."

"Yes. Thank you. It's good to meet you. I hope this is helpful."

++++

Francis played the video for the FBI agent.

The footage was only twenty-nine seconds long and simply panned across a plaid couch that had four white, expressionless masks lying on it. Then four arms reached in, picked up the masks one by one, lifted them out of view, and the video cut off.

"Play it again," the agent told him.

Francis did.

"Again."

This time when it was about halfway through, Agent Bowers reached over and tapped the spacebar to pause the video.

He pointed to something off to the side of the couch in the corner of the frame. "Can you zoom in on this here?"

Francis brought it up, then cleaned up the image, which was mostly obscured by the couch. "That looks like it might be part of a child's backpack, one for school."

"Yes, it does. Is there anything else you can do to enhance it?"

"Let me see what I can do."

++++

While Edlemore worked on the image, he mumbled something about pixelation and vignetting and image degradation, but I wasn't really following. Instead I was surfing on my phone, reviewing the case files of the four missing children and looking for something.

If my memory served me right, that was the same style backpack D'Nesh Mujeeb Agarwai had been carrying on the way home from school when he was taken four months ago.

I found a press photo.

Yes.

Just as I thought. His parents had posted a photograph of a similar pack to help people during the search for their son.

Edlemore finished and leaned back.

It matched. The backpack in the video matched D'Nesh Mujeeb Agarwai's.

In fact there, on the back of it, I could just barely make out three initials. It'd been monogramed D.M.A., just like D'Nesh's pack had been.

"When was this video shot?" I asked Edlemore. "Is there any way to tell?"

"Normally, there would be a time stamp, yes, from codes embedded in the file, but this one has been scrubbed. There's software out there that can take care of that for you. It's really not that hard to do."

"What about location? Is there a geotag of any kind? Can you tell who posted it or where it was uploaded from?"

"I checked the IP address before you came. It was posted from the public Wi-Fi at a coffee shop. Someone put it on YouTube from an account that's no longer active. The upload date was deleted, but it was up and then down a couple months ago. It resurfaced. That's when it came to us."

He told me the name of the account and the coffee

shop and I took note of them. Without a time frame we had little to work from, but if we could decipher a specific time, maybe we could check the place's security camera footage.

++++

Francis wasn't sure what to think.

He'd seen this video at least a dozen times already, had studied it, had thought he'd scrutinized it as closely as anyone could, but this agent had just noticed something that he'd missed entirely, even with all those viewings.

He felt like he'd let the FBI down and wondered how many other things he might have missed over the years, how many other children he might have helped, if only he'd been more attentive, if only—

"Alright." Agent Bowers drew him out of his thoughts. "I'm going to need you to send this to our lab so they can analyze it too. What initially caught your attention about it in the first place?"

"If you enhance the pixelation you can see the faint outline of letters in the background. It's like a digital watermark underneath the image."

"Show me."

Francis worked for a moment to get the resolution sharp enough. Then the two letters appeared: *FT*.

"Final Territory," he said.

"Possibly." Agent Bowers found an office chair at a nearby unoccupied workstation and brought it over, then took a seat. "What do you know about the Final Territory?"

"Nothing really. It gets referenced here and there, but I never thought it was real. Detective Cavanaugh asked me about it. Whoever's behind it has been able to keep it a secret."

"Even from you."

"Well . . . yes."

"Detective Cavanaugh told me you know what you're doing, that you're good at your job. Is that true?"

"I mean . . ."

Tell him you are. He needs to trust you.

No, it would seem like I'm bragging!

But thankfully, Agent Bowers dropped it. "Okay, well, I trust what he said. Mr. Edlemore, I want you to give me a crash course on searching for online predators. Pretend I know nothing about this. Take me through what it is you do here."

25

"Well," Francis told him, "most digital file trading and distribution is done through p2p servers."

"What's p2p?"

"Oh, sorry. Peer-to-peer."

"Gotcha."

"So, that's like when you would have one computer talking with another. Software allows you to share video, pictures, et cetera."

"Right."

"Well, when people want to distribute child pornography, they might set up a server that basically transmits the files to the world—but they're trying to send them out to their consumers while also trying to hide them from law enforcement."

"Which presents a challenge."

"Yes, so they'll rename the images, or maybe embed them into other files. Then there are file-sharing sites—the most famous one over the years has been the Pirate Bay—but they don't host the files, they just index the links."

++ ++

Honestly, the piracy issue has always baffled me. People who would never walk into a store and simply help themselves to the merchandise before walking out again, somehow manage to rationalize doing so when it comes to stealing people's intellectual property off the shelves of the Internet.

Through those file-sharing sites, hundreds of millions of people regularly, illegally download movies, songs, video games, software, and other copyrighted material.

With the warnings about piracy everywhere, it's hard to cut people slack by granting that they might be ignorant of the law. More than eighty percent of people with an Internet connection do it—break international law willfully, unashamedly, repeatedly, somehow justifying it in their own minds in ways I still haven't been able to grasp.

"But," Edlemore said, drawing my attention back to our conversation, "it's really not smart to go through p2p networks if you're distributing child pornography. It's just too easy for law enforcement to see your activity."

"So it's better to use Tor."

"You know about it?"

"A little. From what I understand it's called 'The onion router' because you can keep peeling away layers and never reach the core. Is that it?"

"Pretty much, yes. And there are added levels of encryption and anonymity at every layer. It was developed by the government, but now almost everyone who uses it is trying to avoid being caught by the government."

I asked the obvious question, "What's the purpose of it, then? Why can't it just be shut down?"

"Well, the argument goes that it's important for people in countries controlled by regimes that are politically oppressive to be able to communicate to the outside world. Also, it helps whistleblowers have the ability to anonymously reach journalists."

"But with the proliferation of social media, wouldn't you say that that's not so much an issue anymore?"

"In some instances they use Tor to access Krazle or to blog. But yes, some people have pointed that out, that Tor is becoming less and less essential for the purpose it was designed for."

"And it's also called the Dark Web?"

"Tor is a large part of the Dark Web. For most purposes you can just refer to them interchangeably."

"I heard on the news that the Pentagon is working on a program called Memex that could make it obsolete. Could eliminate anonymity."

"From what I understand that's still in beta." He told me the Dark Web was also referred to as the Darknet and was a tiny part of the Deep Web, or Deepnet, which was much larger than the Surface Web. "You need a special browser to use it," he said. "Basically, it's the black market for the Internet. Human trafficking, credit card scams, drugs, guns, mercenaries, assassins—a psychopath's playground."

++++

Francis waited for a reaction. The phrase "psychopath's playground" had come from a coworker of his who'd resigned six months ago and Francis hoped the FBI agent wouldn't think he was showing off or being overly dramatic by using it, but he liked it, thought it was accurate and appropriate, and had wanted to use it someday.

"There are a lot of sick people on there," Francis added. "A lot of bad people."

"And a lot of porn. Tor has the most hard-core, illicit porn."

Francis nodded. "A quarter of all search engine queries have to do with porn on the Internet as a whole, but over eighty percent of all the traffic on Tor is to child porn sites. That's something Tor advocates don't like to bring up. There's a lot of p2p porn out there that's easily accessible on the Surface Web, but if you want to see someone raping a six-month-old baby, then you're most likely going to find that on the Darknet."

++++

A cold shiver slid through me.

Edlemore hadn't made the comment about the sexual molestation of the baby crassly or offhandedly, and I understood that dealing with that type of material was all part of his daily routine, but when I heard his words I honestly felt like I'd been punched in the gut.

I took a moment to regroup, then asked, "Alright, so how does Tor work?"

"All communication is routed through randomly accessed computers all over the world, with encryption at each level. Once you're on there, you have to assume that everyone you're communicating with is conducting activity that they don't want other people to find out about—whether that's the authorities or the government they might be trying to hide from."

As I listened to Edlemore explain how to navigate through Tor, I was also taking note of his desk.

No pictures of family or friends or pets. No knick-knacks. No fan boy *Star Wars* action figures. Nothing to signify that a unique individual worked here. Just some nondescript office supplies, a half-filled in-box and a full out-box, a computer monitor, and a keyboard.

The only nongeneric thing was a sturdy, well-loved coffee mug from St. Stephen's Research Hospital.

I wondered what kind of personal life you would be

able to have when you worked a job like this. It would be difficult, no question about that.

Even tougher than your job?

Yeah.

Probably.

It would take a certain type of person to do this long-term, that much was for certain.

Either someone who's immune to the images—or someone who's addicted to them.

"Alright." I had an idea. "You mentioned tracing this back to the coffee shop's free Wi-Fi. So you can track IP addresses or p2p servers?"

"Yes."

"Show me."

He clicked on a map of this part of the city, then explained that red lights would illuminate routers or IP addresses where images or videos of child pornography had been downloaded.

Block by block, street after street, it lit up—an intricate, ever-widening, quickly spreading web.

Neighborhood after neighborhood, taking over Manhattan.

He zoomed out as the city became a blur of crimson.

With all the deviance I'd seen in this job, not too many things surprised me anymore, but now I was left speechless. I'd known that the problem was widespread, but I had no idea it was so pervasive.

It was what we would call a target-rich opportunity for law enforcement.

Actually, it was too rich.

There were simply too many consumers of child pornography to arrest them all. It would overwhelm the justice system, especially when you started looking at the exchange of sexually explicit material among minors through mobile devices, sexting, and so on.

The floodgates had been opened.

There was no closing them again.

Already, the United States has the highest percentage of incarceration for its populace of any country on the globe. I couldn't imagine what our prisons would look like if we were to crack down on consumers of child pornography.

But we couldn't just turn our back to the problem either.

Instead, it made sense that we would look for the people producing and distributing the images, for those who were actually molesting children, for those who were actively grooming them for sex.

I asked Edlemore, "Can you show me how it works, surfing the Darknet?"

He shook his head. "They don't want to chance that we would get entangled in any illegal activity, so we're not allowed to go on Tor here at work."

"Okay, so your job is, what, specifically?"

"I evaluate the images that are reported to us. I screen, identify, catalog, and report illicit images. We've created a database with all known images and videos of child pornography—at least from our member countries. There are over seven hundred million. But hopefully more countries will sign on at the summit and donor development banquet next Wednesday."

He took some time demonstrating the workings of the database. We searched for any references to "Aurora's birthday," but nothing came up.

When he mentioned, somewhat offhandedly, that p2p sharing could also be done through video gaming systems if you knew what you were doing, I thought again of Stewart's missing Xbox console and decided it might be useful to investigate any online gaming communities he was involved in. Maybe there was a game platform where they shared the file of Aurora's birthday.

Edlemore showed me around the facility, then introduced me to his boss, a peppy woman in her early forties whose convivial personality reminded me somewhat of a border collie.

She was explaining to me about their mission to help stop child molestation and exploitation when the president of the ICSC, Alejandro Gomez, swept into the room.

++++

Francis had always been impressed by the ICSC's president's charisma. It was evident from the first moment you met him.

He didn't know Mr. Gomez's entire background, but he did know that even though he was Hispanic, he'd grown up in Atlanta. He spoke Spanish and three other languages fluently, but when he spoke English he sounded like a true Southern gentleman.

He was a bit of a chameleon, able to make people of just about any race or religion feel comfortable being around him.

Alejandro appealed to the common concern that spanned borders and cultures and religions—protecting the future by protecting children.

Rather than rattle off statistics about how many kids are abused each year or the percentage of them who end up abusing others themselves one day, he was a storyteller at heart and was able to sift through the data and tell the accounts of one or two children to make the point about so many hundreds of thousands of them who were exploited worldwide.

++++

Alejandro looked like he was in his early sixties and appeared distinguished in his impeccably tailored suit and with his slightly graying hair lightly parted on the side.

When he spoke, it didn't seem like shtick or a sales pitch, but like he genuinely believed in what they were doing here. And, by the end, so did I.

"I understand that you're having a fundraiser?" I said.

"Although we have a public mandate from the countries we work with, we're a private organization and we depend on our donors to keep our heads above water." He reached into his pocket and drew out a pair of invitations. "I'd be honored to have you and a guest join us."

"I can't accept favors. Part of the job."

"As a private citizen, then?"

"Let me think about it. I'll let you know."

"Of course."

He thanked me for my work and I thanked him for his, then he disappeared into his office.

Before leaving the facility, I asked Edlemore to sweep every file in their database for any others that might contain masks—either partials or fulls—and for any images of D'Nesh Mujeeb Agarwai.

He informed me that he'd tried the mask part earlier, but since it required writing up new algorithms, it was difficult and he hadn't gotten anywhere with it. However, he told me he would give it another shot.

Then I gave him the link to the site that D'Nesh's parents had set up. It contained dozens of photos of their son in different situations so that a computer analyst could construct a three-dimensional rendering of his face to make it more likely that they could locate pictures of him online.

Edlemore promised he would find out whatever he could and get back to me.

It was almost one o'clock when I got to the car.

I had two texts waiting for me.

One was from Christie telling me that she'd had a chance to speak to Jodie and had tried to encourage her. "Seemed to help."

"Great," I texted back.

The second was from Tobin asking me to give him a call, which I did.

He explained that he wasn't going to be able to come in at all today. "My mother, she's in a nursing home. She's not doing well. It's a three-hour drive from the city. I didn't want to leave, but they're saying they don't even know if she's going to make it through the weekend. I needed to come. I'm here with her now. She's resting. Sleeping. I'm not sure where things are going to go from here."

"Man, I'm sorry about that. Is there anything I can do for you?"

"No. Just make as much progress on all this as you can. And keep me up to speed."

"I will."

++++

Francis wondered if he'd said the right things.

He hoped that he'd been helpful to the agent, but he wasn't sure. He felt like he should have done more, helped more, noticed more, especially in regard to that backpack.

Now, though, he got right to it, trying to develop an algorithm that would search for images or videos that might contain masks. But it was less than an hour before his two o'clock coffee break. So then, after seeing if the woman was there, he could pick up again looking for the masks and any images of D'Nesh Mujeeb Agarwai.

Just thinking about the possibility of seeing her at the Mystorium made him feel both thrilled and anxious.

Both good and bad.

Like so many things.

26

Lily had stopped crying and screaming and had started trying to figure out how to escape from her imprisonment.

You need to get out of here.

Her eyes had gotten used to the dim, dirty light and she inspected the chain again for any links that she might be able to pry open, or for a way to get it off of the wall, but eventually gave that up as a lost cause.

The chain gave her access to a half circle only ten or twelve feet in diameter. She carefully explored it but didn't find anything she could use to get free.

Everything else in the cellar—the cardboard boxes, the coiled-up garden hoses, the children's bicycles, the cobweb-covered, antique furniture—was all beyond her reach, even when she extended the chain and stretched her arm out as far as she could.

It was almost as if whoever had left her here was mocking her predicament by leaving everything right there.

She was making one final sweep of the area when she saw the camera.

It was hidden in the ceiling joists and wasn't clearly visible from the grimy mattress where she'd been when she woke up, but here at the edge of the semicircle she could just barely make it out.

The red operating light on the lower left-hand corner was on, and she took that to mean that she was currently being filmed.

She gave whoever might have been watching her the finger, then turned her back to the camera and, frustrated, frightened, desperate, put her hands to her head and realized that she still had the ponytail in.

That's what Shane wanted you to wear.

Well, screw him.

She took out the hair clip and shook her hair free. A small act of rebellion, but it felt good to do it.

As she was about to toss the clip aside, she noticed the size and design of the clasp mechanism.

A tiny quiver of hope rose inside her.

Yes, it looked like it might possibly fit.

But first, before anything else, she needed to make sure she would be able to do this in secret, that there weren't any other cameras eyeing her.

Keeping the clip hidden in her hand, she walked the perimeter of the semicircle, carefully studying the ceiling, the walls, and, as best she could from where she was, the other items in the cellar, for any other operating lights that might signify more cameras.

Seeing none, she sat down with her back to the one that she did know about, drew her legs close, and inserted the clasp into the keyhole of the padlock that secured the chain around her ankle.

It did fit, but actually picking the lock was going to be another matter altogether.

27

On my return trip across town from the ICSC, Jodie called and informed me that there wasn't any evidence that Stewart or Wooford had ever been near Beckley, West Virginia, or contacted anyone from that part of the state. The NYPD officers hadn't uncovered anything from their interviews with Stewart's family, friends, and neighbors.

"Any word on the prints from those remote controllers?" I asked.

"Our jumper, Randy McReynolds—on the TV remote. It's confirmed. Stewart's were present too. Nothing more on the mailing list. Did you get anything from the ICSC?"

I told her about the video of the masks and about the backpack. "It's the same style as D'Nesh Mujeeb Agarwai's, it's monogrammed with his initials, and there's a small rip in the corner of the fabric just like there was in the case file's description from his parents."

"So either that's his pack or someone did an amazing job of duplicating it."

"For now we'll move forward with the hypothesis that it is his. I had Edlemore send a copy of the footage to the lab. Some sort of electronic watermark that he was able to pull up contained the letters 'FT,' so it's possible this video came from the Final Territory."

"So, then, if that's the case, then D'Nesh is . . ."

"We can't assume either way," I said, although Jodie was probably thinking the same thing I was: if D'Nesh had been taken by someone from the Final Territory, he might appear in some of their videos.

I didn't even want to think about what his abductors might have done to him—or made him do—if that was the case.

He'd been missing for four months.

That was an awful lot of time to film acts of molestation against a child who was being held captive.

After ending the call with Jodie, I snagged lunch and then phoned Ralph. I figured he would prefer a call to a text, since he liked texting about as much as he liked driving in rush-hour traffic. Or France. The guy just did not like France.

"I was actually gonna give you a shout," he said. "You were right. Maybe you better start trusting your gut."

"I'm not so sure about that. What do you have?"

"Your guy, Randy McReynolds, he was a Marine alright, served in a unit that doesn't officially exist, working missions that never officially happened. Did tours in Iraq, Somalia, Sudan, and at least half a dozen places the United States has never sent any troops."

"Officially."

"Yeah. Officially. And after all that, he decides to off himself by taking a nosedive off a building?"

"He seemed afraid when he jumped."

"Okay, but someone with his background? Afraid? Afraid of what?"

"Well, for one thing, he didn't want to be sent to prison. But he also seemed frightened by what some group would do to him if, or when, they found him." I told him what I knew about the Final Territory, which, truthfully, wasn't very much.

There was a moment of light scraping sounds. It sounded like Ralph was repositioning his phone. "So, any word from the OPR?"

"You heard about that?"

"Well, I know you shot McReynolds in the leg. Obviously, the incident is gonna be under review."

"Neither DeYoung nor the OPR lawyer I met with has contacted me yet today. You know how these things can drag on. I guess I'll just keep doing my job until I'm told not to."

"You want me to put some feelers out, see where things are at?"

"Let's just let it play out. Having any more to do with the review right now would only be a distraction for me."

"Gotcha."

On Friday afternoon in New York City, especially in the summer, people tend to leave work early, and now the crosswalks were packed with pedestrians anxious to get home for the weekend. The stoplights seemed to take forever. Snarled traffic. Cabs clogging the streets. People laying on their horns. Not fun.

Driving around right now while talking on the phone wasn't going to fly. I needed a place to set up shop for a while to read my files.

"Listen," I said, "I gotta go."

"Call me if you need anything."

I wasn't intimately familiar with this part of the city, but I did know that there was a branch of the public library a couple of blocks from here. I worked there sometimes when I was over here and didn't want to work at a coffee shop or restaurant.

With federal plates and an OFFICIAL GOVERNMENT BUSINESS placard in the window, I could leave my car pretty much wherever I could find a spot, but this would give me a legit place to park and a little privacy to sort things through.

28

At two o'clock when Francis left the ICSC building, it felt like a wall of heat was smacking into him as he stepped out of the air-conditioned building.

Walking down the street, he wondered if the red-haired woman from yesterday would be there at the Mystorium. But as soon as he entered, he saw her in front of the register. She had her hands full, juggling her phone, purse, a computer bag, and wallet, trying to dig out some bills to pay for her order.

Francis unpocketed his wallet and did something he'd never done before, something that was completely out of character for him, but something Dr. Perrior would have been proud of him for doing: he said to her, "I'll get that for you," and he offered his credit card to Rebekah, the barista.

"Oh no. I couldn't ask you to do that."

"It's just a cup of coffee."

"But it's a latte. It's, like, five dollars, I—"

"That's very nice of you, sir," Rebekah said, quickly accepting the card from him with a wink. "So, what can I get started for you today?"

Normally, he ordered a small cup of whatever the milder roast was, but now, instead, he opted for a large vanilla latte so that the woman, whose name he still didn't know, wouldn't feel awkward that he was spending more money on her than he was on himself.

She finally managed to get control of all her things and stuck out a somewhat tentative hand. "I'm Skylar."

"Francis."

She squeezed his hand daintily with her fingers rather than actually shaking it.

He handed Rebekah his punch card.

"I guess I need to get one of those," Skylar said to him.

"Well." Francis searched for an appropriate response. "They're good for regular visitors."

Rebekah ran the order and returned his punch card and credit card to him.

They waited for their lattes together at the end of the counter.

"That was kind of you, Francis. To pay for that."

"It looked like you had your hands full."

She sighed. "My friends tell me I'm always trying to do too many things at once, that I need to learn to just focus on one thing at a time, to finish it up, and then move on. I just get flutter-brained sometimes."

"That's good advice." Once again Francis found himself not knowing what to say. "It's always good to finish things up and then move on."

Stupid! That was a stupid thing to say!

Quiet. I'm trying to talk to her!

"Flutter-brained," he said. "I've never heard that before, but I like it."

"Um, thank you."

The drinks came up and Skylar said, "There aren't too many tables open. You're welcome to sit with me—if you want to."

"Actually, I need to get back to my desk. Back to work."

"Oh." She flushed, looked embarrassed. "Of course. Sure. Sorry."

"No, it's okay."

"So . . . Right. It was nice to meet you, Francis."

"Nice to meet you too, Skylar."

Then she offered him one last smile and walked toward the table.

After pausing momentarily, Francis started for the door, but as he put his hand against it to press it open, he hesitated.

Go back and find out her number or when you can see her again. This isn't something you need to be afraid of. This is a good thing, Francis. You should do it.

He stood there at the door debating things long enough for a man behind him to grunt impatiently. Francis stepped aside and the guy shouldered his way past him outside.

Rebekah had a hand on her hip and was giving Francis a friendly scoldy look. With her free hand she was pointing furtively yet emphatically at Skylar, who was setting up her laptop.

It was almost like Francis could hear Dr. Perrior tell him that it would be a good choice, a healthy choice, to go back and speak with Skylar.

And he could hardly believe it, but that's what he did.

His heart was beating so fast he thought it might burst as he approached her table.

Skylar eyed him curiously as he came her way, looking nervous and self-conscious as if she were afraid she'd done something wrong and he'd returned to confront her.

"Maybe tomorrow?" he said.

"Tomorrow?"

"I could share your table with you—I mean, if you're

going to be coming in on a Saturday. You probably don't work Saturdays, but if you do, I mean, if you wanted to, I can—really anytime, but three would—"

"That would be nice."

"It would?"

"Three is fine." She lifted her drink. "I'll buy yours for you tomorrow."

"Oh. Okay." He felt like he should say more but didn't know what that should be and finally just settled on "See you then, Skylar."

It felt good calling her by name, this woman he'd only just met, this woman who'd been a stranger to him only a few minutes earlier. Now he knew her name. Now he could talk to her as if they were friends. Now they were more than strangers.

"Okay," she said. "See you then, Francis."

As he left, Rebekah gave him another surreptitious wink and a thumbs-up of approval.

When he settled into his desk at the ICSC, his heart still hadn't stopped slamming against the inside of his chest.

And with that distracting him, he logged in and began to sort through the images, reminding himself of SICR: screening, identifying, cataloging, reporting.

Yes, there was no one sicker than the people who posted this stuff online.

No one at all.

And he was here to help stop them.

29

A librarian whom I hadn't met on my previous visits here set me up in the "staff only" area where they sorted and received books so I could speak on the phone and not interrupt the other people using the facility.

On our way there I saw that every computer station was in use, but only one person was looking through the stacks browsing for a book.

Typical.

Who knows what role libraries will have twenty years from now—if they're even around anymore.

I suggested that it might be best if I used one of the study rooms, but she had her mind set and I didn't push it.

Over the years I've learned a few things.

One: never catnap for more than twenty minutes or you'll wake up groggy. Two: don't go trail running in flip-flops. And three: don't argue with a librarian. You will never win.

So now, after setting up my laptop, I surfed to the Federal Digital Database and updated the online case files with the information I'd found out during my visit with Edlemore.

While I was scrolling through the updates, I noticed that the autopsy results had been posted.

The cause of death was listed as "catastrophic bodily injuries" caused by "impact-force trauma."

I'd never seen it phrased quite like that before, but the conclusion was no surprise.

As it turned out, the gunshot wound in McReynolds's thigh had not been serious, and if he hadn't chosen to jump, it would've likely healed just fine.

I didn't know how that information was going to play with Aguirre and DeYoung, but at least my conscience was clear about what I'd done when I took that shot.

The toxicology report was what grabbed my attention, and when I read it, I decided to confirm the findings with the medical examiner herself.

I'd spoken with Dr. Coutre during other investigations, and her number was in my phone's address book.

"Is this correct?" I asked her. "McReynolds was poisoned with Tribaxil?"

"An overdose, yes. In small doses it can be used to help you sleep. If he hadn't jumped, he would have died anyway within a few hours."

That might have explained the note he was carrying.

"Would he have known that he was drugged?"

"Well, I don't believe he would've been symptomatic yet when you saw him, if that's what you're asking."

"How is it administered?"

"Normally orally, although some forms of it can be injected."

"So unless someone told him they'd slipped him the drug, or he took it himself, there's no reason to believe he would've known he was dying."

"True. That is correct. But it's not typically a drug someone would slip to someone else. I would anticipate that he knew he'd taken it."

Okay, so did Randy drug himself? Maybe. But if so, then why bother to jump?

He didn't seem suicidal until *after* he found out I was a federal agent.

But if he didn't drug himself, who did?

And why would he have written a note that someone was supposed to open only in the case of his death if he didn't know he was going to die?

More folds.

The origami of death.

The pith of my job.

I thanked Dr. Coutre and hung up.

Randy had seemed frightened that someone was after him. Did he know he was dying? Could that have been what he meant when he said, "I'm dead already"?

I wasn't sure where to let those questions take me and decided that, rather than get caught up in amorphous conjecture, or motive analysis, I would focus on something concrete and specific.

The geoprofile.

I pulled up the notes I'd been working on earlier and searched through the file to identify Stewart's and Wooford's activity nodes.

A few years ago some criminology researchers studied the hunting patterns of great white sharks off the coast of South Africa and discovered that, rather than choosing the ideal location for finding seals, when they were by themselves away from shore the sharks had a consistent area they used as the epicenter for their hunting activities.

In essence, it was a home base, one that the researchers theorized optimized the proximity of the seals as well as the distance from other predators and likelihood of capture rates for finding the seals.

And they're not the only predatory species to do that. Many hunt in ways that appear to be random but aren't random at all.

Research has shown that the same is true for serial offenders—rapists, burglars, killers, arsonists. They base their movement around one of their activity nodes, typically their residence or work location.

Animal predators.

Human predators.

Similar hunting patterns.

And there's a good reason for that, one that's easy to overlook: when we talk about the animal kingdom, we're also talking about the human kingdom. Obviously, we are animals. Whether we're also something *more* than animals is a question philosophers and theologians have debated for centuries.

No doubt that was an important question, maybe the most important one of all, but one I knew I wasn't going to be able to answer at the moment.

Right now I wondered if the findings on patterns of predatory and stalking behavior would apply in this series of kidnappings as well.

I pulled up the information on the four missing children and began to study the data through the lens of a predator looking for his prey.

++++

Lily had never picked a lock before and it didn't seem like she was making any progress. She wasn't sure how long it should take, or if she was doing it right, but it hadn't worked yet and she was getting frustrated.

She kept trying different ways of positioning the end of the clasp and jiggling it around inside the keyhole, but the mechanism in the padlock didn't respond.

Also, she didn't want to stay sitting with her back to the camera for too long for fear that if someone was watching her they might get suspicious and come check on her. So she would work at the lock for a little while, then stretch, pace, curse, cry, all the while pretending for the camera that she was desperate and hopeless.

Acting.

Yes.

Starring in a role that her life depended on her getting just right.

++++

I was analyzing what I knew about the movement patterns and activity nodes of Stewart and Wooford and thinking about the shark research when dispatch called me.

A valet at a condo on the Upper West Side had reported that a woman "may have been in trouble last night," that he thought someone might have been trying to abduct her.

It was all vague and didn't really have the ring of urgency you would think something like that would have.

Normally the NYPD wouldn't have had any reason to let me know about a routine, possibly crank, call like this, but the location was close enough to the Brilington Towers that it raised a red flag for someone at dispatch, and I was glad it did.

The third night in a row. The same vicinity. Timing and location. Something worth looking into.

I thanked the librarian, assured her I would keep reading this summer, something all librarians like to hear, and left for the condo.

30

I arrived just as the two officers who'd initially responded were leaving. They informed me that they'd questioned the young male valet who'd called 911 and found nothing they deemed important or suspicious.

I accepted that but wanted to hear the details from the source.

The valet told me that his name was Joe. He didn't give me a last name. Clean-cut. Stylish glasses. A slight stutter as he spoke. He seemed nervous when I told him I was with the FBI.

I asked him, "If there was a woman in trouble last night, why did you wait until now to call it in?"

"I did call last night, but whoever was there at the police department didn't think it was anything big and told me not to worry about it."

"So you followed up today?"

"I couldn't stop thinking about it."

"Okay, tell me what happened."

"I told those cops already."

"I'm not those cops. I'm here, I'm listening. Tell me."

"Well, this couple came in and I parked his Benz. Nothing weird, right? But when they came back out a couple of hours later, he was helping her, you know, like she was drunk or something. But I've seen a lot of drunk people. She didn't seem drunk."

"So, drugs?"

"I don't know. Yeah. Maybe. But as I opened the door for her, she turned and looked at me and I swear she said, 'Please.' It was something about the way she said it, like she was pleading for her life. And . . . she was dressed up like a cheerleader."

"A cheerleader?"

"Yeah. I've seen that guy a few times before. He always brings in different women. Some of them look really young—one time I thought it was maybe his daughter. Anyway, this lady last night—dude, I don't know, she just looked scared." He was rubbing his fingers together nervously. "I should go. My boss is probably wondering why I'm not working."

"Don't worry about that. I'll talk with him if you need me to. Focus here: the other women this man has been with, were they drunk or drugged or anything when he left with them?"

"Nothing like this. No."

He paused.

"What else?"

"It's sorta weird. I mean, it's probably nothing."

I liked it when people used that phrase. It usually meant something helpful was about to come next.

"What was probably nothing?" I asked.

"One time when I was parking his car I saw a mask on the floor in the front seat on the passenger side."

Now we were getting somewhere.

"A mask?"

"A white one. Plain. Sort of like something from *The Phantom of the Opera* —except this was a full mask. It would've covered your whole face. It's just that it kind of freaked me out. I don't even know why. It stuck with me. That's about it. Otherwise, I don't know. That guy was a good tipper. I know that."

"Describe him—height, race, age, hair color. What did you notice?"

"I don't know. I mean he seemed kind of normal-looking. Around forty or forty-five, somewhere in there, I guess. Maybe younger. About my height."

That would put him at about five-eleven or six feet.

"He was white," Joe added. "Nothing else, really, that I know of."

"No visible scars, tattoos, anything like that?"

"No."

"Facial hair? Glasses?"

"No."

I studied the area. "You guys have security camera coverage of the front of this building, don't you?"

"Sure."

"Take me to your boss."

Joe's supervisor was a balding man who sighed a lot and kept rubbing the back of his neck like he had a knot in it that he was trying to press out.

He was a little reluctant to help me, but I could tell he also didn't want to get in the way of an active investigation and after I explained that his cameras might have captured footage of a woman's abduction, he took me to their security center.

I reviewed the footage from last night at the time when Joe told me the couple had left.

It didn't take long to find them.

Their faces were turned away from the camera, but it was clear that he was helping her to the car, supporting her weight. When he was retrieving his key from Joe, it appeared that their height was indeed similar.

The angle of the car wasn't right for me to see the plates and I "rewound" the footage—a term that makes absolutely no sense when you're dealing with digital videos—to when the unknown man dropped off the vehicle earlier in the evening.

I still couldn't see his face.

That told me three things.

First, he was aware of where the cameras were and knew which way to turn his head to avoid them.

Second, he didn't want to be seen.

Third, he was brazen, since he came in here despite the cameras.

This time I was able to read the New Jersey plates.

I ran them and the owner came up as Ivan Romanoff of 1607 Bradley Road, Princeton, New Jersey. When I showed Romanoff's DMV driver's license photo to Joe, he shook his head. "No. That's not him."

There was also footage of the man and the woman entering the lobby, but his face was turned once again away from the camera as he crossed toward the elevator bay.

The two of them stepped onto an elevator and from there, even though I scanned the different floors, there wasn't any footage of them leaving it.

When I asked Joe's neck-scratching supervisor about it, he explained that there wasn't any footage of the penthouse suite. "The owners prefer their privacy."

"Can you get me up there?"

"Um . . ."

"Wait. I'm sorry about that."

"About what?"

"I should have put it this way: I need to have a look up there. Let's go."

++++

Lily was focused on trying to pick the lock when she heard the rumble of the garage door in the house above her.

A car drove in, then the garage door shut again. Car doors opened, closed.

She waited, her heart thundering in her chest.

They're coming for you. What are they going to do?

They're going to check on you.

Hide the clip.

Pretending she was scratching her leg, she slipped the clip into her sock and strained her ears to discern how many people were entering the house. She knew she needed to get the padlock open, but if they were watching the video of her, she wasn't going to be able to do that.

"I'll be back in a few," one man said. Someone else muttered an indistinguishable reply.

Maybe they've been watching you. They know you're trying to get out.

A door inside the house slammed and then heavy footsteps pounded on the floorboards above her.

No, no, no. The man who took you. He's here.

You need to get out. Now.

But how?

You have—

Then she heard someone crying out and what might have been the sound of feet kicking the floor.

They have someone. They have someone else!

But the cries didn't sound like those of a woman.

"Stop it, you're hurting me!" It sounded like a boy. Maybe eight or nine years old.

A gruff male voice rebuked him. "Shut up or we'll put you in the dark place like we did last week. You remember that place? What happened down there?"

The boy stopped crying out.

"You wouldn't want that, would you?"

Lily heard a faint "No."

"Alright, then."

You need to do something. You need to help him.

Her first instinct was to call out to reassure the boy or to shout threats against the men, but given her situation, it would have been stupid and useless to do either, and thankfully she caught herself before making a sound.

The best way to help the boy, the only way, was to get that lock picked.

++++

In the bedroom of the penthouse suite, I found three marks in the carpet in a triangular pattern pointing toward the bed.

I'd seen this type of thing before.

They were made by a tripod stand.

If this guy brought women here a lot, it might explain why the marks were still visible now, even after the tripod had been moved.

But Joe hadn't mentioned the guy leaving with one, so where was it?

I searched the place and found it in a hallway closet with a mask beside it on the floor.

The camera was gone.

I got on the phone with Jodie, told her where I was and what I'd discovered. "I want to know who owns this condo and if it's the same guy who owns that Benz."

"I'll see what I can find out."

"And get a Crime Scene Unit over here."

"On it."

"Joe, the valet, mentioned that the guy has been here before. Have an officer cross-check Joe's work schedule with the video surveillance footage to see if this guy brought any other women over here who ended up on our missing persons list afterward."

After returning to the security room, I studied the footage again but wasn't able to take anything else away from it.

Wondering if the car's owner, Ivan Romanoff, was connected with Stewart, I went to the case files and searched for his name on Stewart's email list.

Nothing.

But when I went through Stewart's contacts list, I found one for Ivan_r@inova8investments.com.

There wasn't any mobile number listed.

It only took a few minutes of research to find that Romanoff had grown up as a trust fund baby and was an exec at his uncle's investment firm.

The trust fund part might explain how he could afford a Benz and a condo in this price range.

I checked the time, then analyzed Romanoff's Princeton address in relation to the abduction sites and the children's residences, and it came up as a possible location in the hot zone for the abductor's home base.

Nothing certain, but the computer program I used told me there was a sixty-two percent probability for that part of New Jersey being the point of origin for the crime spree.

In other words, if these four missing children really were linked, which the email subscription list seemed to indicate, Romanoff was looking good for this.

Jodie sent me a text confirming that the condo was also in his name.

That gave me some arrows to follow.

Arrows lead to answers.

There wasn't enough to bring Romanoff in, but there was enough to justify having a chat with him.

I asked Jodie to pull up what she could on him while I left to drive to his house.

++++

Things had been quiet upstairs for a while now and Lily was worried about the boy. However, calling out to him would only draw attention to her, and if the men came down here, they might find the hair clip, and then she would have no way of escaping, no way of helping the boy.

Their best hope was for her to get out of here and find help.

As she worked on the lock, she heard a television come on somewhere on the other side of the house, and then, just barely, through a vent about fifteen feet away, she heard the sound of the boy crying.

31

As I drove toward Ivan Romanoff's New Jersey home, Jodie gave me an update on him: Forty-one. Single. Twice divorced. No kids. His money came from his family, not from his work ethic.

Jodie had called in to see if Romanoff was at his office, but they said he hadn't been in yet today. "They told me he keeps his own hours," she informed me.

"I'll bet he does."

++++

The boy would sob for a while, then stop, then start again.

Hearing him cry like that was hard on Lily, especially since she wasn't able to do anything to help him.

The television cut off.

The floorboards above her must have been pretty thin, or there wasn't insulation, because she could hear two men speaking in the room that sounded like it was at the top of the steps.

"We should drug him."

"They want him awake and alert when it happens. They'll be logging on in about twenty minutes. Have you checked the video feed yet?"

"You mean of our girl downstairs?"

"Yes."

"Naw. Not yet." This man sounded like he was from the Bronx. The other, Middle Eastern. Neither of them sounded anything like the man who'd called himself Shane.

"Go peek in on her. See how our little honey's doing. She should be awake by now for sure," the Middle Eastern man said.

" 'The kidnapped cheerleader.' I think it's gonna be a popular one."

You need to hurry, Lily. You need to get out of here!

The door at the top of the stairs opened and a chunky, unkempt man shambled down the steps.

She backed up against the wall and shivered from fear. It wasn't just acting.

He smirked at her and rested his heavy hands on his wide hips. "Hello, Lily."

Then he came toward her and she raised her hand to slap him, but he stopped her by grabbing her forearm. She spit at his face and he shoved her back against the wall.

He wiped the spittle off his cheek. "Just wait 'til you see what we have planned for you. I don't think you'll feel quite so spunky then."

He grunted once, then returned upstairs.

Lily waited a few minutes to make sure he wasn't going to come back down, then turned her back to the camera and desperately probed the padlock's keyhole with the wire of the hair clip.

And without any warning, almost as if it'd been waiting for her desperation to reach a certain level, the mechanism inside the padlock clicked and the shackle snapped out of the body of the lock.

It took her by surprise and she stared at the lock for a long moment before it registered that it was open.

Yes, yes, yes.

You're free.

Frantically, she removed the lock and was about to unloop the chain from her leg and run up the stairs when she realized that as soon as she did that, whoever was watching through the video camera would see that she'd left the mattress.

Think this through.

Maybe there's no one watching it right now. Maybe they're just recording you.

The boy upstairs cried out again.

Go, Lily. Do it now.

No! They'll see you.

Go!

If the men were watching, then she would get caught, but she was already caught and just sitting around here wasn't going to do anything. It wasn't just herself she was worried about, it was the boy too. She needed to help him.

She unwound the chain, crossed the basement, and then clambered up the stairs and tried the doorknob.

It turned freely, but the door didn't open.

No!

It must have been dead-bolted or something from the other side. Even when she threw all her weight against it, the door didn't budge.

Thunderous footfalls from beyond the door some-where. "Muhammad, she's free!"

Oh no, no, no.

The footsteps came closer.

The lightbulb above the stairs was out of reach, but when she held on to one of her shoes, she was just able to reach it.

She smashed the bulb.

Her eyes were used to the dim light, but she was guessing that the man's wouldn't be when he opened the door. The light switch must have been on the other side, but he wouldn't know that the bulb wasn't working until he opened the door, and the shadowy area around her here at the top of the steps would give her just a moment of surprise.

But what was she going to do to him? She didn't have her pepper spray with her. She wasn't a fighter, didn't know self-defense or anything like that.

The stairs. Use the stairs.

She heard the dead bolt slide to the side.

The door opened and she leapt at him, screeching like a wild animal fighting for its life, and by the look on his face it was clear that she'd startled him. She grabbed the front of his shirt and, stepping to the side, yanked him forward and past her.

It was enough to get him off balance and when she pushed him, he went tumbling down the stairs.

She entered the kitchen, slammed the door behind her, and bolted it shut.

You weren't able to open it from the other side, he won't be able to either.

Unless he breaks it down, unless—

There's someone else here. He called for Muhammad.

She could see the front door on the other side of the house through the living room. She darted toward it.

But that boy is still here.

You can get help once you're free. You just need to get out of here.

No! Once they know I'm free, they'll leave or they might kill the boy!

The man she'd locked in the basement was hammering

against the door, cursing and shouting out crude and shocking threats.

"Muhammad!" he hollered.

A voice came down the stairs from the second floor. "I'm in the john!"

"She's out!"

The boy. Get the boy!

Lily ran down the hallway toward the room where, based on the location of the vent in the basement, she guessed he would be.

She cranked the dead bolt, opened the door, and rushed in, only to find that the boy's leg was chained to the wall just as hers had been.

++++

I parked across the street from Romanoff's place.

A heavily wooded park lay nearby.

No traffic. Just a quiet, serene suburban neighborhood.

++++

The boy was seated on a thin, yellowed mat and wore only a grimy T-shirt and underwear.

He gasped when he saw her, but she reassured him, "I'm going to get you out of here." She tugged at the chain, but that was going to be hopeless. "My name's Lily. What's yours?"

"D'Nesh. They won't let me go. They're bad people."

"I know."

She heard the basement door burst open and the man she'd locked down there stalking his way through the house toward her.

"They're coming back," D'Nesh said. "It's too late."

Run or stay, run or stay?

That guy could just lock you in here.

But he didn't lock her in.

Instead he appeared in the doorway holding a wickedly sharp kitchen knife.

"Muhammad, bring the camera," he called. "You're gonna want to film this."

++++

There was nothing dramatic or out of place for the modest, beige two-story house. The Benz wasn't in the driveway, but it might have been in the garage—there were no windows in the door, so there was no way to tell.

The shades were all drawn.

Hard to tell if anyone was home.

Jodie had updated the task force on where I was, but I called in my location to dispatch, then exited the car and headed for the front door to see if Ivan Romanoff was here.

As I approached the house, I noted its layout and mentally compared it to typical floor plans for two-story homes. From this vantage point I couldn't see much of the back of the house, except for the wraparound deck.

I knocked at the front door.

++++

Lily heard someone knocking at the door.

The man with the knife glanced in that direction, then came toward her. She stood between him and the boy, but he pushed her aside, went to D'Nesh instead, and pressed the knife against the child's throat. "You cry out," he said harshly to Lily, "he dies. Do you hear me?"

"Yes."

The knocking came again.

The boy's eyes were wide, silently pleading with her to save him.

"Do you believe me?" the man said in a charged voice.

"Yes. Yes, I do. Don't hurt him!"

She was tempted to run from the room, to go to the front door, to beg whoever was there for help, but then this boy would suffer, would die.

They might kill whoever's at the door too.

++++

Shane realized what was going on and made a decision. It wasn't ideal, but it was necessary.

++++

I heard footsteps inside the house.

A lanky Middle Eastern man with a salt-and-pepper beard opened the door partway. "Yes?" he said impatiently. "Who are you?"

I held up my creds and mentally reviewed the faces I'd seen in the case files.

No. I didn't recognize him, and his frame didn't fit that of the man in the security footage outside the condo. "I'm Special Agent Bowers with the FBI. I'm looking for Ivan Romanoff."

He shook his head. "I don't know anyone by that name."

"This is 1607 Bradley Road, isn't it?" I said, though I knew it was.

"Yes."

"And you are?"

"Muhammad El-Sayed. I don't know any Romanoffs."

"What are you doing in his house if you don't know him?"

"I am not from here. I am staying with a friend," he said, switching his tack and suddenly speaking in stilted English. "This is his old college roommate's house. That is all I know."

"And what friend is that, Mr. El-Sayed?" I took out a notebook. "What's his name?"

"What is this about?"

"A missing person's case." I studied his face, watched his reaction. "A boy named D'Nesh Mujeeb Agarwai. Do you know where he might be?"

He shook his head. "I don't know that boy. Will that be all?"

And that was it.

That's what I was waiting for.

If a federal agent shows up at your doorstep asking questions about a missing boy, you'd typically be nervous and worried. Most people would naturally ask, "What happened to him?" or something along those lines. That, or they would get frightened or nervous and ask why the agent was talking with them, or they might deny that they had anything to do with his disappearance.

We are a curious race, and when someone betrays that instinct, it says to me that something else is going on.

The guilty think that asking questions about a case will make them seem guilty, so they don't. But just the opposite is true. It makes them look suspicious.

"Mr. El-Sayed, may I come in? Maybe we can talk inside?"

"Do you have a search warrant?"

Pretty well-informed for a foreign national just staying with a friend.

"Why would I need a search warrant? Is there something you're not—"

I looked past him and saw it on the other side of the living room: the plaid couch from the video Francis Edlemore had shown me, the one with the footage of the four masks and D'Nesh Mujeeb Agarwai's backpack.

32

Time seemed to slow down.

The pack wasn't there now, nor were the masks, but it was definitely the same couch.

As my gaze shifted back to Muhammad, he must have recognized that I knew something.

"Hands in the—" I reached for my weapon even as he slammed the door in my face.

I tried the knob.

Locked.

Gun out, I took a step back, then kicked hard against the door, planting my heel just to the side of the lock. It took two kicks before the lock splintered and the door flew open, smacking hard against the wall.

For a brief moment I moved to the side to avoid being an easy target, then I whipped around into the doorway and caught sight of Muhammad disappearing up the stairs.

"Stop! Put your hands up!"

"Help!" a boy cried from a room down the hall.

"D'Nesh?" I called. "Is that you?"

"Yes!" a woman shouted. "We're in here!"

Muhammad reemerged at the top of the steps holding an M4.

Oh.

Bad.

He swung the gun into position and fired before I could get off a shot.

I dove to the side around a corner of the wall to get out of his sight line and heard the sound of semiautomatic fire as he sprayed the spot where I'd been standing only a moment earlier.

This drywall wasn't going to give me much protection.

Crouching, I leaned around the corner and got off two shots but couldn't tell if I hit Muhammad or not before going for cover again.

He was yelling in a language I didn't understand. Sounded like Arabic, but I couldn't be sure.

Apparently, I hadn't hit the mark.

I tapped in 911, sent in a dispatch code telling them I was with a suspect and that shots had been fired.

They would send backup, but who knew how long that might be?

I needed to hold out until then.

And I needed to find a way to get to the woman and the boy.

Based on the house's footprint, I guessed that there wasn't another way down the stairs, so unless Muhammad was going to jump out a two-story window to flee, he would need to come back down the steps he'd just ascended.

++++

Lily heard the gunshots.

Moments ago someone yelled for the guy to stop, to put his hands up.

A cop!

He must be a cop!

The man with the knife glanced at the doorway to the room, then at her and the boy, and she had the sense that it was too late. That he wasn't going to chance letting them live any longer.

But the cops are here!

"Take me instead of him," she said.

The man grabbed her roughly, pressed the knife to her throat, and shoved her ahead of him into the hall.

"Drop the gun!" he hollered. "I've got the whore!"

++++

"I'll kill her!" a man in the hall south of me yelled. "If you don't drop your gun!"

I was pinned down between the two men. I needed a play here.

When I was a kid in a snowball fight, my brother would lob one snowball at me and then when my eyes were on it, he'd zing a second one right at my chest.

Misdirection.

I didn't have a second gun with me to throw out there, but unpocketing my Mini Maglite, I turned it on, then spun around the corner and tossed it into the air as a distraction, and as Muhammad was shooting at the flashlight, I fired at him.

Three shots. Center mass. I wasn't sure if all three hit their mark, but at least one did.

He staggered backward into the wall behind him, then drifted limply to the floor.

"Muhammad?" the man in the hallway called.

With my gun level and ready, I edged into the hall. The living room stretched out behind me.

Five meters from me a thickset man stood behind a woman in a cheerleader outfit. He had a knife to her throat.

Though I was a pretty good shot, I didn't want to chance hitting the woman. "Let her go," I ordered him, my weapon directed at his head.

He sneered at me and opened his mouth to reply.

But that was the last thing he did.

His head snapped back and he collapsed as the sound of a gunshot sliced through the air.

I was momentarily confused. I hadn't squeezed the trigger, or had I?

I whipped around and saw a flash of movement as someone ducked out of sight into the other room, apparently fleeing.

But it wasn't Muhammad.

A third person.

Whoever it was had fired the kill shot.

And that was some shot.

Why didn't he kill you?

Chase him or—

No.

Check the victims. Secure the boy and the woman.

She'd collapsed onto the carpet and was shaking, terrified.

I rushed forward, past the corpse of the hulking man who'd been holding the knife to her throat, and knelt beside her. "Are you okay? Did he hurt you?"

"No." Her breathing was ragged, gaspy. "I'm alright. The boy, D'Nesh, he's in the room."

I brought her with me as I went to check on him.

D'Nesh Mujeeb Agarwai was huddled in the corner, sitting on a thin mat, his leg chained to the wall.

"It's okay," I assured him. "You're going to be okay. My name's Pat. I work with the police. I'm here to help you."

He said nothing, just watched me warily.

"You're D'Nesh, aren't you?"

He nodded.

"I'm Lily," the woman said.

"Alright, Lily, tell me: are there any other people here?"

"Not that I know of, no."

With the shooter out there, I wasn't about to chance telling her to run for safety or risk leaving her and the boy here unprotected. I needed to look after these two until backup arrived.

I'm pretty good with locks and I took out my lock pick set and got started on the padlock shackling D'Nesh's leg to the wall.

33

I was still working on the lock when I heard the crackle of flames coming from the hallway.

"Stay here," I told Lily.

Gun in position, I crossed the room and peered into the hall.

The end of it was blocked.

Someone had wedged in a reclining chair and set it on fire, sealing us in. Beyond the chair, through the shimmer of heat and curls of black smoke, I could just barely see the whisper of movement as he—or she—went through the living room lighting the drapes on fire as well.

Okay, change of plans.

There wasn't time to wait for backup.

We needed to get out of here now.

Based on the intensity of the flames, I guessed that the arsonist must have splashed the recliner with gasoline or some other accelerant first, before lighting it.

I rushed back into the room to D'Nesh's side and called to Lily, "Try the window."

She went to the window but found that the slats criss-crossing the glass were steel.

Enough with trying to pick this lock. I wasn't going

to gamble with three lives that I'd be able to pick it quickly enough to save us.

"Check the other rooms in the hall," I told Lily, and she disappeared out the door.

I positioned myself between D'Nesh and the wall so that if the bullet ricocheted it would hit me rather than him, then I lined up the barrel at the hasp where the chain was attached to the wall.

On the fourth shot the link snapped.

I gathered the boy up in my arms as Lily returned. "Nothing," she exclaimed. "The windows in the other rooms are barred too."

We had to get past that burning chair.

I pointed toward the thin, ratty mat that D'Nesh had been sitting on and said to Lily, "Grab that."

It wasn't much, but it would have to do.

Smoke was curling beneath the doorjamb into the room where we were and gathering along the ceiling.

"Close your eyes," I told D'Nesh so he wouldn't have to see the corpse in the hall. Then, carrying him, I stepped over the body.

By now, the recliner was engulfed in flames, completely sealing us off.

I set D'Nesh down for a moment.

I considered barreling forward and trying to tip the chair over or shove it out of the way, but it appeared to be pretty firmly wedged in place, so I took the mat from Lily and draped it across the flaming chair instead.

The flames snaked up around the mat's edges, but the center of the mat remained clear for the moment.

It wasn't going to buy us a lot of time, but hopefully it'd be just enough to get to the other side.

"Crawl over that," I told Lily.

"I don't think I can."

"You can. Go."

After a short hesitation she took a deep, uneasy breath, then scrambled across, crying out in pain as she slipped and her arm brushed through the flames.

"You alright?" I shouted.

"Yes."

I knelt beside D'Nesh. "You're next, okay?"

"I'm scared."

"It's okay. I'll be right behind you."

Lily waited on the other side of the chair to help him. "Hurry!"

But the boy didn't move.

Flames raged up the walls on both sides of the mat.

"We don't have much time, D'Nesh. I want to get you back home to your mom and dad . . ." I searched my memory for other details from the case files. "And your dog, Pepper. She wants to see you."

"Pepper?"

"Yes."

"She misses you. She's waiting for you."

That did it.

A nod. "Okay."

I helped him onto the mat. Lily grabbed his armpits and slid him across to join her, but as she did, the mat caught on his foot and got pulled over to her side. It was burning enough so that she wasn't going to be able to lift it up or slip it back onto the chair.

With the sudden rush of oxygen, the flames on the chair shot higher.

Getting over that chair was the only way out of here.

"Move back," I called.

Lily and D'Nesh took a couple of steps into the living room.

"Farther!"

The chair was too high, I wasn't going to be able to hurdle it.

I backed up and sprinted toward it, then dove head-first through the flames.

If I were more coordinated or knew gymnastics, I might have been able to tuck into a somersault and roll to my feet, but I'm no acrobat and I just ended up colliding ungracefully with the floor, skidding across the carpet, instinctively protecting my face with my arm.

The jarring impact didn't feel great on the arm that'd been wounded in that fight with Randy McReynolds the other day, but I could deal with it.

Now that I was on this side of the chair, I saw a meandering path through the flames to the front door. I told Lily and D'Nesh to leave and pointed the way. Lily reached for D'Nesh's hand, but he was too scared to move.

"Go, Lily." I hoisted him into my arms.

She hustled forward, disappeared around the corner, and made it outside.

I sidestepped a long tongue of fire and was heading for the front door when I saw movement out of the corner of my eye from the man on the balcony, who was evidently not as dead as I'd thought.

Still slumped on the landing, he swung the M4 up and I spun to protect D'Nesh with my body.

The man fired. I felt a slice of pain rip across my left side, but it wasn't enough to put me down, and I hurried through the front door.

Burst outside.

Fresh air.

I carried D'Nesh to the other side of the street, away from the blaze, and set him down on the grass.

Some of the neighbors had stepped outside and were

staring at the fire. Some were filming it. Sirens whined through the day from cruisers on their way here.

I told D'Nesh and Lily, "Both of you stay here. Help is on the way. I'll be right back."

Checking my side, I saw it was just a flesh wound. I put a call through to dispatch that we had one suspect on the run and that we needed to get the neighborhood cordoned off and set up roadblocks. The arsonist had a head start and this was a subdivision near a forested park, which was going to be a pain to seal off, but if we could get units here quickly, we might have a shot at catching him before he slipped away for good.

Analyzing the neighborhood and the street layout in relationship to what I remembered from when I was driving here earlier, I guessed that the most likely escape route for someone on foot was to the west, between the houses, and then through the park.

I ran that direction, scaled a six-foot-tall wooden fence, leapt down on the other side, and scanned the area.

No sign of anyone.

The spot where the bullet had nipped my side was sore, but it wasn't serious. My sliced arm was stinging more than the minor GSW.

Quickly, I traversed the lawn, then looped south around the home to the serpentine street winding through the subdivision toward the park.

Two women had stepped out of their homes. One was holding a baby.

"FBI!" I yelled to them. "Did you see a man come running through here?"

One woman shook her head. The other replied, "No." Then she held up her cell phone and started taking pictures of me.

Damn phones.

A police car and an ambulance screeched around the corner on their way to the Romanoff house.

I sprinted to the wooded area nearby. There was a path leading into it, and if it was laced with trails we might be out of luck.

Who cares.

It was worth a shot.

I took the trail. The woods were thick with summer growth and it was tough to see more than a dozen or so meters in any direction. I followed the path to the top of a small rise, found nothing, and, frustrated, returned, circling around to the burning house again.

By the time I'd made my way to Lily and D'Nesh, an ambulance had arrived and the paramedics were assisting the two of them, giving them oxygen to help them recover from smoke inhalation.

I could've probably used some myself, but right now I wanted to do everything I could to find the suspect. I had a few minor burns, mostly on the backs of my hands and my face, but they weren't serious.

Police cars were arriving, and I told the responding officers what I knew and offered my best guess about the route our guy might have taken.

Then we tightened the net around the area and sent officers to interview neighbors, search homes door to door, and inspect every car that was leaving the subdivision.

34

The man who called himself Shane hid the mountain bike in the underbrush beside the fence, and then opened the lock that chained shut the gate encircling the abandoned, condemned high school two miles from the house he'd just burned down.

Earlier, he'd left some things in one of the classrooms here in case he needed them, in case things went sideways.

And they had certainly done that now.

It'd been close, but he'd made it out of the neighborhood before the police were able to cordon it off.

He knew enough about how law enforcement worked to know that typically in a situation like this they would check cars and pedestrians but wouldn't necessarily take too close a look at cyclists, so he'd grabbed the mountain bike from the garage and hit the trail through the park.

People see what they expect to see, and he'd thrown on a helmet and looked the part. None of the neighbors would even have thought twice about seeing him on that trail.

The ceiling tiles of the old school were falling in. The walls were marked with gang graffiti. The floor was covered with dust and grime. Slivers of light snuck into the hallway from a few open doors, but for the most part it was draped in long, looming shadows.

Some of the lockers were open. Others were locked tight and would remain that way until the building was eventually torn down, holding whatever secrets the students might have left behind seven years ago when the doors to the school were shuttered.

There was less than a week left to put everything into play and Shane wasn't about to let this incident disrupt what they had planned for Wednesday night.

He put in a call to make sure the Benz disappeared forever, then changed clothes, cleaned up, and took off before the police could check the school.

35

We found nothing.

Not in the homes of the neighborhood. Not as officers went house to house interviewing people to find out if they'd seen anyone fleeing.

Not even when we brought in dogs and a helicopter to search the area.

Whoever the shooter was and whoever had started the fire—whether that was a man or a woman, the same person or a different one—had gotten away.

Meanwhile, the fire department had been able to contain the blaze, but they weren't able to save the house.

Thank God there hadn't been any other people in there.

When there's a fire, crime scene and evidence response units work closely with arson investigators to determine the cause of the blaze. In this case, the point of origin wasn't so much in question, nor was there a question about whether or not this was arson, or even if accelerants were used. We didn't know what they were yet, but something had been done to burn that place to the ground quickly, and without an explosion.

D'Nesh Mujeeb Agarwai bore no visible physical injuries, but time would tell how emotionally scarred he was because of what he'd been through since he was abducted.

I watched when his parents arrived and were reunited with him.

His mom was in tears and even his dad fell to his knees and just held his son and wept.

This is a world racked with grief, but interspersed with fleeting moments of almost incomprehensible joy.

And for the Agarwais, this was one of them.

Christie's words came back to me: "You never know what's coming your way . . . Why not celebrate proactively?"

Pain and awe.

And right now, thanksgiving.

But I also felt some regret that the other three missing children weren't also here. We would have to tell their parents that their kids were still out there somewhere, and that was not going to be a welcome task.

But the fact that this one boy was alive was good news. It meant that those other children might still be as well.

Tomorrow, after D'Nesh had been checked out at the emergency room and given a little chance to recover, some officers and a psychologist who specialized in speaking with victimized or molested children would interview him to find out more about his captors. Until then he could just be a boy in the arms of his parents.

And that was okay.

I got a text from Jodie that she was ten minutes out and on her way here.

I assessed things.

We had two dead suspects, both burned beyond recognition in the house, and at least one more on the run.

Even though the penthouse where Lily's abduction had apparently taken place was under Romanoff's name, we hadn't been able to determine yet if he was the person who'd slipped away.

Neither of the men in the house matched Romanoff's description from his driver's license.

A van was in the burned-down house's garage. Externally, it'd been damaged quite a bit by the blaze, but the inside was still intact and that was where our evidence response team would be focusing their attention, looking for hair, fibers, DNA.

According to what D'Nesh had told us before his parents arrived, that's how they'd transported him to the house.

"They moved us back and forth for when they filmed different things," he'd said.

Though we were going to wait to ask about the filming, he had just said "us" rather than "me," so I asked, "Were there other kids there?"

"Yes."

"Do you remember their names?"

"Maggie, Andre, and LeAnne. But I think they're still at the other place."

"And do you know where that is?"

He shook his head. "Uh-uh. But maybe Lizzie lived there."

"Was that another girl?"

"I just heard 'em say her name once when they didn't know I was listening."

I thanked him and told him how things were going to be okay now, and that he was safe.

Before being transported to the hospital to have her burned arm treated, Lily spoke with me.

She explained that she was twenty-one, but when the guy took her to the penthouse he'd told her she looked sixteen. "That seemed important to him, that I looked young. He wanted me to wear a ponytail."

"What can you tell me about him?"

"He called himself Shane—but he also told me that it wasn't his real name." She recounted as much as she could about what had happened in the penthouse and how she'd used the hair clip to pick the lock on the chain that was around her ankle when she was in the cellar.

"You were very brave," I told her. "MacGyver would be proud of you."

"Who?"

"MacGyver, from that old TV show—never mind."

She must not have been a very big television-watcher as a kid.

Then the paramedics took her to the hospital to treat her.

Jodie drove up and looked concerned about my side being bandaged.

"The bullet just grazed me. Really, I'm fine."

She nodded toward the sky. "I'd say someone up there is watching over you this week."

"That may be true."

I related what'd gone down in the house.

"And the guy in the hall?" she said. "His own man shot him?"

"That's what it looks like, yes."

"Any idea why?"

"Motives, Jodie. You know I don't go there."

"So he wouldn't be able to testify against him?" she mused, but I sensed that she wasn't so much asking me as she was thinking aloud. "I mean, everybody talks. If all of this is related—and it sure seems like it is—then Wooford was taken out before he could talk too. I mean, if he was killed."

"I believe he was."

"Based on?"

"What Randy McReynolds told me before jumping off

that balcony. He said we'd failed to protect Ted and wouldn't be able to protect him either. Whoever's behind this doesn't want word spreading about what's happening."

"Sounds like you just identified a motive."

"You really know how to go for the jugular, don't you?"

"What can I say?" A smile. "Did Lily tell you anything helpful?"

"The guy who called himself Shane made a lot out of the fact that she looked young."

"Could be they needed someone younger on short notice and he settled for her."

"That's a possibility."

While Jodie went to talk to the officer in charge of the search, I phoned Tobin and filled him in on what had happened here. When I asked about his mother he told me that she was doing better, seemed to be recovering, and that he was hoping he'd be able to return to the city tomorrow afternoon.

"Don't rush things," I said. "Stay there with her if she needs you."

"Thanks. I will, but I hate not being there now. I'll plan to see you tomorrow night."

"Sounds good."

As I was about to leave, I was surprised to see Assistant Director DeYoung show up, but then, considering how high profile this case had suddenly become, it didn't really shock me so much after all.

I overheard him speaking with the local police chief, assuring him that the Bureau would lend all of its available resources to helping find the suspect who was at large. Then he came over to me and cleared his throat in his typical, distinctive manner.

"So, Pat. It's been quite a week."

"Yes, sir, it has."

"Congratulations here today, on getting those two out of the house."

"Thanks."

"I've reviewed your report regarding the events the other night leading up to the death of Randy McReynolds. I've also looked over the autopsy findings and . . ."

Okay, here it comes.

The reprimand.

Or maybe worse. He might put you on administrative leave.

He said, "There are a few questions I have regarding the incident at the apartment Wednesday evening and the timing of the events that led up to the discharge of your firearm, but in light of everything that's happened today, I think it would be valuable to take a little more time to evaluate that material. We'll talk on Monday. That'll give me the weekend to review things."

"Works for me."

Considering what we were dealing with here, we needed to assume that there were people out there who would not want Lily Keating and D'Nesh to have survived this, so I made sure we put them under protective custody.

I phoned Christie, told her what was happening, and explained that I was going to get Jodie set up at my place and would be over as soon as I could afterward.

36

It was dusk by the time Jodie and I made it back to my apartment. After changing, I grabbed enough clothes to last a week or so and handed my extra key to her. "The lock sticks sometimes. Just jiggle it a little back and forth and you should be fine."

She thanked me, and then I said to her, "You told me earlier that Dell wanted you moved out by the end of the weekend. Do you need help with that?"

"Actually, if you don't mind. Late morning? Ten to twelve or so?"

"Sure. Okay, I'll plan to see you tomorrow."

Then I left for Christie's apartment. I bypassed dinner, figuring I could probably grab some leftovers when I got there.

She was seated in the living room with Tessa when I arrived. Both looked at me expectantly as I walked in carrying my computer bag and suitcase.

"Yes." I anticipated the question. "You're going to hear about it on the news tomorrow. But this time it was good. We saved two people. And two bad guys are dead."

But there are still three missing children. And one guy is still on the run, I thought, but held back from saying that.

"Did you kill 'em?" Tessa asked me.

"The two men were fatally wounded during a shoot-out."

"But—"

"We'll leave it at that," Christie inserted.

"But what was it like?" Tessa asked me. "To be there when they—"

"Tessa," Christie said. "That's enough."

"What? I'm just curious."

"Patrick can't tell you about it. It's related to the case."

"He can tell me how he feels, though."

"I can't share any more details about it, Tessa," I said.

She sighed heavily and headed to her bedroom.

When her daughter was gone, Christie asked me, "Are you okay?"

Back at my apartment I'd changed out of the shirt that'd gotten bloodied when the bullet skimmed my side, and the bandages weren't visible under this shirt, but still, it was a natural question for her to ask.

"I'm good. Yes."

I set my things down and gave her a kiss.

The kiss she gave me back was quick.

Relationships are measured in fractions—fractions of a second, fractions of an inch. Maybe he leans just that close to her and no closer, maybe she hesitates just that much before answering him.

Those fractions speak volumes.

She says, "I love you," and then waits, expecting a certain reply, expecting to hear, "I love you too." But she's listening not just to the words, but to the silence that precedes them.

Is it too long? Does that mean he's unsure about how he feels about her?

Or is it too short? Is he answering like he knows he's

supposed to, but there's no real meaning behind the words?

Timing.

Fractions.

Of course you can read too much into silences, but you can't help reading *something* into them. It's just human nature. We want to be loved and we look for affirmation and affection wherever we can find it.

And now I found myself wondering about the brevity of the kiss, if there was a message there that I should be deciphering.

I put some of my things in the dresser in Christie's bedroom, then stowed the rest in my suitcase in her closet.

Back in the living room, I told her as much as I could about saving Lily and D'Nesh, which basically amounted to what would be on the news.

She listened quietly and when I was done she asked me, "Pat, do you believe in demons? In demon possession?"

At first it seemed like the question came out of nowhere, but considering her faith and the nature of the things I'd just told her, it wasn't really so surprising.

"I don't know. I'd say I believe people can be possessed by evil, though. Some would say that's the same thing."

"Some would. Yes."

"But not you?" I got myself a drink of water from the sink.

"No."

"Water?"

"No, thanks. So you don't believe in spiritual entities? Demons, the devil, any of that?"

"Honestly, I'm not sure what to believe concerning

them." I joined her again in the living room. "In a certain way it would make it easier for me if I did believe in demons. It might help explain some of the things I've seen."

"Some of the evil?"

"Yes."

"Like with this case? The people who took that boy? Who abducted that young woman?"

She seemed deep in thought, but also solemn.

I put my hand on her arm. "Hey, are you okay?"

"It just bothers me, thinking about all this."

"It bothers me too. I'd say that even if demons were able to possess people, I think we're all still responsible for our choices, for the things we do."

"Sure, yes. I understand."

In this job I'd found that some people blame their parents for their actions—they didn't hug them enough, or they spanked them too much. Or the kids at school called them names. Or they were born into poverty or wealth, or whatever. Some people blame their genes for giving them a disposition toward violence. Others blame the devil or demons.

I think we all have baggage, we all have extenuating circumstances, but we're all accountable for the choices we make. If not, there would be no reasonable way to ever serve justice or punish people for crimes. After all, how can you fault someone for doing something he couldn't avoid?

I thought Christie might take the demon topic deeper, but instead she was silent and though I tried to read the pause, what she might have been trying to communicate by it, I failed to.

Finally, I said, "Things cool with you and Tessa? I know you were going to sort some things out with her."

"We're good."

"You mentioned on the phone earlier that you wanted to talk about something tonight with me, and I'm guessing it wasn't demon possession."

"We can discuss it tomorrow."

I didn't like that word "discuss." It sounded a lot more serious than the phrase "talk about."

"Are you sure?"

She gave me a faint smile. It didn't look forced, but it also didn't look like she was particularly happy. "We'll talk in the morning. How about we step out for breakfast? Eight o'clock?"

"I told Jodie I'd help her move at ten. Will that give us enough time?"

"Let's go with seven thirty."

"Okay, it's a date."

"Oh. I almost forgot. I need to do some shopping tomorrow afternoon. Tessa hates shopping. I wondered if maybe you two could spend some time together instead. Get to know each other a little better. Hang out."

Often, stepping away from a case gives you the perspective to see things with new eyes.

The change of pace would be healthy.

"No problem."

"Great. Hey, sit with me, okay?"

I positioned myself on the couch and she leaned into my arms.

I thought of demons and evil and choices and excuses and of the Final Territory and that web of red dots spreading out across the city indicating all the IP addresses that had downloaded child pornography.

We are a strange breed. Study history and you'll see blood splashed all across the pages of our story. We're so confused and backward.

As one of my instructors for my doctoral program once put it, "We choose as a remedy the very drug that worsens our condition."

It's so true. I've seen it over and over. People turn to affairs when their marriages are crumbling, to drinking when they're depressed. They work extra hours to assuage their guilt for not being there enough for their kids. They buy clothes and cars and houses and gadgets to fill their empty hearts, even though they know those games of distraction and diversion will never work in the long run, but will only leave them feeling more hollowed out.

Human nature hasn't changed much in the millennia of our existence. We are just as lost as ever, trying desperately to get back up the hill by running headlong into the valley. We willingly avoid the things we know we need, and desperately embrace the things we know will destroy us.

What lies at the heart of human nature? The quest for happiness as we willingly take roads we already know lead to pain instead.

Those were my thoughts as I held the woman I wanted more than anything else to make happy, but felt distant from her even though she was enfolded in my arms.

++++

With all that had happened today, with trying to help the FBI agent, with meeting Skylar, and then going back to search for the files for Agent Bowers, Francis was feeling disoriented, but at least now good things were happening.

He was helping the FBI. That was good.

He was going to see Skylar again tomorrow. That was good too.

Tonight he did not chat with graciousgirl4 before going to bed.

But neither did he fall asleep right away.

Instead, he went to bed to try to sleep, but he was distracted thinking again of how he'd missed seeing that backpack in the video he'd shown the FBI agent and of how he might have missed other things in the past.

37

Even though the diner that Christie chose was only a block and a half from her apartment, I hadn't been here before.

The place was mostly empty. Since this was a Saturday morning and there were only three other people inside it when we arrived, I couldn't help wondering if their food was going to be any good.

But truthfully, the quality of the menu items wasn't the main thing on my mind. Based on the vibes I'd been getting, I was a lot more concerned about the discussion we were about to have than whether or not my oatmeal was going to be tasty.

While we waited for our order to come up, we made small talk, something neither of us is good at, and that only served to accentuate that something big was going on and that she was trying to feel her way into the topic.

I didn't push things.

"What are you thinking of doing with Tessa this afternoon?" she asked me.

"I'm not sure. I'll do some brainstorming."

"She can be a handful sometimes."

"Oh, I'm sure we'll be fine."

"Of course."

The server brought my steel-cut oatmeal and blueberry muffin and Christie's pancakes and two sunny-side up eggs.

"Now you'll have to help me finish this if I can't make my way through it all," Christie said somewhat mechanically.

"Sure."

She prayed over the meal and we both started into our food.

More small talk: weather, news, sports, nothing that mattered.

Minutes passed.

"I've got one for you," I said.

"You've got one?"

"A tongue twister." It was something I'd thought of yesterday when Lily Keating was telling me about how she'd picked the lock in the basement. "The tip of the clip's clasp. Try it. Five times fast."

She did, then I did, then awkwardness settled in even thicker than before.

Finally, she set down her fork. "On Wednesday night when you came over you promised that you were going to be with me, not somewhere else."

Ah, so that's what this was about. Alright, that made sense. She was upset I'd been distracted.

"I'm sorry, really. I tried to. There's just been—"

"No. That's what I need from you right now."

"Alright." I waited. "I'm here. I'm listening."

She took my hand. "Would you say things are going well between us?"

"Yes. Absolutely."

A fraction of a moment. One that spoke volumes.

"I'm going to have to ask you to make a decision, Pat."

"What decision is that?"

She let go of my hand. "They're eliminating my job."

"What?"

"The owner ran into some financial problems. I don't know the whole story—I think it's fallout from his divorce. He just told me at the beginning of the month about the downsizing. About letting me go."

She prodded her eggs with her fork, then put it down again. "I've been looking into things and I think I found another job. It's doing pretty much the same thing, except with more managerial duties, but . . ."

"Yes?"

"It's not here in the city."

"Is it nearby?"

"It's in Omaha, Pat."

"Omaha? As in Nebraska?"

A nod. "There's a Midwestern firm that's opening up a new division. They want me to head it up."

"And you're seriously thinking about this? About moving to Omaha, Nebraska?"

"You know how expensive it is to live here. I can barely make my rent every month. And as far as saving up for college for Tessa, for the future, I don't have anything set aside. Nothing. It's enough of a struggle just making ends meet every week. The benefits are good, Pat. There's health and dental. They would even pay my moving expenses."

"So you've looked into this pretty closely already."

"Yes."

"How does Tessa feel about it?"

"I haven't told her yet."

"Oh." I found it a bit puzzling that she would be bringing this up with me first. "A minute ago you said you needed me to make a decision. What decision is that?"

A beat of silence. "There's an FBI Field Office there. I looked it up."

"What? In Omaha?"

"Yes."

I was stunned. "Are you asking if I would move out to Nebraska with you?"

"I'm asking where we go from here. I need to do what's best for my daughter, but I want to do what's best for all of us—for all three of us. I want you to be a part of my life, Pat."

"I want that too, but . . ."

She bit her lip. I took it for nerves. "What are you thinking?" she asked.

"I'm thinking this is a lot to process. We're serious about each other, we're close, but we've . . . I mean . . ."

"What does your gut say?"

"I try not to trust my gut."

"Then what does your heart say?"

"That I care about you very much."

That I might just be falling in love with you.

It was the first time those words had strung themselves together in that order in my mind, but I wasn't sure I should go so far as to say them aloud. "That we have something special, something worth holding on to," I said instead.

"Yes. I agree." She waited as if she could read my mind and knew there was more I wanted to say.

"I want the same things you do, Christie: what's best for all three of us. And that you'll be a part of my life. Not just now, but long term."

"I can sense a 'but' coming."

And again I thought something I didn't say, *But my heart says I wouldn't be happy in Omaha. You must know that already, Christie. You must know I belong here.*

"But you're good at what you do. Certainly there are other job opportunities for you nearby."

"That's probably true," she acknowledged.

"I can help you look."

"With the cost of living here, I just don't think I can do any better than I am now—and what I'm doing now isn't enough. I checked around. There aren't any jobs in the income range of what I need to take care of Tessa."

"But you didn't give it a lot of time. You've only known about this for the last couple weeks."

She nodded. "True, but I have to admit, I've been keeping an eye on possibilities for a while. There's just not a lot out there. I haven't been able to get ahead and I can't live from behind forever."

"If it's money you need, we can try to work something out. I mean, I—"

"You don't have any extra money, and even if you did I wouldn't ask you to—" She sighed. "But here I am, asking you to consider moving across the country. I know, it doesn't make any sense."

She picked at her pancakes, and as she was searching for the next thing to say a tear formed in her left eye.

"Hey, don't cry. We can figure this out."

She took care of the tear with the corner of her napkin. "I don't want to lose you."

"And I don't want to be lost."

A sea of emotion swirled through those tragically sad eyes from her turmoil, her questions, her uncertainty. I wanted to calm it but didn't know how.

Life doesn't always offer us good choices, but it

seemed like there had to be other possibilities for her in this case. There just had to be.

"I have to do what's right for my daughter," she told me unnecessarily.

"Of course."

Where to take things from here?

"When do you need to let them know?" I asked. "The firm in Omaha?"

"They're going to want me to start as soon as I can make a decision."

The ground seemed to shift beneath me.

Six years ago I was in L.A. during an earthquake, and I'll never forget that feeling of the earth quivering underfoot, and the way I couldn't get my balance because the very thing I was relying on for support was unsteady beneath my feet.

That's how I felt right now.

An earthquake deep inside me.

What I thought had become a solid, reliable part of my life was trembling uncertainly and I didn't know where to turn, what to lean on to find my balance again.

"When do you think you'll tell Tessa?" I said.

"This week sometime. She's a big-city girl. I know she's going to hate moving. I wanted to wait until I . . . well, I had my ducks in a row before telling her."

"And I'm one of those ducks."

She smiled faintly. "You're the main one."

"I've never been called someone's main duck before."

"There's a first time for everything."

Her smile was short-lived, as the seriousness of the conversation weighed on her again.

"I wish I knew what to tell you, Christie, but I—"

"No, wait." She held up a hand to stop me midsentence. "This isn't right. I put you in an impossible situation. I know, I know. I shouldn't have . . . It was wrong of me to bring all this up to you, to drag you into this. I'm sorry, it's—"

"No, no. It's alright. I understand that you're just—"

But then she was standing up and I could tell that a corner of a napkin wasn't going to be able to take care of the tears that were about to come.

"Christie, I . . ." Words failed me. She fumbled with her purse, but I laid some money on the table and said, "I've got it."

"I . . . I'm sorry."

"There's no reason to be. There's—"

But she avoided eye contact and offered me a manufactured smile.

It hurt to see her trying so hard to be happy.

Trying and failing.

While everything I said seemed to push her further away.

"Christie, please."

"Excuse me, Pat."

She hurried to the restroom and a few moments later I got a text from her: "**Please go. I need some time.**"

Unsure what else to do, I stepped outside, alone, into the piercingly bright summer morning.

38

Back in her living room, I tried to process what had just happened, what she'd asked of me.

New York City was where my life was, my career, my future. I couldn't move with her to Omaha. It was out of the question.

Explaining that to her was going to be tough, and acknowledging that we were very likely not going to be able to remain together if she moved was going to be even tougher.

I wanted to talk more now, to sort things out, to solve this, but she must have gone for a walk because, though I waited for her, she didn't show up.

Being here in the apartment and knowing her situation and her dilemma, her place seemed even more cramped than before—very cramped compared to the wide-open possibilities of life out on the plains.

No, there has to be another way!

It's amazing how quickly your perspective can change.

Yes, yes, in the blink of an eye.

Tessa was in her room.

I didn't disturb her.

I needed to leave in just over an hour to help Jodie. I

could cancel, of course, but maybe giving Christie some time to herself this morning was what she needed.

I texted that I was here if she wanted to talk and that I could tell Jodie I couldn't make it, but Christie replied that I should go help her, that she was okay. Then she reiterated how sorry she was.

Once more I told her that she didn't need to be.

Call her and tell her that you love her. That's what she needs to hear.

No. That was probably the last thing she needed to hear. It would've only made things more confusing, made her dilemma more difficult to sort through.

Right now we needed to think about this rationally, not let impulsive emotions cloud our reason.

She wasn't trying to manipulate me; I didn't get that from her at all. She was just trying to figure things out, to chart out what was best for her daughter and how I might be a part of their future.

In truth, what other option did she have than to bring things up the way she had? Yes, she wanted what was best for Tessa, but she cared for me as well.

Staying here meant mortgaging Tessa's future.

But leaving meant losing me.

Trapped.

Unless you were to go with her.

I found myself asking what I wanted more—the excitement of working here in New York City or the adventure of starting a new life with Christie in Nebraska, or wherever destiny might take us.

Just for argument's sake, let's just say you did move and things didn't work out with her, what then?

Well, first, just getting the transfer wasn't a done deal, and even if I could get a position there, it wasn't like I would just be able to return again to New York City—

things didn't work that way in the FBI. It might take years—if a transfer back here would even be in the cards at all.

And what about the seminars at the Academy? Would I lose the opportunity to teach those as well?

Almost certainly I would. Logistics-wise, teaching at Quantico would be a nightmare if I were living out there.

So, what did I want more—a lasting relationship with an amazing woman who'd taken up residence in my heart, or the career I'd dreamed of for years?

There had to be another option.

There just had to be.

Marriage was a possibility of course, but I saw that as something on the far horizon, not around the next bend.

If Christie and I weren't going to be able to discuss this now, I needed to get my thoughts moving in a different direction before leaving to meet up with Jodie, so I turned my attention to the case.

I logged in to the Federal Digital Database to check the updates on the investigation and saw that Ivan Romanoff was still missing.

Officers were searching for anything on Muhammad El-Sayed and doing their best to identify the other man who'd been burned beyond recognition in the fire, but so far they weren't having a lot of luck.

The psychologist spoke with D'Nesh and the NYPD brought in a sketch artist who did his work on a computer sketch pad to add color to what he was working on. However, neither D'Nesh nor Lily was able to give us anything that matched photos of the persons of interest we'd collected, based on tips called in or leads from other cases that we were thinking might have been linked.

Taking into account the cameras at Romanoff's suite and in his house's basement, the Bureau's Cyber Division was searching for any "cheerleader" videos that might have been posted online featuring Lily Keating in the hours since her abduction.

Nothing so far.

The arson investigator had uploaded video footage of a walk-through of the burned-down home.

I watched it and listened to his preliminary analysis of what had happened.

He concluded that the walls of the house had been filled with some sort of flammable material instead of fire-resistant insulation. It was as if the place had been designed from the ground up to be consumed quickly if it were ever to catch fire.

I sent in a request to Agent Descartes for a complete background on the construction company that'd built the house.

On another front, the computer techs were still trying to mine the data from the USB drive.

Apparently, they'd been able to pull off a few corrupted photos of child pornography—all of which were already in the ICSC database, and none of which were images of the three remaining missing children. However, there was still more than a gigabyte of data they were attempting to access and it was taking longer than they'd anticipated to get through the firewalls and encryption.

Their latest update, entered yesterday at 7:03 p.m., noted that they would post the results of their final analysis "as soon as possible," which, translated, could mean anytime now, or maybe never. I didn't take it as a good sign that they weren't predicting when it would be done.

I put a call through to Harrington's contact at Homeland's Cyber Crimes Center, the one who was in charge of Wooford's case. This time I used his cell number rather than his work number and I was able to reach him at the golf course.

He restated some of the information that was in Wooford's files and told me I could call him next week during office hours if I had any questions, that he would be glad to address them.

But while I had him on the line I went ahead and asked my questions now: if the eight-minute gap in the security footage had ever been investigated, if anyone had visited Wooford in the detention facility prior to his death, what their hypothesis was on why they never found any evidence of the Final Territory on Wooford's computer, what his lawyer's name was—but the agent didn't give me any new information.

"We can talk next week, when I'm at my computer," he told me. "You caught me at a bad time."

And then, before I could reply, he hung up.

After the call, I went back to reading through the online case files.

The lab had analyzed the video that Edlemore had found of the four masks, and they were able to discern that it'd been filmed three months ago, which didn't really help us much because we already knew the date of D'Nesh's abduction.

I sent in a request for Officer Hinchcliffe to review the security camera footage from the coffee shop during the month when it'd been uploaded, and to run facial recognition to see if anyone in our databases might have been there.

Then I shifted my focus to Randy McReynolds and the events preceding his death.

Based on what he'd said to me on that balcony at the Brilington Towers, I wasn't convinced that his suicide note had anything to do with date rape allegations from high school, as his brother, Billy, had speculated.

Agent Descartes was searching through the names of women from Randy's high school to see if any had reported sexual abuse, but so far that had come up empty.

However, in my view, Randy's state of mind and the things he said didn't jibe with a guy who was simply distraught over false sexual assault allegations from a decade earlier.

Based on what he'd said about us not being able to protect Ted, and our discovery of Ted's connection with the Final Territory, it was more logical to begin with the premise that Randy's death had to do with that group and maybe that file that he'd mentioned to me, "Aurora's birthday."

But then why the suicide note?

I pulled it up again and studied it:

Dear Billy,

    I'm sorry it came to this, but it's the only thing I know to do. Whatever you want to believe about me, whatever anyone says, you need to know that I never did the things she's claiming I did. I'm sorry I let you down.

                        —Randy

Apart from the contrast between his blunt denial and his repeated apologies in the note itself, nothing jumped out at me. It seemed a little odd that he'd written "Open only in the case of my death" on the envelope. Why include the word "only," if he was planning to kill himself? But I didn't know where that took us.

Related to all this, we still didn't know for sure that McReynolds killed Stewart. Yes, his prints were on that remote; yes, the knife wounds were consistent with the blade he'd been carrying when he attacked me, but that didn't necessarily mean he was the murderer.

Assumptions are the easiest things in the world to make and the hardest ones to walk back from, so you need to avoid making them even as you move through a case.

You test those theories and discard them when possible as you uncover new evidence.

But sometimes you end up having to go back and pick your discarded hypotheses clean of the facts, and perhaps reconsider them again as you dig up new information.

And so it goes. You cycle your attention into and out of the pool of evidence, sorting, sifting, evaluating, eliminating theories, then reconsidering them, always trying to brush away speculation so the truth can take center stage.

I wanted to know more about which online communities Stewart might have been involved with, so I sent in a request for an agent to look through his credit card purchases to find out what games he'd purchased for his Xbox.

Finally, I worked on the geoprofile. We had a lot of data now to sort through in relationship to the missing children and the crime spree, as well as regarding the location of Romanoff's home in Princeton, New Jersey.

It would take me a couple of hours at least to analyze it all, so I only had time to get the preliminaries done before leaving to help Jodie move.

I could dive into it more in-depth this afternoon with Tobin after he returned to the city and after I'd spent a little time with Tessa as I'd promised Christie I would do.

39

The house where they did so much of the filming was lost.

Lily and the boy were both out of the picture and, with their police protection, they would be difficult—although not impossible—to get to.

And two Associates were dead—Shane had taken care of one of them himself, to stop him from being taken in for questioning. After all, there'd been only one bike there and officers were en route.

But at least they still had the other place, the one in the city.

And at least they still had the other three children.

He tapped the phone number into his encrypted cell phone and the voice answered, the electronically altered voice, the voice of the person calling all the shots, the voice of the Piper. "Hello, Shane."

"Hello."

"I've been watching the news."

"I'm the one who shot Garrett."

"They haven't reported that yet."

"No, I would suppose not. They're going to play this close to the chest. Do you want me to go after the boy and the prostitute? They've seen me."

"A lot of people have seen you, Shane."

"What would you like me to do?"

"I'd like you to make sure everything is in place for Wednesday night. At this point that's what matters most. The boy and the courtesan are of little consequence. Going after them now would unnecessarily complicate things. Let them be. Get the algorithm into the system."

"I will."

"Has it been tested yet?"

"The team is working on finishing it up. It'll be ready in time."

"I'm not pleased that you're cutting it this close."

"It's the best way to avoid early detection."

"And the woman you chose, the one who is . . ."

Shane sensed that the Piper was searching for the right word. "Undercover" wasn't quite it. "Incognito" didn't nail it either, but it was closer.

"She'll come through for us," he told the Piper. "Don't worry."

"I don't need to remind you that some of my clients are more interested in adults than children. You know what that would mean for you if things don't go as planned."

Shane had seen what the Piper did to people, and despite all he'd done to others himself over the years, he felt a shiver.

"I won't let you down."

He waited for a reply, but the Piper had already ended the call.

Shane kept the ringer on just in case, and went online to email the team in Russia to see if they were almost done with the algorithm.

40

Jodie had rented a small moving van to transport her things to a storage unit.

Thankfully, Dell had left for a few hours, so there wasn't the added stress of having her around while we carried the boxes to the van.

Agent Descartes and another friend from work had shown up to help, and Jodie had relatively few possessions so it was going pretty quickly.

When it was just the two of us in the room, she said, "I've been wondering a few things about the case."

"What are those?"

"First of all, with his Special Forces background and training, would Randy really have left tool marks in the lock to Stewart's apartment?"

"It's hard to say, but yes, that's a good point."

"And maybe that's how he was able to disappear too. I mean for the last six months—because of his training."

Now that she pointed it out, I had to admit that, regarding his history, we might never learn where he'd been living or what he'd been doing since January.

A thought struck me. "And he was also trained on how to kill someone."

"Yeah, which you almost found out the hard way."

"No, I mean, why was there so much blood in the apartment and so much of a struggle? Stewart made it to the bedroom before his attacker was able to fatally wound him. They fought loud enough for a neighbor to hear them and contact the police."

"You're saying McReynolds would have been a lot quicker, a lot more efficient about it if he were the killer?"

"There's nothing to indicate that Stewart had studied martial arts, close combat, or self-defense, and yet he was able to hold his own in a hand-to-hand fight with someone as skilled and experienced as McReynolds, who was also armed with a knife? It doesn't fit."

"So someone else killed Stewart."

"I think that's something we need to seriously consider. Maybe someone else left the tool marks." It was a thought I'd toyed with briefly earlier in the day. Up until this morning we'd been working from the hypothesis that McReynolds was the killer, or was at least present at the time of McReynolds's death. Now a whole new set of variables came into play.

Assumptions.

So easy to make.

So vital to set aside.

"What else have you been wondering?" I asked her.

She loaded up her trophies from her college swimming meets and closed up the box. "If he was so motivated to find this file, why would he kill himself first?"

"That is a good question."

"And why would Stewart be killed if he was a part of this group? Was he looking into things?"

"That's a motive we may never know."

The other movers returned for more boxes and we finished getting Jodie's things loaded up. A few of her friends had already signed on to help her unpack at the storage unit, which was good because it freed me up to spend time with Tessa.

Once again, Jodie thanked me for letting her stay at my place, then we agreed to touch base later and I returned to Christie's apartment to meet up with her daughter.

Tessa was in the kitchen waiting for me, munching on a carrot, when I came through the door.

"So, do you have anything in mind for this afternoon?" I asked.

"No. You?"

"I brainstormed a few things."

"You brainstormed them?"

"Yes."

I pulled out my notepad.

"And you felt the need to write 'em down?"

"I wanted to be thorough."

"Oh boy." She eyed me cautiously. "Alright, read it to me."

"Well, first, I was thinking we could visit Ellis Island."

"Oh, I see, sarcasm."

"No, I was being serious."

"Do I look like a Japanese tourist to you?"

"What about Central Park?"

"Sunlight and I don't get along."

"Times Square?"

"Been there a million times. Next."

"How about a matinee? Something off-Broadway?"

"Too expensive."

"A movie?"

"Weak."

"Um, how about an art museum?"

She peered at my list, reading it upside down. "That's not even on there."

"I'm improvising. So, what do you think about a little culture?"

"I'm not into art. It's too predictable."

"How is art predictable?"

"Just look for three things: penises, breasts, and eye-balls. There you go. It's all you need to know to interpret art."

"I'm afraid you're going to have to walk me through that."

"Penises stand for male dominance or suppression; breasts for fertility and femininity; and open eyes for see-ing things in a new way—new opportunities, doorways, insights. Closed eyes equals blindness, naïveté, repres-sion. It's tiresome. The art world needs an injection of creativity."

"Huh. Looking for those three body parts isn't exactly something I'm guessing they typically teach you in art appreciation class."

"Yeah, well, I wouldn't know. But I do know that any-time you have to be *taught* to appreciate something, it's either lame to begin with or you can be pretty sure they're actually doing the opposite."

"How's that?"

"Are there any classes on superhero movie apprecia-tion? Or stand-up comedian appreciation? Or video game appreciation? No. And I'll tell you why."

"Why's that?"

"Because they don't need it. They're art forms that stand or fall on their own. Just like all art should. They don't need to be analyzed or interpreted. They entertain hundreds of millions of people and they're popular be-cause *they connect with the audience*. If your art form doesn't do that, what's the point of it anyway?"

I'd never thought of superhero movies, stand-up comedy, or video games as art forms, but when I considered what she had to say, I could certainly see where she was coming from.

"Oh, or what about literature?" She obviously wasn't finished with her rant yet. "Go ahead, interpret the crap out of this novel. Dissect this short story. Imagery. Symbolism. Spit out the themes. Whatever. It's sickening. And it always works backward. When you overanalyze something you end up hating the very thing you're supposed to be learning to love."

I had the sense that there might be a deeper meaning to what she was saying, but I couldn't quite decipher if she was trying to tell me something beyond the obvious or not.

I put the notepad away. "So, what would you like to do?"

"I don't know. Take me to where you work."

"The FBI Field Office?"

"Uh-huh."

"It's a government building, Tessa. By definition, it's a boring and uninteresting place."

She shrugged. "I'm interested in it. How many times have you ever heard me say I'm interested in *anything*?"

"You do have a point."

"Look, as long as we never go into any restricted areas and you escort me the whole time, we can at least walk through the Field Office's museum on the twenty-eighth floor of 26 Federal Plaza."

"How do you know about that?"

"There's this crazy thing they invented called Google. You can look stuff up on it. You should check it out sometime."

"Ah. Now, that was sarcasm, right?"

"Um. No."

"But that was?"

"What do you think?"

"Wait—was that?"

She looked at me disparagingly.

"Alright, I'll take you to the museum."

She finished her carrot. "Excellent."

"You're sure Central Park is out of the running?"

"Fresh air makes me break out in hives."

"And here I thought you were Miss Nature-Lover Girl."

"You pretty much suck at this, don't you?"

"At what?"

"Communicating with a teenager."

"I admit I'm still on my training wheels."

She slung the messenger bag she used as a purse over her shoulder. "Alright, I promise to hold on to the handlebars for you the whole time."

++++

A flood of colors and scents from fruit stands and street vendors circled around Francis, along with the sound of people bustling past, talking into phones, leaving snippets of their conversations trailing behind them in the air.

Sights. Smells. Sounds.

It was overwhelming.

No, it's healthy. All this is healthy for you.

I know but it's also a little overwhelming.

Don't argue, Francis. It doesn't become you.

Last week he'd told Dr. Perrior that he was going for a walk every other day and, even if he wasn't going to be able to see his psychologist anymore, he wanted to keep his word and do what he'd said he was going to do.

So ten minutes ago he'd left his apartment and walked to an open market at a park near his home to get his exercise in.

He enjoyed the cool/warm/cool touch of air on his skin as he passed from shadows into sunlight, and back into shadows again.

Darkness.

To light.

To darkness again.

He kept his walk brisk and his mind occupied.

Last night he'd heard about what happened in Princeton: the missing boy and the prostitute being found alive, the fire, everything. Someone had leaked the name of the FBI agent who'd saved them and it was the same man who'd come by the ICSC office in the morning, Agent Bowers.

I helped him.

Not really. All you did was show him the video.

But that was something. Something right, something good.

Because of that, albeit minor, contribution—even though Francis hadn't had anything to do with the events there in New Jersey—he felt like he *was* a part of it, like he'd provided at least a small hand in helping them piece together the bigger puzzle.

Shadow and sunlight.

Shadow.

And light.

But he could do more.

He could really make a difference if he could find the Final Territory.

To do that he would need to use the Dark Web.

He couldn't search it at work, so then he would do it at his apartment.

You shouldn't go on there. You might see something illicit or illegal.

But what could be worse than what I have to look at every day at work? No, I'll be alright.

He could at least get started before his three o'clock meeting with Skylar at the Mystorium.

He turned back toward home, skirting through the shadows thrown down around him by the buildings that owned that part of the day.

41

I parked in the underground garage, and Tessa and I headed up to the Field Office's entrance.

"So tell me more about what you do," she said. "I mean, I know you work for the FBI—obviously. And I know you help track down serial killers and stuff, but that's about all. Nutshell it for me."

"I didn't know 'nutshell' was a verb."

"Training wheels, Patrick."

"Oh. Sorry. Well, basically, when there's a series of linked crimes, I help law enforcement agencies analyze the data points related to the crime spree to narrow down the search parameters by identifying the most likely home base for the offender."

"What do you mean by data points?"

"For example, the victims' residences or places of work or any applicable primary or secondary crime scenes. By taking into consideration the timing, location and progression of the crimes I—"

"So, math, basically. Algorithms."

"Yes. And logic."

"I like logic. Maybe I can help you."

"Um, I'm afraid you'd need to graduate from the FBI Academy first."

"How about this: I give you a logic problem. If you can solve it, you have to let me help you. If you can't, I'll shut up and forget about it."

"If I can't . . . ?" I tried to process her request. It seemed backward to me. "It doesn't quite work like that, Tessa. But go ahead, give me your logic problem. I'll see if I can solve it."

"I need to make it up first."

She dug a small journal out of her bag and as we walked up the stairs, she jotted down some ideas.

I checked my texts as we waited to get through security. In following up on my request from earlier, an officer texted me that Jamaal Stewart had recently purchased a video game called Exo-Skel IV.

After we'd made it past the checkpoint, we rode the elevator to the twenty-eighth floor, then exited it and entered the Field Office's museum.

For the time being Tessa put the notebook away.

To say it was a museum was accurate but also misleading. It was really only one large room, but the plaques and artifacts from past investigations, the materials recovered from the 9/11 site, and the history of the Bureau was detailed and specific and informative.

But it wasn't something I would have typically thought a teenager would be interested in.

"Okay." I gestured toward the walls. "You obviously did your research or you wouldn't even have found out this place was here, but what do you know about it already?"

"Just basic stuff mostly. Names, dates, numbers, stats: this is the Bureau's largest Field Office, each of its six divisions are the size of a typical FBI Field Office in other major cities, they cover the thirteen million people in the New York metro area. Blah, blah, blah. Whatever. I want the inside scoop. What they don't tell you online."

"Well, there's a reason those things aren't posted on-line, Tessa."

"Oh, lemme guess: it's inside information."

"Bingo."

"Please don't say 'bingo.' It makes you sound even older than you are."

"Oh."

"And trust me, you don't really wanna go there."

"Gotcha."

She was studying the plaque that told the history of the FBI here in New York City. In 1910 the original New York Office was in the old post office in what is now City Hall Park.

"Okay, some hidden gems, then," I said. "Let's see. There's an old saying in the Bureau, 'As New York goes, so the FBI goes.'"

"Okay, good. Give me more of that. Any other sayings?"

"Well . . . Let's see . . . 'We specialize in utilizing yesterday's technology tomorrow.'"

"Ha-ha." It wasn't quite a laugh, but it wasn't quite derision either. "What else?"

I tried to think of things that a teen might find interesting. "Did you know that we have to qualify on the gun range four times a year, or that at the Academy we all get pepper-sprayed in the face so we know what it's like?"

"Oh, that would seriously suck."

"Yeah. It did. Oh, and in real life we talk about 'actors' or 'offenders' rather than 'subjects' or 'UNSUBS' or 'perps' like they do on TV crime shows. There's also a dress code."

"What's that? Look as lame as possible in a ten-year-old suit?"

"Well, that's the unofficial version. It's basically to

dress professionally, although we need to fit in too. I mean, you wouldn't go down to South Central wearing a suit. That would not be a good call."

"Understood."

She turned her attention to the detailed history of the Evidence Response Team, which was established after the 1993 World Trade Center bombing with the mission to "identify, document, collect, and preserve evidence pertaining to FBI cases."

There was a mannequin dressed in one of the thick protective full-body suits—it almost looked like a space suit—that ERT members wore when recovering evidence from the 9/11 site.

"Or, how about this," I said, "when developing sources we look at the acronym CRIME—Compromise, Revenge, Ideology, Money, and Ego. Normally, it's a combination of factors."

"Sources? You mean like informants?"

"Yes."

"Cool."

"And of course the Bureau loves acronyms: AOR: Area of Responsibility. HVE: Homegrown Violent Extremists. OCONUS: Outside Continental United States. I think someone just sits around coming up with these things."

"An IUOTM."

"What's that?"

"Idiotic Use of Taxpayer Money."

"I'll remember that one."

"You can use it. You don't even have to credit the source. You have my permission."

"Thanks."

"If you let me help you."

"Nice try."

She pointed to the exhibit on USERT—the Underwater Search Evidence Response Team, which uses sonar, metal detectors, and lift bags that can bring up a two-ton vehicle from the depths. There are four USERTs—one here at the NYFO, then ones in Miami, Los Angeles, and Washington, D.C. "There you go again," she muttered. "More acronyms."

Then she went from exhibit to exhibit, reading, processing, and asking questions, which I fielded as best I could.

Her curiosity was insatiable.

When she was done, I gestured down the hall, where a small store with FBI paraphernalia was located. "Do you want to swing by and pick anything up? An FBI hat, water bottle, T-shirt?"

"Naw, the whole reason I'm with you is that I hate shopping, remember? Oh, wait, that's not the whole reason. It's also because my mom wants us to get to know each other better, right?"

"That is true," I admitted. "Hey, listen, you wanted to help me?"

"Yeah?" she said hopefully.

She might know. She's a teen, a digital native. She might even have experimented with it.

"Well, speaking of acronyms, have you ever heard of the Tor?"

She groaned.

"What?"

"It's 'The onion router.'"

"That's right. So?"

"So don't call it 'the The onion router.' It's like when people talk about ATM machines: Automatic Teller Machine machines. Really? Are you that stupid? Or they say they're gonna type in their 'PIN number.' Personal Identification Number number. Or SAT test—"

"Scholastic Aptitude Test test."

"Precisely. Pleonasms."

"Pleonasms?"

"It pretty much just means redundant phrases."

"Or, what about 'The *La Brea* Tar Pits'?"

"The the tar tar pits," she said reflectively.

"Yes. It should just be *La Brea* Pits."

"Huh, I hadn't thought of that one. I like it."

When we were back at the car she scribbled a few more notes to herself, then crossed them out and rewrote them, connecting them to each other with arrows, and said, "Okay. I've got it. You like geospatial stuff, right?"

"Sure."

"So here's your puzzle: John, Amy, George, and Linda all arrive at a crime scene. They work as the fingerprint analyst, detective, paramedic, and undercover officer—but not necessarily in that order."

"Okay."

"Your job is to figure out the name and job of the person who got there first."

"Alright, give me the clues. Lay it on me."

"'Lay it on me' falls in the 'Bingo' category. Avoid at all costs."

"Right."

"Anyway, here you go. You get two clues. First, the detective arrived after the undercover officer, but before John and Linda arrived. Second, the paramedic left before his wife arrived, after talking with the female detective."

"Hmm. That's nice. It's clever, simple, elegant."

"Nice? What does that mean—*nice*? Did you solve it?"

"Yes. But you made that up?"

"You're stalling."

"I'm not stalling, I'm just—"

"You are *so* stalling."

"George, the undercover officer, arrived first," I said. "But it's really impressive that you—"

"Man, I knew it was way too easy," she grumbled. But then a light seemed to go on. "It might have been luck. Tell me how you figured it out."

"Well, since, according to the first clue, the detective arrived after the undercover officer but before Linda and John—and there were only four people—we know the undercover officer had to have arrived first—and also that this person couldn't be Linda or John. Consequently, George has to be either the detective or the undercover officer. But, as you said, the detective was female. George is a man's name, so—as I said, he arrived first. Then, Amy the detective got there, followed by John the paramedic and Linda the fingerprint analyst."

"Yeah, *way* too easy. I'll think of a better one."

"You want some ice cream or anything?"

"Ice cream? Seriously?"

"Sure. Everyone likes ice cream."

"Not vegans."

"Oh. Right. Sorry. Italian ice?"

"I don't care."

"And that means yes, right, in teen-speak?"

"Now you're catching on."

As long as the car was already parked, we walked to a little Italian ice spot nearby, then returned to the parking garage and took off.

"Well." She took a substantial bite of her dessert. "You solved it, so I guess I get to help you."

"Hang on . . ."

"That was the deal." She smiled slyly.

"So you made it easy on purpose," I concluded. "You were only pretending just a couple minutes ago about how you should have made it harder."

"C'mon," she implored, "let me help you solve something. I know it's probably illegal and everything, but I won't tell."

"Hmm. You know, now that I think about it, there might be something you can help me with after all."

"What's that?"

"I have an idea, but first we need to do a little shopping."

"For what?" she groaned.

"An Xbox."

42

Francis was early at the Mystorium.

But he didn't have to wait long for Skylar.

She got there early too.

Since she was buying, Francis ordered a small coffee so she wouldn't have to spend so much on him.

She ordered the same.

Rebekah wasn't working today. Francis didn't usually come in on weekends, so he didn't know the man who was filling orders behind the counter, but he wondered what he might be thinking about them, about this woman buying his coffee for him.

He'll think you're friends.

Francis liked that.

Hoped it would turn out to be true.

Once they had their drinks and were seated, Skylar said, "So, what do you do, Francis?"

He'd thought about this on the trip over, considered how much he should really tell her about his job.

On the one hand, he wanted to be open and honest with her, but on the other, when you worked at the ICSC, there were certain things you didn't tell people, things they didn't need to know.

For example, explaining to someone that you spend

eight hours a day sorting through and categorizing child pornography wasn't probably the best way of striking up a friendship.

"I work in technology," he said rather vaguely. "File analysis. What about you?"

"I'm an archivist for the Brooklyn Museum." She sighed. "Boring, I know. But I'm hoping to start my own business someday."

"Really? What kind of business?"

"I always thought it would be neat to sell beads. I don't know if I could ever make a living at it, but just creating and selling jewelry, handmade jewelry, it'd be nice. Anyway, it's probably too late." She lowered her voice. "I'm coming up on thirty."

"That's not too old." Francis liked how she told him her age, something women normally don't share. "It's never too late to pursue your dreams," he said, quoting one of the past development campaign slogans from the hospital.

That campaign was Jasmine's.

It ended four years ago.

Her poster was the one right above his couch.

Skylar sipped her drink and asked Francis about his hobbies and he told her about changing the posters and doing balloon animals for the children at St. Stephen's Research Hospital.

"That's awesome, helping with the kids like that."

"I'm not very good at the balloon tricks," he admitted. Then he added, "Oh, and I've started to go on walks."

She remarked that she liked going on walks too, even though she didn't have a dog like everyone else in her neighborhood seemed to have. "Do you have any pets?"

"No. But I did when I was younger."

He avoided dogs at all cost, since there were bacteria in dog bites that could quickly become fatal for people who'd had a splenectomy, like he'd had when he was eleven.

He didn't mention that.

And before he knew it, Francis found himself sharing things about himself he'd never told a stranger before, or even a casual acquaintance—that when he was a boy he used to have a pet turtle and had wanted to be a herpetologist when he grew up, but had gotten into computers instead. "I started off playing video games and it just moved on from there."

"Turtles, huh?"

"Yes."

"For me, when I was a kid, it was always rabbits," she said. "I had two of them." Then she told him about Hopper and Nibbles and how she'd kept them in a hutch out behind her house in Ohio.

And the whole time Francis was with Skylar, he didn't think about missing and exploited children.

Or even about graciousgirl4.

43

When we were back at the apartment, Tessa shook her head. "I seriously can't believe you just bought an Xbox."

"It's for research."

"Riiiiight."

I held up the game I'd purchased with the console. "So, do you know anything about Exo-Skel IV?" I'd picked it out while she was distracted checking out some guy at the store who looked about four years older than her.

"It's pretty popular," she replied.

"Did you ever play it?"

"A little."

"You like it?"

"I dunno. Not really. It's okay, I guess."

"Tell me about it."

"Why'd you get it if you don't know anything about it?"

"I've heard of it," I said, leaving out any reference to the case. "I figured it was worth a try."

As I set up the system, she explained, "It's a first-person shooter game where you basically play a high-tech soldier wearing this robotic exoskeleton, so you can run superfast and do all sorts of things normal people wouldn't be able to do—tipping over cars, smashing through walls, deflecting bullets—stuff like that."

"And it's interactive?"

"Yeah, sure, I mean you create an avatar and then play against other people around the world. There are ways to chat with them. You can share files, techniques. I don't know, exchange armor, weapons. Whatever."

"When I was a kid it was—"

"Please don't say Pac-Man."

"Pong."

"Ha. Even you're not that old."

"Thanks. I guess. Anyway, I was just going to say that with video games it wasn't such a social experience. If you played against other people at all instead of just the computer, they were right there in the room with you."

"Well, games today—it doesn't matter, I mean, whether they're first-person shooter games, or strategy games or fantasy games—they're community-based. It's not just how many terrorists can you blow up, it's how many can your team take down. In South Korea they'll get tens of thousands of people together in a stadium to watch people play video games on giant screens."

"That's just . . . That never would've happened with Pong."

"Puh-lease."

"But it's crazy that video games have become a spectator sport."

"You just say that because in the world you grew up in, football and basketball were the spectator sports. It's still the same thing—a bunch of people in the bleachers watching a bunch of other people show how good they are at trying to beat other people at something that doesn't ultimately matter."

I'd played sports in high school. "I'm not sure that's quite how I'd put it."

"Okay, then what about concerts? You have tens of thousands of people watching someone bang on the drums or play a piano keyboard. What's the difference between that and watching someone at a computer keyboard or game console?"

"Entertainment value?"

"But people *are* entertained by watching the games, by seeing the strategies, how they play out, all that."

I wanted to refute her, but, to my mild annoyance, I actually found myself admitting that she had a point.

Once the system was connected and ready, I said, "Show me how it works."

She walked me through the steps of setting up my avatar.

"So, there's different weapons you can choose, different shielding. Every time you get hit with a bullet or something, it decreases your lifespan and when it reaches a certain level you need to get medical attention, or get a new suit, get repairs, whatever."

Even in the video trailer preceding the game, the graphics were stunningly realistic.

It felt like I'd stepped right into a war zone: the bullets tracing through the air, the spray of blood when they found their target, the brutal sounds of urban warfare echoing all around us.

She picked up one of the controllers. "On this first level there are six of us and we're trying to find and then access a house in Baghdad where some terrorists have taken two journalists captive."

"And the other characters are played by real people?"

"Just the infiltration team, not the journalists or terrorists. But if you level-up you can join other teams on other missions. Sometimes you work with them, sometimes you try to beat 'em. I don't know. I'm not an expert."

"A lot of your friends at school play it?"

"Whoever said I have a lot of friends?" Her defensive tone made it almost sound like she was upset or that I'd just accused her of doing something wrong.

"I just mean, since it's popular. Like you mentioned a few minutes ago."

"Yeah, some people are into it. Why all the questions anyway? I feel like I'm being interrogated."

"No, it's just that . . . I found out some people use the game to share files that contain content that's not . . . well, appropriate."

"Oh. Lemme guess: drug drops or porn."

"The second one in this case." I didn't specify that the images had to do with children.

"And so you're, what? Checking into this game instead of people's cell phones?"

"Why do you say that?"

"I mean, if you wanna share porn it's a whole lot easier to do it through your phone than through some sort of file-sharing thing from a video game."

"So sexting is common among your friends?"

She looked at me with genuine confusion. "You keep referring to my friends. How many people do you see me hanging out with on a daily basis? Did I win a popularity contest somewhere that no one bothered to tell me about?"

"I'm just wondering about the extent of sexting among other kids at school."

"How much does it happen? Um—all the time. Every day. So what else is new? Girls send pictures of their boobs. Guys . . . well . . . you know."

"Do you realize that every time that happens, it's the illegal distribution of child pornography?"

"I mean, I guess." She seemed taken aback by my question. "Nobody really thinks of it like that." I had the sense that she was going to delve more into that, but she shifted gears. "Speaking of sexting, how serious are you about being with my mom?"

Although I wouldn't naturally have moved from talking about sexting to the topic of serious relationships, I could understand how, to a teen today, the idea of sexting and a relationship would go hand in hand.

"Pretty serious."

"Like, moving-in serious? Getting-married serious? What?"

"It's a little premature to start thinking about moving in or getting married."

What about moving across the country?

I didn't bring that up.

"Is that how she sees things too?"

"Well . . . I'm not exactly—"

"Come on. Gimme a break. You must talk about this. You're both single and you're not getting any younger."

"We're only in our mid-thirties, Tessa."

"Yeah, that's what I mean. So, are you looking for something long term here or are you just out playing the field?"

"I don't play the field."

"Well, other guys have told me that they were serious about her too."

"And?"

"And they were serious about getting into her pants, beyond that, not so much." She folded her arms. "So, have you slept with her or have you two been chaste?"

Now I was the one who felt I was being interrogated.

"That's a bit of a personal question, Tessa."

"Yeah? So? Have you slept with her?"

"It's really not—"

"Don't say 'appropriate.'"

"Well, it isn't any—"

"Don't say 'of your business.'"

"No."

"No, you haven't, or no, it's not any of my business?"

"No." I figured I'd just answer her question so we could move on to another topic. "We haven't slept together."

"Why not?"

"Well, as you know, your mom has strong convictions about people having intimate relations outside of marriage."

"She's pretty religious, huh?"

"I respect that about her."

"Uh-huh. So's that the only reason, then? Because of her"—she made air quotes as she said the next two words—"strong convictions?"

"Tessa, I'm not sure this is all—"

"Do you want to make love to her?"

"Do I . . . ?"

"Want. To make love. To my mom."

"She's very special to me. I wouldn't want to ruin that by pushing things in a direction she's not comfortable with."

"Uh-huh. But you do want to, right? Just tell me."

I could see I wasn't getting anywhere with this and gave up. "When the time is right."

She looked satisfied. "Thought so."

I couldn't tell if that was her way of judging me or her way of giving my attraction to her mother her seal of approval.

An incoming text caught my attention: Tobin was back in the area and wanted to know if I could come over tonight to discuss the case. Sixish? he wrote.

You can work on the geoprofile there. No one else knows as much about the missing children as he does. Maybe he can help you with it.

I was replying that that'd be fine when Tessa said, "Tomorrow's Father's Day."

"Oh, that's right." I set the phone down. The fact of it being Father's Day tomorrow wasn't really on my radar screen and I'd forgotten about it until she brought it up.

"I sometimes think about him on Father's Day, my dad, you know."

"That's understandable."

"And how much I hate him."

Oh.

"I guess you're wondering what the deal is with him, though, huh? I mean, why he's not around. And, if Mom's so into being chaste, well, how did she end up pregnant as a teenager?"

She didn't wait for a reply. "It was consensual—I mean, she wasn't raped. She doesn't talk about it much. She's never really told me the whole story, but basically he bailed on us. End of story."

Despite her obvious disdain for her father, I sensed that she wished that he would have stayed a part of her life. She said she hated him, but by the way she said it, I got the feeling that she wished she would have at least been given the opportunity to love him.

"You know." She picked up her controller. "Let's play for a while. I think I've had about all the soul-baring crap I can handle."

44

Christie came in to find us playing Exo-Skel IV.

"Hey," I called.

"Hey."

Out of the corner of my eye I saw her set a few shopping bags onto the kitchen counter. When I glanced her way, I failed to see an enemy combatant leap up from behind an empty oil drum and he got a shot off at me before I could take him down.

His bullet slammed into the side of my neck, and my life points took a major hit. If it hadn't been for the exoskeleton's energy-infused Kevlar shielding, I would have been in serious trouble.

"What's this?" she said.

"Patrick bought an Xbox," Tessa informed her.

"Really?"

"It's for research," I explained.

"I see."

"We went to the Field Office." Tessa didn't look away from the screen. "To the museum there."

"Well, that sounds nice."

"It didn't completely suck," Tessa admitted somewhat amiably.

"How are you?" I asked Christie.

"Good." She gestured toward her bedroom. "Hey, can I talk with you for a sec?"

"Sure."

I set the controller down and when we were alone in the bedroom I anticipated what she might want to talk about.

The Xbox.

"It seemed like a way we could connect," I said. "I'm trying to enter into the mindset of someone in one of my cases. I guess I should have asked you first before we started playing this game, though, huh? It's pretty graphic, pretty violent. Sorry, I wasn't thinking. I was just—"

"No, no. It's okay. I'm sure it's not any worse than what's on TV." She seemed distracted. "I'm not mad. I was just surprised."

"What is it?"

"I'm going to tell Tessa."

"About Omaha?"

"About the possibility of it. Yes. This isn't to put any pressure on you. Like I said earlier, I stuck you in an impossible situation and it wasn't right. But I need to talk it through with her. I probably should have spoken with her right away."

"Tell you what, I'll clear out, give you two some space. Tobin wanted to get together at six or so. Maybe I'll just head over there a little early to work on the geoprofile and get him caught up on the case."

I told her about his situation: that his wife and daughter were gone, and that it looked like his mother was dying.

"Is there anything we can do for him?" she asked concernedly.

"I'm not sure. I'll ask him."

"Let me send some food along."

"Don't worry about that. I'll pick up some wings or something on the way."

"Please tell him I'll be praying for him and for his mother."

And see? This was one of the reasons I liked this woman so much.

"I will."

"And you'll be back later, then?"

"Yeah. I'm not sure when."

"I'll be up."

"I'll see you then."

After a quick kiss good-bye, I gathered my things, and as I was passing out the door I heard Christie say, "Tessa, pause the game for a minute. We need to talk."

PART III

Dark Web

45

Tobin greeted me at the door to his house, which lay across the river in New Jersey where home prices weren't quite as stratospheric as they were in the city.

"How's your mom doing?" I asked him.

"Her condition hasn't worsened."

Inside the living room I told him about Christie's sentiments and that she would be praying for him and his mother.

He said nothing and I wasn't sure how to take that.

"Is there anything we can do for you?" I asked.

"No, but thank you for asking."

I held up the take-out bag from Rita's Wing Joint. "I've got garlic Parmesan, barbecue, and ragin' Cajun."

"Great." He invited me to the kitchen.

On the way there we crossed the hallway to the bedrooms.

A door about halfway down the hall had a sheet of paper taped to it with Adrienne's name drawn in colorful crayons and with the awkward, blocky letters that a child might use. A golden sun looked down on the letters from the top right corner of the page. Three happy stick figures stood holding hands at the bottom of the page, beneath the letters.

He never took it down.

All these years and he left that sign on her door.

The other day he'd told me how hard it was to move on.

The sign bore out how hard it really had been for him.

Love sets us free. But in many ways it also holds us captive.

It looked like his love and the lack of closure from never finding Adrienne's killer had kept a part of his heart imprisoned all these years.

Once we were in the kitchen, he said, "You didn't really get a chance to finish your beer the other night. You want one?"

"Naw. I'll need to drive back to Christie's later. But go ahead."

"I think I have some root beer in here. Sound good?"

"Sure."

He found two bottles of Barq's in the fridge and after uncapping them, handed me one.

"Thanks."

We spoke for a few minutes and I told him about my day with Tessa, about taking her to the museum and trying to relate to her. "Any advice on talking to teenagers?"

"I'm as much in the dark on that front as you are."

It didn't take us long to polish off the wings and while he was cleaning up, I used the bathroom. When I returned he said, "So, what does that discerning eye of yours see here so far?"

"What do you mean?"

"What have you noticed about my place that other people wouldn't have?"

"Is this a test?"

"Just curious."

"Um . . . well, there's no indication that you live

alone. The bathroom has women's soap, moisturizer, body lotion. There's children's bubble bath by the tub. You still subscribe to Misty's magazines and keep them beside your couch."

"The mailing labels? You saw them when you walked in?"

"Yes."

"And?"

"And you have photos of your wife and daughter—at least I'm guessing that's who they are—in every room I've seen so far. In fact, I'd have to verify it, but by their orientation to the doorways, it appears that a picture would be in your line of sight as you entered any of the rooms from any direction."

He sat quietly for a moment, then went to the counter and picked up the photo of him with an attractive blond woman and a little girl who looked like a miniature version of her. All three were smiling. They stood on a boardwalk along the beach. A gently rippling ocean spread out behind them.

He turned the photo so I could see it better. "This was taken about a month before Adrienne was abducted. We'd been thinking about moving—had our place here listed with a realtor, held an open house and everything. We'd visited the shore, thought we were going to move over there. Ended up staying. I've been here ever since."

"This house holds a lot of memories for you." I left it up to him to decide where to take things from there.

"I know—some people would have wanted to move, to escape the harsher ones, to start over, start fresh. For me, though, staying was important. It kept me focused."

"Focused?"

"Yes."

I waited. He didn't elaborate, but he did set down the

photo, then faced me and got right to business. "So, tell me about the case, about what happened yesterday, what you've been thinking about this guy who got away."

It took more than an hour to fill him in and address all of his questions. We perused the online case files and found that when the man who'd abducted Lily Keating had brought other women to the condo, he'd managed to avoid the cameras each time. Officer Chip Hinchcliffe had posted that he hadn't been able to identify anyone at the coffee shop who might have uploaded the masks video.

I spent even more time showing Tobin what I was doing with the geoprofile. He seemed very interested in understanding as much as he could about my approach.

Finally, the conversation drifted off into a natural eddy and in the silence that followed he said, "Hey, listen, do you play pool?"

Actually, I welcomed a breather from the case. "I've played a little over the years, but I wouldn't say I know the game very well."

"I think you'd like it. The timing and location of your shots mean everything. Very geospatial. Come on, I have a table in the basement."

I followed him down to the rec room.

"Break?" he asked.

"Go for it."

We racked the balls and he showed me where each one should go when you're setting up for the break shot. He rolled some chalk onto the end of one of the cue sticks and walked to the far end of the table, lined up on the cue ball, and fired away.

When the cue ball hit it, the triangle of balls exploded apart, splaying across the table. Two striped ones dropped into a couple of the pockets.

"I guess I'm solids," I said.

"So you do know how to play."

"Just the basics."

"Well, it's all about planning your next shot before you take your current one. You want to set yourself up to take advantage of the position of everything else on the table." Like always, there was a solemnity to everything he said, although I could sense that he really did enjoy the game. "And all the while, you try not to disturb the other balls that don't have anything to do with the shot you're setting up."

"There's an art to it."

"A strategy at least." He eyed down the cue stick at the eleven ball. "Listen, Patrick, I have to admit, one of the reasons I invited you over was to apologize."

"For what?"

"For the other night when we were at Mally's Pub and Toffee Shop, for getting into the whole story of what happened with Adrienne and Misty. For dumping it on you out of nowhere."

"That's nothing you need to apologize for, Tobin. I was just honored you felt comfortable sharing it with me."

Earlier, Christie had been apologizing to me, now Tobin was, both for something they hadn't done wrong—trusting me, being honest, sharing something deep—Christie about her future, Tobin about his past.

He took his shot and banked the eleven in, and the cue ball rolled gently into place to allow him to drop the fifteen into the side pocket. This man had clearly played this game before.

"Do you know the story of the Pied Piper of Hamelin?" he asked.

"I'm afraid my folktale repertoire is a bit limited, but that's the one with the rats, right?"

"Yes. In Hamelin, Germany, the town's official record begins on June 26, 1384, and here's the first line: 'It is 100 years since our children left.' That's how it begins."

"That's chilling."

"No kidding. And no one knows what happened to the children. The way it's phrased—I mean, it doesn't say they died, but that they *left*. Well, it's stumped historians to this day."

He put in the fifteen, walked to the other side of the table to take aim at the nine.

"And that inscription," I said, "is that what the story grew out of?"

"The story might have come first, no one knows for sure. According to the most common legend, the village was infested with rats, and the people tried everything they could think of to get rid of them, but nothing worked."

He called the nine in the corner pocket and delivered, then said, "So one day a stranger from out of town appears dressed in these colorful clothes—that's what the term 'pied' refers to. He makes a deal that if he can rid the village of the rats, the people will have to pay him a certain amount, an exorbitant amount, actually."

"And they agree because they don't think he'll be able to pull it off."

"Right. Well, he plays the flute—the pipe, that is—and when he does, the rats follow him. He's able to lead them out of the city and into the hills. So he delivers Hamelin from its plague of rats."

"But that's just the first part." It came back to me now. "Then he lures the children away."

Tobin nodded.

With his next shot he sank the twelve ball and set himself up for a perfect bank with the fourteen.

"The people of the village refuse to pay him for getting rid of the rats, and then he returns and plays a new tune. And this time, yeah, it's the kids who follow him out of town. And they're never seen again."

He pocketed the fourteen and the cue ball rolled into position, offering him a chance to finish off the game by dropping the eight ball with a straight shot across the length of the table.

I wasn't getting much of an opportunity here to pick up any practice. He hadn't missed a shot and now he was about to win without even giving me a reason to chalk up my cue stick.

"And they still don't know what really happened to those children?" I said.

"Right. But according to an inscription found on a stained glass window in the town from the early 1300s, one hundred and thirty children did disappear."

"The plague, you think? The Black Death?"

"That didn't break out in Europe until after these events in Hamelin occurred."

"Huh."

He lined up and stroked smooth and easy at the cue ball. It rolled across the table, tapped in the eight ball, and then followed it, falling into the pocket as well.

He clicked his tongue and shook his head. Based on how effortlessly he'd cleared the table and how accurate his shots had been, it didn't seem likely that he would have made that mistake by accident and I wondered why he'd just handed the game to me.

Also, I wasn't clear on why he'd brought up the story of the Pied Piper.

"That last shot is always the kicker. Everything depends on how you wrap up the game." He leaned his cue stick against the wall. "I also needed to tell you that I'm sorry about my mother."

"Your mother?"

"For lying to you about that."

"What are you talking about?"

"I wasn't at a nursing home with her yesterday and this morning. She died two years ago."

"Where were you?"

"I need to show you something, Pat." He gestured toward what I assumed to be a guest bedroom.

Without another word he opened the door.

"Where were you, Tobin, if you weren't with your mom?"

"You'll understand when you step inside."

He ushered me into the room.

46

The walls were covered with photos of children, some from missing persons posters, others from case files, still others from newspapers or printouts of websites.

A large road map of the Northeast seaboard hung on the wall. Eighteen pushpins had been stuck into it in locations ranging from Maine to North Carolina. Strings connected them, creating an intricate web. The nexus of the web was in a location in New Jersey.

This city.

And, if I was correct, this address.

A pile of overstuffed file folders sat on a desk in the corner of the room.

"This is about Adrienne, isn't it?" I said softly.

"They wouldn't give me the case, Patrick. They told me it would be too personal."

The conclusion was obvious: "So you've been digging into things yourself, all these years, looking for her killer."

"I couldn't just let it be. You understand that, don't you? She was my daughter."

I pointed to the pushpins. "These are all child abductions?"

"Those are sites where their bodies were found. Eighteen of them over the last decade."

"And you think they're related to Adrienne's case?"

"Yes. I was looking into one of them yesterday."

"I don't like being lied to," I said.

"The lies end here."

"Tobin, if you found anything specific regarding any of these cases, you need to pass that along to the detectives assigned to their investigations."

"Oh, I have. Believe me. Everything I find, I share, and it gets put into the system."

"But"—I anticipated what he was going to say—"it's a big system."

A nod. "Things get lost in the shuffle, officers get reassigned, new cases take precedence over older ones, time marches on. In the eight years since Adrienne was taken, her case has been handed off to four different detectives, but each one has eventually been transferred or retired up until this current guy, and his caseload doesn't give him a lot of time to look into an eight-year-old cold case."

"Okay, tell me what you have here."

He pointed to the pins. "Eighteen children of different ages, races, and socioeconomic backgrounds spread across nearly as many states over the course of ten years and four months, killed different ways, abducted under different circumstances."

"Both sexes?"

"Yes."

"So there's nothing on the surface linking them?"

"No."

"What about Stewart's mailing list?"

"Their names don't appear." He picked up the stack of file folders. "What I have here aren't solid leads. It's more like the back of a rug—you know, where you see the tangle of threads. You realize there has to be a pattern there, but you just can't see it."

"Until you turn the rug over."

"Right."

"Who else knows about this? About what you're doing here?"

"No one."

"Why are you showing me this, Tobin? Why are you telling me all this?"

"I want you to help me flip over the rug."

"Why me?"

"From what I can tell, you see things—patterns, relationships, connections that other people miss. You have an eye for it. And location and timing—it's your specialty. And that's what we have here. I've been looking at all this for so long by myself that I need a fresh pair of eyes on it. I want you to help me find the person who took my daughter."

"What makes you think all these deaths belong to the same rug?"

As I asked the question I was scanning the maps, the missing children's posters, and the newspaper articles regarding when their bodies were found.

Timing and location.

Timing and—

Aha.

I answered my own question: "They were all kept alive for at least six months before they were killed. That's what ties them together."

"See what I mean?" He sounded pleased that I'd picked up on that. "It took me sorting through hundreds of pages of case files to pull that out."

"That's not something that would show up on ViCAP. It's good work on your part."

If we were on the right track with this, it was huge.

"Someone is taking children," Tobin said, "keeping

them locked up for months or even years, and then killing them. He's been doing it for a decade and I think he did it to my daughter."

Based on what'd happened to D'Nesh, it might be related to our current case as well.

"Have these children's pictures appeared online? Any record of them in the ICSC database?"

"No—at least not where we've been able to see."

So that linked them together as well. Lack of evidence where you'd expect it is evidence in itself.

"Why did you tell me the story of the Pied Piper?"

"In many of these cases, the abductor led the children away right under the eyes of their parents. I've found images of flutes and passing references on the Dark Web to someone out there whom people refer to as the Piper. I think whoever that is, he's engineering all this. Maybe even modeling his work after parts of the folktale."

"And there, in Hamelin, one hundred and thirty children were taken."

"Yes."

A deep chill.

"You think the Piper might be the one behind Adrienne's death?"

"I do." He walked over to his desk and picked up a file folder. "Because of this."

47

He laid out the papers. They were copies of official police reports from a variety of law enforcement agencies. I didn't ask how he'd gotten them. With his job and his connections, he could simply have requested most of them. He might have called in favors for the rest. Right now I didn't worry about that.

He indicated the top police report. "The last of the eighteen bodies found: a four-year-old girl, Haley Furman. She was abducted from her home in Maryland while her parents were sleeping just down the hall. It happened two states away and seven years later, but it's the same m.o."

"As when Adrienne was taken?"

"Yes."

"If I'm going to help you with this, Tobin, I'll need you to tell me the details of Adrienne's disappearance. Are you up for that?"

"Yes." But he didn't answer right away.

"You sure?"

"Yeah."

"Alright, first, tell me exactly how she was taken."

"It was April. The twenty-fourth. Misty and I were asleep in bed and I heard the front door close. At first I wasn't sure if I was just imagining things, you know how, when you're somewhere in between being awake and asleep, and you think you hear something but it's really just your mind playing tricks on you."

"Sure."

"But then Misty grabbed my arm and asked if I'd heard something and I knew that it was real, that it was happening. I checked the time, 3:52 a.m. I had a Glock under the mattress, so I grabbed it, then I told Misty to stay in the room and lock the door, and I went to investigate."

"And you two were in the master bedroom at the end of the hallway, past Adrienne's room?"

"That's right. Her room is between ours and the front door, so I checked that first, but she wasn't there. Just a pile of blankets on her bed. Then I heard a car engine fire up out by the curb, so I rushed outside. A sedan with its lights off was pulling down the street."

"Plates?"

"Too dark to see. I went back in, grabbed my car keys, and took off after it."

"Were you in your cruiser or your personal vehicle?"

"My cruiser. My pickup was in the garage. And that's when I called it in, to get a unit to my house while I was en route."

"So you pursued the sedan."

"Yes.

"Did you have a visual on it the whole time?"

He shook his head. "As I'm sure you noticed on your drive over here, we don't live far from the interstate, so I lost sight of him briefly, but then I saw a sedan turning onto a side street that led to the onramp."

"The same car?"

"I couldn't tell. Not for sure. I merged onto the highway and pulled him over. The driver was male. No one else in the vehicle, not in the backseat, not in the trunk. Nothing. Adrienne wasn't there. It was the wrong car. The guy claimed he hadn't been to my house, that he had no idea who I was or what I was talking about. I didn't care, though."

"You arrested him anyway."

"I detained him. Yes. Put him in the back of my cruiser. I wasn't about to take any chances. I know what you're probably thinking, but I can't imagine there was time for him to switch cars or transfer her to another vehicle. I mean, it's possible, but I'd say it's highly unlikely. And the guy checked out when it was all over and done."

I considered that. "So you returned here, to the house, with him in the backseat?"

"Yes. The whole drive I kept telling myself that this was all some sort of mistake, that Adrienne was really back at home, that I just hadn't noticed her: she was probably just lying under that pile of sheets and blankets, or maybe she was hiding under the bed or in the closet or something. She was just scared and that's why she hadn't said anything—that's what I kept repeating to myself. Over and over."

His gaze shifted away from me into a distance that didn't exist down here in the basement and he started talking as if things were happening right now, right here. "She would probably be even more scared now, with all the yelling and with the police coming in, but I would take her in my arms and hold her and tell her it was okay, that everything was going to be okay, and then Misty and I would let her sleep in bed beside us, like we sometimes needed to do when she got scared of storms, or of bad dreams, or when she thought there were monsters under her bed."

Then he looked at me again. "I told myself those things, even though I was on the radio with dispatch the whole time. I knew she was gone. I just couldn't accept it. A unit was already at the house and others were being sent to the neighborhood. I knew that in more than seventy-five percent of the cases when children are taken in nonfamily abductions, they're killed within the first three hours."

I tried to imagine what it would have been like to be in his shoes, but I couldn't.

Most people don't know the stats.

In his case, knowing them would have only made things more difficult.

"The three hours passed. Then three days. Three weeks. Three months. Misty spiraled off into depression. And I already told you about how a jogger found Adrienne's body. It was almost two years to the day from when she disappeared."

"Where was she found?"

"Just off a running trail in a park about five miles from here. We looked into the guy who found her. Nothing. He was clean."

I processed what he'd told me, thought about the distances from his bedroom to Misty's room and then the distance from there to the front door, and then down to the curb . . . thought about the timing of how long it would take to have the brief exchange with Misty and then to check Adrienne's bedroom, get outside, start up the cruiser . . . thought of the layout of the neighborhood, the proximity of the onramp to the side streets that I'd taken to get here . . .

There's a back door through the kitchen. One that leads to the backyard.

But the front door was the one that closed. That's what woke them up . . .

Tobin's pickup was in the garage. His cruiser was in the driveway.

It was one of those details that would be easy to miss.

"And the front door—was it unlocked?"

"It was locked but not dead-bolted. Evidently, he picked the lock to get in. I figured that we lived in a good neighborhood, and since I was a cop and I was home, I could defend my family. I kept my cruiser parked in the driveway every night. You'd think that would be deterrent enough."

"Yes." I was deep in thought. "You'd think it would be."

Or an invitation.

Depending on how you look at it.

I had an idea.

"Come on." I headed for the stairs.

"Where are we going?"

"I have a thought, but I want to walk this through."

48

Upstairs in his bedroom, I scrolled to the stopwatch function on my phone. "Let's reenact what happened. I'm going to time you. I want you to go through what you did that night from the moment you woke up. Try to do it at the same speed, or at least whatever feels right to what happened eight years ago."

Tobin lay on the bed.

"Okay." I started the stopwatch. "You wake up wondering if you really heard something. Take it from there."

He sat up. "I speak to Misty. She's heard it too. I glance at the clock, then go for my gun."

He reached under the mattress and produced the Glock he still kept within reach.

"Then I go to clear Adrienne's room."

I followed him, keeping one eye on the time as the seconds ticked by. Studies have shown that, even though people think they have a good conception of the passage of time, they really don't. They almost always underestimate the amount of time pleasurable activities take, and overestimate the time it takes to get through unpleasant ones.

He checked his daughter's room, then moved through the hallway, ran outside, came back in, and went directly to the key holder board near the door. After snatching up his key ring, he bolted out again to his cruiser and started the engine. When the door closed behind him, it didn't sound loud enough to have woken up two people in the bedroom at the end of the hall.

I joined him outside. "Okay. Thirty-four seconds."

"Alright." He stepped out of the car.

"It's cutting it pretty tight."

"What is?"

"The timing. For someone to get down the driveway to the sedan, get Adrienne inside it, then climb in, start up the engine and leave before you could catch them."

I looked around the dewy night. A neighbor's dog barked, then another one farther down the street followed suit. "Did any dogs bark that night?"

"Honestly, I don't remember."

"Okay."

We went to the front door. It was recessed in a small vestibule.

"Was the porch light on?"

"Yes. I remember noting that later in the police report."

However, even now with it on, taking into account the location of the exterior light, because of the way the vestibule of the house was designed, a swath of shadows would have allowed an intruder as much time as he needed to pick the lock without being visible from the street.

"And this is the same door?"

"Yes. Do you have something?"

"I'm not sure yet. I want you to go through it again. I'll pretend to be the abductor."

"Alright."

"This time I'll actually close the front door. When you

hear it, go through the steps again. Play it out until you get in your cruiser. I'll meet you outside by your car."

He agreed, then disappeared into his bedroom. I went to the front door and started my watch, then sharply closed the door.

I slipped into the kitchen and watched down the hallway as Tobin appeared and entered his daughter's room. A few seconds passed, then he quickly traversed the hallway, passed through the living room and out the front door, burst back inside to where he kept the keys, then left the house again.

I went out the back door and walked around the house through a row of hedges. He'd started his car, but now when he saw me, he shut off the engine. I met up with him by the driver's door.

"Where were you?" he asked.

"I went out the back."

"What are you thinking?"

"A couple things. First, why'd he turn it off?"

"What?"

"The car. Why not just let it idle? Why chance letting someone hear him start up the engine? And what about the car doors?"

"I thought about that before. I should have heard at least one of them closing, or at least the trunk if Adrienne was put in there."

"But you didn't."

"No."

"Because she wasn't."

"Right." He looked at me curiously. "What else?"

"Why bother to close the house door behind you? It would be hard enough to do so while carrying a child and it would make no sense if you're trying to get away without being discovered."

"Adrienne could have been walking."

"True, but that seems doubtful, wouldn't you say?"

"I would. So where does that leave us?"

"I'm thinking the guy you pulled over in the sedan might not have been so innocent after all. I'm not convinced he ever got out of the vehicle in the first place. But based on the road layout and the timing, it's likely that it was the car you saw leaving your street. Do you have a file on him?"

"Sure. Downstairs."

We returned to the basement and he dug through the folders, pulled one out, flipped it open, and showed me the top page.

"That's him." I hadn't expected this, but it did fit, and it revealed a part of the rug I hadn't even known was lying there right in front of me. "He was at Romanoff's house. That's the guy who was holding the knife up against Lily Keating's neck."

49

"What?" Tobin exclaimed. "The man who was shot in the head by the unknown assailant?"

"Right."

According to these files, his name was Garrett Higgs. I quickly flipped through the pages, committing some of the dates, times, and locations to memory.

"So it's all connected." Tobin sounded like he was deep in thought.

"Somehow, yes."

"That means Adrienne's abduction has to do with the Final Territory."

"It certainly looks like it."

This gave us more threads that were knotted together on the back of the rug. Now we just needed to see the pattern on the front.

"How did you know it was the same guy?" he asked me.

"I didn't."

"A hunch?"

"Not even that."

"Then how did you . . . ?"

"The pieces didn't fit. I don't believe in random crimes. In any abduction there's a convergence of desire, availability, and choice. People make rational decisions based on perceived risks and rewards. So if the people behind Adrienne's abduction knew you were a cop—and the cruiser out front would have been a pretty good indicator of that—they would likely have anticipated that you would be armed."

"Sure, that makes sense."

"And what would be the best way to escape with the daughter of an armed law enforcement officer?"

It hit him. "To draw me out of the house."

"Yes. Remove the primary threat first. Misdirection. And that would require more than one person."

"You think Adrienne might have still been in the house when I left it?" A deep tremor ran through his words. The idea that he might have been lured away while his daughter was in the home with a second abductor obviously shook him to the core.

And knowing that he'd very likely had one of the kidnappers in his custody and then let him go must have been unbearable.

"Closing the door loud enough to wake both you and Misty up—it seems like a mistake someone planning a crime like this wouldn't make, unless they *wanted* you to wake up."

"But if they closed it loudly on purpose, I mean, why chance that at all?"

"To make sure they could get you off the site. To toy with you. A power trip. I don't know. But to pull all this off, they would've needed to know the inside layout of your home."

But how would they have found out the . . . ?

"The open house," I muttered.

"The open house?"

"You mentioned earlier that before the abduction you

were thinking of moving, that you held an open house. Burglars sometimes attend open houses to scope out their marks, take note of security systems, the presence of dogs, do threat and target assessment, or plan out their entrance and exit routes. Kidnappers have been known to do the same."

"But the guy in the sedan, Higgs, he never came to the open house. I would have remembered him. I'm certain of it. So . . ." He considered the implications. "His partner might have come. I never kept track of who attended. It could have been anyone."

"Listen, I need to know something and I want to apologize beforehand for having to ask it."

"Go ahead."

"Have you checked the ICSC database for images or videos that might have included Adrienne?"

"Yes. There were no matches to her on any of their files. Thank God."

It was at least a small gift that photos or video of her being molested hadn't made the rounds on the web.

"Could the abductor have been someone who knew you from a previous case?" I asked.

"I've asked myself that a thousand times over the years. I went back through every case I'd ever worked looking for any connection to this, to people who might have been trying to get back at me by striking at my family. Some names came up, but when I dug deeper there was nothing there."

Scanning the maps covering the walls, I studied the location of the sites where the bodies had been found, then said, "In order to reduce the risks of being caught, killers tend to leave the corpses of their victims in areas they're familiar with. Typically, the farther a body is from a road or trail, the more prominent the role that location plays in the cognitive map or awareness space of the offender."

"Because he's more confident there."

"Yes."

"But these sites, they're strewn all over."

"So," I said, "perhaps the killer wasn't necessarily the one to dispose of the bodies."

"Or there was more than one killer."

"Or that." I checked the time and saw to my surprise that it was already after ten. "Listen, I don't want to take off right now, not considering where we're at with all this—but I don't want to get back to Christie's too late either, so—"

"You can sleep here, no problem."

"All I need is a couch."

"Then I've got you covered."

I called Christie to tell her that I was going to remain here tonight, but first I asked how the conversation with Tessa had gone regarding Nebraska.

"Not as well as I would have hoped, but about as well as I expected."

"So she wasn't thrilled about the prospect of moving to Omaha."

"She shared her views in rather colorful and unequivocal terms. We can talk about it later."

"I'm sorry she was upset."

"She'll be alright."

"Hey, something came up that's related to the case this week and to the murder of Tobin's daughter eight years ago. It looks like it's all tied together. We want to take a closer look. Do you need me back tonight? Otherwise, I was thinking of staying here so we can work late."

"A breakthrough?"

"A possible one."

"No, of course, that's fine. You don't need to come home."

The phrase struck me: "come home" rather than "come back."

It sounded so natural when she said it and I couldn't help wondering what it would be like to do that, to come home to her every night. I don't even think she noticed what she said.

However, now was not the time to think about all that.

Since she had church in the morning, we made plans to meet tomorrow afternoon. I could work here with Tobin beforehand and then spend some time with her before diving into preparing for Monday morning's briefing.

We said good-bye and good night, then I turned to Tobin and gestured toward the stack of file folders. "Alright. It looks like I have a bit of catching up to do. Let's get started."

50

Francis's day had passed quickly.

The three o'clock coffee with Skylar had turned into a four o'clock walk and then a five o'clock dinner at a nearby Thai place.

"We both have to eat, right?" Francis had said.

Skylar had agreed with that. Certainly she needed to eat. They both did. Why not do it together?

He'd been amazed: even after two hours together it didn't seem like she was growing tired of being with him. And he was definitely not growing tired of being with her.

It felt good.

It felt right.

And even though they barely knew each other, he felt comfortable with her, more so than he'd ever felt with any other woman.

Finally, at seven, they'd exchanged phone numbers. Then he'd given her a slightly awkward half hug, which she returned to him.

Francis couldn't believe how easy it was to talk with her. She listened to him, really, really listened without pestering him or accusing him or condemning him like the voice in his head so often did.

No. She's just pretending. She couldn't really like being with you, Francis.

Be quiet! Yes, she does.

You'll hurt her. You'll do those things you think of sometimes. You'll—

I'm not going to hurt her. I would never hurt her!

Before he left the restaurant, he'd invited her to join him tomorrow at the hospital when he was going to be visiting one of the children. "His name is Derek," Francis had explained. "You might've seen his face on billboards or on a poster somewhere around town. He's a minor celebrity."

"I'm not sure I have."

"There's a slogan: You can make Derek's dreams come true."

"Maybe, I can't remember for sure, but I'll keep an eye out. In either case I would like to come."

They agreed to meet at four in the lobby of St. Stephen's Research Hospital's children's wing.

Now, back at home, Francis had been trying to get something called "The Tor Browser" to work on his laptop so he could research sites on the Dark Web to try to help the FBI, but he hadn't had much luck.

The download kept stalling out and wouldn't load.

Frustrated, he set it aside for a minute, checked his phone, and found a text from Skylar. She'd sent a link to a news story about how the tortoise population in the Galápagos Islands was recovering. "Thot u mite like this :)"

She remembered he liked turtles.

Yes, she remembered.

Even before reading the story, he texted her back to thank her for sending it, then added that he was glad he'd spent the afternoon with her.

On the computer, a chat request came in from gra-ciousgirl4, but he didn't answer it.

Instead he closed the Krazle tab on his browser.

Then he sat beneath the posters of the children and started to read about the tortoises.

Skylar texted him back that she was glad she'd met him too and as they texted back and forth, twenty minutes passed and he still hadn't made his way through the webpage.

At last they signed off with each other and he finished the article.

The tortoises had been on the brink of extinction, of disappearing forever, but they were on their way back. There was hope for them once again.

They had been given a second chance.

Tomorrow, he told himself, tomorrow he would get the browser to work, but for now, he could go to bed thinking of how things were finally going right in his life.

And how much Dr. Perrior would approve.

51

The man who chose to call himself Shane had killed twenty-one people, mostly children, in the last decade.

These days he was the one the Final Territory called on when things were over, when they needed to wrap everything up.

But it hadn't always been that way.

He'd started off by himself.

Working solo.

The first girl had been the hardest. He hadn't really wanted to kill her, but she'd shrieked and screamed so much when they were alone together in the shed that he had to find a way to keep her quiet or else someone might have heard her out there behind the house.

He warned her to be quiet, to *please be quiet*, but she wouldn't listen, so he had to do something about it.

It was messy and he cried for a long time when it was done.

But then, when it was over, when he'd washed the warm blood off his hands and put the body in the ground, when he was back at the house holding the hand of the woman he was married to at the time and watching television beside her on the couch, he realized that he had felt more alive while taking that girl's life than he ever had before.

The dance of life and death, of power and breath and finality.

There was something about the fear and the excitement and the thrill of it all, and the surge of those primal emotions and desires.

It felt like a drug high. One he could easily get addicted to.

It'd been hard to go back to normal day-to-day life afterward. Everything seemed black and white and dull compared to the color-rich world of the blood and the stark resonance of those cries for mercy.

He tried to ignore the urge to experience those feelings again, of when life had split open into full, rich color before him.

He managed to make it five months.

Then he saw the girl at the state park, and he realized that he had his chance to feel that way again.

Right then. That very day.

He was walking his golden retriever, Duke, along the beach when he saw the girl, no older than seven or eight, watching him.

After a few minutes he found himself on his way toward her and then he was saying hi and introducing Duke and telling her that she could pet him if she wanted to.

And she asked was he nice and would he bite?

And he told her that yes, he was nice. He was a good dog. And no, he would never bite anyone. Then he reached down to pet Duke to show her how friendly and not-dangerous at all he was.

Duke stood obediently, docilely by his side.

The girl came to them, placed her hand on Duke's back, and stroked his golden hair.

"What's your name?" Shane asked her.

"Samantha."

"Where is your mother, Samantha?"

She was still petting the dog. "Over there." She pointed vaguely in the direction of the water. He didn't see anyone in particular, though. No one was keeping close tabs on the girl. A few women were sitting beneath large beach umbrellas talking. Samantha might have been pointing toward them, he couldn't tell.

A voice inside him told him what he could do, how this could work, how everything could play out.

Just to his left was a rise and a trail through the sand dunes. He and Samantha could take that back to his car. The hill would hide them from view of anyone on the beach.

You could bring her to the shed. Just like Trixie.

"Well, shouldn't you be getting along, then?" he said to her.

She shrugged. Kept petting. "It's okay."

He felt his chest tighten and his pulse race, and the moment seemed to stretch to infinity and he found himself scanning the beach and realizing that no one was close by, no one was watching. For all practical purposes he was alone with Duke and the girl.

Yes, he could take Samantha to his car.

He could do this.

Right now.

"Would you like to see my other dog?" he asked her.

"You have *another* one?" She sounded astonished, as if owning two dogs would be the most amazing thing in the world.

"Yes. He's in my car." Shane pointed toward the trail. "It's not far. When we're done, I'll walk you back to your mother."

"Okay."

But as they started down the trail, she'd hesitated, so

he had to use his hands and hurt her so that she couldn't cry out.

Then he carried her in his arms, as if she were his own daughter and had simply fallen asleep and he was taking her upstairs to her room.

That time was easier than the first. Quicker. Not so messy.

And he didn't cry nearly as much when it was over.

So she was number two.

The remaining children came later.

After a while he didn't cry at all when it was over. He just looked forward to the next time.

Once you developed a taste for it, it was hard to say no to those urges.

The Internet makes it easy to find people with the same tastes, and eventually, through the Dark Web, he'd made the connections that allowed him to foster and pursue his growing interests. Consequently, he'd been contacted by the Piper and given his current duties.

Without the anonymity that Tor provided, he never would have met the people he needed to meet.

Now, tonight, he went to bed thinking of how, when everything went down on Wednesday, things would be so much safer, of how the risk of law enforcement entanglement would drop to its lowest level since he'd started living life in full color.

And his pastime would be easier than ever to pursue.

52

Last night Tobin and I stayed up until nearly two o'clock turning over the rug, going through his files looking for patterns and intersecting factors between the crimes, trying to see if we could find any additional links between the eighteen homicides he'd charted in that spare bedroom in the basement.

We put in a call to the family of Haley Furman, the girl who'd been taken from her home last year in a similar manner as Adrienne, to see if they'd been planning to move and might've held an open house so we could find out if Higgs had perhaps attended that one. They had, in fact, had some showings, but they didn't recognize Higgs's picture when we emailed it to them.

I thought there might be a connection between the fact that Stewart had a real estate email list, and at least two families that were going to move were targeted, but I wasn't sure what it might be.

Since it was Sunday morning, contacting other realty companies about open houses or showings for the remaining children would need to wait until business hours tomorrow.

Admittedly, however, I wasn't holding my breath about that line of inquiry.

Most people keep notoriously sketchy records, and there was no compelling reason why anyone who was up to no good would use his real name while attending an open house he was using as a scouting trip in preparation for a child's abduction.

Potential home buyers don't have to show an ID to realtors. There's no background check. It's one of the few times when we allow people we don't know into our homes, often giving strangers carte blanche to wander through our residences, even allowing them access to our children's bedrooms.

Most homeowners don't even give it a second thought that the person might be a burglar, a child molester, or a potential kidnapper when they open up their houses like that.

Though Higgs hadn't had a criminal record when Tobin pulled him over, he'd picked up a litany of minor offenses over the last couple of years, but nothing related to the case we were looking at.

We studied his background and used that to compare his known addresses with the times and locations of the other abductions. Although there were no definitive connections, there was a stronger correlation than chance would allow between the places he'd lived and the sites of four abductions and three sites where bodies were found.

During our late breakfast, I asked Tobin the question that'd been scratching around in the back of my mind since last night. "You still haven't told me where you were on Friday and on Saturday morning," I said. "You weren't with your mother—what were you doing?"

"I was looking into something that I thought might relate to the case."

"And that was?"

"Someone named Blake. He might be affiliated with the Final Territory, I'm not certain. I went undercover to some bars I heard he frequented, but either my informants didn't have accurate intel or they were leading me on a wild-goose chase. In any case, I didn't find anything. It looks like he's going to be hard to get to."

"Why didn't you tell me that right off the bat?"

"I was wondering if Blake might be someone in law enforcement. I wasn't sure who to trust."

"But you trusted me."

"Yes," he said without hesitation. "I did."

We took a little time to analyze the online case files and update them with what we'd discovered last night regarding the identity of Garrett Higgs.

While I was studying a calendar, looking at the timing of the most recent abduction, I noticed today's date and recalled Tessa telling me how, on Father's Day, she often thought of her dad and of how much she hated him.

Figuring that wishing Tobin a happy Father's Day would only bring back painful memories, I said nothing, but I did make a mental note to call my own dad later on. Though we weren't estranged, I honestly couldn't recall the last time I'd spoken with him.

On a case this sweeping and complex, there are a lot of moving parts, and staying informed on all of them was proving to be an ever-growing challenge.

The forensic evidence left in the van at the site of the fire indicated that both D'Nesh Agarwai and Maggie Rivers had been in it. The team was still looking for evidence that it might have been used to transport the other two missing children as well. Nothing from Descartes on the names of any women who might have accused Randy of sexual abuse in high school. Officer Hinchcliffe had managed to find the name of one registered sex offender on Stewart's mailing list but he was living in Florida and wore an ankle monitor. He was at home during the crimes.

As we came up on noon, I said, "Let's step back for a minute."

I filled Tobin in on the great white shark hunting pattern research that I'd considered on Friday when I was looking for the home base of the person behind the four recent abductions.

"What about Stewart's mailing list?" I asked. "Is there anything there that we might have missed?"

"I've been over it forward and backward, analyzed it every way I can. There's nothing there."

"Hmm . . . Well, what if that list isn't the one we're looking for?"

"What do you mean?"

"I mean, people buy and sell mailing lists all the time. What if Stewart bought or maybe sold that list to someone else? That might be the link we're missing here."

"Hinchcliffe knows that list best. I'll have him look into it, see if he can dig anything up—especially anything dealing with realtors."

"Good."

He called it in.

Then we contacted the parents of the three remaining children—Maggie Rivers, Andre Martin, and LeAnne Cordett—to see if any of them had been planning to move or had held showings or open houses prior to their children's abductions.

Just one family had—the Martins. But they didn't recognize Higgs's photo when we sent it to them. So even after all that, we weren't any closer to identifying who might've been scouting out the homes of potential victims.

After lunch, I hopped onto the interstate to head back to Christie's apartment.

On weekends like this when cases come at me from every side, I sometimes wish I had normal hours off. Some agents are free on weekends, with nine-to-five weekday hours.

In my job, things don't often play out like that—not to mention the fact that I have a hard time turning off cases once they crawl into my head.

Occupational hazard.

Something I needed to work on.

On the drive I called my dad.

He and Mom lived in Denver and I didn't see them much except for the times I was able to sneak out there for the holidays or for some rock climbing.

Now as we spoke, I found myself struggling to say the two things that you should tell your father on a day like this: that you're thankful for him and that you love him.

Instead I simply said I hoped he was having a good day. He asked me about baseball, which I don't follow, and then he told me about how well the Rockies were doing and I didn't know where to go with any of that.

Because of case confidentiality, I couldn't really talk about my job, and since my future with Christie was quite likely in flux, I didn't want to get into that either.

That didn't leave us a lot of common ground, and we ended up circling back to baseball and how much he hated the Yankees. I wasn't sure if they actually played the Rockies or not, but either way I listened to his rant without interrupting.

Before I knew it, we were saying good-bye and getting

ready to end the call. "Hang on," I said. "Dad, I love you."

Silence on the line, then, "I love you too, Pat."

After we hung up, I realized that now I just needed to sort out if I could—or should—say those words to Christie.

But did I love her? Or did I only desire to be in love?

Right now I wasn't certain. And I wasn't even sure how to tell the difference.

++++

That morning, Francis had been able to get on Tor.

He'd promised the agent that he would look for files with masks, and so he'd started with what he knew: the masks, the Final Territory, and the video containing the missing boy's backpack.

He also searched for any other files that might have had the letters *FT* embedded in them or digitized in the background, and he looked for other instances of the hash values for that file with the backpack. In the end, apart from a few scattered references to someone named Blake, he didn't come up with anything.

He didn't know if Blake was a first name or a last one, but he figured he could at least contact Agent Bowers tomorrow morning and share that much with him.

Before closing up his laptop, just out of curiosity, Francis went to Krazle, logged in to his account, and read through the dozen or so messages from graciousgirl4 asking him where he was and why he wasn't replying. Had she done something? Was it something she said? Didn't he want to chat anymore?

On the one hand he wanted to reply, to reassure her that it wasn't her fault, but on the other hand he felt like doing so would have somehow been a betrayal of his feelings for Skylar.

He closed the tab without responding.

Instead he practiced balloon animals. The how-to book he'd checked out of the library explained how to make twenty different animals. Some were a lot more complicated and required multiple balloons twisted together. He stuck with the simpler ones, but truthfully, even those were a challenge for him.

At last, taking a small bag of the balloons and the book along with him, he left to meet Skylar at St. Stephen's Research Hospital to visit Derek, the boy whose posters he had put up just last week.

53

Christie was making some falafel burgers for a midafternoon lunch for herself and Tessa, who must have been in her room, when I came in.

"Did you eat?" she asked.

"I grabbed something earlier." I set down my things and gave her a kiss. "How are you doing?"

"Good."

"How was church?"

"It was nice." She flattened out one of the burgers. "I guess."

"You guess?"

"I'm not sure if I agreed with the sermon, but it made me think."

"Now you've got me curious."

"First, how did it go? The things you were looking into with Tobin?"

"The pattern on the rug is starting to take shape."

"The rug?"

I explained the analogy.

"Ah. Makes sense."

"So now, what was this thought-provoking sermon about?"

"Temptation." She sprinkled some spices on the burgers, flipped them, then put a slice of pepper jack cheese on hers.

"Okay, and?"

"Here." She handed me the spatula. "Watch these for me." She had the habit of taking notes in her Bible rather than on another sheet of paper or in a notebook, and now she dug it out.

"The pastor called the sermon 'Manacled Hearts.'" She was flipping to the New Testament. "There's a Bible verse in James that says basically that people are tempted when they're dragged away by their own evil desires and enticed. Then, after those desires have conceived, they give birth to sin; and sin, when it's fully grown, well, it gives birth to death."

I found the imagery profound—what is conceived in evil develops into sin and eventually gives birth to death. The counterposition of giving birth to death was striking.

"What didn't you agree with?"

"He said you can step out of the cycle anytime, but the longer you let evil desires lead you around, the stronger their chains on you become."

I actually agreed with that.

Our previous discussion concerning demons came to mind.

This verse, however, seemed to say that temptation came from our own desires rather than being something we can blame on the devil. But either way, whether the temptation came from another source or emerged from within, there was no denying that we're all tempted to do things we know we shouldn't do, and the more we give in to them, the more power they exert over us.

Chained souls.

Manacled hearts.

Sounded pretty spot-on to me.

For example, regarding this current case, people often get drawn into porn one mouse click, one seemingly innocent image, at a time. After a while, though, the tamer images aren't enough, don't satisfy them anymore, and they turn to more and more deviant images or videos.

And the chains don't discriminate. You'll find truckers, doctors, teachers, rabbis, cops, the wealthy, the poor, all races, all ages, none of that matters.

I thought of the pedophile Hal Lloyd again, as I had the other day during Tobin's briefing.

Talk about manacled hearts. Lloyd had been drawn in, not only to the images, but to reenacting the violent and twisted sexual acts he saw online.

And now he was serving a twenty-year sentence at the Albany Federal Penitentiary.

"And you don't agree?" I said, getting back to the conversation with Christie.

"I don't agree that we can step out of the cycle anytime—at least not by ourselves."

I anticipated where she was going with this. "So you're saying we need God's help."

"I believe we're born with chains and it takes more than just a concerted effort on our own part to shrug them off."

So how much do we need God to break us free from our own evil desires, and how much responsibility do we have for doing it on our own? God's sovereignty versus human accountability. Some of history's deepest thinkers have spent their lives grappling with that conundrum.

I didn't have the sense that we were going to resolve it this afternoon.

I slid the falafel burgers onto a plate and shifted the

discussion away from temptation and its implications. "So, how's Tessa? You told me your talk with her didn't go as well as you'd hoped it would."

"She's giving me the silent treatment. She's been in her room all day. When I asked her if she was sulking, she told me, 'If you have to ask, then the answer is obvious.'"

"You think maybe she's just studying for her exams?"

"I doubt it. She doesn't need to. School is easy for her. I wish I could remember half of what that girl does."

Christie found two buns, then turned to the fridge. "I thought maybe if I made falafel for her it might help thaw things out between us."

"Do you have an avocado?"

She took one out of the vegetable crisper. "Great minds."

"If that doesn't start the thawing, I'm not sure what will. After all, the way to a girl's heart is through an avocado."

"I'm not sure that's quite how the saying goes, but let's hope it does the trick in this case."

While she took the food to Tessa, I set up shop at the kitchen nook, spread out my papers, and went online.

Checking the Federal Digital Database, I found that the psychologist who consulted with the NYPD and had interviewed D'Nesh yesterday had posted the transcript of their conversation.

I studied it and took careful note of what the boy had to say.

D'Nesh mentioned that most of the people who were with him wore masks the whole time except, as it turned out, the two men from Romanoff's house—Muhammad El-Sayed and Garrett Higgs—who were primarily in charge of transporting the children from one place to another.

Dr. Perrior: "Can you tell us about the other place where they took you?"

D'Nesh: "We had hoods. They made us wear hoods over our heads when they drove us around, but there were pillows on the walls."

Dr. Perrior: "Pillows on the walls?"

D'Nesh: "They looked like pillows, but they weren't really pillows. I saw 'em when they took off the hood."

Dr. Perrior: "What does that mean, D'Nesh? Pillows that weren't really pillows?"

D'Nesh: "I don't know. And there were windows where they watched us. Are the other kids okay?"

Dr. Perrior: "We're doing everything we can to help them."

I read the entire transcript, then, in preparation for tomorrow morning's briefing, updated the case files with what Tobin and I had discovered last night and earlier today at his house.

54

With Skylar by his side, Francis knocked on the door to Derek's room.

Skylar had brought along a small paper bag and hadn't shown Francis what was inside it. "It's just something I made for Derek," she told him cryptically. "You'll see what it is."

"Come in," Derek called.

They entered together.

There was nothing particularly memorable about this hospital room. It had the prerequisite mechanical bed, a couple of chairs, a television mounted on the wall, medical apparatuses, a window with heavy drapes that could be used to shut out the daylight when desired.

In this case, though, a cluster of cards surrounded the five stuffed animals that lounged together on the counter beneath the window.

"Hello, Derek," Francis said.

Derek sat up on the bed, his bald head glaring slightly from the overhead light. The last time Francis had been here, the ten-year-old had told him he should bring sunglasses next time so he wouldn't get blinded, and when Francis asked if he really wanted him to, Derek had needed to explain that he was only joking.

"Hey, Mr. Edlemore."

Francis had told him more than once that he could call him by his first name, but Derek kept reverting to the last name just to be polite, since, as he noted last time, his mom had taught him not to call grown-ups by their first names. So Francis didn't push things.

"This is my friend Miss Shapiro," Francis said.

She smiled. "Hi, Derek."

"Hi."

"I brought you something."

She gave him the paper bag. Derek opened it and drew out a beaded bracelet. The multicolored beads were threaded onto a tawny leather cord.

"I tried to make it look nice for a guy," Skylar told him. "I didn't use any girlie beads or anything, but—"

"You *made* it?"

"Yes."

"It's awesome." Derek tried to tie it onto his wrist one-handed, but when he fumbled with it, Skylar leaned over and tied it for him.

"Thanks."

"Of course."

Francis asked Derek how he was doing, the boy told him fine, then Francis held up the bag of unblown-up balloons he'd brought.

"Do you want me to make you a dog?" he offered, since that was the one he'd practiced the most.

Derek shrugged, then asked Skylar, "What do you want him to make?"

"Oh, he can make something for me anytime. This one should be something special for you."

"But if he *was* gonna make you something, what would you want it to be?"

"I've always been partial to rabbits."

"That's what I want, then," Derek announced to Francis.

Though the book did offer step-by-step instructions for doing rabbits, Francis had only tried making them a few times. "You sure you don't want a dog?"

Derek folded his arms. "Nope. A rabbit."

"Okay. What color?"

"Pink."

"Pink? Really?"

"Yup."

"Okay. One pink rabbit coming up."

It took him a few attempts, but by consulting the book, Francis was finally able to pull it off.

Its ears weren't perfect and it was a bit lopsided, but Derek accepted it.

"It kinda looks like it got run over by a truck," the boy said.

"Thanks," Francis said.

You should make another one.

No, he was just joking.

It wasn't a joke, he—

"Just kidding. It's nice." Derek held it out to Skylar. "Here."

"Um . . ."

"I want you to have it."

Finally, she graciously accepted.

"*Now* you can make me a dog," Derek said to Francis.

"Okay."

While Francis worked on it, Skylar told Derek a joke: "How come there are no seven-foot snakes in the world?"

"I don't know. Why?"

"'Cause snakes don't have feet."

"Ha-ha. What happens when you run after a car?"

"Hmm. I don't know."

"You get exhausted. Get it? *Exhausted*?"

"And when you run in front of a car you get tired," she replied.

He smiled. "I like you, Miss Shapiro."

"I like you too, Derek."

Francis finished the dog for Derek and handed it to him.

"Show me how to do it," Derek said.

"Okay."

"But let's do rabbits instead of dogs."

"Whatever you want."

Half an hour later, when they had a pile of half-twisted rabbits and accidentally burst balloon pieces strewn across the floor, Derek told them he was getting kinda tired. "They gave me some medicine before you came. It makes me sleepy."

Skylar leaned over and gave Derek a gentle hug. "It was nice to meet you."

"Are you gonna come back?"

"Sure. I promise."

Derek smiled and settled back on his bed. "Don't forget your rabbit."

She held it up to prove that she had it. "I won't."

As Francis and Skylar were leaving the hospital, he said to her, "You were great in there. You're good with kids."

"Thanks. I don't know what it means that I still like the jokes I heard in third grade. I guess I never quite grew up."

Tell her that you like that about her.

No! Then she'll think you're calling her immature.

"He liked you," Francis said. "Derek did."

"Do you come here much?"

"Whenever I can."

"Not too many people would visit kids with cancer and make them balloon animals on their days off from work. You're a sweet man, Francis."

She took his hand.

When she touched him he felt a rush of adrenaline and fire that he never wanted to end.

They walked toward the subway station entrance and he asked if he could see her again tomorrow afternoon at the Mystorium and she said sure, that would be nice.

She was still holding his hand.

They arrived at the top of the stairs.

He liked it that she held his hand.

He liked it that she hadn't let go.

Then, rather than say good-bye to him, Skylar asked if he would like to come over to her place for a little while, just to hang out or talk—if he wanted to, only if he wanted to, or if he wasn't doing anything else, 'cause she didn't want to keep him from anything he might need to do.

But he was too nervous to say yes and so he politely declined.

"Sure. Okay." It sounded like she was both embarrassed and disappointed. "I'll see you tomorrow, though, right?"

"See you tomorrow."

He gave her his email address at work and told her to let him know if her plans changed, then he offered her a hug like he had the other day and she reached up and gave him a swift kiss on the cheek when they were done.

"That's for being so nice to that boy," she said, then turned and disappeared down the steps.

Francis nearly floated home.

He kept replaying those last few moments with her—holding her hand, the invitation to her place, the hug, the kiss.

He thought of just how much he enjoyed being with her, being near her.

Though he barely knew her, she'd already brought out something in him that was right and true and that he didn't have when he was on his own. It was like he could actually be himself—and that he could even somehow be *more* himself than when he was *by* himself.

Next time she asks me to go to her place, I'm going to say yes.

If there is a next time. If she wants to see you again after tomorrow.

Stop it! She will. We had fun.

When he got home, Francis looked on Krazle to see if Skylar had a profile, if he could friend her, maybe chat with her that way.

He found her page and sent a friend request under his real name rather than Jared4life73, because they were friends, right? And if you're friends in real life, why wouldn't you be friends on Krazle too?

55

Monday, June 18

The briefing started promptly at nine o'clock.

Jodie was there, as were the other joint task force members from the NYPD and FBI who were working this case. The police chief and several officers from Princeton, New Jersey, where Romanoff's house was, also joined us.

Assistant Director DeYoung came too, and, to my surprise, even Maria Aguirre, the Office of Professional Responsibility lawyer, showed up. Perhaps she was interested in what I would have to say about the second shooting incident I was involved in over the course of less than a week.

Last Thursday, Tobin had indicated to his team that they were going to meet again Monday morning. He'd also made the grooming video available for them to watch over the weekend, and, according to our records, nearly all of them had done so.

However, in light of what'd happened on Friday, the entire tone of today's briefing was different. Now, rather than being informative in a general sense, it was specifically focused on what had gone down on Friday and what we'd all learned over the weekend.

There was a lot to cover. We dove right in.

Tobin summarized what he and I had dug up, highlighting how we'd identified the person of interest who'd been caught driving away from his home on the night of Adrienne's abduction eight years ago as Garrett Higgs, the man who'd been shot by the unknown assailant in Romanoff's house.

Then he pointed out the connection of how the other eighteen deaths were linked. "The cases are all intertwined. My daughter's, the current abductions we're looking into, the deaths of Wooford, Stewart, and McReynolds."

Chief O'Toole from Princeton looked skeptical. "And you're basing this simply on the fact that the children were all kept alive after they were abducted?"

"In nearly ninety percent of nonfamily abductions, the children are killed within the first forty-eight hours. The odds of a series of crimes like this being *unrelated* are astronomical."

"But you're talking about abductions involving different-aged children in a dozen states over the course of a decade—not to mention the two recent suicides." O'Toole consulted the notes we'd handed out. "Some of the children were strangled, others stabbed, one was shot."

"We're not saying that all the children were necessarily killed by the same person," Tobin replied.

"Then what are you saying?"

"That the children were killed by the same group."

"The Final Territory?"

"That's our working theory, yes."

"With all due respect, Detective, I think your personal interest in this case has clouded your judgment."

I spoke up: "Then it's clouded mine as well."

Everyone looked my way. The chief gave me an especially icy glare. "What action steps would you propose?"

I counted them off on my fingers as I listed them.

"One: Romanoff—we need to locate him. He's the key to finding those three remaining missing children and he can lead us to the Final Territory. Two: realtors—see if any of the eighteen families had open houses before their children were taken. Three: locate known associates, and check occupations and residences of Garrett Higgs. Four: Tribaxil—Either Randy McReynolds took it himself or it was administered to him. In either case, someone obtained it. I want to know how hard it is to get, where it's distributed, and where you might be able to get it on the street. And five: finish processing the lab results from the deaths of Stewart and McReynolds last week."

Assistant Director DeYoung handed out assignments to team members.

When he was done, I went on to explain the geoprofile to everyone, and as I got into the spatial analysis and the kernel density interpolation I could see their eyes start to glaze over. "Okay, let me put it this way: taking all the locations into account, studying the timing of the abductions and the sites where the bodies were found, we're going to be looking for a different location other than Romanoff's house as the home base for this crime series."

"But I thought that's where things pointed?" Maria Aguirre said.

"For the current crimes, yes. But that was before I had all the information about the timing of the previous abductions and the states where their bodies were found. Note how they move south as the year gets cooler."

"What does that mean?" Chief O'Toole's curiosity was touched with cynicism. "Our guy was migrating south for the winter?" He seemed to say it as a joke, but no one laughed.

The guy was really starting to get on my nerves.

"It means that whoever was responsible might have worked a seasonal job, heading south as winter rolls in and then back up north again in the spring."

"A seasonal job?" Officer Hinchcliffe asked. "Like what?"

"Landscaping or construction, for instance."

"Building the homes of the victims?"

"The timing doesn't work for that, but seeing if any of Higgs's friends worked seasonal jobs would be a place to start."

He offered to look into it.

The conversation tilted toward the Final Territory.

Tobin took the floor again. "The people who run international human trafficking organizations are incredibly well funded, often reside in countries that don't have extradition treaties with the West, and are experts at using Tor and at covering their tracks. They know the Dark Web's hidden corners and back alleys and they capitalize on that knowledge. Some of these groups cross from child porn trading to hosting live molestation of children."

DeYoung asked, "What do we know for sure about this one?"

"Very little, definitively," Tobin admitted. "We're looking for a private site, a secure, closed online community. It's likely we'll need to find someone to invite us to join it. They'll have encrypted SMTP servers."

"So how do we get invited to one of them?"

"It's not easy. There's usually a pretty extensive vetting process. There's a whole online culture that you have to be able to navigate and understand. They're good at weeding out newbies and law enforcement officers who might be trying to infiltrate their groups. A common membership requirement is that you have to upload a certain number of files or videos to their collection."

Ms. Aguirre put the pieces together. "So that makes sense, then, when you hear about someone being arrested with a couple hundred thousand images or videos on his computer—like the Wonderland Club or others similar to them."

"Yes. In most Western nations it's illegal for law enforcement officers to possess or distribute child pornography."

"Makes it pretty tough to infiltrate those groups."

"It does, because unless you share those images, the site's administrator won't give you the access credentials to download their material or communicate with other group members. And once you've posted them, you're facing jail time. Depending on the nature of the images or videos you upload, you could be looking at life in prison."

The more Tobin spoke, the more an idea took shape in my mind about how we might be able to move forward on this.

In total, the briefing went nearly two hours.

After we'd closed things up and the team members were rising to head off to their assignments, I said to him, "We need to talk to someone who knows his way around Tor. Not someone from law enforcement. Someone who knows those back alleys and hidden corners you were talking about."

"But how are you going to get access to one of these communities without uploading images or videos of child pornography?"

"By getting someone to help us."

"Who?"

"A person who's done it before."

"And you have someone in mind?"

"Yes. Hal Lloyd." During the briefing I'd pulled up his file and now I spun my laptop toward Tobin so the screen faced him.

"He was a computer consultant that Cyber called on sometimes," I said. "Turned out he was as perverted at using the Internet as he was gifted at navigating it. I knew the agent who originally worked his case. They found more than ten thousand images of child pornography on Lloyd's computer but suspected he'd cached a lot more that they were never able to find on the Dark Web. He was arrested for propositioning an eleven-year-old girl. They found out he'd also molested an eight-year-old. If anyone can get us an invitation and log-in credentials to the Final Territory, it's him."

Assistant Director DeYoung and Ms. Aguirre were talking with each other in the corner. She glanced my way and I sensed that they were talking about me.

Tobin read off some of the charges against Lloyd. "Two counts of lewd or lascivious exhibition, four counts of transmitting images harmful to a minor, using a computer to solicit a child for sex, contributing to the delinquency of a minor . . . Unlawful sexual conduct with a minor . . . Criminal child molestation . . . This guy's a real piece of work. How much time did he get?"

"He was sentenced to twenty years."

"So, maybe he serves ten or twelve with good behavior?"

"Yeah." I hated the way the system worked. "Maybe." So far he'd been in for three.

"And why would Lloyd be willing to help us?"

"I'm still working on that."

"So where is he? Rikers?"

"Albany Federal Penitentiary."

DeYoung left, but Ms. Aguirre was watching me from across the room. When I made eye contact with her, she started walking my way.

Great.

"That's a bit of a drive," Tobin noted.

"Probably three hours or so, depending on traffic. I'll head up by myself."

"No. I'm coming along. I want to talk to him too. When are visiting hours?"

"I'm a federal agent. They'll let us in as soon as I ask them to."

"I like the sound of that." He pulled out his phone. "Let me make a couple calls first, clear my plate."

When Tobin stepped away to do that, Ms. Aguirre saw her chance and addressed me. "Agent Bowers."

"Ms. Aguirre."

"Do you have a moment?"

"Actually, I was just on my way out."

"We need to talk."

"Now's not good. As I said, I'm about to take off."

"With Detective Cavanaugh?"

"Yes."

"First thing in the morning, then. Eight thirty. I'll be in my office."

Something to look forward to.

"I'll see you then," I said.

She strode away, her heels click-clattering briskly against the floor.

Tobin returned. "What was that about?"

"We're going to have a little sit-down tomorrow morning," I said. "I'll probably get a reprimand."

"Well, at least you know the ropes."

That was the same phrase Jodie had used with me last week. "You've been talking with my partner."

"That is possible."

I might have glimpsed a smile.

He summarized his phone conversation: the realtor who'd been in charge of his home was no longer with the firm, and when he followed up with her, he found that she was living in North Carolina and had no records of who might have attended an open house eight years ago in New Jersey.

So, a dead end.

Before leaving, I had some of the guys from Cyber download onto my laptop the special browser needed to surf on Tor.

While they were working on that, I checked my email and saw a note that Mr. Edlemore over at the ICSC had found some references to Blake. There wasn't anything specific for us to follow up on, just a few more arrows pointing in his direction.

Tobin and I contacted the Albany Federal Penitentiary warden and had him send us Lloyd's prison records, which would include his visits to the infirmary, time in solitary confinement, and the specification of any additional charges that might have been leveled against him since his incarceration.

A little light reading for the trip.

Finally, we touched base with Jodie, who was heading off with Agent Descartes to the investment firm where Ivan Romanoff, the man who owned the house in Princeton where I'd found Lily and D'Nesh, worked. They were going to talk with his coworkers to try to find out anything they could that would help us zero in on his current location.

Then Tobin and I climbed into my car and left for the Albany Federal Penitentiary.

56

First thing that day after getting to his desk, Francis had called the psychologist whom Dr. Perrior had recommended to him to find out if she could get him in sometime this week.

It went to an answering service, and he left his name and number, requesting that she call him back as soon as possible.

All morning and all through lunch he'd been distracted thinking about Skylar.

She hadn't responded to his friend request on Krazle.

It might've been that she just hadn't checked her account.

Or it might have been that she didn't want to be his friend.

Now, at his afternoon coffee break, as he kept an eye out for her to come into the Mystorium, he thought of her and of graciousgirl4.

There was something about spending time with an actual person, not just chatting with someone online, that made it seem even more real than an online relationship.

Graciousgirl4 is just someone I've chatted with, that's all.

No, she's more than that. You know she is.

But I like Skylar better.

Why don't you meet graciousgirl4 and see which of them you like more?

I don't know.

All you have to do is meet her. You don't need to do anything else, just go and meet her. See her. Say hi. She told you she was eighteen.

I know, but what if she's not? What if she's younger?

Then you just leave. Walk away. You're not the kind of person to take advantage of a teenager.

No, I'm not.

But if she is old enough, then you can maybe spend some time with her. Get to know her a little bit better. After all, what does age have to do with love? Who's to say that—

But I'm not in love with her. And what about Skylar? I like Skylar. And she's my age, or at least closer to my age, but—

Go online and look up graciousgirl4. Just to see. Then you can be done with her. Tonight, at home, you know how to do it. Check, and then it'll all be over and you can move on with Skylar.

No, it wouldn't be right.

You just need to see her before you end this.

I shouldn't be thinking these things. I shouldn't be wondering these things.

You haven't done anything. You wouldn't do anything.

But how can you say that? I might. Anyone is capable of making a mistake. If they're in the wrong place at the wrong time. It can happen to me. It happens to people every day.

Not to you. It won't happen to you.

Thoughts wrestling with each other.

Tugging him back and forth.

Skylar didn't come in the door of the coffeehouse and

Francis wondered if maybe, since he hadn't said yes to going over to her place yesterday, she might be feeling hurt or offended or might have thought he wasn't interested in her.

He hadn't heard from her all day: no calls, no texts. Maybe she'd changed her mind about him, about getting together today.

That's why she didn't reply to your friend request on Krazle.

If he lost her, all he had was graciousgirl4.

He remembered telling Dr. Perrior last week that it was like there was a line in the sand.

To see it is one thing.

To know it's there, to approach it and stand there, maybe sliding your toe up to it, or maybe kneeling down and tracing it with your finger.

That's one thing.

And that's what you've been doing with your chats, Francis. You've been seeing how close you can get without stepping over.

This far and no farther.

This close and no closer.

Safe on the side you're supposed to be on.

If there was anyone who should've known that, it was him. With what he did at work. With all he'd seen, yes, he should.

Yes, he did.

So that was one thing.

Seeing the line.

And then there was crossing it.

He knew the tactics abusers use to get close to children.

Yes. It would be possible for him to see graciousgirl4 even if he didn't set up a time to meet her.

Just back-trace her IP address and turn on her comput-
er's camera. You can do it without making the light go on.
Just get a glimpse of her. Then you'll be able to tell how old
she is. Then you can stop chatting with her.

But what about Skylar?

This'll be it. The last time with graciousgirl4.

I need to end things with her. I have Skylar now.

You don't have Skylar now. She doesn't know you. If she
knew you, she wouldn't like you. Not if she really knew you,
what you see, what you think, what you—

Stop!

It was ten minutes after two.

Skylar still hadn't come, hadn't texted.

She's not coming. She changed her mind. She doesn't like
you.

Okay, tonight.

Just to make the voice go away, just to make the questions go away.

Yes, tonight he would back-trace to graciousgirl4's IP
address, get his answers once and for all about her, and
then be done with her before he crossed the line for
good.

But that is crossing the line.

No, it's just finding out how wide it is.

If nothing else, at least those voices in his head would
stop. Then he could move forward getting to know Skylar better and maybe even visiting her place or inviting
her over to his.

Maybe they would even be together someday. He'd
never been with a woman before, never in that way. It was
something he wanted before he died, no matter how
soon or how far out that day might be.

As he was thinking about that, Skylar pushed open the
door, scanned the room, and as soon as she saw Francis,

she made a beeline for him and apologized, "I'm so sorry I'm late. Don't be mad. Were you waiting long? Oh, I hope you weren't waiting long."

"No. I just got here."

"Oh, good."

"It's good to see you."

"You too."

"Do you want some coffee?"

"Yes. Please."

While they ordered their drinks, she explained that she'd forgotten to charge her phone and it'd died and she'd missed the train she'd been hoping to catch and she would have let him know she was running late if she could have, but that she was glad he was here because she did want to see him today. She really did.

She didn't say anything about not accepting his friend request on Krazle.

He didn't bring it up.

Though he'd been looking forward to seeing her, now that she was here he was nervous too, because he'd been thinking about that other woman.

Skylar didn't know about graciousgirl4.

And she never needs to.

No, she didn't. And Skylar never needed to know about his chats either, or the things Francis sometimes thought of doing and the dark temptations he sometimes had to try so hard to resist when he was chatting with graciousgirl4 on Krazle.

Some things were best kept secret, especially when they might hurt someone else—so that's what he quietly told himself as Skylar recounted her day and her hectic trip across the city to see him.

57

On the drive to the prison, Tobin and I took turns alternating driving and looking through Hal Lloyd's records.

Now, only a few miles from the penitentiary, Tobin was at the wheel and I was perusing Lloyd's list of visitors over the last three years. One name jumped out at me: Jewel Vernett.

She was the woman who'd been living with him at the time of his arrest. Evidently, she'd stayed close to him over the years, visiting him every other Saturday like clockwork.

Flipping a few pages forward, I noted that Lloyd was currently in solitary confinement for having a shiv made out of a screwdriver found in his cell.

We arrived, parked, and went to the security checkpoint.

Normally, prison guards wouldn't allow anyone to take in a phone or a laptop when interviewing an inmate, but thankfully that didn't apply to federal agents or law enforcement officers, so we were in the clear.

However, we both did have to leave our weapons with the guards there at the checkpoint.

In most federal and state penitentiaries in the United

States, even though tower guards are armed with high-powered rifles, the prison staff who have daily contact with the inmates don't carry firearms—after all, it would be far too easy for prisoners to overpower someone, take his weapon, and use it against him or against other prisoners.

When someone is sent to prison for the crimes Lloyd had committed, the warden's office screens all their mail. They don't want to enable the prisoners, facilitate their fantasies, or give them a chance to relive their crimes. So, no pictures of children are allowed. No correspondence with minors.

Also, there's no Internet access for people like Lloyd, even though some advocacy groups claim that access to the Internet is "a basic human right."

Thankfully, the courts have rejected that argument.

At least so far they have.

Labeling Internet access as a basic human right would pave the way to requiring prisons to provide it to inmates, and that would have incalculable negative effects in contributing to criminal enterprises worldwide.

Unintended consequences.

But real, nonetheless.

As a result, Lloyd hadn't been online in three years.

Technology is advancing exponentially every year, so I wasn't sure he'd be able to get us the information we needed, but he'd been an expert at finding his way around the Dark Web in the past and I figured there was at least a fifty/fifty chance that he was going to be able to help us find the Final Territory.

We were led to a visiting room usually reserved for inmates to use when speaking with their lawyers.

The exchanges in these rooms were confidential, of course, but were filmed so that guards could monitor the conversations to make sure that nothing was passed from one person to another.

However, there was no audio recording of the rooms, and the lawyer was situated in such a way that his or her face wouldn't be visible to the camera so lip readers wouldn't be able to tell what he was saying to his client.

After we'd taken our seats on one side of the wide steel table that'd been bolted to the floor, two guards led Hal Lloyd into the room.

On the drive up here I'd seen his photo, but those pictures had all been taken during the trial or at his intake into this facility, and I could see that the last few years of prison life had not been kind to him.

He'd lost a lot of weight, fifty pounds at least, and his narrow face looked decidedly gaunt and bloodless. His nose had obviously been broken at least once while he was in here and it hadn't healed properly. A jagged scar that hadn't been present before his conviction trailed across his right cheek and down to his neck. The upper half of his left ear was missing. From the case files I knew it'd been bitten off.

They say that child molesters do not have an easy time of it in prison. Lloyd's injuries bore that out, and that wasn't even considering the other kinds of abuse he might have suffered in here.

Prison is hard enough on anyone.

But the last thing you'd want in here was ending up at the bottom of the totem pole.

Hal's hands were cuffed in front of him, standard-issue cuffs that both Tobin and I could have freed him from. When the guards positioned him in the chair across from us, they secured the center link of the handcuff chain to the table before exiting the room and leaving the three of us alone.

"Mr. Lloyd," I said, "I'm Special Agent Patrick Bowers with the FBI. This is Detective Cavanaugh."

Lloyd scrutinized me, then asked Tobin, "Who are you with?"

"NYPD."

"Neither of you two were at the trial, were you?"

"No," I said.

"Where's Ferguson?"

Donald Ferguson had been the agent in charge of the investigation that led to Hal's arrest. Donald had drowned in a boating accident last year.

"Agent Ferguson is no longer with the Bureau," I told him.

"Uh-huh." Lloyd's gaze shifted to the camera mounted in the corner of the room behind us. "And so, what is it that brings you gentlemen in here today?"

"We're currently investigating a website that provides footage of children under the age of twelve being molested." We weren't exactly sure what all the Final Territory provided, but I figured that phrasing things like that would get Lloyd's attention.

"And so you decided to come talk to me."

"Considering your background, we felt you might be able to offer us some assistance."

"Assistance."

"Yes."

"With what, exactly?"

Tobin answered, "With tracking down some people who deserve to be in solitary confinement even more than you do."

"I see. And what possible reason could I have for helping you? Wait, let me guess: The chance to see justice done? To do the right thing? Or maybe to protect some innocent little lambs from the big bad wolves? What's on the table here?"

"Detective Cavanaugh, can you go have them turn off the video cameras to this room?" I'd waited to make the request so Lloyd would know we weren't going to be filmed for the rest of our conversation.

"My pleasure."

Lloyd eyed Tobin as he left, then his somewhat wary gaze shifted to me again.

I said, "There's a site on the Dark Web we're trying to gain access to."

"Right, well, let's say I was to help you. What are you willing to offer me in exchange? You know how these things work. Tit for tat. How're you gonna scratch my back if I scratch yours?"

"I can put in a request to get you out of solitary confinement."

He turned his head to show me what was left of his chewed-off ear. "And what makes you think I would want that? Nobody eats me while I'm living alone."

"Right now you're stuck in a twenty-three forty-five and you don't want that long term. Take it from me. I've seen what it can do to people."

In prison lingo a "twenty-three forty-five" means that you're in solitary confinement for twenty-three hours and forty-five minutes in your cell—they would call it your "six by nine"—alone, and then you have fifteen minutes to shower.

Some prisons provide you an hour of exercise in a caged-in area outside. This one did not.

"Okay," he said, "here's what I want: I help you, I get my sentence reduced."

Deals like that are made all the time. For the right

testimony or information regarding a case, sentences are shortened or commuted, people get parole, probation, time served. But I didn't cut deals like that.

I shook my head. "That's not going to happen."

"Ferguson would've swung it for me. Without a reduced sentence, I have nothing more to say to you."

"As I said, that's not—"

"What happened to Ferguson, by the way?"

Tobin returned. "Video is off. It's just the three of us."

"He's dead, isn't he?"

I told Lloyd, "We know about Jewel Vernett."

He worked his jaw back and forth slightly but didn't respond.

"I see from your visitors list that you two have stayed close."

Lloyd still didn't answer, but I could tell I definitely had his attention.

"It isn't what's in it for you," I said to him, "it's what's in it for her. At the trial she said she had no knowledge of your online activity. She made that claim while she was under oath."

"And?"

"And Detective Cavanaugh and I have reason to believe that the prosecution didn't dig as deeply as they could have into verifying certain aspects of her testimony. What if I told you we have recently come upon some evidence that contradicts her claim?"

"What are you talking about?"

"Four years ago on November thirteenth at eleven fifty-two p.m. when you took pictures of your genitals to email to the eleven-year-old girl you were grooming for sex, there was a window behind you, but it was dark outside."

"So?"

"The glass acted as a reflective surface, Hal, and guess whose reflection appears next to you in the background of the shot?"

He was quiet.

"Jewel was there with you when you were chatting with the children you abused, wasn't she? How involved was she in setting up your meetings with them? It was never clear who drove you to the—"

"Okay. That's enough."

"That photograph alone is enough to get her perjury, and if she's convicted of conspiring with you or taking you to the meets she'll get at least—"

"I said that's enough! What exactly do you want from me?"

"I want you to get me an invitation and access code to a site called the Final Territory."

He scoffed. "You're entering a world you know nothing about." He tapped his forehead. "There's no delete key up here, Agent Bowers. You can't unsee what you see. Once the images are in there, you'll never be able to shut them out."

Tobin leaned forward. "On the drive here I looked over the record of your visits to the infirmary. You and the doctors in there must be on a first-name basis by now, huh?"

Lloyd said nothing.

"Do you know Carlton Lyota? Over in cellblock four?" Tobin studied Lloyd's face. "Yeah, I thought so. Everyone knows Carlton. We go way back, Carl and I. Did you know I'm the one who put him in here? I saw in your prison files that you've had a few run-ins with Mr. Lyota over the years. Do you know how easy it would be to let word get around that you were visiting with us? That you were helping the Feds and the NYPD with a case? You know what happens to prison snitches. When Carlton hears about that, how long do you think it'll be before you're—"

"They would never allow me access to a computer anyway, so I couldn't help you even if I wanted to."

"No, they wouldn't." I pulled out my laptop. "But I would."

He gazed at it intently. His tongue licked across his upper lip. I wasn't sure if he was consciously doing it or not.

"The video camera in here is turned off," I reminded him. "It's just the three of us. There's no one watching."

"And you'll leave Jewel out of it?"

"I give you my word."

"Uncuff me so I can type."

"Make do."

58

There wasn't any Wi-Fi in here, but I was able to use my phone as a hotspot to get online.

"Do you have The Tor Browser?" Lloyd asked as he positioned the computer in front of him.

It was quite a name: The The Onion Router Browser. Didn't quite roll off the tongue as well as Safari, Firefox, or Chrome.

"It's on there but I haven't used it yet."

"Well, let's see how much things have changed over the last couple years."

He used the browser while also pulling up a script box at the bottom of the screen in which he started to enter code. Most of it was indecipherable to me.

The browser window didn't look too much different from a typical web browser for navigating the Surface Web, but the script box didn't look like anything I'd seen before. I wasn't sure if it came with the browser or if it was something he'd downloaded to help him find what he was looking for.

To make sure he didn't access any images of children, I stood over his shoulder monitoring every page he went to.

Lloyd muttered to himself as he typed, mentioning

some of the things Tobin had covered in the briefing earlier, "You gotta know how to navigate through this world. You don't use the right terms, the right lingo, the right phrases, they'll sniff you out in an instant."

That's why we were here. Because Lloyd didn't smell any different than they did.

After about twenty minutes, he nodded. "Okay, now comes the tricky part. They've changed things around a bit. They're going to try to vet me, see if I'm law enforcement."

"Be honest. Tell them you're not."

"Yeah, I will, but as far as the Final Territory, I still haven't found anything specific. I might know of someone, though, who can help you. Name's Blake."

"Blake?" Tobin said. "What do you know about him?"

"Not much. Just that he's been around for a while. Used to be based out in Los Angeles. I don't even know if that's his real name. If he's not in prison these days, he might be the best guy in the area to help you out."

Lloyd studied the screen thoughtfully. "I had an online identity that I never told Ferguson about. Obviously, it hasn't been used in a while, but let's see if it still holds any currency."

He skillfully navigated past a series of firewalls and screening questions meant to identify people in law enforcement.

"And here we go."

"Did you find the Final Territory?"

"Something called Flute. Watch this."

He hit the spacebar and the word "flute" morphed into Final Territory, with the *f* and the *l* turning into the first and last letters of "Final." The *u* disappeared, and the *te* formed the first two letters of "Territory."

Flute.

Just like the Pied Piper.

"If you want me to keep going," Lloyd said, "I'm just letting you know—from here on out there are going to be images coming up. Pictures you're probably not gonna want to see."

"Even before we access the site?" I asked.

"Think of it as allowing people to window-shop. The pictures are there to keep you clicking."

Manacled hearts. Here it was, right in front of me, a system that championed freedom of expression but that ended up only adding to people's chains.

Tobin was more used to this kind of material than I was, and he turned the screen so Lloyd couldn't see it, then took over at the keyboard. "We move forward, but I'll take care of it."

He went through the questions, replying to them by using the phrases and jargon Lloyd told him to use.

As Tobin typed, I studied the stoic look on his face and wondered what was going through his mind.

He worked these kinds of investigations on a weekly basis, but still, it had to be tough, and I wondered what effect seeing those images might have on him, what effect it might have on anyone.

Maybe he'd found a way to shut it out. Some people do.

Others get jaded.

But based on the depth of love he still had for Misty and Adrienne, I didn't think that was the case with him.

No, he wasn't jaded.

Tobin was focused.

Finally, he finished with the data entry and Lloyd asked, "Is the screen clear? I mean, of pictures?"

"Yes," Tobin told him.

"Let me see it one more time."

"Why?"

"I need to type in an access code."

"Tell it to me."

"This one I'll need to do. Agent Bowers can watch me, but I can't let you enter these codes."

"And why is that exactly?"

"Let's just say it's for personal reasons."

"That's not good enough."

"It's gonna have to be."

Tobin debated things for a moment, then dialed the screen in Lloyd's direction and I made sure no images came up as he entered the alphanumeric password.

"There." He slid the laptop toward me. "It's done."

"Now what?" Tobin asked.

"Now we wait."

"How long?"

"They'll get back to you when they get back to you. If this worked—and that's a big if—and if you're accepted—and that's an even bigger one—well, if all that happens, they'll send access credentials to that email address I gave you. Then you'll need to come up with a way to pay that matches my online identity. But I'm telling you, these are people you do not want to mess with."

"I think I'll be alright," I said.

"Well, at least I gave them what they wanted. They'll be happy about that."

"What do you mean? What does that mean you gave them what they wanted?"

"They require fifteen thousand images for membership. I sent them a link to my archives. There's more than enough to get you in. Now—"

"What?" I gasped.

"It's done, Agent Bowers. I knew you wouldn't say yes to it. But it's the only way you're going to—"

I spun the laptop around to face him again. "Undo it."

"It's not undoable. The request was sent in. They have access to the pictures. Now, though, at least you'll be able to report them to the ICSC. Without coming here today you never would have found 'em or been able to report 'em, so you should actually be thanking me. It won't do any good to tell these people, 'Oh, hey, you know what? I changed my mind. Please don't look at those photos after all.' You're in this for keeps now, Agent Bowers."

Before doing anything else, I emailed the link to Francis Edlemore at the ICSC so he could analyze the images, but just the thought that Lloyd had used my computer to send a link to over fifteen thousand files of child porn made me physically ill.

However, there was some truth to what he'd said. Without this visit today, those images would have remained hidden deep on Tor and we wouldn't have been able to sort them, record their hash values, and search the web for other instances where they might have appeared. If we could identify offenders related to the images, we might end up saving children from molestation. Maybe some exploited children would be helped by this in the end.

"Okay," Lloyd said. "I did my part. Now you leave Jewel alone."

"No one will be contacting her," Tobin replied. "And no one will know you were here talking with us today. Not Carlton, not anyone."

"What about solitary confinement?" I asked Lloyd. "Do you want in or out?"

"I'll get out when I get out." He cocked his head at me. "You never answered my question, Agent Bowers. How was Ferguson killed?"

"What makes you think he was killed?"

Lloyd scoffed. "You really have no idea who they are, do you? What you're getting into here?"

"I never know what I'm getting into. Goes with the job."

"Yeah, and how far are you willing to follow this?"

"All the way to the kids who've been hurt. All the way down the rabbit hole."

"Uh-huh. Well, it's gonna take you places you won't want to go."

I've already been places I don't want to go, I thought.

Tobin spoke up, "Did you ever hear of a girl taken in New Jersey eight years ago?"

"There are a lot of girls taken."

"She was five. Caucasian. Blond hair."

"Yeah, and?"

"Whoever took her kept her alive for a year and a half before killing her. Her name was Adrienne."

"Aha." A slight grin. "She was yours, wasn't she, Detective?"

Tobin leaned forward. "She was."

"I see." Lloyd's gaze went to the camera behind us, the one Tobin had told the guards to turn off.

"Do you know anything about her abductors?" Tobin asked him.

"Nothing pops to mind."

"Get the guards, Agent Bowers," Tobin said. "Tell them we're done in here."

"Are you sure you're—"

"Go on, Patrick." His eyes were glued on Lloyd.

I left them alone. As the door was closing behind me I heard Tobin asking Lloyd about Adrienne.

It took me a few minutes to locate the guards, who were playing cards in a room down the hall. As I approached the door, one of them said, "I heard five billion a year."

"But how do they know that?" the other guy replied. "It's not like the child porn industry reports its income or pays taxes. And if so many videos and images are free, where's the money coming from?"

I knocked on the door, which was already ajar. "Excuse me. We're finished with Lloyd."

A blank video screen on the desk gave testimony to the fact that Tobin had convinced them to shut off the camera in the room.

"Okay," the stouter guard said to me, then answered his friend, "Downloads, access to hidden content." He punched in some security codes and then a password in order to bring up the video. "Members-only areas, DVDs, phone sex, and pay-per-view and personalized videos."

"Personalized?" The slim guard set his cards facedown on the table and stood.

Okay, this was quite a conversation I'd interrupted here.

"'Customized' might be a better term for it." The video monitor was taking a moment to wake up. "You basically choose from a drop-down menu what you want the models—well, porn stars—to do, and then they'll film the scene for you. They'll even add your name in there if you want."

Man, I was glad I didn't have this job.

Or Tobin's.

When the monitor's screen finally came on, it showed Tobin standing over Lloyd, who'd been uncuffed and lay crumpled and motionless on the floor.

"What the hell?" the guard beside me exclaimed.

We raced down the hall and back to the interview room. I arrived first and wedged myself between Tobin and

Lloyd to separate them while the guards knelt to assist Lloyd, who was groaning.

"You better check the floor," Tobin said to the guards, his voice cool, impassive. "It's a little too polished. There's a slick spot over there."

When I put a hand on Tobin's shoulder he roughly shrugged it off.

"Lemme guess," the thin guard responded. "He slipped when you uncuffed him to get him ready for the transfer back to his cell."

"Precisely."

Lloyd was licking at his bloodied lip.

"That what happened?" the other guard asked Lloyd.

"Yeah," he said. "I slipped, just like the good detective said."

Tobin was quiet as we exited the prison and crossed the parking lot to the car.

I hit the unlock button on the key fob. "You alright?"

"I'm alright."

I took the driver's side as we climbed in. "What happened in there, Tobin?"

"After you left, he started telling me what he would do to a five-year-old girl if he had 'access' to her for a year and a half."

"And you lost it."

"No. If I'd lost it, he never would've gotten up from the floor again."

"Did you ask him about the Piper?"

"Yeah. I asked if he'd ever heard of him and he just looked me in the eye and said, 'What do you think?' That was all."

"Did he know anything about who might've taken Adrienne?"

"No. I asked him a couple different ways and he said no each time. That was it. Then you guys arrived."

I pulled out of the parking lot and drove in silence. I wasn't about to judge Tobin for taking his anger out on Lloyd. There was a time early in my career when my fist had found the jaw of a serial killer who was mocking the death of one of his victims. I broke that guy's jaw and I've never regretted it.

No, I couldn't condone what Tobin had done. But neither could I condemn him for doing it.

When we were merging onto the highway I said, "Why would Lloyd have asked about how Ferguson was killed? His death was listed as accidental. We need to find out the circumstances surrounding it, if there was ever any suspicion of foul play."

"We'll look into it. Was any of that true, by the way? What you said in there? About Jewel's reflection in the window of the chat? I saw the same photos you did on the way over here. I didn't even notice it."

"The darkened window was true."

"But not the image of Jewel?"

"No."

"So you made that up?"

"I speculated."

"But what if you'd been wrong?"

"I would have speculated something else."

"On the spot?"

"Sometimes it's the best place to do it," I replied. "What about you? What you said about Carlton Lyota?"

"Never heard of him before today. On the drive up here I saw his name on the warden's reports."

"Yeah." I remembered that report. "He was the guy who chewed off half of Lloyd's ear."

"Exactly."

"But you didn't put him away?"

"No."

"So you made that up?"

"I speculated that Lloyd wouldn't want another run-in with him."

"I like the way you think, Tobin."

"The feeling's mutual, my friend."

59

On the drive back to the city, we touched base with Jodie and found out that she and Descartes had met with Ivan Romanoff's boss and learned that Romanoff had remotely logged in to his computer over the weekend to delete his files.

"I'm having Cyber look into it," she informed us.

"Still no word on his whereabouts?"

"No. And as far as seasonal jobs for Higgs, Hinchcliffe is still checking."

I dropped Tobin off at NYPD headquarters, where he'd left his car. Then, since it was already after office hours, I grabbed a quick bite at one of my favorite street vendors that sold chicken ranch bacon wraps and drove to Christie's place.

When I walked in, I got the impression that she and Tessa might have patched things up a bit because they were playing Exo-Skel IV with each other.

So.

Good.

A little mutual destruction to let off some steam.

I greeted them, then asked Tessa how her exams had gone.

"Fine. Whatever." She didn't look away from the screen,

where she was engaged in a firefight with some hostiles. "They were stupid. Easy and stupid."

I put my things away.

Both Christie and Tessa seemed engrossed in the game, and since I'd been sitting around all day in meetings or in the car, I needed to stretch out and get some exercise in, and I knew just the place to do it.

At the climbing gym where I was a member.

The Hangout.

Despite the sting in my arm that was recovering from the knife wound and the minor injury in my side, it felt good to climb again, to enter that delicate dance of balance and strength, to disappear into the mental space of being one with the rock, even though, here, it was only artificial. Pulling plastic, they say.

After an hour or so I returned to the apartment. Christie was sitting by herself on the couch, quietly reading.

She was into the Christian mystics and had even started to get me interested in them. Tonight she had one of her old volumes in front of her. When she closed it up and set it aside, I asked what she was reading.

"Some of the works of Hildegard of Bingen."

"Who's that?" I asked.

"Actually, Hildegard is one of my heroines. I can't believe I haven't told you about her. She was a composer, a writer, an artist, a healer. She's the first composer we have biographical information on."

"What—the first composer *ever*?"

"Yes. She was an abbess in Germany, collected books about medicine and herbs, and wrote music for the nuns to sing."

Admittedly, I hadn't read too much of the mystics' work so far, but from what I had read, I liked how they taught that the pathway to God was through love, not through theology; through an active faith lived out in the world, not a sterile faith that had no roots in relationships or in serving other people.

"Love without hands and feet to help a hurting world isn't love at all," one of them had said. I agreed.

"Tessa's in her room, writing in her journal," Christie explained.

"How'd the game go?"

"I don't know, exactly. We killed a lot of terrorists."

"That's always a good thing. So, how are things between you two?"

"Could be worse," she said, defaulting to a common saying from her native Minnesota. "How was the climbing gym?"

"Not as good as the real thing, but close enough to get me through until I can get to the crags again. At least it gave me a chance to think."

"About your case?"

"About us, actually."

"Ah. Us."

"Yes."

"And how about that? I've been thinking about us too."

"What did you come up with?"

"You first."

I took a breath. "Well, I think raising a daughter as a single mom here in the city must be terribly difficult. I think that if it was just a money issue, we could maybe live together—in the same apartment, I mean, share the space, the costs, just to save money . . . You'd still need to land another job, but maybe there'd be something you could find here that would help you—us—get by."

"So you're saying you think it would be best for me to stay?"

This was not going to be easy. "Honestly? No, I don't. I think it would be best for *me* if you stayed—but for Tessa, for you? When you're thinking about the long term of what's best for your family, if the money is right and the benefits and everything, it would probably be best for you to take this job in Omaha. Tessa has two more years of high school, so it's a good time to move if you need to. What's keeping you here, really? You don't have family in the city, you just work here. This isn't your life."

"She is."

"Yes."

"And you are."

"Well, I'm here, yes, but . . ."

"But?"

We're not a "we" yet, Christie, I thought, but I was worried how it would sound if I put it like that. "But we're not . . ." I was struggling here. "Being together is something we've both thought about, it may even be something we both want, but—"

"No, no, I understand."

Tell her you love her.

Do it, Pat. Say the words.

But are they true?

It wouldn't have been enough to just say that I liked her, but I didn't want to say that I loved her either because those words carried a promise that I wasn't sure I was ready to make.

I didn't want to deceive her or pressure her to commit to something she wasn't ready to commit to, so I kept my feelings to myself.

"Okay," I said. "Your turn."

"Tessa is my main concern, but I would never want you to think I'm involved with you just because I want what's best for her."

"I don't think that at all."

"Good. I will say, however, just out of honesty, that she's never had a father figure, a positive male role model— at least none that have stuck around for more than a month or two. I know she only has a couple years left being at home, but that's one of the reasons I want her to have a positive influence from a man now, before she moves out and goes to college, or decides to live on her own. That's not by any means the main reason I want to be with you, but it is something that's important to me."

"I would want that for her too," I said, "if I were you—I mean, I do want that."

A small smile. "I know what you mean."

"Right."

"As far as sharing a place, you remember what we talked about yesterday—temptation. I'm afraid moving in together might put pressure on our relationship, might bring up temptations that, well . . ."

"I hear you. I get that."

"I should tell you, Pat, they're flying me out on Sunday, the firm in Omaha is. I have some meetings on Monday."

"Oh. Okay."

"Tessa will be staying with a friend."

I wasn't aware that Tessa had any, but Christie might have been talking about one of her own friends. I didn't ask her to specify.

She went on, "It doesn't mean I've decided, it just means I'm keeping the option open. Just to see if there's the right kind of chemistry there for me to work with them."

"Yes, that makes sense," I said agreeably, but that feeling hit me again—the one of the ground under me quaking. I needed my footing, wasn't sure how to regain it.

"Listen, Pat, I know it's a lot to think about. I don't want this to get between us. I want it to be something we can sort out together."

"I want to help sort things out, I do, but right now I can't see myself moving out to Nebraska."

There it was.

I'd said it.

"Of course," she replied, "and it wasn't right of me to even bring that up."

"No more apologizing for trying to find a way for me to remain a part of your life."

"Agreed." Then she took my hand. "Come here."

I drew her into my arms. She held me tight, as if she were afraid I might slip from her life forever if she let go of me right now.

Then we kissed and it felt right and comfortable and the way things were supposed to be.

But they might not be this way for long if she decides to move.

I pushed that thought aside.

The longer I held her and the longer we kissed, the more I wanted to keep going. At last I said softly, "You remember when we were talking about temptation?"

"Uh-huh." She was breathing deeply, as deeply as I was.

"This would be one of those times."

"Yeah."

"If we keep this up I'm not going to want to stop."

She closed her eyes, took a long breath, then opened them again. "Yeah. Me too."

We continued looking deeply into each other's eyes for that fraction of a second that spoke volumes.

And then a little longer than that.

Neither of us pulled away.

"Okay, then," I said.

"Right."

We eased back from each other, even though it was clearly something neither of us wanted to do.

Yeah, it would be tough living with her if all we were doing was sharing finances. That was just not going to work.

Even though it wasn't late, she told me that she should probably be getting to bed and then went to take a bath first.

Oh man.

I felt like I could have used a cold shower.

There was a lot on my mind and I didn't expect that I would be able to get to sleep for a while, so, hoping it would help me relax, I grabbed a glass of wine. Then I went online and looked into Ferguson's death.

According to the official report, he was alone when he died. He'd been canoeing. When he didn't return home, a search team went looking for him and found his canoe overturned and his body floating in an eddy in the river.

What exactly happened was never established. The medical examiner's report listed drowning as the cause of death and labeled it accidental, but just like so many of the aspects of this case, it seemed like an all-too-convenient explanation.

I wondered what Ferguson might have known, if he might have been murdered, or if, maybe, I was starting to see conspiracies around every corner and if his death was really just an accident after all.

60

Francis checked Krazle to see if Skylar was his friend yet.

She wasn't.

While he was on the site, the voice came to him again: *Graciousgirl4 will be online at this time of night. You can do this, get it over with, and then move on.*

What if she's younger than eighteen? What then?

Then nothing. You're done with her. You move on.

But then I would have done something wrong.

No, she told you she was eighteen.

He tried his best to turn away from all this, to quiet the voice that was telling him to hack in to graciousgirl4's computer's camera, but even as he argued against it, he found himself typing on his laptop, going through the steps to back-trace her through Krazle, to check her IP address, and to turn on the camera.

He knew the steps.

From his work, he was aware of what pedophiles and hebephiles sometimes did in order to watch the boys and girls during their chats, or maybe to catch them changing by turning on their phones' or computers' cameras around bedtime.

Yes, he knew those things.

It was part of his job to know them.

It'd been a hard day. He'd received a link from that FBI agent, Patrick Bowers, that had led to thousands of images that needed to be screened and cataloged.

It was always tough when things like that came in. But it had already led to some positive IDs of known missing children and it looked like it might possibly lead to some more as well.

It felt like things were spinning out of control, like he was driving a car that'd hit a patch of ice. He still had his hands on the wheel, but no matter how tightly he gripped it or which direction he steered, the car was caught in a skid, his life was caught in a skid, and it was going to go where it was going to go and there was no stopping it.

He was sliding headlong toward the ditch and had no way to steer clear of it.

Maybe it was the stress of the day, maybe it was just the desire to get rid of the voices, but whatever it was, Francis kept going, kept typing in code.

Don't do this, it's betraying her friendship. What if she's in her pajamas or something? You shouldn't—

But then the time for argument was over. He was tired of the voices arguing in his head, tired of the questions, tired of the pressure pulling him in two directions at once. He wanted to be with Skylar, but he also wanted closure here.

The line in the sand.

The net around his feet.

What would Skylar think?

She won't know. She'll never know.

His screen flickered for a moment as the video from the other computer came on and sharpened into focus.

From what he could tell, the laptop must have been on a table in the dining room near where things opened up to the living room. An open bag of cheese curls lay nearby. A sofa sat in the background and a widescreen TV hung from the wall beyond it.

No one was sitting in front of the computer, so graciousgirl4 must have stepped away for a moment.

Then someone who was probably her dad walked through the other room, picked up the remote, and started channel-surfing on the television.

Francis felt his chest tense up. He didn't want her dad to see them chatting. It wasn't smart of her to leave the chat window open like that. What if he came over and looked at some of the things they'd typed to each other in the past couple of weeks?

You were careful. You never said anything that broke any laws or—

I know, but we shared things with each other. Things that were just meant for the two of us.

And when he thought of that, he felt ashamed because he wanted Skylar to know those things. He wanted her to know his secrets, to know him. A real woman. A real friend.

Still, Francis's chats had been meant for graciousgirl4, not for her dad, not for anyone else, so he was nervous about her computer being left out there on the table.

As soon as she came back, he could ask her to please take her laptop into her room so they could chat in private.

But you don't really want to chat with her in private tonight, do you? You just clicked on here to see her. Right?

I guess. I—

*Maybe she needs to have her computer out here. Maybe that's the rule at their house. Maybe her dad doesn't let her have it in her room because he wants to protect her, to make sure she doesn't end up chatting with people she shouldn't be chatting with—*And then the next three words came, the words he didn't ever, ever, ever want to think: *people like you.*

No, I'm not like that. I'm—

Francis hated that he was thinking these things, that he had become someone whom others might fear or want to avoid.

Turn it off. You've seen enough. You shouldn't be doing this.

But he didn't turn it off.

He waited.

The seconds ticked by as the man in the other room flipped through those channels.

Just for another minute. She'll return. You can see her, and then it'll be over.

Finally, the man landed on a channel and stayed there. It was a car chase scene through the streets of downtown New York City, which Francis recognized from living here.

He didn't know the movie, but he did know the city.

His city.

The man turned up the volume, set down the remote, picked up a bottle of beer that'd been sitting by the couch, and then approached the computer.

No, no, no.

He'll see the chats! He'll see!

He pulled a chair up to the table, took a long drag from the bottle, then had a handful of cheese curls and began to type.

As he did, the words came up on Francis's computer: "Jared4life73. Where ru? Where have u been? I miss u!"

He's pretending to be graciousgirl4!

That was Francis's initial thought.

But then the truth hit him all at once, hard and solid like a rock slamming into him—something he should have guessed, should have anticipated—maybe it was something he'd even subconsciously known but had been keeping from himself.

This man wasn't *pretending* to be graciousgirl4.

He *was* graciousgirl4.

She doesn't exist. It's just some guy who gets off pretending to be a teenager chatting with people like you.

Francis felt a dip in his stomach like the ones he used to feel when he was younger and would go on roller coasters at the theme park outside Dallas and the coaster would plummet down a steep drop.

Down and down and down. People screaming all around him. And some of them would raise their hands into the air, but Francis would always hold on. He would grip the bar or the seat in front of him as tightly as he could.

The earth rising up toward him, picking up speed, picking up speed, and then—

The man took another mouthful of cheese curls, then suddenly stopped chewing and stared directly at the camera.

Swerving.

To the side.

A corkscrew.

And Francis realized that he had never entered the code to turn off the camera's light.

The man leaned close, then narrowed his eyes and cursed vehemently before putting a hand up to cover the camera.

Francis slammed his laptop shut.

Heart hammering.

Twisting.

Turning.

That dip in his stomach growing tighter as if he were in a free fall.

He sat there staring at his computer like it was a foreign object, like it was something he'd never seen before.

A mixture of shame and dread overwhelmed him.

Shame, because he'd been so stupid, so stupid, stupid, stupid to chat with this person online and share the things he'd shared, hope the things he'd hoped with someone he didn't even know. And also, shame because of the feelings he'd developed for her, even though he knew she was out of bounds, might have been too young, was probably too young.

But now he found that she wasn't even real.

She'd never existed at all.

In an online, anonymous world you can be anybody.

In the real world you had to be yourself.

And he felt dread too, yes, because of the way the man had looked into the camera.

He feared that if there was some way for that guy to find out Jared4life73's true identity, he might get in trouble or lose his job or something.

But how could he know who you are? All he could see was that the light of his chat camera was on. You're safe. You're fine. It's over. The Krazle profile you made up wasn't real. There's nothing real about any of this. You were both caught up in a fantasy world, and now it's over and you've learned your lesson and what's done is done is done. There's nothing else to say about it and there's nothing to worry about.

But what if he knows how to—?

There is no if. It's over.

However, just to make sure, just to make *absolutely* sure, Francis opened up his laptop, went back online, deleted Jared4life73's Krazle profile and his browser's history, then did a complete wipe of the free space on his computer to get rid of any residual file fragments and cookies that might have still been there hiding in the shadows, fragments of his past that the computer didn't want to let go of.

Using the skills he'd picked up over the years, he made them go away.

Made them all go away.

She was gone now.

Graciousgirl4 was no longer a part of his life.

She never was.

She was never real.

Move on, Francis, just move on.

He went to bed and tried to fall asleep, tried, tried, tried, tried, tried, tried, tried, but all he could think of was the threatening look on the man's face as he stared into the camera right before Francis closed his laptop to end the chat.

He texted Skylar good night and when she replied, he read her text aloud to himself, over and over, to try to make it seem like she was there with him, telling him in person that she was glad he was her friend.

61

On his computer, Shane typed in the sixteen-digit password, and clicked through three levels of data encryption to get to the site where the Piper left him instructions, and where he could access the video of the three remaining children.

They were still here in the city, would be until Wednesday night when everything went down.

After that, he would be free to do whatever he wanted to with them and then post it for all the world to see with no recriminations whatsoever.

If all went as planned.

A sturdy chain manacled the left leg of each child to the wall of their separate rooms.

Some nights he would watch them sleep, like he was doing right now.

Sometimes they would awaken and cry, but for the most part, those days were over. They really didn't weep or scream or beg so much anymore. You only scream so long. You only cry so much. Then, after that, it's time to accept your place, accept the way things are.

That was what Shane had done: accepted his place. Things were the way they were. It was as simple as that.

In all that he did, he was only following his desires.

That was it. He did not believe in ethics or morality or God, that there was, or had ever been, a divine being. The universe didn't need a designer. It needed only time.

Time.

And chance.

And natural laws.

And, of course, without God there was no such thing as evil, just as there was no such thing as good. There was utility, yes. There was survival and instinct and there was pain, yes, in the natural world.

There was pain.

But there was no evil.

To call something moral or immoral, good or evil, just or unjust in a godless expanse was to put a value judgment on something that was ethically neutral.

There was no driving purpose behind evolution. An individual had no value beyond itself, no existential meaning beyond the role it played in evolution. Survival, yes, that was the *result* of evolution, but it was not the *intent* of it. Without a designer, without a god, there was no design, there was no intent.

To act—not to rationalize—this was our role. To act and pursue the instincts evolution has given us.

And he felt the instinct to kill.

So Shane did not feel the need to justify his actions to himself, to the world, to God.

He glanced at the blades he'd laid on the counter in front of him, then directed his thoughts back to the children, to the moments he would have alone with them when the Associates were done with their filming.

No, it wasn't just a professional interest.

It was something a bit more personal than that.

Living in full color.

Using his encrypted cell, he made the call to the person he'd hired to get them into the system.

"How's it coming?" he asked.

"We'll be ready. Trust me."

"There's a lot riding on this."

"I know. I'm moving forward. It'll come together. Just be ready when it does."

He observed the knives again, specifically the one he'd used to kill Jamaal Stewart last week when they found out he was going to be sharing more with the world than he needed to be.

I'm ready now, he thought.

No, he didn't want to wait, but patience carried with it its own rewards, and after the donor banquet on Wednesday night, time would be on his side.

He hung up and went back to watching the children.

++++

As I was closing up my research for the night, I checked my email one last time and found a message from an unknown sender that read, "We have received your request and we would like to set up a personal meeting."

It'd been sent to the email address Lloyd gave me, and forwarded automatically to my account.

There was a hyperlink at the bottom of the message.

I copied it, went to the Dark Web, and pasted it into the browser's search box.

A page came up with an address in the Bronx and a message: "1:00 p.m. tomorrow. Come alone. Ask for Blake."

That was all.

I looked up the address.

A bar.

Even though it was now after eleven, I didn't care. I called Tobin, who must have had his phone by his side because he picked up after only one ring. I told him what I'd just found.

"It doesn't make sense," I said, "not if Lloyd's email account was anonymous like he told us it was."

"You mean, how would whoever sent it know that you would be in this area of the country, that you'd be able to make it to a one o'clock meeting tomorrow in New York City?"

"Exactly."

"Maybe it's just that Lloyd's identity package wasn't as secure or confidential as he thought. I mean, it was several years old. It could be that he wasn't as thorough by today's standards at hiding his tracks."

"That may mean they know who I am."

"Regardless, it's telling you to ask for Blake. You have the chance to meet him and he's our link to the Final Territory."

"And he thinks I'm the one who sent a link to over fifteen thousand images of child pornography."

"That is true."

Tobin's words from yesterday came to mind, his suspicion that someone from law enforcement might be involved in this at some level.

They might have access to the Federal Digital Database.

I wasn't exactly sure where that left us, and after brainstorming for a few minutes and not coming up with anything specific—beyond me attending that meeting—we ended the call.

Okay, tomorrow at one I would ask for Blake at that pub and we would see where that took us.

As I lay back on the couch to try to get some sleep, I wondered if there was any way for these people to know who I was, and I figured that, yes, it was possible—especially if Blake had some sort of connection to law enforcement.

First thing in the morning I had a meeting scheduled with Maria Aguirre, the OPR lawyer.

I wasn't about to take any chances, not when we were this close to uncovering something that might lead us to finding those three missing children and deciphering who was really behind the Final Territory.

I knew what I had to do.

I made my decision.

Tomorrow morning when I met with Ms. Aguirre, I would ask her to put me on administrative leave.

62

"What do you mean you want me to order your suspension?"

I was in Ms. Aguirre's office at headquarters and even though I'd been through this once already with her, it hadn't quite sunk in.

"I'm hoping that the man I'm going to meet after lunch today will lead us to the Final Territory."

"Blake."

"Yes."

"And you want to go undercover."

"Not exactly, but yes."

"Not exactly, but yes."

"As I said, Blake might already know I'm an agent, but if things go well with him it could lead us to the three missing children. D'Nesh said that he'd seen them, he'd met them in another location."

"But Blake knows you're an agent?"

"Well, he might. I'm not sure. I think that perhaps he, or someone he works with, might've been able to access the Federal Digital Database."

"That's impossible."

"Wooford was being protected by the Justice Department, so who could have gotten to him if it wasn't someone with a connection to law enforcement?"

"I thought that was ruled a suicide."

"The evidence points in another direction. Tobin also suspects that Blake might have someone from law enforcement helping him."

She evaluated that. "And this man, Lloyd, who you went to see yesterday—he entered information into the Final Territory website on the Dark Web?"

"Yes."

"So it's possible that he might have alerted someone that the authorities are looking for them?"

That was something I hadn't considered. "Actually, that is possible, yes. Right now we don't know who's involved, but if they do have a way to get onto the Federal Digital Database, or a way of identifying me, they'll never trust me unless there's a strong reason to."

"And being put on administrative leave will do that?"

"Depends on how you word things in the report, but yes. I think you could pull it off."

She rubbed her jaw. "I don't know."

"Listen. We have three missing children to consider. This is our chance, today, to meet with Blake. I don't know if we'll get another one, especially not soon."

"Is DeYoung on board with this?"

"I haven't spoken with him yet. Since my review is in your hands right now, I decided to start with you. I can talk with him, or you can. It doesn't matter to me. I have the sense that he'll follow your recommendation, whatever it is."

She stared out the window, obviously deep in thought.

"I need it official," I told her. "Whatever they do know or don't know about me, this group we're looking into,

I'm guessing they can spot law enforcement and undercover agents a mile away. That's how they stay one step
ahead, how they stay out of prison. I need them to think
I'm dirty. That's the only way I can meet up with Blake."

"Alright." She rose. "I'll go speak with the Assistant
Director."

"And no one else. On the paperwork, make it look like
you don't trust me at all."

"If we go that far, you know you'll have to turn in
your credentials and your firearm. You do know that,
don't you? If I expedite this like you're saying, we'll need
to go all the way to make it believable."

"I know."

"I'll talk to him. I'll let you know what he says."

Back in my office, I put my things in order with the
expectation that I might not be back in here for some
time.

Then I called the Homeland Security agent I'd caught
at the golf course on Saturday morning. "Have you had a
chance to look into what we spoke about the other day?"

"Yes." But he sounded annoyed that I was following
up. "There's no record of anyone visiting Wooford while
he was in detention."

*Only someone with inside connections could have pulled
off seeing him without filling out any paperwork.*

"Anything else?"

"Wooford worked for a construction company for a
couple years. Some of his chats with minors were done
from his work computer. I'll see if I can find the specifics
and get them to you. I'll let you know if I come up with
anything else."

I met with Tobin and Jodie and told them what was
going on.

"If this works out," I said, "you two are going to be my eyes and ears. We'll contact each other through burner phones or radios so there's no record of our calls on our personal cells."

We picked up some behind-the-ear radio patches that were nearly invisible and would give us hands-free communication if we needed it.

It took the rest of the morning for us to convince DeYoung, and then for Maria to submit the appropriate paperwork. Finally, rather unceremoniously, I handed the Assistant Director my creds and my gun.

"To make it official," he said, "I'll need to announce this to the media. They're already chomping at the bit wondering what happened to the agent from last week's shooting incident with Randy McReynolds. I'll tell them it's an ongoing review, that you've been placed on administrative leave as per our policy."

"That'll work if you put a reprimand in my file."

"I have a three o'clock press conference scheduled. Should I try to do something earlier, before your meeting with Blake?"

"No. Earlier would be too convenient and conspicuous. It might reveal our hand."

"You have to know, Patrick, this is not going to help your reputation, even if we clear things up soon. People hear things on the news and those impressions stick, even when the truth comes out later."

"I'm not worried about what people think of me. Let's just make some progress on this case. Let's find those missing kids."

"I'll want you to report directly to me about this. You can't come in to your office. You won't have access to your federal account, the case files, or your email."

It would be ideal if we could backdoor things, but it wasn't worth taking the chance.

"I'll have Tobin and Jodie keep me up to speed. Maybe meeting with Blake is all I'll need to do. Maybe by tomorrow this'll all be over."

"Maybe." He didn't sound very optimistic. "Let's hope so. And I want you wearing a wire."

"I can't do that. It's one of the first things they'll look for. I need to go in quiet on this."

DeYoung rubbed his head and squinched up his eyes as if all this was giving him a headache, which might very well have been the case. "Tobin stays close to you every step of the way."

"What about Jodie?"

"You can keep her in the loop, but she and Descartes are spearheading the search for Romanoff and I want her to stay on that."

Before I left, he requisitioned some cash in case I needed it on the street, then I took off for my meeting with Blake.

++++

Francis heard back from Dr. Tignini, the psychologist that Dr. Perrior had recommended to him.

"Hello, Mr. Edlemore. I have the referral notice here on my desk and I did receive your messages. I would be glad to see you, but I don't have any openings for the next two weeks."

"But Dr. Perrior said you were just getting established, that you would be able to help me."

"Well, I'll be happy to help you, but I'll be attending a conference and won't be in town. However, can I write you down for July second?"

No, no, no.

"Yes, I mean, that would be good. How much does it cost—because that's the main reason I need to see someone else, not because things weren't going well with Dr. Perrior."

"I see. Well, we can discuss that. I work on a prorated basis. I'll do all I can to help you out."

"Thank you."

"I'll see you next month, then."

"Okay."

Francis tried to sort things through.

So much was happening.

He was trying to help the FBI, trying to catalog the new files that'd been submitted, and also wrap up what he could before the gala tomorrow night.

And then there was graciousgirl4, who wasn't a girl at all.

And Skylar, whom he couldn't get out of his head.

He really wished he could see Dr. Perrior.

"Honesty is the best policy," he'd told Francis once.

He'd never forgotten that.

Honesty, honesty, honesty.

Yes.

That was the key here.

You need to talk to someone.

And the only person who came to mind was Skylar.

Francis decided that maybe sorting through things with her would help.

He phoned her to see if she could meet at two o'clock during his coffee break.

"It doesn't look like I can get away this afternoon," she said, "but can I see you for dinner maybe? Maybe after work?"

"Alright. Yes. That would be nice."

"Are you okay? You sound upset. Are you mad at me? I'd come if I could, I just don't think I can get—"

"No, no, no. I'm just . . . It's something here at work. It's not you."

"Okay. So you're alright?"

"Yeah. I'll see you tonight for dinner. Six?" Then, a bit to his own surprise, he added, "If you want, we can meet at my place."

She told him she would enjoy that and could they make it seven and did he need her to bring anything?

"No. I'll make spaghetti, okay?"

"Sounds great."

Then he passed along his address and the plans were set.

She was going to come over to his apartment tonight.

A real woman.

Yes, honesty is the best policy.

And when she did come, he would tell her about graciousgirl4 and then things would smooth out, the stress would go away, and everything would be less overwhelming, once it was all out in the open.

63

I entered the pub.

The yeasty stench of spilled beer hit me right away.

Despite the time of day, there were four men seated around the room, nursing their drinks. I couldn't help but wonder what was going on in their lives for them to feel the need to start drinking this early in the day, unless, of course, they were here to help protect Blake.

Two didn't even bother to look my direction, but the other two guys stared at me from the time I came in until the moment I arrived at the bar, where a beefy, scraggly-faced Latino bartender was wiping down the counter. An open bag of sour cream and onion potato chips sat beside him.

He slid a napkin onto the counter in front of me. "What can I get you?"

"I'm looking for someone. I think you can help me."

He eyed me coolly as he picked up a beer glass and began absently drying it with a towel, even though it didn't appear to be wet.

In the real world, information doesn't always come without a price and I laid a hundred-dollar bill on the bar.

"His name is Blake," I said. "I was told I could find him here."

"Yeah, and who told you that?"

"I got an email."

"An email."

"Yes."

"Uh-huh. Well, there's no one named Blake here."

"And see," I said, "I think there is."

The bartender stopped wiping the glass, set it down, placed both hands on the bar, and leaned forward, getting close enough for me to smell his sour cream and onion breath. "I think it's time for you to walk out that door you came in."

I set another bill on the table. "Tell him Patrick Bowers is here to see him. Tell him that we share a mutual interest."

"And what interest is that?"

"Aurora's birthday. The email I received told me to meet him at one o'clock. Go on, before he thinks I got here late."

He appraised me once more, then slid the two bills back in my direction. "If Blake's not expecting you, I'll just take 'em off your body when he's done with you. If he is expecting you, he's not gonna want to see you passing me bills. I don't want him to think I'm on anyone's payroll."

Then he left, disappearing into a door behind the bar.

I pocketed the money and took the opportunity to assess the room and develop an exit strategy in case I ended up needing to get out of here in a hurry.

One of the guys was still staring at me. I wondered if he was involved in this, if he might even be Blake and this whole deal with the abrasive bartender was a setup, but then he went back to his beer and I faced the bar where

I could still keep an eye on him through the mirror behind the counter.

While I did, I turned the rug over in my mind to look
at the patterns that were there, the ones that were so easy
to miss.

Wooford's supposed suicide.

Ferguson's supposed boating accident.

Randy McReynolds's overdose.

I thought of that note I'd found on Randy's body, and
allowed myself to venture, for the moment, into the
realm of motive. Why would he have written a suicide
note to Billy when they were estranged and hadn't spoken in two years? Why would he say he was sorry he'd let
him down? Wouldn't it make more sense to apologize for
whatever had caused the rift between them, to address
that issue rather than what some woman said he'd done
years before?

But, just like all forays into motive, I didn't come up
with anything solid.

I still had Billy's business card. Maybe he would be
able to give us something. He'd offered to help us if he
could. That might be something to check up on.

But you're on leave, Pat.

Well, that didn't mean I couldn't visit a radio talk
show host and ask him a couple questions.

As I waited, I thought about what I might say to Blake
and decided I'd need to mostly play it by ear.

Nearly ten minutes passed before the bartender reemerged and gestured for me to come with him.

Stepping around the end of the counter, I followed
him through the door and into a narrow hallway leading
into the bowels of the building.

64

Beer posters with bikini-clad models lined the 1970s-style paneled walls.

We passed two doors, one of which was slightly open. A woman wearing black fishnet stockings and high heels sat inside the room on the edge of a bed covered with crumpled, stained sheets. "Now, don't be too rough." She had a pair of handcuffs dangling from one of her fingers and giggled as someone else closed the door.

An enormous bouncer who would have dwarfed most NFL linemen stood sentry in front of the door at the end of the hall. The bartender passed me off to him and he simply said, "Spread 'em."

He patted me down, found that I wasn't carrying and, satisfied, swept me for a wire, took my cell phone, and then opened the door and stepped aside so I could pass by, which, considering how much of the hallway he took up, wasn't easy.

A man in his mid-fifties with a carefully trimmed beard stood in the middle of a wide windowless room, hands clasped behind his back. Athletic build. Caucasian. He studied me with deeply perceptive eyes but didn't say a word.

The bouncer closed the door behind me, leaving the two of us alone.

Well, not exactly alone.

Ten female mannequins also stood in the room. Some were missing arms, others heads. Most were unclothed, some were wearing lingerie—bras, panties, panty hose.

The mannequins were arranged in a variety of poses—some leaned forward slightly, others stood ramrod straight and tall with their arms outstretched, others had their hands slung, with attitude, to their hips.

Sterile, hairless bodies. Blemish-free faces. I couldn't help but think of corpses, unabashed and mute, standing around me, frozen as if in midstride.

For something as innocent and commonplace as mannequins, it created an eerie scene.

The man spoke first. "Rodriguez tells me your name is Patrick Bowers."

"Yes."

"It's *Agent* Bowers, isn't it?"

I didn't have a physical description of Blake, so I didn't know if this was him, or perhaps another gatekeeper between me and the man I was looking for.

The computer screen on his desk showed the security footage from inside the bar. A facial recognition program was running and my face was on the screen. Somehow he was logged in to the Federal Digital Database.

Okay, this guy definitely had connections.

"Yes, it is," I said. "Are you Blake?"

He raised both hands in a gesture of mock surrender. "And so, here we stand before each other with our true identities out in the open. Always a good place to start. Can you drink while you're on duty?"

"I'm not on duty."

"So, then, whiskey?"

"Sure."

"Administrative leave, huh?" he said. "As of this morning?"

"They haven't announced that publicly yet."

"No, they haven't." He walked to his desk. "And all because of a shooting incident?"

"I get a little carried away sometimes."

"Then it looks like we have something in common."

At a liquor cabinet near his desk, he poured each of us a glass from an ornate decanter, then handed one to me.

"What's the deal with the mannequins?" I asked.

"The silent ladies. You like them?"

"It's a little eccentric, if you don't mind me saying so."

He smiled. "Not at all. Rodriguez told me that we share a mutual interest. I looked at the files you uploaded. I believe he's right."

"There's a particular file I'm looking for."

"Aurora's birthday."

"Yes."

He showed no reaction. "And what makes you think I would be in possession of this video? How's the whiskey, by the way?"

Ah, so it *was* a video.

"Excellent," I told him, although I didn't really have an opinion one way or the other. "And regarding the video—from my sources it sounds like you have the connections to locate certain items that are difficult for most people to put their hands on."

"Your sources."

"That's right."

"Is this a request of a professional nature?"

I evaluated what to say, which direction to take this. "It's for personal use."

"I need to make sure it was you who did it."

"Who did what?"

"Shared the link to those images."

"I'm the one."

"How many were there?"

"Sixteen thousand and forty-two." I knew the number only because I'd reported them to the ICSC. "I want in to the Final Territory."

"Yes. So it seems." He took a slow sip of his drink. "This video and the access credentials to enter, that's what brings you here."

"The email I got is what brought me here. I didn't expect to have to meet with someone in person. It's highly unusual."

"Well, certainly, you can understand how, with you being a federal agent, and me being an entrepreneur who does business with people who prefer to work in anonymity— well, you can see how I might be reticent to carry this conversation any further. Confidentiality is one thing my clients value quite highly."

"I can help you."

"And how can you help me, Agent Bowers?"

"Through my contacts at the Bureau."

"You're on administrative leave."

"My contacts aren't."

"Maybe that's not something I'm in need of."

Alright, so he'd basically just told me that he had a contact at the Bureau, which could explain his access to the Federal Digital Database.

He might be bluffing.

At this point I doubted it.

Unsure what he did know and what he didn't, I went with the truth. "There's an NYPD detective who has your name on his radar screen. He's on the joint task force. I can take care of him, point him in a different direction. He's good. He's persistent. He will be coming for you. I can do more than find information for you, I can make it go away for good."

He took another sip, then rested the glass in the outstretched hand of one of the mannequins beside him. "People who enter into partnership with each other need to be able to trust each other, wouldn't you agree?"

"Of course."

"You have to admit that the timing of your suspension and the shooting, your uploading the files, all of it does raise some red flags."

"I'd think it would do the opposite. You know that Randy McReynolds was looking into things. He told me a lot when we were there in Stewart's apartment alone."

"What did he tell you?"

"Let's just say it was enough to get me interested in meeting you." I drained the glass. "I did my due diligence on you, I posted the link to the photos, and here I am."

He rubbed two fingers together as if that would help him sift through my words and find any lies lurking within them. "I would like some reassurance of our mutual dependence on each other. A good-faith gesture."

"Go on."

"The woman you're seeing. She has a daughter."

"What?"

"Christie Ellis. Her daughter is what? Fifteen? A little footage is all I ask. I'll provide you with the camera. It'll be discreet. Just hide it in her room before she changes clothes. She'll never know it was even there. After I have the footage we'll talk again."

"How do you know about Christie?"

"Your phone records, Agent Bowers. I ran them while

you were waiting for Rodriguez to return to the bar. It was all right there: a man doesn't call a woman that often and at those hours unless he's more than friends with her."

That's something I would have looked into.

This man approached things the way I did.

That was an unsettling thought.

Maybe he was ex–law enforcement.

Or ex-FBI.

"Her daughter's name and phone number are on her account," he explained. "Running the girl's name through the school district's database gave me her age and their address. Simple."

Okay, this guy knew his stuff.

You can fake the footage somehow. You can make this work. There's too much at stake here. Three children, maybe more. This is your best chance to break into the Final Territory.

"When do you need this?"

He opened his desk drawer and took out a button-size camera. "Let's say by five."

"I can't get it by then. She doesn't even get home from school until four or so. She wouldn't be getting ready for bed until at least ten."

"Just ask her to try on a different outfit. Use your imagination. You're a clever man. I'm sure you'll think of something."

He showed me how to use the camera, then asked if I knew why Randy McReynolds had been in Jamaal Stewart's apartment Wednesday night.

"I believe he was looking for the video of Aurora's birthday," I said.

He was quiet. "Be careful who you trust, Agent Bowers. The truth that's right in front of you is often the hardest to see."

"I'll keep that in mind."

I retrieved my phone from the hulk in the hallway, and then, back in the bar, I nodded toward the bartender, who was apparently named Rodriguez.

"Next time, then," he muttered. I had the sense that he was talking about the money, that he'd hoped I wouldn't return from my visit with Blake and his silent ladies.

I caught up with Tobin two blocks away in his undercover car. "We might have a problem," I said.

65

Tobin stared at me incredulously when I told him about Blake. "He had access to your and Christie's phone records and to the Federal Digital Database?"

"Yes."

"So he might very well have someone at the Bureau or the NYPD in his pocket."

I nodded. "Obviously, I'm not going to film Tessa changing clothes, but if we're going to move forward on this we need to figure out something that'll fool him."

My first inclination was to call Christie, to tell her what we needed to do—just use Tessa's room and get an undercover agent to impersonate Tessa, but Blake had access to my phone records and might be suspicious if he saw I'd called her, so I used Tobin's phone.

She didn't answer.

I knew that she had meetings this afternoon, but I figured she would be checking her messages in between them, so I left a voicemail for her to call me, then texted her the same.

There was a lot at stake here—this was our first real shot at getting into the Final Territory, at piecing together where those three missing children might be.

"Could we fake it?" Tobin asked. "Use another room? Stage things with a female officer or agent?"

"That's what I was thinking, but Blake knows I'm seeing Christie, knows where she lives, and that she has a daughter. He intimated to me that he had a source in the Bureau. With those kinds of connections, I'm guessing that he and his people might find out about the agent we were using, or if we weren't actually in Tessa's room."

"I might have an idea. Tell me a little about Tessa. Height, weight, race. That sort of thing."

"Caucasian. Five foot five. A hundred and fifteen, maybe a hundred and twenty pounds. Shoulder-length black hair."

"Do you have a picture of her?"

I pulled out my cell and found a photo of Tessa and Christie taken a couple of weeks ago. Christie was smiling warmly. Tessa looked bored in her endearingly sullen way.

I wasn't quite sure how she did that.

"There's an officer from the Port Authority whom we've used before," Tobin said. "She's twenty, but looks a lot younger. She's helped Hinchcliffe and me in a number of undercover and sting operations. I'd say she's a little taller than Tessa and she's blond, but I think with a wig and the right clothes we might be able to make it work. Since she's not with the Bureau or the NYPD, I think we can do it without alerting anyone who might be compromised."

Even though a person needs to be twenty-one to be an NYPD officer, the age is lower in New Jersey and for the Port Authority, so sometimes for undercover assignments when they need young-looking officers, the NYPD uses officers from other jurisdictions.

"You think she can pass for a fifteen-year-old?"

"She has in the past."

"And she's good?"

"She's good." He had his phone out. "Let me see if she's available."

++++

Rather than going through Shane at this point, the Piper contacted the Associates in Russia directly, the ones in charge of finishing up the code.

The Russians were some of the best in the world at getting around Western security protocols. Really, it was the ideal place to base operations out of.

"Is it finished?" the Piper asked.

"Finished and waiting to be downloaded."

"I want it tested. I made that clear earlier."

"It has been. It'll do what you want. All you need to do is have him download the file."

"Is it traceable?"

"What do you think? It's rerouted through more than a dozen servers around the world, each with its own level of encryption. No one will track it back to us and no one will track it back to you."

"We move on this tomorrow. Cocktails are served at six. The dinner begins at seven. Gomez will be speaking at eight or so. That's when I want it to happen."

"I'll make sure the timing is set. If it's not downloaded until after that, it'll automatically initiate its protocols as soon as it's opened. Just let me know the email address, and when you want me to send the link, and it'll be on its way."

"And what about uploading the files when it's finished?"

"That'll be up to you. There are hundreds of millions of files. Give it fifteen minutes. I'll email you the password."

66

Officer Naomi Morgan met us at a wig shop three blocks from Central Park.

Tobin had been right, she did look remarkably young for her age.

I still didn't have Christie's permission to use her daughter's room for all this, but I was moving forward for the time being as if I did.

I figured she would call back any minute and we could set up the details to make this work.

To do this without attracting attention, and because we thought that Blake might have contacts in the Bureau or the NYPD, we didn't officially call this in, but I did notify DeYoung to keep him in the loop.

The shelves along each wall of the shop were lined with dozens of mannequin heads each wearing a wig of a different color, style, or length.

It didn't take me long to find one that satisfactorily matched Tessa's hair.

As Naomi made sure it fit, she asked, "Is there anything I should know about her? Music? Friends? Clothes? What's she into?"

"She likes death metal bands," I said, "doesn't really have too many friends. She tends toward black fingernail polish. Sometimes black lipstick. But she doesn't really go full goth."

"Steampunk? Emo?"

"I'm not exactly sure what those are."

"Okay. What about scars? Piercings? Distinguishing marks?"

"She has pierced ears. I'm not aware of any scars or anything."

"That'll work. Does she wear hats?"

"Not usually, no."

"Glasses?"

"Not prescription, but she does go with sunglasses sometimes—although she's not one for fresh air, sunlight, that sort of thing. Though she is a pretty committed neoliberal environmentalist."

She detoured to a sunglasses rack in the corner before checking out. Tobin and I followed her and we all spoke in hushed voices. "Hmm." She scrolled her finger across the sunglasses, came up with a pair, and tried them on. I shook my head and she stuck them back on the rack, then chose a different pair.

"Maybe. I don't know." I was starting to have second thoughts about this whole thing. "I'm not sure about this, Naomi."

"Trust me. I can pull off a teenage girl." She went for another pair. "These?"

"I think so, but you don't really look like her."

"Forgive me for putting it so bluntly, Agent Bowers, but knowing what kind of people you're dealing with here, once I start changing clothes they're not going to be looking at my face."

That was true enough.

After we'd purchased the wig and sunglasses and left the store, Naomi asked, "How are we going to get in?"

"I have a key to the place."

"And you have permission from the girl and her mother?"

"Not yet, but I'm working on it."

I checked for any texts from Christie on Tobin's phone or my own.

Nothing.

"Can we wait, then?" Naomi said. "Put this into play later? Maybe tonight or tomorrow when we have the green light from her mom?"

Tobin, who'd been quiet up until now, spoke up. "Blake gave Patrick a time frame. It needs to happen this afternoon."

"What time?"

"By five," I answered. "And you're willing to be filmed changing clothes?"

"I'll keep on my bra and panties," she said matter-of-factly. "Listen, I've worked undercover as a prostitute, passed as a high school sophomore to investigate a teacher who was bedding his algebra students, and been involved with four stings to catch online sexual predators who'd been setting up meetings with underage girls. I think I can change clothes in front of a camera."

"Okay. Point taken."

I tried Christie again to get permission to use her apartment, but again the call went to voicemail. Not really wanting to leave a message about what we were hoping to do, I simply left another request for her to call me.

I didn't like this.

It was a bad idea on any number of fronts, but the deadline of five o'clock didn't give us much wiggle room. Christie wouldn't be getting home from work until five thirty or six, and if I couldn't get in touch with her first, we would need to pull this off before Tessa came home.

But then there would be explaining it all after the fact, a prospect that did not at all thrill me.

There are three other children out there. This is your best chance to get into the Final Territory, your best chance to find them.

Naomi sensed my hesitation. "It's your call, Agent Bowers. What do you want me to do? Are we a go on this or not?"

Wait, Pat. Talk it over with Christie, with Tessa. Clear it with them first.

But then I reminded myself of what was at stake. I could resolve everything with Christie later. Right now we needed to make a decision. Just getting across town, getting the camera set and Naomi in place was going to be cutting it tightly enough.

"Yeah," I said. "We're a go."

++++

Tessa Ellis finished her last exam of the day in twenty-two minutes, not that she was counting, or that she even cared, it was just that she happened to glance at the clock and since she was the first one done, she went over her answers again just so it wouldn't look weird with her handing it in so early.

But there wasn't really any need to. She was pretty sure she'd aced it, except for one question about Willa Cather that she wasn't quite sure about.

Finally, she'd had enough sitting around waiting, and she turned it in and took off for the subway entrance.

Maybe, if she was lucky, she could catch a train without too much waiting and make it back to the apartment by three forty-five or so.

Ever since her mom had dropped the bomb on her Saturday night that they were most likely going to be moving to the middle of nowhere, she'd felt like she had the wind knocked out of her.

Unbelievable.

Nebraska? *Seriously?*

New York City was her home. She could be anonymous here. She could be herself and no one cared. She could fit in by not fitting in and that was okay.

And it was like her mom had made the decision without even talking to her first, which was maybe what bothered her the most.

Plus, it seemed like this move would probably make three people miserable—her, her mom, and Patrick. And what was the point of that?

Sure, okay, she could understand how they needed money. But there had to be another way. What was the point of screwing up three people's lives when the only thing you needed was a little extra cash?

Maybe you could get a job? It might help, at least a little.

Yeah, right. As if, at fifteen, she would be able to find a job in New York City that would make enough money to help keep her and her mom afloat.

MetroCard in hand, she descended the steps into the subway tunnel to catch the train that would take her to the stop two blocks from home.

67

Just in case Blake had people watching the apartment, I went in alone to set up the camera while Naomi and Tobin waited down the street in an unmarked car.

Although I'd been in Christie's apartment by myself before, I'd never yet been in Tessa's room, and now as I entered it, I had the sense that I was betraying the trust Christie had placed in me when she gave me a key to her place. But, honestly, I wasn't sure what else to do.

It's going to be okay. Just get this over with. You can talk it through and sort things out later. Right now you're just doing what needs to be done.

Tessa's walls were covered with posters of the bands I'd heard her mention: House of Blood, Boomerang Puppy, Trevor Asylum, and Death by Susie. All such positive influences. No posters of boy bands, pop stars, or teen idols, but she did have one of a somber-looking Edgar Allan Poe.

The room smelled faintly of bubble gum and perfume, which surprised me since I'd never really noticed Tessa wearing perfume before. And I hadn't seen her chewing gum either.

A pile of well-worn leather-bound journals sat on her desk. A coffee mug half-filled with coffee beans served as a pencil holder and contained a highlighter, pens, pencils, and an X-ACTO knife.

To my surprise, her bed was scrupulously made. A teddy bear sat beside her pillow, reminding me that even though she was fifteen, she was still, in many ways, just a child.

That realization made this even harder.

"Pat?" Naomi's voice came through the radio patch I was wearing behind my ear. "Are you there?"

"Yeah."

"How's it going?"

"Give me a second."

I studied the layout of the room and chose a bookshelf across from Tessa's dresser, positioning the camera so that it wouldn't catch the corner of the mirror and there would be less chance of them seeing Naomi's reflection.

I held back from turning it on for the moment and radioed back to Naomi that things were set.

"Look in her drawers and her closet for me," she said.

"What? Why?"

"I'm going to have to put on some of her clothes to make it believable."

For some reason, even though I knew that it was the whole reason for doing this, it hadn't really registered that she would be digging through Tessa's dresser or shuffling through the clothes she had in her closet.

Man, if Tessa ever finds out, she is not going to be happy.

"I need to know where things are," Naomi explained. "I doubt Tessa would have to root through her clothes looking for what to put on."

"I'm not going to go through her things." Just being in here was bad enough. "It's believable that she might sort through her drawers looking for what to wear. You can pull it off. I trust you."

A pause. "Okay, I'll figure it out. Where's the camera?"

"It's on the south wall in the bookshelf, third shelf from the top. There's a plastic skull. I set it right next to that. If you turn slightly to the left as you enter the room they shouldn't be able to see your face." Then I added, "Alright, I'm going to start recording. We'll need to stop talking."

I turned on the camera and set it to wirelessly transmit its signal, just as Blake had shown me before I left his office. "She got done with her exams early," I said for Blake's benefit, making up a reason for why we were filming now, since I'd told him earlier that Tessa wouldn't be home until four. "She's on her way."

This was happening.

It was officially in play.

Naomi and I met outside Christie's place in the hall near the elevator, and I handed her the apartment key.

She said nothing, but nodded, then slung a book bag over her shoulder, walked up, and unlocked the door.

++++

Blake sat at his desk, sipping whiskey, surrounded by his silent ladies, watching the video feed of the girl's bedroom on his computer's monitor.

Bowers had started the transmission, had indicated that the girl was coming home early.

Now, on the screen, the door to her room opened and she stepped inside.

With her sunglasses on, Blake couldn't see her face all that clearly, but the people who were going to purchase this video weren't going to be very interested in that little detail anyhow.

If he sold it.

That was yet to be determined.

He might just post it online and let the world watch it for free.

68

On the subway, Tessa plugged in her earbuds and escaped into the sardonic lyrics of House of Blood, then found a seat and dug her journal out of her backpack.

She wasn't into writing on her laptop—not *writing* writing. Assignments, sure. Whatever. But sorting out her feelings? That she did by hand in her journal.

There was just this way of looking at the words, of processing them, of moving ideas from her mind to her fingertips that happened when she handwrote stuff that didn't happen when she typed.

She flipped to the last entry that she'd written.

It was from the point of view of her namesake, St. Teresa of Ávila, a Christian mystic her mom was into back in the day when she got pregnant with her. Tessa had tried to climb into the mind of the saint and sort out how she might feel about God, about the Bible.

She glanced it over.

> *The word-heat of your story*
> *causes blisters on my eyes.*
> *I'm seared into a new way of seeing.*
> *Of being.*
>   *Of dreaming.*

> *I can't touch the page anymore*
> *or my skin might just*
> *burst into love and*
> *grow scars that look like yours.*

> *Whenever I close my Bible,*
> *steam presses out of the cover.*

She liked that phrase "word-heat of your story." It seemed to really capture what a saint might be feeling.

It wasn't so much that Tessa *didn't* believe those things about Christianity like her mom did, it was just more like she wasn't sure *what* she believed.

How do you know what you know, and how is that different from believing that you know it? At what point does doubt become faith, and belief become knowledge?

It was all sort of twisty and hard to put your finger on.

House of Blood raged their lovesick angst into her ears. Fire and malaise in every word. It made her feel right at home.

She flipped to the next page, a blank one, then jotted down a few words, reworked them, and let the rhythm of the writing unearth where the poem should go.

Normally, she wasn't into stuff that rhymed, but this time it was as if the words wanted to come together that way and she wasn't about to pick a fight with them.

> *The night is as black as an eel.*
> *The day is as long as the night.*
> *My heart has been wrapped up in steel.*
> *I can feel the vampires bite.*

> *Time has been taunting and turning.*
> *The streams in my soul have run dry.*

The vision is clouded and blurry.
The past wants to wake up and die.

Oh, dread of the heartache and venom,
*   the vision scrawled under my skin.*
The future is pregnant with glory,
*   but the present is weary and thin.*

Just one more stop and then a two-block walk home.

She toyed with some of the words, "venom" especially. It didn't feel quite right, but at the moment the rest of the poem seemed pretty much on target, like she'd captured what was going on in her heart: the confusion and questions, the uncertainty and anger about her mom and their future together.

The train jostled, and the person standing beside her bumped into her elbow, causing her to draw a meaningless line across the center of the page, as if she were scratching out everything she'd just written.

She glanced up severely at the man who'd banged into her, and he just flipped her off.

So maybe he'd done it on purpose.

She tugged her earbuds out. "What's your problem?"

"No problem, honey."

He fake-blew her a kiss.

Jerk.

She was tempted to tell him off, but the train started to slow and she held her tongue and just closed up the journal instead and stuffed it into her pack.

They rattled to a stop and she stood.

Only one day of exams left and then she was finally free for the summer.

But come autumn, where would she be in school? Here? Or in Omaha?

Man, it was just too much to deal with right now.

She filed into the anonymous crowd of people leaving the train, making sure she accidentally-on-purpose stepped on Mr. Kiss Blower Guy's foot as she passed by him.

Then she headed for the steps that led to the subway exit.

++++

"Okay," Naomi's voice came through the radio. "It's done. I'm in the hall."

Nearly fifteen minutes had passed since she'd entered Christie's apartment.

"What took you so long?" I asked into the radio.

"I needed to sell it. A fifteen-year-old girl isn't just gonna come home after school, change clothes, and then leave her bedroom. I'm not even sure why she would change clothes at this time of day anyway, unless she was planning on meeting someone—but that doesn't matter. Point is, she'd hang out, at least for a little while. Text her friends. Chill, listen to some music, whatever. I'll be down in a minute. I'm on my way to the elevator now."

69

From where Tobin and I sat in the sedan halfway down the block, we could see Naomi exit the apartment building wearing a different outfit from before, but one that I recognized as consisting of Tessa's clothes.

I looked out the car windows in both directions, studying the people who were on the sidewalk to see if there was anything out of the ordinary, or if there was anyone I recognized as being part of the case—and I saw one of the men who'd been at the bar earlier.

Ah.

So they *were* checking up on this.

Once he noticed Naomi, who was wearing the wig and sunglasses and really could have passed for Christie's daughter, he pulled out a cell phone, made a call, and started walking away from the apartment.

And that's when I saw Tessa coming this way on the other side of the street.

Oh.

No.

It didn't appear that the man took any notice of her.

She isn't supposed to be home yet!

She'll see Naomi wearing her clothes!

"Turn around, Naomi," I said into my radio. There

was no one close to her, so I told her to drop the apartment key for me.

She immediately turned and slipped the key out of her pocket, flicking it onto the sidewalk.

"What is it?" she asked.

"Tessa."

"What?"

"She's on her way home, take the next left. Go around the block. I don't think she saw you."

Tessa continued toward the apartment building's entrance.

That camera was still in her room. If she went in there now, Blake, or whoever might be watching the video, would know she wasn't the one who'd changed clothes a few minutes ago. It would jeopardize everything.

I needed to get up there and stop her before she went into that room.

Exiting the car, I crossed the street, jogged down the block, snatched up the key from the sidewalk, and then hurried into the lobby just in time to see the elevator doors close behind Tessa.

Taking the stairs two at a time, I raced to the fourth floor and emerged as the elevator opened at the end of the hall.

Tessa had her head down and was staring at her phone texting someone or playing one of the word games she liked when she emerged from the elevator, but I clearly wasn't going to make it into the apartment and into her room before she could get in there or before she would look up.

"Hey," I called, trying to sound nonchalant.

"Patrick?" She looked at me quizzically. "What are you doing here?"

"I needed to swing by and pick something up. How was school?"

"Stupid. What did you need to pick up?"

We walked toward the door to the apartment. The whole way I was brainstorming for a believable way to keep her from entering her bedroom until I'd had a chance to remove the camera.

Nothing popped into my mind.

"Hello?" she said somewhat impertinently. "I asked what you forgot, what you came back to get."

I wasn't about to say, "A secret camera that's hidden in your bedroom," but I didn't want to lie to her either. "It's just something for work," I told her. "Do you know where your mom is?"

"At her office, obviously. Unless she decided to move to Omaha without me." Tessa eyed me. "You do know about that, don't you?"

She unlocked the door.

"She did tell me about the job offer, yes."

We entered the apartment.

"When?"

"When?"

"When did she tell you?"

"The other day."

"What day?"

"Saturday."

"What time?"

I didn't think it would go over very well if she found out Christie had told me about the possible move first. "About eight or so." I didn't specify that it was a.m.

"But you were at that detective's place."

"Cell phones are amazing things," I said evasively, and I was glad she didn't press it further.

"So, what's up with you and her, anyway? I mean, is it just gonna be over or what? Long-distance romances suck."

"Both of us are exploring our options."

"Your options, huh? Options of what? It's not like you're gonna move out there with us, is it?"

"I don't really know what the future is going to bring."

"Okay, whatever," she said dismissively. "I'm not into vagaries and deflection. If you don't wanna talk about it, fine, we won't talk about it."

She headed directly for her room.

"Tessa, hold up a sec."

Okay, how to do this.

I didn't know if the camera in her room would pick up the sound of us talking in the hall, so I wanted to be careful what I said and how loudly I said it.

"What?" She had her hand on the doorknob.

Even if Blake hears you, though, he won't necessarily be suspicious. He might think you just want to get the camera out before she goes back into the room.

"Don't go in there right now," I said.

"What are you talking about?"

My phone vibrated in my pocket. An incoming call.

I had a burner phone with me too, but this was on my personal phone and I wondered if it might be Christie.

"Hang on."

I unpocketed my phone and glanced at the screen.

The number was listed as private, but there was also a text that popped up even as the phone was ringing.

Answer it, Agent Bowers.

"Why don't you want me to go into my bedroom?" Tessa said.

Tell her. You're going to have to tell her.

"There's something in there that doesn't belong."

"What? What are you talking about?"

I tapped at the screen to answer the call. "Hello?"

"I received the footage." It was Blake's voice, but I couldn't tell from his tone whether he thought the video was truly of Tessa or if he was onto us.

"Eh-hem." Tessa cleared her throat emphatically. "Didn't anyone ever tell you it's rude to answer a call in the middle of a conversation?"

I raised a finger to indicate that I needed a second, then said into the phone, "I gave you what you wanted. Now I want the credentials to get onto the site. And access to the video."

Tessa opened her mouth, but I shook my palm to signal for her to stop right away.

I couldn't slip into the other room to talk privately or else she might go into her bedroom, but I couldn't very well stand here talking to Blake with her listening in.

Tessa threw a hand to her hip and looked at me with a mixture of confusion and defiance.

Blake gave me a location that was nearly a mile and a half away. "We'll want you there in ten minutes. We'll find you."

"I can't make it by then, I'll need more—"

The line went dead.

"Are you gonna tell me what's going on here or not?" Tessa belted out.

There was no elegant way to put this, no way to finesse my way out of this situation.

Do it. You just need to take care of it.

"I can't explain right now."

As I approached her, she opened her bedroom door and I said, "I need to check first, before you go in there."

Without waiting for a reply, I slid past her, briefly acted like I was inspecting the room for something, then ended up at the bookshelf, snagged the camera, turned it off, and dropped it into my pocket.

"What was that?" Tessa said. "I saw you grab something."

"A camera."

"What?"

"I'll explain everything later. Right now I need to go."

"What do you mean it was a camera?"

As I left, I heard her call after me one more time before the closing door behind me shut out the sound.

With traffic, there was no way to guarantee that we could drive to that intersection in time.

But there was a way to bypass traffic.

I checked the time on my phone as I flew down the stairs and then out the front door, and by the time I hit the street I was already in full stride on my way to the corner Blake had specified.

70

I sprinted down the street, weaving through the stream of pedestrians.

I had no idea how I was going to explain all this to Christie and Tessa, but right now I was more concerned with just making it to the intersection in time so I wouldn't miss out on whatever Blake and his crew were going to tell me or hand off to me.

From my early morning runs when I stayed over at Christie's, I knew this area of the city pretty well and there was a park nearby that I could cut across and shave off enough distance that I might be able to make it to the corner in time.

As I ran, I radioed Tobin and told him to wait for word from me.

Thoughts of the case flipped through my head. The stakes. The timing. The video of D'Nesh's backpack that had led us on the path to where I was here today.

There were four masks on that couch.

Four hands reached in to pick them up. All Caucasian. What was different?

Three right hands and one left hand, and based on the location of the masks and the arms, they came from four different people.

It hadn't seemed relevant at the time, but earlier Blake had used his left hand to pour and then take his drink.

That doesn't prove anything.

No. But it was something to keep in mind.

The corner was close, just one more block.

Ignoring the walk signal and an oncoming taxi, I shot across the street in front of it, bouncing slightly off the front bumper as the cab skidded to a stop. The blaring horn told me how happy the driver was about that.

Four masks in that video.

Four.

Four hands, four people.

But the camera in the video had panned across the couch. It wasn't static, wasn't on a tripod, so someone was holding it.

A fifth person was present in the room, watching things from behind the lens.

Half a block.

Don't assume too much.

Don't give in to conjecture.

At last, I made it to the street corner and I paused, trying to catch my breath after running full out for nearly a mile and a half. Under ideal conditions I could have done it in the allotted ten minutes, but navigating through the crowds and across busy streets had not been ideal at all.

I glanced at the time.

I was late. Not by much, just thirty seconds or so, but I didn't know if, to these guys, that might make all the difference in the world.

I searched the crowd for Blake.

My phone rang and immediately I answered it. "I'm here." I was still out of breath. "I'm at the corner."

"I see you. Turn around."

I spun.

Looked for him.

Nothing. No sign.

But I did see the gargantuan bouncer who'd frisked me in the bar's hallway. He was walking my way, but was staring past me, pretending not to recognize me.

Five meters away.

I flexed, ready for a fight, as I studied his hands for a weapon. It seemed outrageous that he would attack me here on this busy street in broad daylight, but I didn't want to put anything past him.

"Just be easy, Agent Bowers," Blake said into my ear, as if he could read my thoughts.

Two meters.

One.

I was ready.

The gorilla bumped into me as he passed, and then lumbered down the sidewalk and disappeared into a nearby restaurant.

"Now what?" I asked Blake.

"Check your pocket."

I did.

In my left front pants pocket I found a key identical to the one that'd been on Randy McReynolds's body last week.

Okay, that big guy was good. I hadn't even felt him deposit the key into my pocket.

"What's it a key to?" I asked Blake.

"Everything."

I flipped it over and saw that a time was written on the back with a thin-line permanent marker: 9:00.

"What about the video?" I said. " 'Aurora's birthday'— can I get a copy?"

"Just keep the key with you."

"Morning or evening?"

No reply.

"Blake, are you there? Is it nine o'clock in the morning or at night?"

But the line had gone dead.

I visually swept the area again. He'd said on the phone that he saw me, but he wasn't on the street. I scrutinized the windows of the buildings around me, but I didn't see anyone staring down.

Thinking that maybe his bouncer might be able to give me some answers, I went to the restaurant and looked around, but he wasn't anywhere inside.

Fire codes: there has to be another exit out the back.

Instinctively, I reached for my creds to show them to the people in the kitchen as I passed through it, but found my pocket empty.

Of course, since I'd turned the creds in to DeYoung earlier in the day.

Oh well.

I made do, excusing my way past the angry line cooks who were rattling off what I assumed to be invectives at me in Korean, and I burst out the back door.

Down the block, the bouncer was squeezing into the back of a taxi.

It pulled forward, wove around an executive car that was dropping someone off, and then accelerated down the street.

For a moment I thought about trying to catch up with them, but then realized that if I were a dirty agent trading in child porn, I wouldn't have any reason to. I had the key. Things were moving forward.

I didn't really want to walk all the way back to Christie's apartment, so I called Tobin to have him pick me up.

"What did you learn?" he asked me.

"I'll tell you when you get here."

++++

Blake had watched Bowers from the button camera that his bodyguard, Mannie, was wearing.

Just giving Bowers the time for now was enough. Let him be vigilant when nine o'clock rolled around.

71

On the drive back to Christie's place, I filled Tobin in, showed him the key, and told him about the bouncer and Blake's phone call and Tessa seeing me take the camera.

"And you don't know anything more about the time listed on the key?" he asked me.

"No."

"What are you going to tell Tessa and Christie?"

"I'll think of something."

"Go with the truth when you talk to Christie. Trust me, Patrick. Just lay it out there. Don't lie to the woman you love."

"What makes you say I love her?"

He seemed surprised by my question. "I mean, the familiar way you speak about her, the fact that you're staying at her place. I guess I just, well . . . I assumed you two were in love."

Maybe you're right, I thought. *Maybe we are.*

"I don't know you very well yet," he said, "but I have the sense that you're not someone who does things half-way. You're all in or all out. Am I right?"

"Possibly." I steered the conversation away from my feelings toward Christie. "In any case, I do think going with the truth in this case is the best call. I've been told I'm not a very good liar."

I phoned Christie and finally caught her. She told me she'd been in meetings all day and hadn't been checking her messages. "What's going on? Are you okay?"

"I'm okay, but there are some things I need to talk to you about. Do you know when you'll be home?"

"I'm on my way there now. When I got all your messages and then this frantic call from Tessa a few minutes ago, I left work early. Can you tell me what happened? I haven't heard her that upset in a long time—not even when I told her about the possibility of moving. What's this about a camera in her room?"

"It's a long story, but I can tell you that no pictures were taken of her. No footage either."

"Who put the camera in there, Pat?"

"I did."

There was a long pause.

"It's for a case," I explained, although I had the sense that I wasn't really helping things.

"I'll see you in twenty minutes," was her blunt reply.

Then she hung up.

"It's not going to be good, is it?" Tobin said.

"No. I don't think it is."

I wasn't sure I wanted to show up at Christie's apartment before she got there, so Tobin and I met up with Naomi at a restaurant nearby.

While she was in Tessa's closet she'd stuffed her own clothes into the backpack she'd been carrying and had since changed back again. She handed Tessa's clothes to me folded up neatly and placed in a plastic shopping bag.

We thanked her, and after she left, Tobin and I were discussing the fact that there were five people present during the filming, when he got word from Agent Descartes that the construction company that'd built Romanoff's house twenty-three years ago was in the clear. "The paperwork was filed with the city of Princeton that the place was up to code," he told Tobin, and then Tobin told me.

"Well, someone took that insulation out," I said.

"A remodel?"

"Yeah. And a major one at that. Have him scour Romanoff's bank records and see if he can find anything."

He relayed the request to Descartes.

When Tobin checked the online case files, he saw that Officer Hinchcliffe had posted a note that one of the realtors he'd interviewed remembered someone using the name Shane. "Could be the same guy who abducted Lily Keating. I'm looking into it."

I'd been hoping that we might be able to track the Tribaxil back to someone who might've obtained it to administer to Randy McReynolds on the night he died. We perused the files, but there was nothing so far on that front.

A few minutes later, I heard from Christie that she was home, and then Tobin dropped me off at her apartment.

++++

Blake got on the line with his contact. "He has the key," he explained.

"Do you think that was a good idea?"

"I think it'll be easier to get him alone this way to find out."

"And the package?"

"I'll use a courier service, get it to him in the morning."

++++

Sitting in Christie's living room with her and Tessa, I told them the story of what had happened.

I was as honest and upfront as I could be without revealing the specifics of the case or the identity of the Port Authority officer we'd called on to change in Tessa's bedroom.

Tessa just gasped. "Seriously? You went into my room without my permission? You invaded my privacy? And you had this woman go through my things and *change into my clothes*!"

I showed her the bag I'd brought with me. "I got them back for you, it's just—"

"I don't care about the stupid clothes! That's not the point. The point is, you didn't respect me!"

Going out a bit on a limb, I mentioned that this case involved three missing persons. "Children who have been gone for months," I said. "They might still be alive and this might be our best chance at finding them."

Christie hadn't said anything yet and I did not take that as a good sign.

"Okay," Tessa said impatiently. "I get it that this was important, but you should have waited and *asked* first." She looked to her mom for support and finally just shook her head. "Screw this." She stomped down the hall to her room and slammed the door loud enough to accentuate how she truly felt.

"Well." Christie laid her hands on her lap. "I'm not sure what to say."

"Listen, I'm sorry. I tried getting in touch with you. I know that doesn't excuse—"

"Before you say another word."

"Yes?"

"You need to know that I'm not angry."

"You're not?"

"This case, this investigation, I realize that there's a lot more at stake than Tessa's privacy or the fact that you had this female officer change into some of her clothes. I get that."

I hadn't been expecting this from her. I wasn't sure how to respond.

"However," Christie continued, "it appears that my daughter doesn't see things the same way. It may take some work to patch things up on that front."

"Yeah. I'll have to see what I can do."

"I need to ask you something, though, and I want you to be completely honest with me."

"Go ahead."

"Do you think this was a good call? To do this, to film this here today?"

"No," I told her frankly. "It wasn't a good call. There were no good calls here, Christie, not this time. It's just what we had to work with at the moment. It wasn't a good call, but it was the right one."

She considered that. "Okay."

"Do you think I should go talk to Tessa?"

"Now might not be the best time."

"Right."

I tried to put myself in Tessa's shoes and I could certainly see why she was upset. What would get me un-upset, though, if I were her? That really was the question.

Christie pointed to my head. "I can see the wheels up there turning."

"I think I might have an idea of how to start bridging the gap."

"What's that?"

"Come up with something she can't solve."

She looked at me quizzically. "Something she can't solve?"

"Yeah. A puzzle. A challenge. Logic." I pulled out a notebook and a pencil and got to work.

Christie stood. "Alright, well, in the meantime, let me go speak with her."

72

Tessa threw her pillow against the wall.

How dare he!

This was her room. This was her stuff.

A knock on the door. "It's me," her mom said. "You okay in there?"

"Oh, I'm brilliant."

"Can I come in?"

"No."

"Please?"

"Leave me alone."

"Tessa, please."

"What!"

"I need to talk with you and I don't want to do it through a closed door."

"Fine. Whatever. Come in. I don't care."

Her mom eased the door open, entered, and closed it behind her. "I can understand how you'd be upset."

"Oh, well, in that case, that solves everything. Thanks for being there for me, Mom. I appreciate it. I guess you can leave now."

"Let me ask you something."

Tessa said nothing. Waited for her to go on.

"If we would have asked, would you have allowed it?"

"What do you mean?"

"If Patrick had gotten ahold of me and we would have been able to clear this with you first, would you have had a problem with it—with this undercover operation happening in your bedroom?"

"Oh, I get it—this is one of those 'It's better to ask for forgiveness than permission' deals, is that what you're saying?"

"That's not what I'm saying. But I want to know, would you have given us your blessing to go ahead with this?"

"Yeah," she admitted. "Of course. I mean, if it'll help save some kids."

"Then we need to find a way to move forward and trust each other again."

It annoyed Tessa that she agreed with her mom right now—even if it was just to a minuscule degree. It wasn't fair that she was making a good point. Seriously not fair.

"Every family ends up with collateral damage," her mom said. "You can't live with someone for any length of time without hurting those closest to you by the things you do or say. It's what happens afterward that makes all the difference."

"You said 'family.'"

"What?"

"You said 'every family.'"

"I guess I did."

"But we're not a family yet."

"No, no. We're not."

Neither of them spoke.

"Okay," Tessa muttered. "I'll reconsider hating him forever."

"That's a good place to start."

73

Francis had never made dinner for anyone before.

Spaghetti wasn't that hard, though. That's what he told himself. How can you mess up spaghetti? You boil some water, drop in some noodles, make sure they're not overcooked, microwave some sauce, and you're done.

He'd bought some garlic bread too, and had spent nearly half an hour at the grocery store picking out just the right ingredients for a salad that he'd mixed together when he first got home from work an hour ago.

He didn't want Skylar to think he was weird or that something was wrong with him, so now, while the water boiled, he took down the posters of the children that covered his wall and hid them in the closet.

There was also a pile of them by the window that wouldn't fit in the closet, so he turned the top one over so Skylar wouldn't see what he had collected. Then he set some books and a house plant on the stack.

It'd been nearly eight years since his walls were bare, so it made him a bit uncomfortable and made the room look strange, but Skylar didn't need to see the walls covered with posters of dead children, especially when he told her what he was planning to share.

You could tell where some of the posters had been. The paint looked a different color, slightly more white.

He scrubbed the wall down and it helped a little, but it was still noticeable and he just hoped Skylar wouldn't say anything about it.

He put the garlic bread in the oven and was opening the package of noodles when Skylar buzzed him from the front door of the apartment building. She'd arrived a few minutes early and he was glad he'd decided to take care of the posters when he did.

He buzzed her in.

She'd dressed up and put on makeup.

"Hello, Francis."

"Hello, Skylar. You look very pretty."

She blushed. "Thank you."

Along with her purse, she was carrying a bottle of wine.

"Come in. Please."

As she did, she handed him the wine. "I didn't really know what kind to get, but you said we were having spaghetti. The lady at the liquor store said this would go with it. It's red. A Chianti."

"Okay."

He'd given up drinking because Dr. Perrior said it lowered his inhibitions, but he didn't want Skylar to know about that, so he accepted the wine and put it on the counter.

The water was at a rolling boil when he checked it.

"I guess it's time for the noodles." He dumped them in. "The secret to making good noodles is making sure they're in boiling water the whole time."

"Do you cook a lot?"

"I just read it," he admitted. "It was in the cookbook."

"That's nice. I mean, that you looked that up."

He heated up some sauce and when the noodles were done "al dente," as the cookbook had said, he drained them and carried them to the table, where Skylar took a seat across from him.

He'd prepared a salad, spaghetti with marinara sauce, and garlic bread.

A real meal.

He poured them both some wine.

There was a lot he wanted to tell her—what he really did at work, how he'd been chatting with graciousgirl4, that he'd turned on the camera and discovered that it was really a man there instead, but truthfully, he had no idea where to start.

Honesty is the best policy.

As they began the meal, they talked casually about the hassles of their day the way people familiar with each other might do, and eventually Francis said, "I need to tell you something, Skylar. I mean, if we're going to be friends."

"We're already friends, Francis, aren't we?"

"Yes, but there are some things you should know about me."

"What are those?"

"Well, in my job—I told you I work with file analysis— well, what I do is, I have to . . ."

She picked up on his hesitancy. "You don't have to tell me if you don't want to. It's alright."

"No, I do. I analyze files, but they're not just computer files."

"Okay."

"Well, I help sort through files that people report to the place I work for—the International Child Safety Consortium—photos that might involve children being molested."

"Oh."

"I try to help the children, you know?"

"How do you help them?"

"By working to identify them so the police can try to rescue them." He went through the acronym SICR explaining each step to her: "So I screen the files, then try to identify if the images have appeared somewhere else online. Then I catalog them for law enforcement to use, and report them to the authorities."

"How do you do it?"

"How do I do it?"

"Look at those things."

"I just tell myself I'm doing something good. That I'm making a difference. They've made a lot of arrests because of my work. A lot of bad people are in jail because of it."

Hundreds of molesters, he thought, *serving almost ten thousand years in prison.*

"I'm glad you told me, Francis. That you felt like you could share that with me."

"There's one other thing . . ."

No, don't tell her! She'll hate you. You couldn't even tell Dr. Perrior about what you think sometimes. You can't tell—

"What is it?"

"There was a girl I was chatting with, I mean, a woman. So, she said she was eighteen, but she wasn't a woman at all."

"I don't understand. You have a girlfriend?"

"No, I—"

Don't!

I have to now that I started telling her. I have to!

"I wanted to meet her," he told Skylar.

"So you were chatting with a teenager and you wanted to meet her?"

"To see how old she was."

"But you said she was eighteen?"

That's not all! You wanted to—

Francis could sense that even though Skylar hadn't leaned backward, the distance between them was widening. "She might've . . ." he began. "I mean, well . . ."

He kept thinking that he wanted to be honest, but if he was, he might turn Skylar off from wanting to spend time with him.

"So what happened?" she asked.

"She wasn't who I thought she would be."

"What does that mean? You met her?"

"Sort of."

Skylar looked at him quizzically. "Francis, you're not making a lot of sense. You said she wasn't a woman after all. Was she a girl? Were you chatting with a girl?" Now her tone had moved from simple curiosity to something else, something Francis didn't want to name.

"It was a man," he said, "pretending to be an eighteen-year-old woman."

"Oh."

"I just wanted to tell you. I didn't want there to be any secrets between us."

"But why did you want to meet her?"

"Why did I . . . ?"

"I mean, if you thought she was eighteen. That's pretty young. I mean—unless, how old are you?"

"I'm twenty-eight."

"Okay. But you wanted to? And you weren't sure she was even that old?"

"I guess, I mean . . ."

This was going badly and he didn't know how to fix things. "It's always been hard for me to talk to women," he said, but sensed that all this honesty was only driving a wedge deeper and deeper between him and Skylar.

Maybe honesty wasn't the best policy after all.

Maybe secrecy was.

"Is it hard to talk to me?" she asked.

"No. It's different with you."

"You said sort of."

"Sort of?"

"A minute ago you said that you 'sort of' met this person, this man. What did you mean?"

"I did something I shouldn't have."

A pause. "What's that?"

"I went online and back-traced to the IP address. Then I turned on the computer's camera so I could see her—well, as it turned out, him."

"You were spying on her?"

"I mean, it was just to see who she was."

"Oh." She slid her chair back. "I think maybe I should go."

"I just wanted to tell you the truth."

"Okay."

"I would never do anything to hurt you."

"Why would you even say that, Francis?" There might have been a hint of fear in her words. "Why would you even think you needed to tell me that you would never hurt me?"

"Please, just." He took a deep breath. "I need to—"

But she stood and went for her purse, which she'd left near the door.

"Skylar, I'm sorry."

"I should . . ." she mumbled. "This wasn't a good idea." He couldn't tell if she was talking to herself or to him. "I mean, we barely know each other, right? We should have spent more time together before I came over here."

"Please. I'm really sorry."

She stopped at the door, and just before reaching out for the doorknob she turned and faced him. "For what, Francis? What are you sorry for?"

It wasn't that he was sorry for telling her all that. He was sorry for being weak, for giving in, for chatting with someone who he thought was too young for him, even if she had been an eighteen-year-old woman.

It didn't feel right to him.

And so it wasn't right for him.

"What are you sorry for, Francis?" Skylar asked again.

Tell her about the cabin and what happened to you. Tell her about—

No!

"I'm sorry for not saying no," he said softly, "for not stopping when I should have."

She didn't come any closer to him, but she didn't leave either. "Go on."

"I was lonely."

"Francis, that's—"

And before she could finish her sentence, he interrupted to tell her the things that he hadn't even been able to tell Dr. Perrior.

"It was my uncle," he began.

"Your uncle?"

"He would take us to his cabin. He lived in Vermont. Out near the mountains. He would take my brother and me there when we were kids. We lived in Texas, but he would fly us up there in the summers."

The images came back all at once, flooding their way through his mind, a series of pictures that he had not threaded together—not like that— not for a long time.

"What happened at the cabin, Francis?"

He remembered it vividly now: summer and how green everything got up there, but also how the temperature would drop in the evenings and then his uncle would start the fireplace. "Gonna be a cold one," he'd say.

And Francis remembered the rough sounds, the frightening sounds, that his uncle would make when it happened, and then how dirty and lonely and scared he felt afterward.

He remembered waking up in bed with his uncle beside him, touching him in places where he didn't want to be touched, and then making him do things he didn't want to do.

No, don't tell her!

But I have to be honest with her. People who care about each other tell each other the truth, don't they? They find someone they can tell their secrets to. Honesty is the best policy.

"Francis, what happened up there in Vermont?"

"My uncle was a bad man." He saw that his hands were trembling and he felt dizzy, like he needed to sit down, but he stood there instead and stuffed his hands into his pockets so Skylar wouldn't see them shaking. "He shouldn't have done those things he did to me and my brother."

A long moment passed. Neither of them said anything.

His uncle was dead now.

Seventeen years gone.

His brother too. They'd both died in that car accident on the way to the airport. Francis had survived.

Well, not at first. He'd died, then they brought him back.

A second chance.

Just like those tortoises in the Galápagos Islands.

It'd never seemed fair to him, never seemed right to him. His uncle should have died, yes, that would have made sense, but his brother should have lived.

He wanted to say more, to explain more to Skylar. He

wanted to tell her that he wasn't bad, he wasn't sick, he was just hurting and he wanted to be loved, but he didn't know how to find that, how to find someone to love him in the right way, but in the end he said nothing except, "I'm sorry. This was a mistake. Thank you."

"For what?"

"For listening."

She was still standing by the door.

He didn't know if she was going to leave or stay.

"And that's why you do what you do, isn't it, Francis? To protect other kids from having those things happen to them."

"Yes."

She set her purse on the counter. "Remember when I gave that bracelet to Derek?"

"Yes. That was nice of you."

"I made one for you too." She took it out of her purse. It was similar to Derek's but a little more rugged-looking. "I hope it doesn't get in the way when you're typing at work."

"No. It'll be okay. I know it will."

She came close enough for him to smell her perfume, sweet and touched with a hint of vanilla. He'd smelled it briefly earlier when she came in, but now it was more evident, now that she was so close to him.

She wrapped the bracelet around his wrist and then tied it off. It didn't seem like she hurried. She wanted to get it right. When she was done, she didn't back up right away but peered into his eyes.

"You're a good man, Francis."

"I'm—"

She put a finger to his lips. "You are."

Then she took him in her arms and he could feel her heart beating right beside his.

She leaned back slightly and tilted his head so that he was looking directly into her eyes. "You can kiss me. If you want to, I mean. It's okay."

The only other time he'd ever kissed a girl was when he was in primary school and he'd kissed Megan Pepaj on the cheek because his friend Bruce Smythe had dared him to do it and he didn't want to lose the dare. Megan had cried afterward and told the teacher and he'd gotten in trouble.

Skylar closed her eyes. Francis didn't close his, but watched her carefully as he kissed her, afraid that she would back away. At first he couldn't quite figure out what to do, but then she opened her mouth and she was touching her tongue to his and it was as if he suddenly did know what to do.

He closed his eyes then, and everything was new and exciting and terrifying at the same time. It felt like all of his life had led up to this moment and even if this was his last moment, it would have all been worth it just to live long enough to kiss this woman who had heard his secrets and had not walked out the door.

PART IV

The Piper

74

I knocked on the door to Tessa's room.

"What?"

"It's Patrick."

"I'm not talking to you."

"Okay, but can I open the door for a second?"

"Why? I told you, I'm not talking to you."

I didn't point out the inconsistency in her statement. It probably wouldn't have helped matters at the moment.

"I want to give you a logic problem I came up with."

Silence.

"Well?" I asked.

Nothing.

"If you can solve it, I'll give up meat for a week."

A pause, and then, "A month."

"Two weeks."

"Three."

"Alright," I agreed. "If you can solve it, I'll give up meat for three weeks."

"Tell it to me through the door."

"Four brothers live at the crossroads of a well-traveled intersection. Lots of people stop and ask them for directions since the beach lies in one direction and the mall in another. But not all the boys tell the truth."

I paused.

"Go on."

"The thirteen-year-old tells the truth exactly half of the time, the fifteen-year-old tells a lie exactly half of the time, the twelve-year-old always lies, and the fourteen-year-old always tells the truth. From the following three clues, can you figure out which direction it is to the mall, and the age of each of the boys?"

When she didn't answer right away, I wasn't sure if she was going to let me keep going.

Then, at last, her voice came from the room: "Give me my clues."

"One: when you ask which way the beach is, Eric is the only one to point to the right. Two: when you ask which way the mall is, John is the only one to point to the right. Three: John is older than Paul, but younger than Matt."

"Read them one more time."

I did.

Even for Tessa that was a lot to process.

"And am I facing them?" she asked. "So their left would be my right?"

"Let's say it's the same, so their left is yours and your right is theirs. Do you want me to copy this down for you? Slip the clues under the door?"

"No. I got it. I'll get back to you. But I'm still not talking to you."

"Okay. Good-bye."

"Good-bye."

Back in the living room, Christie asked me, "So, how did it go?"

"Not too bad. She told me she isn't talking to me, though."

"She does that."

I checked the time.

A couple minutes after eight.

That gave me just shy of one hour before nine o'clock rolled around. I still didn't know what I was supposed to do or where I was supposed to be when it arrived, but I figured Blake would contact me again, so I kept my phone handy.

In the meantime, I told Christie that I'd been put on administrative leave and that she might hear about it on the news.

"Is this because of what happened last week?"

"I can't go into the details—and I should tell you that it's just temporary—but my schedule might be a little, well, unpredictable for the next few days."

"Fair enough. When I got involved with an FBI agent, I knew things would be a bit crazy, but . . ."

"You had no idea they would be like this."

"Bingo."

"Don't say 'bingo' around Tessa or she'll call you old."

"Gotcha."

I slipped into Christie's bedroom where my suitcase was, ostensibly just to change clothes, but while I was in there and out of earshot of Christie, I called Jodie on the burner phone to tell her what was going on. I caught her as she was leaving the Y, where she'd just finished swimming.

I filled her in.

"Thanks for the heads-up," she said. "By the way, as you know, DeYoung has had me looking for Romanoff. It looks like his files were never backed up on the server before he deleted them, so that's no good. Also, I checked the case files just before I started my laps: the doorman at Romanoff's condo building remembered him but not Shane, which is awfully convenient. And I should mention, at this point I don't think Romanoff was the shooter in the house."

"You mean the guy who killed Higgs?"

"Right."

"Why do you say that?"

"From where he had to have been standing, based on the house's floor plan and your account of the shooting, someone doesn't make a shot like that without practice and there's no record in Romanoff's credit card statements of any gun purchases or visits to shooting ranges. There are no firearms registered to his name. He doesn't have a carry permit from any state."

"So what are you thinking?"

"We're looking for someone who's an expert marksman with a handgun."

"So, quite possibly someone in law enforcement or the military."

"I know you're not one to work off assumptions, but . . ."

"No, it's a good place to start, given all that we know about this case."

I mentally sorted through things.

"Alright," I said, "this is all intertwined and the only people who knew I was going to that house were the ones on the task force. Tomorrow I want you to take a look at the task force members. Do it under the radar, but see if anything comes up. Check if any of them are on Stewart's mailing list or have reprimands for downloading porn at work, anything."

"Are you serious?"

"Yes. And qualification scores on the firing range."

"Some of that information will be confidential. Only someone from the Office of Professional Responsibility would have access to their personnel files."

"Call Maria Aguirre in the morning."

"Is this really a can of worms you want to open?"

"No, but it might be one we need to peer into. Also, have Tobin take a closer look at Hal Lloyd, see if he can find any connection between him and Higgs, Stewart, or Wooford."

She offered to let Assistant Director DeYoung know what was going on.

"I'll contact him," I said.

At the dining room table, I went on my computer and had just started an email to DeYoung when my phone vibrated. A text from Tessa: "It's not bad. Not great but not bad."

I doubted that many teens used proper spelling and punctuation when they texted, but I had the sense that Tessa wouldn't have had it any other way.

I texted back, "So you figured it out?"

"It's nice. It's clever, simple, elegant," she replied, choosing the same language I'd used on Saturday when I was talking about the logic problem she'd made up.

"Nice?" I typed, echoing what she'd said the other day. "What does that mean? Did you solve it?"

"Yes. But you made that up?"

"You're stalling."

"I'm not stalling," she texted back.

"You are so stalling," I replied.

"The mall is on the right. The beach is on the left. Eric is twelve; he always lies. Paul is thirteen and tells the truth half the time. John is fourteen; he always tells the truth. Matt is fifteen and lies half the time."

Man.

She was good.

It wasn't the easiest puzzle in the world and I was

curious how she'd solved it so quickly, but since she'd nailed it and I knew she'd never seen it before—since I'd just made it up tonight—clearly, whatever technique she'd used had worked.

I texted her, "Does this mean you're talking to me again?"

I waited.

Finally, she typed back, "No."

"But you're texting me."

"This doesn't count. I'm not moving my lips."

"Training wheels," I texted.

"Enjoy not eating meat."

When I set my phone down, Christie said, "Well?"

"It looks like it's going to be an ongoing project, but I think the foundations are in place."

As I was finishing the email to the Assistant Director, I recalled that Blake had access to my phone records. I wasn't sure if my email account had been compromised as well, so I used an alias account to send my report to DeYoung. Then I turned to a more personal matter.

I wanted to put this whole prospect of moving with Christie on the table, to examine the possibility and see if it got my juices flowing, so I pulled up some online maps of Omaha and started poring over them, studying the cost of apartments in different neighborhoods, especially those near the Field Office.

However, rather than finding the prospect of relocating intriguing, it just made me feel anxious.

I was caught up in my thoughts about that when Christie said, out of nowhere, "I never told you what brought us to New York City."

"No. You didn't."

"I was trying to start fresh. I'd met a guy and I thought maybe . . . Well, I came here to be close to him and it didn't work out. By then I had a job and I decided to stay."

I wondered why she was explaining this to me now, but then she pointed toward my computer screen where the website of Omaha real estate was visible to her. "Moving to be close to someone doesn't always go as planned," she said softly.

"Are you telling me this to dissuade me from coming with you?"

"Just to make sure you don't make a mistake."

"But see, was it really a mistake for you to move here? If you hadn't, we never would've met."

"That's one way to look at it, but I think our paths still would've crossed."

"Why do you say that?"

"When people are meant to be—" she started, then caught herself and said, "I just mean, I believe there's a bigger plan at work. If people—whoever they are—are destined to be together, it'll . . . I'm digging myself a hole, aren't I?"

"Not really. I kind of like the idea that we were meant to be together, that it's part of a bigger plan."

A call came in. I checked the screen.

Tobin.

"Hang on. I need to take this." I went to the other room. "What do you have?"

"I think someone found out about our visit with Lloyd in prison yesterday."

"Why's that?"

"About an hour ago he was found dead in the shower. Blunt force trauma. Someone bashed in the back of his skull with a fire extinguisher that'd been stolen from the kitchen."

Though I wasn't thrilled to hear that Lloyd was dead,

considering what he'd done to those children, I didn't mourn very long. "And I suppose no one knows anything about this—any of the other inmates, I mean?"

"According to the official report put out by the warden, no one saw a thing."

"Of course not."

The prisoners knew that if they did report anything, they might be next.

"So," I said, "someone wasn't happy that he was talking to us. Someone with connections."

"Connections—you mean someone in law enforcement?"

"Maybe. Jodie's doing some checking into the task force. Stay in touch with her."

"The task force?"

I summarized the reasoning.

He heard me out, then said, "As far as task force members and the mailing list, I already checked that out. Chip wasn't on Stewart's list, but he did get real estate emails. When I talked with him he told me, 'Retiring on the pension of a cop? No thanks.' He subscribes to half a dozen newsletters for investment opportunities."

"Huh."

"Maybe it's something, maybe it's not. We can't discard it, but when I looked into it, it didn't lead anywhere."

"Okay."

"Listen, I've been thinking about the fact that there were five people present at the filming of the video with the masks. I mean, we can't presume too much, but according to D'Nesh, the two guys who were in Romanoff's house didn't wear masks. That leaves us with, what? Blake? Shane? Romanoff? The Piper? And someone else we don't know about yet?"

"There's no evidence that they're all different people," I said. "Romanoff might be the Piper. Blake might be Shane. But yes. Any way you slice it, there are a lot of people involved in this. We need more information."

"I'll see what else I can pull up on Lloyd."

"Since the key they gave me had nine o'clock written on it I might be in for a busy night. We'll see."

"Keep me updated as best you can."

"I will."

I kept my phone ready and my email open, but nine o'clock passed by without Blake contacting me. I continued to work and gave him until ten thirty, then finally called it quits for the day.

While I lay on the couch trying to fall asleep, I thought of all those names we'd listed, all the people who might be involved with the Final Territory.

I sometimes wonder if offenders think about getting caught, if they ponder the consequences of their choices. I've heard of instances in which killers were apprehended after years or even decades on the run and they didn't fight the police or try to flee. They just went along willingly.

Back in the 1980s when the police arrived to capture one serial killer twelve years after his crimes began, he simply said, "It's about time."

So how does a person go about day-to-day living knowing that at any moment he might be caught and sent to prison for the rest of his life?

Waiting.

Watching.

For the day when the police show up and you say—or at least think— "It's about time."

Desire. To enticement. To death.

Chained souls.

Manacled hearts.

Blake had told me that the key I now had was the key to everything, but we still didn't know what it actually opened.

I kept it beside me as I closed my eyes and wondered what exactly "everything" might entail.

75

I slept in my clothes just in case I was called out for some reason.

But I was not.

And I did not sleep well.

The images in my dreams weren't quiet and reassuring, but rather, were marked with the madness of this case.

I saw myself surrounded by tongues of fire like those from the other day in the burning house. Higgs was there too, being consumed by the flames, then his head snapped back from the bullet hitting his forehead, and he fell to the floor. I watched prison bars rise around me and razor wire from the Albany Federal Penitentiary hem me in. It curled into me and then twisted its way out of my chest, the coils covered with glistening blood.

When I finally awoke, I was glad Christie and Tessa were in their rooms and didn't see how tense I was as I tried to shake off the residue of my dark thoughts in the night.

*   *   *

We all got ready for the day, and as Tessa finished up her breakfast, I said, "Are you talking to me now?"

"Yes. But I'm using small words."

"Okay. So, tell me how you solved that logic problem last night."

"Well, the two who lie and tell the truth half the time would need to point the same direction for each question, whereas the other two would have to switch. And since John has a younger brother, he can't be the twelve-year-old who always lies. Therefore he must always tell the truth."

Amazing.

I'd thought it would be more confusing, but when she put it like that, it sounded so simple.

"So, how long did it take you to figure out?"

"I waited for a while before I texted you. I didn't want to hurt your feelings by making you think it was too easy."

"Oh. Well. Thanks for that. So, this is your last day of exams and then you can finally enjoy your summer, huh?"

"Yeah. Finally. And you won't be eating meat for the first three weeks of it."

"Maybe we should go double or nothing."

"What do you mean?"

"Come up with another one," I said. "See if I can solve it."

"And you'll go six weeks?"

"Or none."

"If you solve it."

"You mean *when*."

"Yeah, right."

"So is it a deal?"

"Okay, deal. I'll text it to you."

"I'll be waiting."

Christie appeared, grabbed her purse, wished me a great day, gave me a kiss good-bye, and in a rush and a whirl they were out the door. And then they were gone.

A blunt silence enveloped the apartment in their wake.

Being on administrative leave without access to my office and not knowing what nine o'clock might bring, I wasn't sure if I should stick around here or go out somewhere.

In the end, I figured that before anything else, I would sneak in a workout here at the apartment since this might be my only chance today to do so. I went with chair dips, sit-ups, push-ups, planks, and fingertip pull-ups on the doorframes—as much as I could with that gash in my arm from last week.

The same kind of workout prisoners do.

And that's what was on my mind as I exercised—what it would have been like to do all this behind bars.

++++

Francis stared at the ceiling, trying to believe that what had happened last night had actually happened.

Skylar leaned up on her elbow and laid her other hand on his arm. "I don't usually do this," she said softly.

"Neither do I."

He didn't tell her that he'd never been with a woman before. He didn't want her to think less of him, that he wasn't a real man.

Maybe she would feel special if she knew she was the first one?

No! She didn't say anything last night about you not knowing what you were doing. You don't need to ruin things by bringing that up now.

They were adults, they liked each other, they'd each

had, perhaps, a little too much to drink. And things had gone in a direction he'd never anticipated when he first invited her over for spaghetti.

That was it.

That's what he told himself.

Sunlight eased in softly through the window and he knew that he needed to get going if he was going to make it to work on time, but he didn't want to leave. He wanted to just stay right here by Skylar's side and let the world outside circle around them, go on its way, and leave them alone.

Just the two of them.

Forever.

"Are you okay?" she asked.

"Yes."

But she must have thought that he seemed distant. "Did I say something? Is something wrong?"

"No, no. Everything's perfect."

He looked past her and saw his closet where he'd stored the posters he'd taken down before she came over last night, and he thought of them and of secrets and of the things we keep hidden.

Maybe you should show them to her after breakfast?

Yes.

Definitely.

No more secrets.

Honesty is the best policy.

"I like you, Skylar. I feel like I can be myself with you."

"Me too."

So maybe he *would* be a few minutes late for work. It would be the first time in eight years.

He was probably long past due.

Skylar gave him a kiss. "I need to use the bathroom."

She rolled over and slipped out of bed, then grabbed her clothes and disappeared down the hall.

Francis took a deep breath, closed his eyes, and let himself smile.

He felt exhilarated and at peace and vulnerable and unconquerable. Somehow all of them, all at once.

It was going to be a busy day, getting everything ready for the donor banquet tonight, but it was also going to be a good day.

Maybe you can ask Skylar to come tonight? It's probably not too late to get her an invitation. Just talk to Claire and—

There was a knock at the front door.

Francis sat up.

Why on earth would anyone be coming to his apartment at this time of day?

The knocking turned to pounding. "Open up!"

After tugging on his pants and slipping into a shirt, Francis went to the door and peered through the peephole. A fierce-looking man in his forties stood outside the threshold.

Francis latched the chain lock and eased the door open a crack. "Hello?"

The man threw himself violently against the door, and the meager chain that was holding it snapped. He burst into the room, shoving Francis to the side and then throwing the door shut behind him.

"Where is she?"

Francis scrambled to get in front of him. "There's no one here," he lied.

"Oh, I know she's here. Where? The bedroom? Skylar!"

"I told you there's no one here."

She stepped out of the bathroom wearing her clothes from last night. "Ivan, you didn't need to—"

The man went directly to her and punched her brutally in the face, sending her reeling backward and colliding into the wall.

She cried out, slid to the floor, and cowered by the bathroom doorway.

"Stop it!" Francis ran toward the man she'd just called Ivan and pushed him to make him stop hurting her. "Get away from her!"

Ivan seemed amused by Francis's feeble attempts to get him to move.

Francis had never been in a fistfight before. Though he'd been beaten up more than once when he was young, he'd never thrown a punch at anyone, and now as he swung at the man's face, Ivan easily deflected his hand.

"Every time you hit me, I'll hit her. Go ahead, see if I'm bluffing."

"Don't!" Skylar gasped, holding one hand against her face where Ivan had punched her. "He'll do it."

Francis stood there feeling helpless, unsure what to do. "Who are you?" he demanded, although he thought he might already know: her boyfriend.

Her husband?

No reply.

"I'll call the police," Francis threatened.

The man shook his head. "I don't think that would be a good idea."

"Oh? And why not?" Francis knelt to help Skylar to her feet so he could lead her to the bedroom where his phone was, and where he could call 911.

As she stood she glared at Ivan. "Why did you hit me so hard?"

"It was the best way to make this believable."

Francis looked from Ivan to Skylar, trying to process things, but he felt like he was one step behind whatever was happening. "What's going on?"

"Francis," Ivan said, "I'm going to need you to do something for me."

"I'm not doing anything for you! You just attacked Skylar."

"No. *You* did."

"What?"

"You're going to receive an email at work this afternoon. It has a link that you're going to open. A file will download to your computer. When it does, all you have to do is open it. The algorithm will do the rest."

"What are you talking about?"

"At work. At the ICSC today."

Francis had that plunging feeling in his stomach again, just like he'd had on Monday when he saw that man chatting as graciousgirl4. "I don't understand."

"Francis, the firewalls at the International Child Safety Consortium are very good. The best way in wasn't to breach the firewalls." He pointed to Francis. "It was to breach you."

"To breach me?"

"Last night you sexually assaulted a woman you barely knew after luring her to your apartment."

"What? No, it was—"

"You were rough with her, you punched her in the face to keep her submissive."

"I'm sorry, Francis." Skylar went to stand next to Ivan. "It had to be like this."

"What? You were in on this?"

Spinning and twisting.

Dipping and diving.

Corkscrewing downward and out of control.

Ivan said, "If you don't do as we say when you get that email, Skylar will claim that it wasn't consensual last night. And with those bruises, and since I was never here, who's going to doubt her? After all, considering what you do for a living, the images you look at every day, it would be quite believable that you would decide to act out some of the things you've seen."

Francis told himself that he must be dreaming and tried to wake up, tried to make all this go away.

"You're going to help us," Ivan continued. "Do you know how much prison time you could be facing for raping this lovely young lady?" He slid his finger down Skylar's cheek and then along her jawline.

"Don't touch her!" Francis yelled.

Skylar brushed the man's hand away, but said to Francis, "You need to listen to him. You're in over your head here."

Ivan glanced at his watch. "You better get going, Francis, or you're gonna be late for work. And with the big fundraiser tonight, they won't be very happy with you if that happens."

"No," Francis said defiantly. "I won't do it. I won't compromise our system no matter what you do to me. Even if Skylar lies, even if I get in trouble, I'm not going to do it because it's not right and I won't do something that I know is wrong. Not purposely. Not ever."

Ivan looked at Skylar. "Is this guy for real?"

"I would believe him. He has an honest heart."

"Uh-huh. Well, in that case, there's something I need to show you, Francis."

He reached into his pocket, produced a bracelet, and tossed it at Francis's feet.

It was the one Skylar had made for Derek and had tied onto his wrist Sunday afternoon.

Or at least it looked like the same one.

She could have made two. It might be a duplicate. Maybe she made it because she knew this was going to happen.

"When did you get that?" Skylar asked Ivan.

"I paid the kid a visit last night."

"That wasn't part of the—"

"Don't you worry about that." He turned to Francis. "Next time I'll bring you the arm it was attached to. Test me if you don't believe me."

"I believe you."

"Listen, Francis," Skylar said. "We don't want to hurt anyone. The people behind this can get good care for Derek, they can help him, help with the research. If you do this for us, I'll make sure they do."

"We don't have permission to offer him that," Ivan countered.

"I have some sway." Then she addressed Francis again. "You have a simple job. When you get the email, click on the link, download the file, open it, and Derek will be fine and all this will go away."

"A virus."

"A file," Ivan said. "That's all you need to know, and if you call the police or the FBI we'll know about it and we will hurt Derek in ways you don't even want to imagine."

Francis was quiet.

"Come on," Ivan told Skylar. "It's time for us to go. Francis needs to get ready for work. We wouldn't want to make him late. Not today."

She went to gather her things. "Don't be angry, Francis. It isn't personal. I like you. And we really can do good things for Derek if you help us. I promise."

76

I finished my prison workout, took a shower, and got dressed.

Without access to my work files, I felt a little direction-less, and if Blake didn't follow up on something here at nine, I wasn't sure what I was going to do for the day.

Yesterday, I'd contemplated visiting Billy McReynolds. That was always a possibility.

Checking my email, I saw that DeYoung had replied to my message from last night, thanking me for keeping him in the loop.

As I read through his reply I could almost hear him clearing his throat every sentence or two.

I put on some Ethiopian Yirgacheffe from Blessed Nir-vana Roasters and settled in to see what I could figure out about the file sharing options on Exo-Skel IV.

++++

On his way to the subway tunnel, Francis tried to make sense of what had just happened at his apartment. Skylar

had betrayed him. He was in big trouble and he didn't
have any good options.

Either he downloaded the file or Derek might be
harmed, killed even.

He was passing a newsstand when the headline of one
of the city's newspaper's caught his eye.

It announced that the FBI agent who'd shot a man last
week had been put on administrative leave.

There was a photo of Agent Bowers, the man Francis
had met on Friday, the one who'd sent him the link to the
cache of more than sixteen thousand images.

He was suspended?

It was a little hard to believe. He'd seemed so honest
and professional and perceptive, especially about the
video that had that backpack.

In fact, it was almost like he knew exactly what to look
for.

Well, people aren't always who they appear to be.

Bowers wasn't.

Skylar wasn't.

Graciousgirl4 wasn't.

*Maybe no one is who they appear to be when the masks are
finally ripped away.*

Who are you, Francis? What are you capable of?

What masks are you wearing?

++++

I was looking for clues to anyone who might have shared
a video called "Aurora's birthday" on Exo-Skel IV's community forum when I glanced at the clock and realized
that it was just a couple minutes before nine.

Still no word from Blake.

Tobin called and I picked up.

"Anything more on Lloyd?" I asked.

"No. Remember how we had some officers checking to see if any other women who'd been brought to Romanoff's condo had disappeared?"

"Yes."

"Well, as far as we can tell, none did—which is good news, but it doesn't help us any."

"I'll take any good news I can get it."

Someone buzzed Christie's apartment number at the front of the building. "Hello? I have a package for Dr. Bowers in 416."

I checked the time.

Nine o'clock exactly.

"Hang on," I told Tobin. "I need to get this."

77

Still on the line, I buzzed the courier into the apartment building.

"What is it?" Tobin asked.

"Someone's here. He's on his way up now. There's a package for me."

"But who even knows you're staying there with Christie?"

"Blake might—if he had me followed."

Who else? Well, Tobin and Jodie. Agent Descartes was helping her move the other day; he might have overheard something.

"Interestingly enough," I said, "the delivery guy said the package was for Dr. Bowers, not Agent Bowers."

"Does Blake know you have a PhD?"

"He might. It's not something I usually put out there, though." I recalled that Maria Aguirre had commented on my PhD when I first met with her on Thursday. Really, since my academic history was detailed in my personnel file, anyone with access to it could have known that.

Or anyone who'd read either of my two books.

Tobin told me that he was going to spend the morning looking for any connections between Lloyd and the other people we knew of who had ties to the Final Territory. "What are you up to today?" he asked me.

The doorbell rang.

"I may be about to find out," I said. "I'll talk to you later."

"Okay. Be careful."

"Always."

Though I'd had to turn in my Bureau-issued firearm, many agents own a personal handgun, and I was no exception.

So now I had the .357 SIG P229 ready as I answered the door and found the deliveryman standing there holding a package about the size of a shoebox and wrapped in plain brown paper. He also held a clipboard with a form for me to sign.

I didn't aim the gun at him, but I was holding it ready by my side and let him see that I was armed. "Set the package down."

He gulped, eyes on the gun, but didn't move.

"Just set it down. Do it slowly."

Finally, he did, then stood again and, quivering, held out the clipboard. "I, um . . . I normally, I need you to sign for . . ." He was still staring at my SIG. "But I can always just take your word for it."

With my free hand I scribbled my name on the line.

There was no return address on the package. "What can you tell me about the person who gave this to you?"

The guy shook his head. "They just hand 'em to me at work and I deliver 'em. I have no idea who dropped it off."

"Alright. Thanks. You can go."

He nodded, then backed a few steps down the hall

before turning and hurrying the rest of the way to the elevator.

I picked up the package and went back into the apartment, closing the door behind me.

I put the gun away, set the box on the table, and studied it.

With the potential that there was something toxic inside it, I opted not to open it in here and chance exposing Christie's place to whatever that might be.

It'd be best to open it somewhere else, somewhere out in the open where I'd be the only one in any danger.

The park I'd cut across yesterday when I was running to meet up with Blake's man had some secluded areas that were almost always free of foot traffic and pedestrians.

Ideally, it might be best to have a bomb squad open this box, but I was pretty sure there wasn't a bomb in here.

Not positive.

But satisfied enough to go for it.

Decision made, I slipped my laptop into its bag and grabbed my burner phone and my personal cell. Then I slid my folded-up automatic knife and the key from Blake into my pocket, and, carrying the package, I left for the park.

++++

Tessa was distracted during her history exam as she found herself thinking about what kind of logic problem to come up with for Patrick.

She wanted something different, but also something that could throw him off.

A twist.

That's what she needed.

Something that would lead him in one direction, play to his expectations, and then turn them against him.

She had two other finals today and didn't intend to cram for either of them. Hopefully, that would give her enough time to come up with something good.

++++

As I traversed the sidewalk, I kept an eye out for anyone who might have been following me, especially any of the men who'd been in the bar yesterday when I met up with Blake.

I saw no one.

At last, confident I was alone, I slipped through the trees and found the most remote part of the park, made sure no other people were around, and laid the box on the grass.

I flicked out my automatic knife.

Carefully, I removed the brown paper that the box was wrapped in.

It appeared to be just a plain corrugated cardboard box with the top flaps taped shut.

I cut the tape, and as I opened the flaps, I found myself holding my breath.

But there was no bomb, no poison, no anthrax spores. No tarantulas or copperhead snakes.

No needles, thank God.

Nothing dangerous.

Instead, nestled on a bed of silky black cloth was a white mask identical to the ones that appeared in the video that contained the image of D'Nesh's backpack.

I examined the mask carefully before removing it. Beneath it was a notecard that read *Tonight at nine. 54 North Worthy Drive.*

Handwriting different from Randy's suicide note.

When I took a closer look at the black cloth, I realized that it was actually a hood.

I could certainly have these items checked for fingerprints and DNA, but that's probably not what a dishonest agent hoping to get into the Final Territory would do.

No, if we were going to make this happen, right now I needed to engender Blake's confidence, and he quite possibly had a contact at the Bureau, perhaps on the task force, who would be able to find out about any tests I ordered.

I wrapped the mask in the black hood to preserve prints, put it in my computer bag, and discarded the box and paper in a recycling bin on the edge of the park.

Then I went to a coffee shop to go online and look up who lived at 54 North Worthy Drive.

78

Francis arrived at work.

Ivan had told him that the email would come in the afternoon, but at the moment, Francis had something else on his mind other than viruses and compromised computer systems.

He called St. Stephen's Research Hospital to check on Derek. The receptionist connected him to the boy's room.

"Hello?" Derek answered uncertainly.

"Derek, this is Mr. Edlemore. Are you alright?"

"Oh. Yeah. I'm okay."

"Good, good. Do you still have that nice bracelet Miss Shapiro gave you?"

"No. I had it last night, but when I woke up this morning it was gone! Somebody *stole* it!"

That was not what Francis wanted to hear. He'd been hoping that the one Ivan had shown him this morning was simply a duplicate.

"I'm sorry someone took it," he told Derek.

"Maybe she can make me another one."

"Maybe."

"When are you coming back?"

"Soon."

"Is Miss Shapiro coming with you? She was nice."

"We'll see."

"She promised to."

"I know."

But we're not friends anymore, Francis thought. *She lied to me. She's working for some very bad people.* But he didn't say any of those things, of course. "We'll get you another bracelet," he told Derek. He was looking at the one on his own wrist as he said the words. "An even better one."

After the call, Francis managed to remove the bracelet that Skylar had given him.

If nothing else, he could give it to Derek once all this was over.

Why did you ever trust her?

Well, just like Derek said, she was nice.

Just because someone is nice doesn't mean you should trust them!

Francis tried to process everything.

Ivan had snuck into Derek's room last night while he was asleep and had taken the bracelet.

Just thinking about how he'd invaded Derek's room like that, and then how he'd punched Skylar in the face, made Francis angry all over again—even though he knew she wasn't to be trusted, that she was on the wrong side of this.

Maybe Ivan and his people were threatening her. Maybe that's why she was doing this.

Yes. That's it. That has to be it.

He couldn't think of any other reason why she might have helped them.

Maybe she's just bad, Francis. There are bad people out there. You know that better than anyone. And she's one of them.

No, she's not!

Yes. Francis. Yes, she is.

Preoccupied by his thoughts, he took the St. Stephen's Research Hospital mug from his desk and went to the break room to get some coffee.

Ivan had warned him not to contact the police about what was happening, but what about telling them that someone was sneaking around the hospital stealing things from children who were dying of cancer? Did that count?

Of course. These people aren't going to want you talking to the police about anything.

At the coffeemaker, Claire approached him and smiled. "All ready for tonight?"

"I was just about to get started on my work," he said distractedly.

"Of course. Well, I wanted to tell you that I decided to let everyone off a little early today. This way we can have time to get ready for tonight."

"How early?"

"I'll be closing the doors at four, but if you need to leave earlier, that can be arranged."

Four?

No, what if the email comes in after that?

Certainly when Ivan said it would arrive in the afternoon he meant before four.

Maybe not. You don't know that for sure!

"Well." Claire gave Francis's shoulder a friendly chuck. "Let me know if you need anything today."

"I will."

It'll be okay. The email will get here by four.

But what if it doesn't?

Well, there was nothing he could do about it either way at the moment.

After filling his coffee mug, he took it to his desk and turned his attention to the computer screen.

He had some time. He needed to make sure he was caught up on his other projects or else Claire might think something was wrong and take more careful note of what he was doing today.

But even as he started his work, he wondered what he was going to do when that email from Ivan did arrive—open it or report it?

And, despite how much depended on his answer, he really didn't know what it would be.

++++

I could hardly believe who lived at that address on North Worthy Drive: Marcus Rockwell, the billionaire entrepreneur who'd started the groundbreaking social networking and web search engine, Krazle, six years ago, when he was only twenty-five.

Krazle's ads stated that their vision was to create a community where you could find "anything on the web or beyond it," and based on the company's meteoric success, they were doing a pretty good job of reaching that goal.

Blake wants you at Rockwell's house tonight at nine?
Is Rockwell somehow involved in all this?

That seemed highly doubtful to me, but I didn't want to discount anything.

Last Wednesday, Randy McReynolds had told me, "They know things. They can find out things. You have no idea how far this goes."

Did it go all way to the CEO of Krazle?

Was that even possible?

Krazle's corporate headquarters was just outside Silicon Valley, but they also had offices here in New York City, and apparently that's where Rockwell primarily worked out of when he wasn't involved in humanitarian efforts around the globe.

It wasn't difficult to find photographs of Rockwell's sprawling estate at 54 North Worthy Drive, half an hour outside the city limits. The grounds used to be a boarding school and the main building had been renovated, apparently with a ballroom and catering facilities, ideal for hosting events.

Rockwell's Wikipedia page noted that he gave millions of dollars to charities and public service organizations. The ICSC appeared first on the list.

After a little more searching, I found that Rockwell's upcoming media appearances included being a guest on Billy McReynolds's radio show this morning.

Interesting.

Hyperlinked to the article was information about the International Child Safety Consortium donor banquet that their president, Alejandro Gomez, had invited me to last week when I was at their office, meeting with Mr. Edlemore.

Rockwell was hosting the gala at his mansion tonight.

And so.

More threads woven into the rug.

But more questions too.

Is the Final Territory going to stage some sort of protest? Have they infiltrated the ICSC?

The best way to find answers to those questions would be to attend the event tonight.

When Gomez had invited me, I'd declined since I didn't want it to appear that I was receiving perks or special consideration from him during an active investigation.

However, now that I was on administrative leave and since I'd received this mask and hood, we had a legitimate reason to suspect that something untoward might occur during the fundraiser. I figured I could go, and it might make sense for us to have an even bigger presence there.

How to frame this . . . ?

I contacted the ICSC to see if they could get me in touch with Gomez. When I told the receptionist who I was, she immediately patched me through to his personal line.

I didn't mention that I was currently suspended, and I hoped he hadn't been following the news. Stretching the truth slightly, I told him, "We have credible intel that there's a group that might be planning a demonstration or disruption at the fundraiser tonight."

"Agent Bowers, if something like that were to happen, it would just provide us with even more exposure and media coverage—a bigger audience to hear our message of hope for the children we work so hard to protect worldwide. I'm not going to cancel the event, if that's what you're suggesting."

"No, I'm not. At this time I don't have any reason to believe that you or your guests are in any kind of danger. That being said, we're going to want some agents under cover at the event. We'll work with your security team. We'll be unobtrusive, I promise. But I want some people on-site just in case anything goes down."

Thoughts flashed through my mind, what was best for everyone, what was safest for everyone.

You could order police protection for Christie and Tessa while you're there, or . . .

I recalled Saturday night when I was at Tobin's house and we were postulating about how Adrienne's abductors had pulled things off—they drew Tobin out of the house, likely to remove the primary threat first.

Misdirection.

Now, this morning, someone who knew I was staying

at Christie's had given me a time and a location where they wanted me to be while she and Tessa were likely going to be someplace else.

Maybe all this is an orchestrated attempt to get you away from them tonight . . .

But of all the people involved in this, who can you trust?

Off the top of my head I couldn't think of too many task force members who I was confident weren't involved.

The list was strikingly short: Tobin, Jodie, DeYoung.

If all this is going down tonight, the safest place for Christie and Tessa wouldn't be at home alone under police protection, but close to you and in a group with other people around.

"Did I lose you?" Gomez asked me. "Are you still there?"

"Sorry. Yes. I'm . . . What were you saying?"

"We were talking about unobtrusive security for tonight."

"Right. Just a few other agents."

"Certainly. I'd be a fool to ignore the threat you've identified and an even bigger fool to turn down the offer of the FBI's help with our security. How many invitations do you need?"

"Five."

"I'll have them waiting for you when you arrive. They'll be under your name."

"One will be for a guest under twenty-one. Will that be a problem?"

"No, there'll be nonalcoholic beverages available." Then he added, "It is a black-tie event, so if your agents wish to remain unobtrusive—as you said—I would suggest they dress accordingly."

"Good to know. Thanks."

He told me that cocktails started at six, followed by dinner, and then a short presentation at around eight. "I look forward to seeing you there, Agent Bowers."

After Gomez hung up, I called Tobin to tell him what was going on.

He took it all in. "So they gave you a mask and a hood?"

"Yes. It looks like I've been officially invited to join the Final Territory."

He was quiet. "I can certainly come to the event tonight and I'll see if Jodie can as well, but I don't like this, Pat. Let me have the lab take a look at the hood and mask, check them for prints and DNA."

"I should probably keep them with me for now."

"And you think it's a good idea to have Christie and Tessa there tonight?"

"Right now I don't know who to trust. This way I'll be able to keep an eye on them. There'll likely be dozens, if not hundreds, of people there. Safety in numbers."

"And when you put on that mask and hood at nine o'clock and they take you to wherever they want to take you—I mean, assuming that's what's going to happen—what then?"

"Then I'll leave Christie and Tessa under your watchful eye. Or maybe Jodie's. Either way they'll be safe. Hey, listen, I was thinking about how, when you're working on a puzzle, after you've taken a glance at the big picture, sometimes it's good to go back to the beginning to review what led you to that place."

"You mean return to Stewart's apartment?"

"Yes. I'd like to poke around a bit, then head over to Billy McReynolds's studio and talk with him. Last week he offered to help us out if we needed it. Maybe there'll

be something else about his brother that he's remembered that'll better prepare me for this meeting tonight
with the Final Territory people."

"All that sounds good, except the part about you going back to the apartment. It's still a sealed-off crime
scene and you're currently suspended."

"Hmm." That was true. "How about this. Jodie's
been there before. Why don't you see if she can go back
and have a look around?"

"I'll talk to her."

"And I'm going to want you to find out everything
you can about Marcus Rockwell. Any links to Stewart,
Lloyd, or Wooford."

"You seriously think he might be involved?"

"We need to eliminate that possibility. By the way,
have you heard from the tech team about the contents of
that USB flash drive from Stewart's place?"

"Not yet. I'll swing by in person and find out where
they're at, make sure they know we need those results
ASAP."

"Alright. I'll go meet with Billy and see what he can
tell us."

79

I sent a text to Christie telling her about the donor banquet tonight and asking if she and Tessa would be able to attend with me. "It's for the ICSC," I explained. "They work to stop child molestation and abuse around the world."

I included a link to their website.

Then I left for Billy McReynolds's BranchWide Studios.

On the way, Christie called me, asking for details about the event.

"Everything starts at six," I said. "They're serving cocktails, and then dinner. It's a formal event, so we'll need to dress up."

"And Tessa's invited too?"

"Yes. I made sure it would be okay."

"Let me contact her. I'll let you know."

++++

Francis was at his desk when the email came through, but it wasn't the one he was expecting.

"I know it was you," it read. "I know where you live. If you recorded me at my computer, you're going to delete the file or I'll make sure a record of all your chats finds its way into the hands of your superiors."

It was signed graciousgirl4.

Francis felt a deep chill.

Somehow the man who'd been posing as the eighteen-year-old woman had tracked him down, and had even found out his work email address.

He's involved in what's happening with Ivan and Skylar! He's a part of their team! This is all a setup to blackmail me!

No, Francis, think about it. That doesn't make sense. How would they know you would back-trace to his account? This is separate from what's happening with Ivan and Skylar.

Well, whoever this man was, he'd done something Francis didn't think was possible: he'd located him—at work even.

And also threatened him.

That seemed to be happening a lot today.

You were careful. Whoever he is, he must be an expert at finding his way around the Internet.

Now what?

Call the police. I should call the police.

And tell him what? That you hacked in to a Krazle account and saw a guy sitting there? You'd either get in trouble or they'd just laugh at you and tell you that it served you right. Besides, you can't contact the police or Ivan will attack Derek.

Okay, so this guy was threatening to let his boss know about the chats. Francis figured he might lose his job if that happened, but he had a lot more to worry about today than that.

He'd lose it anyway if he purposely downloaded a virus.

He deleted the email without replying to it.

++++

Battling traffic, I didn't make it to the BranchWide Studios until nearly eleven.

It was across the street from the docks near Jamaica Bay and situated in a warehouse district next to an old auto repair shop, but the studio building itself was clean and recently refurbished.

Inside, a slightly overweight woman in her late fifties sat behind the reception desk. The name plate in front of her read ELLE LACHMAN. I recognized her as the person who'd picked up Billy McReynolds at Presbyterian Central Hospital after our meeting in the morgue last week.

"May I help you?" she asked.

"I'm looking for Billy McReynolds." I showed her the business card he'd given me. "My name's Patrick Bowers. I spoke with him on Thursday. I'm with the FBI, looking into the death of his brother."

It wasn't quite the whole truth, but it was enough for now.

"He's on-air right now, I'm afraid."

"Do you know when he'll be done?"

"His show is live from nine to noon, but I might be able to get you in to see him during one of his commercial breaks—if it's urgent."

"That would be great. Yes. This is important."

"Let me check with our call screener and see what I can find out."

I took a seat in the corner of the reception area, and while I waited to talk with Billy I connected to the studio's Wi-Fi and emailed DeYoung, telling him about the mask and the hood and the event this evening. "I've asked Tobin and Jodie to come too," I wrote, then waited for his reply.

++++

Tessa was on her way to her next classroom when she noticed a text from her mom: an invitation to some sort of dinner tonight.

It looked boring.

"No, thanks," she texted back.

Then went in to take her algebra exam.

80

11:00 a.m.
10 hours left

Ms. Lachman told me that Billy had a short commercial break at quarter after the hour and could speak with me then.

"He's interviewing Marcus Rockwell," she said proudly, obviously excited that they'd been able to convince the billionaire to stop by and be on the show.

"That's what I heard."

The minutes ticked by, and at twelve after she led me down a hallway with recording studios on either side. The thick soundproof glass offered me an unobstructed view of Billy and Marcus, who were seated across the table from each other with a mic in front of each of them.

A neon ON AIR sign glowed red above the door. Billy's call screener was working across the hall in another studio.

I asked Ms. Lachman, "How did Billy pull off an interview with Marcus Rockwell?"

"There's an event that Mr. Rockwell is hosting tonight. He wanted to promote support for the International Child Safety Consortium, and my husband has a listening audience of nearly five million people. The ICSC works to stop child exploitation across international borders."

"Yes, I'm familiar with—I'm sorry, did you say your husband?"

"I know, different last name. We got married later in life." She held up her ring finger to show off her wedding band. "But it's been two years now, come August."

"Congratulations."

She smiled. "Thank you."

"Did you know Billy's brother very well?"

"I'm afraid not. I was working here before Billy's show started, so I only met Randy once, right after Billy and I started dating. They weren't especially close. Still, it has been hard for him this last week. They were brothers, after all."

I thought of my own brother and how things had been strained between us as well, over the years, and of how many times I'd wished we were closer. "Yes," I said, not really sure how else to reply. "It would be hard."

Ms. Lachman glanced at the call screener, who gave her a thumbs-up. "Should be ready in just a moment."

From where Billy was seated, he could see us through the glass, and his gaze was level and flat and a lot more hostile than it'd been when we first met last week in the hospital when he came in to identify his brother's body.

The call screener held up five fingers, then four, then three. Two. One.

The ON AIR sign went black, Ms. Lachman opened the door for me, and I entered Billy's studio.

He removed his headphones and rose. After briefly introducing me to Marcus Rockwell, who had blond, surfer-style hair and a breezy way about him, Billy stepped to the side with me and lowered his voice. "I've read the news feeds. You didn't tell me that you shot Randy before he died last week."

"It might sound strange, but it was to protect him, to stop him from jumping."

"Uh-huh." He didn't sound convinced. "Well, I saw that you were put on administrative leave for taking that shot."

"Yes."

"Did you ever think that shooting him might have startled him or frightened him? Maybe that's what caused him to jump. I haven't ruled out a wrongful death lawsuit against you and the Bureau."

Through one of the speakers just above the sound-absorbing baffles on the far wall, the call screener said, "Billy, you have one minute and thirty-five seconds before you're back on the air. One minute thirty."

"Why are you here today, Agent Bowers?" he asked me tersely.

"I wanted to know if you might have thought of anything else that could help us resolve the circumstances regarding your brother's death."

"I think they're pretty clear."

I held up the key I'd received that was identical to the one found on Randy's body. "Do you recognize this?"

Billy took it and inspected it carefully. "No. Should I?"

"Your brother had a copy of it on him when he died."

"I have no idea what this is a key to."

"One minute," his screener announced.

He gave me back the key.

"I'm sure you received the autopsy results," I said to him.

"Yes. Randy was poisoned. Do you have any idea who did that?"

"No. So despite the suicide note you think someone else was trying to kill him?"

"I don't know what to think anymore."

"—Forty-five seconds—"

Mr. Rockwell glanced our way and I guessed that, even though we were both speaking quietly, he could probably still hear us.

"Do you know the name Hal Lloyd?" I asked Billy.

"No, I don't think so. Was he involved in this business regarding my brother?"

"What business?"

"—Thirty seconds—"

"I just mean, whatever he was into."

"We're not sure what Randy was involved with," I said. "Were you able to remember the name of the woman who brought those sexual assault allegations against your brother? You'd mentioned Beth maybe?"

"No. I'm—"

"—Fifteen." Urgency in her voice now.

"My lawyers will be contacting your superiors," Billy told me. "Elle will show you out."

"Ten!"

He returned to the table, put on his headphones, and Elle and I went into the hall. The call screener counted the last five seconds down with her fingers as we watched through the glass.

The neon sign flashed ON AIR again.

"I'm sorry about that," Ms. Lachman apologized. "I knew he was upset, but I didn't know he was going to be, well, to say those things."

"He did just lose his brother. I would be upset too."

Outside the studio, I checked my phone and saw a text from Christie that she was on for the banquet tonight and that she had invited Tessa as well. "She declined," Christie wrote. "I'm not sure a formal fundraising dinner is really her thing, anyway."

I didn't really want Tessa to stay at home—especially not by herself. My plan had been to have them both there so I could keep an eye on them.

"Give it another shot," I texted back. "I really think she would enjoy hearing about the work of the ICSC."

Jodie phoned me from Stewart's apartment, where she and Agent Descartes, who'd been working with her this morning, were. "Is there anything specific you want us to look for?"

"Check the blood spatter one more time. See if it makes sense to you that Stewart could have fought off Randy McReynolds, like we were talking about the other day."

I told her that nothing had really come from visiting Billy, other than finding out he might be going after me in court for shooting his brother.

"Okay." I could tell there was something else on her mind. "Pat, there are a couple things you should know. I went to Ms. Aguirre, as you suggested, to get the task force members' personnel files."

"How did that go?"

"She's considering my request. On another front, Descartes found out that Romanoff did hire a company to remodel his home eight years ago: Hearre Construction. So they might have taken out the fire-resistant insulation. We're looking into it."

"The agent at Homeland's Cyber Crimes Center told me that Wooford had worked for a construction company," I said. "What other places did Hearre Construction renovate?"

"They're not in a very sharing mood. For that we're going to need a warrant."

"Talk to DeYoung, see what you can do."

After the call, I checked my laptop and saw that I was still on the station's Wi-Fi. I pulled up my email's in-box and, ironically, found a message that DeYoung had sent me only a few minutes ago, informing me that Maria Aguirre would be attending the event tonight as well, that he had made all the arrangements with Mr. Gomez.

What? Why would DeYoung want an OPR lawyer there?

Maybe to keep an eye on you?

Unsure what to make of that, I drove a couple of blocks and, deep in thought, swung into a Mexican restaurant just on the edge of the warehouse district to grab lunch.

81

In the cafeteria, Tessa saw that her mom had texted her another invite to the thing tonight.

Okay, so that was annoying.

This time she'd included a hyperlink to the group putting on the dinner—something called the International Child Safety Consortium.

Tessa clicked on the link.

They helped stop human trafficking and child abuse and tried to catch people who molested kids. So, alright, that was pretty awesome.

Free food was a plus—as long as they had veggie options.

And who knows, maybe you can even score some champagne when Patrick and Mom aren't looking.

It wasn't like she had anything else going on.

Might be kinda cool.

Alright, whatever.

She replied that she would go.

Then, for the rest of lunch, instead of studying for her last final, she started working on creating the logic puzzle, taking some inspiration from the algebra word problems she'd just tackled.

++++

While I waited for my burrito, Christie forwarded me a text from Tessa: an affirmative reply to the invitation about the dinner tonight.

Good. I'd be able to protect them both.

At least until nine.

Well, then Tobin and Jodie could take over.

My food came up and I slipped off to a corner of the restaurant to monitor the two phones.

++++

Francis watched the clock tick to ten minutes past noon.

He knew only that Ivan and his people were going to send him the email this afternoon. He wished he had more specifics, but he still hadn't decided what he was going to do when it did come in, so maybe it was good that it hadn't arrived yet.

Derek is in danger, I'll have to open it.

You can't! It's a virus! It'll compromise the ICSC's system. It might open it up for hackers to get in. Maybe that's what they want, to hack in on the day of the fundraiser.

But I could be saving Derek's life.

But it could be ruining lots of other kids' lives. If their abusers can access this system and find out personal information about who's been identified over the years, you might be endangering all of them.

Maybe—but I don't know that. Not for sure.

Francis found it hard to concentrate, but reminded himself of his job: Screen. Identify. Catalog. Report.

SICR.

There was no one *sicker* than the people who were filming those things.

And stopping them was what he was here to do.

And that's what he was going to do.

That last one was the key.

Report.

But in this instance, if he couldn't report it to the FBI or the NYPD, then who could he contact?

++++

I got a text message from Tobin that he might have something. "Call me when you get a chance."

When I phoned him he said, "The video that I was showing my team last Friday, the one about how to groom children for sex, I think we found the narrator."

"Tell me."

"I want Jodie and Angela on the line too."

"Angela?"

"Angela Knight from the Bureau's Cyber Division. I'd sent her the video to examine. She's the one who found the narrator."

I'd heard of Angela, heard she was good. She was a bit famous—or infamous—for nicknaming her computer Lacey and referring to it as if it were an actual agent.

It was somewhat idiosyncratic, but considering the recent strides in AI, voice recognition, and EAAs, or electronic audible assistants, it was becoming more and more common for people to refer to their machines using masculine or feminine pronouns. They already did it with their phones and GPS units. Maybe Angela was just ahead of the curve.

To make sure I'd have enough privacy for this conversation, I took my meal to-go and sat in the car. Then, using the burner phone, we set up a four-way call.

Or, well, five-way if you counted Lacey.

I wasn't sure exactly how that worked.

"So," Angela said, "as Tobin may have mentioned to you, I believe Lacey found the woman who recorded the voice-over for the video."

"How did she do that?" I asked, playing along that Lacey was real.

"She was sweeping the web, doing a voice analysis on videos uploaded within the last year. Turns out the narrator is an actress named Gabrielle Livingston, does voice-over work, audiobooks, that sort of thing. She looks clean."

I could hardly believe that anyone who was just trying to pay the bills would have gotten involved in a project like that, narrating a how-to video aimed at helping potential abusers get away with child molestation, but it's amazing what people will justify when the paycheck is attractive enough.

"Do we know where she lives?" Jodie asked.

"She's based out of L.A. but splits her time there with work in New York City. I'll email you her contact information."

"I'll go talk to her," Tobin offered. "See if she can at least tell us who hired her. Maybe they have ties to the Final Territory."

"Good work, Angela," I said.

"Thank Lacey."

"Thank you, Lacey."

"She says you're welcome."

Okay, this could get weird.

Once Angela was off the line, I said to Tobin and Jodie, "You know what, let me go talk with Gabrielle."

"You're on admin leave," Tobin reminded me once again. It was his new hobby.

"Yes, and that's exactly why this makes sense."

"That, you're going to have to explain to me."

"Despite what Angela said, it is possible that Gabrielle is involved with these people. If you go and speak with her, they could easily get spooked about tonight, about meeting with me."

"If they're even the same people."

"True," I acknowledged. "But if I meet with her, I can feel things out. If it seems like she's involved, I'll warn her that you're onto her, that she needs to be more careful. That'll make me seem dirty, cover for both of us."

The line was silent.

"He does have a point," Jodie told Tobin.

The email from Angela containing Gabrielle Livingston's address and phone number arrived.

"Alright," Tobin agreed. "Go ahead. Meanwhile, I did find one thing: when I was analyzing any connections between Stewart and Rockwell, I saw that Stewart bought his mailing list from someone—Dr. Evan Madera. I think we should speak with him."

"Do we know who he is?" I said.

"I've run into him before. He's an online anthropologist."

"Online anthropologist?"

"He studies online culture, web-based communities, and the behavior of individuals on the Internet. Specializes in research on destructive and deviant behavior: how-to sites on self-harm, suicide, Ana and Mia, and pedophilia."

"What's Ana and Mia?" Jodie asked.

"Anorexia and bulimia."

"Wait—there are how-to sites?"

"Yes. With tips on how to purge, hide your thinness, fool doctors, and so on. Their bloggers claim that doing it shows you're self-controlled and that it's proof of your willpower. They call it 'thinspiration.' "

"Girls slowly committing suicide, thinking it's their pathway to empowerment?" Jodie's voice was laced with both concern and anger. "That's just plain wrong."

From working with her over the last couple of years, I knew she was a strong proponent of both women's rights and freedom of expression, but in this case I could see things cutting both ways. When exactly do you curb freedom of speech for the common good?

"Well," Tobin said, "Dr. Madera, he's a self-professed pedophile. Remember at last Thursday's briefing when I mentioned the lawsuits to lower the age of consent to twelve years old? That was Madera's brainchild. He's careful to tell you that he's a 'nonoffending' pedophile, though. That's a big deal to him. He's an advocate for removing age-of-consent laws."

"Unbelievable," I said. "How did you meet up with this guy?"

"Defense attorneys of accused pedophiles love to quote from his writings. I've had run-ins with him before. While you go talk to Gabrielle Livingston, maybe Jodie and I can speak with Madera."

"Where are you now?" Jodie asked him.

"At headquarters."

"And Madera—where does he live?"

"Long Island."

"I'm with Agent Descartes now. We're a lot closer. How about the two of us go instead? Save some time?"

"Good. That'll give me a chance to look into some things here."

We ended the call and I phoned Gabrielle at the number Angela and Lacey had dug up.

"Hello?" she said.

"Ms. Livingston, my name is Patrick Bowers. I'm looking for someone to do a voice-over for a video. I'd like to speak to you about your work. Could we meet?"

"Did you say you're Patrick Bowers?"

"Yes."

Silence.

"Ms. Livingston?"

"I'll meet with you. We need to talk—but not on the phone."

"Okay. Where are you?"

"I'm at the hospital."

She gave me the address. "I'll be there as soon as I can," I said.

++++

"Francis?"

Startled, he looked up to see Claire beside him.

He had no idea how long she'd been standing there.

"Yes?" he answered.

"Are you alright?"

"Yes. Sorry. Fine. I'm fine." It was twelve fifty-five. Still nothing from Ivan's group. "I have a lot on my mind. I'm just excited about the donor banquet."

"Well, that's what I came to talk with you about." She laid a large manila envelope on his desk. "I need someone to deliver this to Marcus Rockwell. I'd like you to take it over there. He'll be quite busy tonight, but this will give you the chance to meet him for yourself. He's a legend in the computer technology industry and I know how much you value your work and . . . Well, I thought you'd enjoy meeting him in person."

"But I'm in the middle of a project here."

She looked at his clean desk, empty in-box, and clear home screen on his computer. "What project is that?"

"Um . . . trying to get caught up."

She patted his shoulder in a warm and encouraging manner. "You're a hard worker, Francis. I'm sure you're caught up just fine. I've seen your reports. There's nothing in your work queue that can't wait."

From his invitation to the gala tonight, he knew where Mr. Rockwell lived, and it wasn't nearby. "Even in a taxi, getting over there might take an hour."

"We need this delivered. It's important."

He seesawed back and forth.

You'll be okay. There'll still be time.

I have to stay here at my desk, wait for the email!

You should be back by three thirty or so. If it comes in before then, you can just deal with it when you get back. Maybe slipping away will be good for you, help you figure out what to do.

"Francis?"

"I'll take it for you." He picked up the envelope.

"Thank you, Francis. You're a very faithful employee. I appreciate that in you. I always have."

82

While Descartes drove, Special Agent Jodie Fleming read through Madera's website where he rationalized pedophilia, blamed society for "victimizing" children by holding them back from "their instinctual curiosity about their bodies." Madera argued that pedophilia was natural and was really a sexual orientation rather than simply a sexual interest.

For Jodie, since she was a lesbian, this topic of sexual orientation was sensitive to her and hit close to home.

Redefining pedophilia as a sexual orientation instead of a sexual interest would have devastating consequences by undermining the prosecution of those who molest children. Offenders would just claim that they couldn't help it, that they were born that way. After all, who's to say it was wrong for them to act on their natural instincts?

Madera claimed that by forcing children to postpone happiness by the way they touch themselves and others, we teach them that their bodies are bad, and that by doing this we disrespect them, that it propagates the idea that adults have ownership over them, and that the children don't have ownership over their own bodies and their own choices.

According to him, the emotional damage is done long before adolescence. As the René Guyon Society, an adult/child sex advocacy group, says, "Sex before eight, or else it's too late." They assert that if you waited until puberty, the children will be indoctrinated into society's norms of shame and victimization and will never be free to be fully liberated or to truly understand their own bodies and the ways they wish to pursue pleasure.

It was hard for her to read all this without feeling sick to her stomach.

Jodie hadn't been to church since she came out when she was in college, but she remembered people quoting a Bible verse to her at the time: "Woe unto them that call evil good, and good evil."

They'd shared it with her in regard to her homosexuality, but she'd never seen a clearer example of that principle than here on this website where one of the greatest evils imaginable—raping children—was portrayed as the greatest good—liberating them.

All of Madera's arguments ignored the fact that minors cannot meaningfully consent to sex, that there's always a power differential between adults and children that allows the child to be taken advantage of.

Also, his work turned a blind eye to the troves of research from sociology and psychology that showed that sexual contact with adults confuses children and often causes years, or even a lifetime, of shame, guilt, anxiety, and depression. Being molested as a child doesn't lead to a healthy self-image, but exactly the opposite.

Calling evil good.

Calling good evil.

"Did you watch that video that Tobin posted last week?" she asked Descartes.

"Just what he showed us in his briefing. You?"

"Yeah. It deals with the same issues as Madera's website."

"You think Madera wrote it?"

"Let's ask him."

Descartes pulled around the corner and they arrived at a modest home across the street from an elementary school playground.

83

Jodie led Descartes up the driveway toward Madera's front door.

"How does a guy like this get a house across the street from a grade school?" Descartes asked her disgustedly.

"He's not a registered sex offender. Since he's never been arrested for anything, he's free to buy a home wherever he wants."

"So a self-professed pedophile and advocate for removing age-of-consent laws gets to buy a house where he can watch children play all day across the street?"

"Antidiscrimination ordinances," she said. "What are you gonna do?"

She knocked, and a few moments later a Caucasian man dressed in designer jeans and a pink Polo shirt appeared.

"Dr. Madera?" she asked.

"Yes?" It was both an answer and a question.

"I'm Special Agent Fleming. This is Special Agent Descartes. We're with the FBI."

She showed him her creds.

He looked uneasy for a moment, but then quickly recovered. "Ah. A knock and talk. Well, come in. Feel free to confiscate my computer. God knows it won't be the first time. But I don't have any illegal content on there, I'm quite careful."

"I'm sure you are," Jodie said.

She entered.

Descartes came in behind her.

The walls of Madera's home were filled with photos of children, all professionally framed and neatly arranged at eye level.

"Were those taken with the parents' permission?" Descartes asked.

"They were all purchased from a photo-sharing site. I have the receipts. I can get them for you, if you desire."

"That won't be necessary." Jodie looked around. Madera had his laptop resting open on the dining room table. A few crumpled bags of pretzels and cheese curls and a slew of empty beer bottles sat beside it.

A Krazle chat window was open.

"I understand you're an online anthropologist?" she said.

"Yes. I used to teach at CUNY—Baruch College. Now, mostly, I speak and write. Freelance. I'm an activist. Listen, I know you didn't come here to look at the pictures on my walls or to review my curriculum vitae. Why are you here?"

"You're an advocate," Descartes said.

"Yes. For equal rights, now—"

"And by that you mean the right of children to consent to having sex with adults."

"All we're seeking is the empowerment of children."

"And the acceptance of pedophilia as an 'alternative sexuality.'"

"Fifty years ago there was a stigma in most of mainstream America toward being gay. Now look at how things have changed. Fifty years from now there won't be any stigma to intergenerational romance. Liberation takes time. But we're patient. One small victory at a time."

Jodie truly hoped he was wrong about that.

"And that's what your website is for." Descartes was eyeing the photos on the wall.

"I just try to provide a supportive community for like-minded people."

"As well as resources to promote your cause."

"As would anyone who has a cause he believes in."

"But if people were to follow the advice provided on your website, more children would be sexually assaulted."

"It's not assault if it's consensual and if someone is of the age of consent."

"And that's why you want the laws changed."

"Yes."

Descartes narrowed his eyes. "And you call that *empowerment*?"

"Yes. To learn to understand and appreciate their own bodies and what brings them pleasure. And to make their own decisions."

"And all this because of your sexual interest in children?"

"You mean sexual orientation toward them," Madera corrected him. "We're born this way. It's no different from someone being born straight or gay."

"Really?" Jodie said.

"It's not something to be cured or condemned. How could we fault someone for being who he was born to be?"

"You mean a pedophile."

"A child lover, yes. Or gay. Or straight. Bi. Trans. Whatever."

"Even if pedophilia were a sexual orientation," she replied, "you can't excuse deviant behavior by saying that you were compelled to act that way, that you had no choice in the matter."

"You call it deviant. I call it perfectly normal."

"I read some of the articles on your website, Dr. Madera. I'm not here to debate morality with you."

He smirked as if her refusal to argue vindicated his reasoning. "I see."

Alright.

He wanted to do this.

She could do this.

"The laws of any just society," she told him, "should always err on the side of protecting the innocent. If there's any question about whether a four-year-old or an eight-year-old or a thirteen-year-old should be protected from an experience that will likely, according to the most rigorous research, end up traumatizing them, perhaps for the rest of their lives, they should be protected from that experience. That's called being responsible. That's called being the adult in the room."

He just scoffed. "That's the same argument antiabortionists make—that if there's any chance fetuses are alive we shouldn't abort them."

"Really?" she said. "You want to go there?"

"What?" His disdain was clear. "Are you one of them?"

"Them?"

"An antiabortionist?"

"Please, Dr. Madera, we both know it's a baby."

"It's a fetus."

"After a miscarriage no one walks around saying, 'I lost my fetus.' And during pregnancy visits the doctor never asks the woman, 'Who's the fetus's producer?' He says, 'Who's the baby's father?' So we, as a society, accept that it's a baby—and there's no question medically about whether or not the child is alive. The question is political—

what rights, if any, should we extend to the unborn child, and what rights, if any, does the mother have to end the life of that child?"

Dr. Madera opened his mouth as if he were going to reply, then closed it again. "Look," he said at last, "what is it you came here for?"

Descartes said, "We want to know about a mailing list and a video."

"Go on."

"We believe that the list you sold Jamaal Stewart has been used by people who are abducting children."

A pause. "Abducting them?"

"From what we can tell, this group is kidnapping children, keeping them captive for months on end, and then killing them. Have you ever heard of the Final Territory?"

He was silent.

"And there's a video," Descartes added. "It's used for grooming pedophiles and hebephiles. We want to know if you wrote it."

"I don't write any videos, but I might have heard of Flute, well, the Final Territory."

"You might have?" Jodie said.

"Look, you may not agree with me, but I don't want to see children harmed in any way. I want to change the laws, not break them. I want to free children, not destroy them."

It struck her that he was a true believer.

He really buys in to this stuff. He believes his own propaganda.

"Then help us," she said. "We know of eighteen deaths in the last decade. Now three more children are missing. We're hoping that they're still alive and that if we move on this quickly, we might be able to save them."

"Let me get my files."

84

2:00 p.m.
7 hours left

Francis had taken a taxi to Marcus Rockwell's mansion. Now, as he approached the front gate, a security guard came to the window. "Yes?"

"I have an envelope here for Mr. Rockwell," Francis told him. "It's from Claire Nolan at the ICSC."

"And what is it regarding?"

"I think it has something to do with tonight's donor banquet. It's important."

"Wait here while I call up to the house."

++++

I knocked at the door to the exam room, and a woman's voice from the other side told me to come in.

Inside the room, an NYPD officer was taking down the statement of a diminutive red-haired woman in her late twenties who was seated on the exam bed.

"May I help you, sir?" When the officer asked me the question he made it sound more like a threat than an offer of assistance.

"I called you on the phone," I said to Gabrielle. "I'm Patrick Bowers."

"It's okay," she told the officer. "Can you give us a minute?"

"I'll be right outside, in the hall, if you need me." He left the room and brusquely closed the door behind him.

A deep bruise purpled one side of Gabrielle's face. "Ms. Livingston," I said. "May I ask what happened?"

"First of all, I just record under the name Gabrielle Livingston. My real name is Skylar Shapiro. You can call me Skylar."

"Alright, Skylar." With a great name like Skylar Shapiro, it surprised me she would choose to record under the name Gabrielle Livingston. "The bruise. Are you alright?"

"A man I know did it, but right now that's not what matters. You aren't really here to speak with me about voice-over work, are you?"

"There's a video out there that's targeted at people who . . . well, groom children for sexual interactions with adults." I tried to phrase things in as generic and non-judgmental a way as possible to fit the role I was here to play. "You did the voice-over for it. Do you know which one I mean?"

She lowered her voice. "Did they send you?"

"Did who send me?"

"We both know who."

I evaluated how to respond. "What can you tell me about them?"

She turned the bruised side of her face toward me. "Ivan did this to me."

"Romanoff."

"Yes. I was helping them, but I want out. I heard about you. You're with the FBI. Can you help me?"

I wasn't sure if this was some kind of test. She certainly seemed to be telling the truth. "I know people who can protect you, people I trust. I need you to tell me where the children are."

She swallowed hard.

"The three children that were taken, Skylar. Where are they?"

She shook her head. "It's too late."

"Too late for what? Are the children still alive?"

"Randy was too close. That's why they poisoned him."

"Who poisoned him?"

"At the LeBange. Don't let them know I told you. I've said too much already." Then she called out to the officer in the hallway, "You can come back in! We're done!"

"Tell me about the children," I said urgently. "Do you know who Shane is? Have you met the Piper?"

"I shouldn't have . . . I've seen the garage. You can't tell them we spoke."

"I won't. What garage? What else do you know about Randy?"

But then the officer had returned. He informed me unequivocally that it was time for me to leave.

"Stay with her," I told him.

"What?"

"I'm with the FBI." I hoped he wouldn't ask for my creds. "Patrick Bowers. Call it in if you need to. Talk to Assistant Director DeYoung, but don't let her out of your sight."

++++

Jodie scanned the printout from Dr. Madera. There were more than ten thousand names and email addresses. This was going to take some time.

She looked for Rockwell's name, but it didn't appear.

"We'll need the records of everyone you've bought lists from or sold them to."

"Anything I can do to help."

"When we first got here, you offered to let us inspect your computer. I think I'll take you up on that."

He seemed less enthusiastic now about the prospect of handing it over than he had when he flippantly offered it to them when they first arrived, but in the end he did.

Outside by the car, Descartes asked her, "So, what now?"

"We cross-reference the mailing list with names from the case and get this computer over to the lab to see if they can pull anything off it."

"I'll take care of it. I know you need to head to that dinner tonight."

"Thanks. Let's get it to headquarters and move on from there."

++++

The guard opened the gate and waved Francis and the taxi driver through.

"This is some layout," the cabbie said to Francis as they wound up the long circuitous drive that led to the front of the house. "Who is this guy?"

"Someone who's doing a lot of good for a lot of people."

"It seems like he's doing pretty well for himself too."

A servant greeted him outside the front door.

"I have something for Marcus Rockwell," Francis told him.

"You're the one with the envelope?"

"Yes."

"Please, follow me."

He led Francis into the mansion.

The place was stunning, with crystal chandeliers, inlaid marble floors, and sweeping spiral staircases leading up to the second floor, where a balcony overlooked the ballroom on one side and the perfectly manicured grounds on the other.

Out back, through the open French doors, Francis noticed servers setting up tables on the lawn. A cellist was practicing nearby.

Francis was taking it all in when he heard someone behind him say, "I understand you have something for me?"

He turned.

Marcus Rockwell strode toward him, smile wide. He wore flip-flops, jeans, and a torn T-shirt. Francis had never met a billionaire before, but he didn't anticipate that this was the way most of them would've dressed.

Mr. Rockwell extended his hand. When Francis held out the envelope to him, he laughed lightly. "I was just hoping to shake your hand."

"Oh."

Francis shook his hand.

"You're Mr. Edlemore?"

"Yes."

"Alejandro has wonderful things to say about you and your team. Thank you for the work you do."

Just the thought that you could be on familiar enough terms with Mr. Gomez to call him by his first name was impressive to Francis.

"Thank you for supporting us," Francis said.

"Of course. Now, Claire said you were sending me the paperwork?"

"Here." Francis handed over the manila folder.

"Thank you. I'd show you around, but I need to take care of a few things, get ready for tonight. However, I can have someone give you a tour of the grounds, if you like."

"I need to go. I have to get ready too."

"Of course. My people have paid the tab on your taxi. Is there anything else I can do for you?"

He's one of the richest and most powerful people in the world. If anyone can help you, it's him. Tell him what's going on.

No! If I do anything they'll hurt Derek!

"No, thank you. Sir."

Mr. Rockwell rebuked Francis lightly, " 'Sir' is a term reserved for my dad. I'm just Marcus, okay?"

"Okay."

"So, I'll see you tonight?"

"Certainly. Yes. I'll be here."

++++

I phoned Jodie from the hospital lobby, but even before I could tell her about Skylar, she launched into a summary of her visit with Dr. Madera. "We're on our way to headquarters to have his laptop checked out," she explained. "He seemed pretty confident that there was nothing incriminating on there, but it's worth a look. He also gave us his mailing list, but it's going to be a bit of work analyzing it. Did you learn anything from Gabrielle Livingston?"

"First off, her real name is Skylar Shapiro. She told me she was involved in this, but that she wanted out. I think she can help us. I want a protective detail over here to watch her."

"I'll call it in right away."

"She knew about Randy being poisoned, said he got too close and that's why they went after him. She mentioned a garage and the LeBange. I looked it up a minute

ago—the LeBange is a restaurant. We need to have someone review their security camera footage on the night
Randy died, see if we can identify him entering it. I don't
know what the garage was about—she wouldn't elaborate. I asked the officer to stay with her. Hopefully, she'll
feel ready to tell us more."

"Okay, I'll have someone contact the restaurant. I
should tell you, I heard from Maria. She gave me limited
access to the task force members' personnel files, but I
haven't had the chance to review them yet."

"Alright. I think that since Blake was able to get into
the Federal Digital Database and Wooford was killed
while in custody, we should check if any task force members had the day off when Wooford died. I want to know
if anyone had time to travel down to D.C. to visit him."

"I'll see what I can find out."

"I didn't bring any black tie-event clothes over to
Christie's, so I'm going to swing by my place to change."

"I might see you there," she replied. "I need to change
as well."

85

Before she left school, Tessa turned in her textbooks.

There.

One thing taken care of.

Now just get home, change, and then finish up the logic problem on the ride to the banquet so she could save a few innocent animals from Patrick's murderous, carnivorous appetite over the next six weeks.

Hopefully, she and her mom would still be around here in New York City when those weeks came to an end.

But that wasn't guaranteed.

With this job offer in Nebraska, it didn't even seem likely.

++++

Out in the taxi again, Francis checked the time.

Already after three.

He really hoped the email hadn't come to his computer yet.

Considering that it would be an hour drive back to the ICSC offices and that Claire had told him she was going to close the doors at four, he needed to do something.

He phoned her and explained that he needed to grab a few personal items before they locked up for the day.

"I can wait until four ten at the latest," she said, "but then I will need to leave."

++++

On the way to my apartment, I called Tobin to catch up and told him about my meeting with Skylar and her warnings to me.

"Do you want me to go over there to the hospital?"

"There's an officer with her, and Jodie called in a team to go stay with her. I think she'll be okay. And Jodie's having an agent look into the LeBange security footage. Skylar said Randy was poisoned by them. We need to find out when he got there and who was with him."

Tobin explained to me that they had finally gotten a list of Tribaxil distributors and were comparing it to names related to the case. "There's a lot to get through. I might be late tonight."

"No problem. Jodie and I can handle it. Also, Maria Aguirre will be there."

"The OPR lawyer?"

"Yeah. DeYoung set it up."

I figured that with traffic at this time of day, I might not make it to Rockwell's until after five, but I wanted to be there early enough to have a look around at the security before Christie and Tessa showed up.

Once I got to my place, I dug out my best suit and quickly changed. Then, with the key in my pocket, and the mask and the cloth hood in the trunk of my car, I left for 54 North Worthy Drive.

I also brought my .357 SIG P229 with me.

And my automatic knife.

Just in case.

86

4:00 p.m.
5 hours left

Tessa entered the apartment.

Her mom had come home from work early and was sorting through a bunch of dresses, trying to figure out which one to wear.

Tessa wasn't really into the whole idea of dressing up. "Can't I just wear what I have on?"

"It's a formal event. We need something nice. What about that dress we bought in the spring for that awards banquet for students on the A honor roll?"

"Oh, you mean that stupid pot roast dinner thing for geeks that you made me go to?"

"That would be the one." Her mother found the dress in the back of Tessa's closet and pulled it out. "Here it is. You look lovely in it. Come on, let's get ready."

++++

Francis saw Claire standing by the door, ready to lock things up, when the taxi dropped him off.

She glanced at her watch. "Tell you what, Francis—

just lock up after yourself, okay? I need to get going. I'll show you what to do."

She trusts me.

You've been working here for eight years. She ought to by now.

She demonstrated how to set the alarm.

When she was done, he waited by the glass front doors, watching until she was past the hedges and out of sight down the street. Then he went to his desk, logged in, and, taking a deep breath, opened up the email program to see if the message from Ivan's people had come through.

Nothing.

Empty.

He called the hospital to check on Derek, who answered, and was doing fine.

Okay, so Ivan had said the email would come this afternoon. That probably meant sometime before five.

You can't just sit here waiting. You need to do something!

What about graciousgirl4? The guy sent that threatening email. Maybe I can figure out who he really is.

Somewhat anxious about what he might find, Francis set to work trying to identify the IP address that the email had been sent from.

++++

While I was driving to the banquet, Tobin called to tell me that he'd spoken with the NYPD officer who'd interviewed Skylar Shapiro at the hospital, but that she had slipped away and was gone. "I'll see what I can do to find her," he said.

"Stay on it. I won't look for you tonight. We need to locate her."

"I'll put a BOLO for her and get officers to her home."

++++

Wearing her official geek-meal dress, Tessa left in a taxi for the billionaire's house with her mom, who actually looked pretty stunning for someone as old as she was.

Tessa took advantage of the ride to finish pulling together the puzzle for Patrick.

++++

Francis was still trying to trace graciousgirl4's true identity when he received the email from Ivan's people, just before five o'clock.

87

5:00 p.m.
4 hours left

At first glance it looked like an official correspondence from the Los Angeles Police Department, but rather than provide him with links to potential sites according to their normal reporting procedures, it had just one link listed.

The form looked so realistic that later on, after the fact, Francis figured he would be able to claim that he thought it was all legitimate. Even with all his years of experience, it wouldn't take much to convince Claire that he'd been rushed in getting everything done before tonight and just hadn't taken the time to read through it carefully enough.

Well, he *could* say those things, but he wouldn't.

No, he wouldn't lie about something like that.

Then you can't open it either!

But Derek's in trouble. Ivan told me they would bring me his arm. Besides, Skylar said the people she worked for could help him.

Yes, but if you let someone hack in here, that could be devastating for other kids all over the world.

Was that worth Derek's life?

Then Francis had a thought, and he was shocked by how cruel and heartless it seemed. He hated himself for even thinking it: *Derek is dying anyway. Would they really be able to save him? To help him?*

Ivan hadn't told him how much time he had to download the file, and before Francis did anything, he wanted to make sure he did the right thing, or at least the *best* thing.

Whatever that was.

So he made two lists, writing down the good and the bad parts of each choice, creating a chart in a way that Dr. Perrior had taught him for organizing his thoughts before making important decisions.

++++

I arrived at Rockwell's place.

It was valet parking only.

After dropping off my car, I took some time to study the grounds and walk through the mansion. On the way past the library, I ran into Alejandro Gomez.

"I'm glad you could make it, Agent Bowers."

"Glad to be here." I glanced around. "Looks like things are almost set."

"Just a few little wrinkles to iron out." He held up a stack of about half a dozen notecards. "And I should run through my speech a couple more times, just to make sure. Don't worry," he assured me, "it'll be brief."

As self-assured and confident as Gomez was, I doubted there would be any problem. "I'm sure it'll go fine."

"Are your other guests here yet?"

"They should be here soon."

"Well, let me know if you need anything."

"I will."

Jodie drove up only a few minutes later. She must have gotten to my apartment to change soon after I left.

"I didn't have much time," she informed me, "but I did glance through the personnel files from the task force. So far no red flags. No one off the charts on their shooting range qualifications. Tobin had the highest scores. Descartes and Officer Hinchcliffe were up there too. If I can, I'll slip away and look them over more in-depth tonight. The tech guys are inspecting Madera's computer now. They think a couple of hours."

"Any word on who was off duty on the day Wooford died?"

"Maria kept those parts of the personnel records confidential."

Great. And that was the most important part.

Well, she should be here tonight. Maybe I could ask her about it in person.

"I'm going to go meet with Rockwell's security detail," Jodie said. "I'll see you in a few."

+++⊦

The chart helped.

Francis decided what to do.

From their exchanges the other day, he had the agent's cell number.

++++

My personal cell rang.

"Hello?"

"Agent Bowers, this is Francis Edlemore. They said I couldn't contact the police or the FBI. But you're on administrative leave. You can't tell them."

"I can't tell who?"

"The people who sent the email."

"What email? What's going on, Mr. Edlemore?"

"I'm in trouble and I don't know what to do."

Then he told me the extraordinary story of what had happened this morning at his apartment. "The woman I was with, Skylar Shapiro, she's working with them. And she's going to claim I assaulted her."

"Wait a minute. Skylar Shapiro?"

"Yes, but I'm not even sure that's her real name. She might have been lying."

The rug, with so many disparate strands, had a pattern more complex and intertwined than I'd imagined.

"I just got the email," he told me, "and I don't know what to do. Ivan said he'd go after Derek."

"You can't download the file, Francis. There's no telling what it might do."

"But Derek is in danger. They might hurt him."

"I'll get an officer over there to watch him. Meanwhile, don't open it. There's someone who I think might be able to help you."

"Who?"

"Her name is Angela Knight. She works with the Bureau's Cyber Division."

"No. They said they'd know if I contacted the FBI."

"She isn't on the task force. Just talk to her, no one else. I'll make sure she doesn't tell anyone."

He was silent.

Still unconvinced.

"Will you be at this number?" I asked.

"Yes, but hurry. Please. I don't know how much time I have before they're going to suspect something. And make sure Derek is safe."

"I will."

Before he hung up, Edlemore told me the name of the hospital and the boy's room number.

I called Tobin and he agreed to phone their head of security and then go by personally to check on Derek.

Then I contacted Angela and gave her Francis's phone number, emphasizing that all this needed to remain confidential.

++++

Francis heard from Angela Knight.

She said that she and her partner, Lacey, would analyze the email. "Forward it to me. We'll take a look."

"Agent Bowers didn't mention Lacey."

"She can be trusted. In the meantime, stay there by your desk in case we have any questions. We'll get back to you."

++++

With Angela helping Francis, Tobin on his way to check on Derek, and officers looking for Skylar, there wasn't much else I could do on any of those fronts right now.

A text from Christie told me that they were five minutes out.

A line of limos and town cars stood backed up in the circular drive in front of Marcus Rockwell's mansion, dropping off dignitaries and guests.

I wondered about the people coming here, how much wealth and influence was collectively represented. And I also wondered—couldn't help but wonder—what connection any of them might have to the Final Territory.

And what would happen when nine o'clock rolled around.

++++

Surrounded by his silent ladies, Blake decided to post the video that Patrick Bowers had provided of the young woman changing clothes. He would offer it without cost to the world.

He knew the best sites to place it on, and as he did, he listed her name and age:

Tessa Bernice Ellis/15

Then he watched as the number of views almost immediately began to rise.

++++

When she stepped out of the taxi, Christie took my breath away. The evening gown she wore was silky and red and formfitting and she made it work in all the right ways.

Tessa wore a black dress with a lace fringe on the bottom. She looked much older than her fifteen years.

I took Christie's hand. "You look amazing."

"Thank you. You clean up pretty well yourself."

"Tessa, you look great too."

"Okay." The compliment seemed to make her uncomfortable. "I'm done with your logic problem, by the way."

"I'm not sure I'll have a chance to work on it tonight, but text it to me. If I can look at it, I will."

As we crossed the walkway to the house, Christie said, "No drinking tonight, Tessa."

"What if they offer me some champagne?"

"Then you politely decline."

"I wouldn't want to hurt anyone's feelings."

"How gracious of you."

"I'm big-hearted, what can I say."

"Just soda, dear."

"Fine," she grumped. "I didn't want any anyway."

Then the three of us ascended the steps to the ballroom.

88

6:00 p.m.
3 hours left

An ornate balustrade ringed the balcony.

Women in elegant, shimmering dresses chatted amiably with men in freshly pressed tuxedos. I felt like I'd stepped into the realm of beautiful people, the elusive world of the rich and influential and famous.

A world I wasn't exactly at ease in.

In the northeast corner of the room, a cellist played. Near her, Billy McReynolds and his wife stood talking with Marcus Rockwell, who was laughing, apparently at a joke Billy had just told him.

Billy didn't look too excited to see me, but I thought Tessa would like to meet Marcus, so I went over and introduced Christie and Tessa to the three of them.

After we'd left, Tessa said, "Was that seriously the guy who started Krazle?"

"That's him."

"Cool."

Waist-high round tables had been set up throughout the room for guests to set their wineglasses or hors d'oeuvres plates on as they mingled. Waitstaff were discreetly clearing the tables of empty glasses and plates as other servers passed through the ballroom offering appetizers to people.

One of the servers approached us with a platter of sparkling crystal wineglasses.

"May I interest you in our select wine for tonight?"

"I'm good," I said.

"Me too," Tessa told him. "I guess."

Christie looked interested. "What are you serving?"

"Sailler-Cipolla Osanner Kirchlay. It's from a small, select, family-owned vineyard in Germany."

She took a glass, went through the whole swirling and sniffing routine, then tasted it. "A classic Mosel Riesling. Very crisp. Dry. A solid and bombastic bouquet."

The server nodded, pleased with her assessment, then stepped away.

"How can a wine be dry?" Tessa asked. "It's wet. It's a liquid."

"She does have a point," I noted.

Christie sighed lightly. "If I try to explain myself I'm just going to end up sounding like a wine snob."

"That is true," Tessa replied.

Christie eyed me, one eyebrow raised.

"Wine *expert*," I said. "Never a snob."

She winked. "Good answer."

++++

Tessa tapped at her phone's screen and sent the puzzle to Patrick.

It wasn't brilliant and it was more math than logic, but it did have a slight twist in it, a little misdirection that might trip him up.

But honestly, there was something even bigger than the logic problem on her mind. She needed to talk with

him about Nebraska, regardless of whether or not he
solved what she'd come up with.

++++

I glanced at Tessa's text.
    Her puzzle.
    Written with excellent punctuation.
    No surprise there.

In South America, there is a certain river that
flows 5 miles per hour in a northerly direction
past the village of Gooma. One day, a Goomian
boy decided to try swimming south to buy a bag
of tortilla chips at the local general store 15 miles
downstream. In still water he could swim at 1
mph. After half an hour he got tired and hopped
into a canoe, which he paddled at 4 mph. After
half an hour of that, he called some friends who
helped him paddle a war canoe at 10 mph. After
half an hour in that canoe, did he reach the
store? Will he ever get his tortilla chips? How far
south was he?

By the time I'd finished reading it, she'd sent me another text: "I'm not giving you forever to solve this. Let
me know your answer by breakfast."
    Well, it didn't appear too tough. Right now I was pre-
occupied with everything that was going on, but once I
had a few minutes I would take a closer look at it.
    "No problem," I texted back. "Meat, beware. Here I
come."
    "That's just disgusting."
    Christie said, "You two are standing side by side. Why
are you texting each other rather than just talking?"

"Seriously, Mom," Tessa said. "Enter the twenty-first century."

"As long as they have good desserts." She gave me a peck on the cheek. "Listen, I'll be right back. I need to find the ladies' room."

When she was gone, Tessa spoke to me in an insistent whisper. "Patrick, you have to make her stay here or else you have to come with us."

"What are you talking about?"

"To Omaha. To Nebraska. You need to make her stay here in New York or you need to come along."

"Now's not the best time to get into all that."

"No, no, listen. I mean it. She needs someone. She needs you. She would never admit it, not in so many words, because she would think it'd be pressuring you, manipulating you, but she loves you, okay? I haven't quite figured out why yet, I mean, no offense."

"None taken. She loves me?"

"Um. Yeah." She looked at me disbelievingly. "Hello. It's obvious. You don't read women very well, do you?"

"Well, I guess, I . . ."

"Didn't think so. Listen, I want someone to take care of my mom. She deserves someone, and for whatever reason she's settled on you. I guess she could do worse."

"Thanks."

"I want her to be happy, okay? She wouldn't be happy living there if you were here. So what is it? Will you come with us?"

"I need to think about it."

"How much of a puzzle would I have to make up to get you to move out to Omaha? Because I swear to God, even if it took me a year to write it, I'd do it if it'd make you come along."

"She means that much to you?"

"She means everything to me."

So what would happen if you moved to Nebraska and things didn't work out with Christie?

Life would move on.

Just like it always does.

Just like it would do if you both stayed here and things didn't work out.

If people are meant to be together, if there's a bigger plan at work, they will be. Right?

So maybe you should tell her yes . . .

Claire Nolan from the ICSC was on her way toward me with a man in tow. I had the sense that I'd seen his face before, but I didn't think we'd ever met.

"We'll figure something out," I told Tessa. "Okay?"

"Sure." She sounded disappointed. "I need a drink."

"Soda."

"Right. Soda."

She walked off and a moment later Claire greeted me. "Agent Bowers, I'm thrilled you could make it."

"It's good to see you, Ms. Nolan."

"Have you met Dr. Perrior? I believe he consults with the NYPD. He's one of the counselors whom some of our . . ." She backpedaled as she must have realized she was about to reveal more than she should have about who was seeing a therapist. "Some of our colleagues highly recommend."

I shook Dr. Perrior's hand.

"Oh!" Claire's eyes leapt around the room. "I see someone I need to talk to." She squeezed his elbow, then mine. "You two can get to know each other." And then she was gone.

"She's an enthusiastic woman," he said to me.

"Yes, she is."

"So you're an agent?"

"I'm with the FBI." I decided to take advantage of the moment alone with him. "Forgive me for bringing up work at a party like this, but I read the transcript of the interview you did with D'Nesh Mujeeb Agarwai on Saturday."

"Yes." He nodded. "He went through quite a devastating experience, but his parents are supportive. He's actually blocked out much of what happened to him." Dr. Perrior tapped the side of his head. "Our minds, they're amazing things. Sometimes forgetting is a blessing. It protects us from suffering."

"And sometimes remembering is a blessing," I replied.

"How's that?"

"Because it heals us from the lies we tell ourselves. I've always believed that finding out the truth is worth the pain of remembering it."

He chuckled. "If everyone was as astute as you are, I'd be without a job."

"A world as broken as ours will always need people like you."

He raised his glass in a small toast to what I'd said.

I excused myself and met up with Christie again.

"Pat," she whispered to me. "I have to say, I don't feel like I belong here."

"Just because these other women can't even hold a candle to you, I don't want you to feel too out of place."

She eyed me flirtatiously. "You keep talking like that and you never know where things might lead."

"I could come up with a few ideas."

"I'm sure you could."

Tessa rejoined us, carrying a glass of cola, and I was glad to have them both close by where we could stick together, especially since Tobin wasn't going to make it tonight.

++++

Shane heard from the Piper that the file the Russians had come up with hadn't been downloaded yet.

He tried to contact Skylar, but she didn't pick up, so he called Ivan Romanoff. "Francis Edlemore hasn't opened the file."

"Hmm. Well, I might know a way to convince him."

"This needs to happen tonight or there won't be a hole deep enough for either of us to hide in."

"Where is Edlemore?"

"From what I understand, he's at his office."

"Okay, leave it to me. I'll get that file downloaded for you."

++++

The Piper discreetly watched the video that Blake had posted, realized the person changing in the girl's bedroom was not Tessa Ellis, and contacted Shane to see if he could figure out who it really was and take care of things.

++++

Jodie was coming toward me, picking her way through the crowd. After a quick greeting, she pulled me aside for a moment.

"I just got word," she said. "That boy, Derek, he's fine. Tobin assigned a couple of officers to watch his room until this is over."

"Any sign of Skylar Shapiro?"

She shook her head. "Angela and Lacey are still working to identify the virus that was sent to Edlemore, trying to figure out what it would do if it were downloaded.

Descartes is analyzing Madera's mailing list. And something a bit out of the blue: remember how some officers were looking into tattoo studios that might have done the work on Randy McReynolds's hand?"

"Yes."

"Well, Hinchcliffe decided to call some studios in West Virginia near where Randy was living. Turns out one of them had a record of giving that tat to him eighteen months ago."

"Eighteen months?"

"Yes."

"Hmm."

"What is it? I can see a light going on."

"At the morgue, Billy mentioned that he hadn't seen his brother in two years, yet he knew about the tattoo."

"Maybe he was just off on his dates."

"Yeah. Maybe."

Or maybe not.

"Tell Tobin to prioritize that LeBange footage," I said. "And look for either of the McReynolds brothers."

"Either of them?"

"Humor me."

As seven o'clock approached, the servers ushered us outside to the lawn, where a sea of round tables and folding chairs had been set up. A line of tables along one side held an array of chafing dishes and hot plates containing different entrées for people to help themselves to.

I kept an eye on Billy McReynolds and tried to decide if I should ask him about the tattoo.

I could think of good reasons to do so and good reasons not to.

For now, I stuck with Christie and Tessa.

People began moving down the food line.

The three of us went over to join them.

89

As we got our plates, Tessa asked one of the servers which options were vegan.

He looked a couple of years older than her. He was a handsome enough guy, and her eyes weren't exactly on the food as he pointed out the options that would be safe for her to eat.

While we were getting our food, Maria Aguirre approached me. "Patrick, could I have a moment?"

After quick introductions, I told Christie that I would be right back, then, carrying my plate, I followed Maria to the balcony overlooking the lawn and the wide, sweeping garden filled with flowers that were in full bloom.

With the gentle glow of the city in the background, and the tiki torches lit along a path that led through the garden, it looked serene and somewhat surreal.

A light breeze brought the scent of the flowers and the distinctive oily burning odor of the tiki torches circling around us.

Ms. Aguirre produced a cigarette and a lighter from her clutch purse. "I don't know how many times I've quit."

"Some habits are hard to break."

"Habits, addictions, it's not always easy to tell them apart."

From this vantage point I could see Christie and Tessa leaving the food line and searching for a table. "What did you need to talk to me about, Maria?"

"Two things. First, this request from Agent Fleming. You had her look into the task force members' backgrounds and firing range qualification scores."

"Yes."

"And that was because you suspect one of them of working with Blake?"

"I don't suspect anyone of anything until there's a reason to. We're just looking for any sign of those reasons."

"And you wanted to know their days off—that was part of the inquiry too?"

"I wanted to see who might have been able to get down to D.C. and kill Wooford."

"I only have access to the Bureau's files, not the NYPD's. None of the agents on this case were off that day."

Hmm.

"What's the second thing?" I asked.

"Detective Cavanaugh."

"What about him?"

"When I was looking into all this, I spoke with a counterpart of mine in the NYPD Internal Affairs Bureau. Perhaps you already know this, but there's an ongoing investigation concerning him."

Internal Affairs investigations are highly confidential, so I was shocked she would even share this with me. "I was not aware of that."

"Do you have any idea what that might be concerning?"

"No. And I'm not even sure I should be discussing this with you."

"Are you aware of his extracurricular activities?"

"What are you talking about?"

"It seems he's conducting his own investigation." She puffed on her cigarette. "Off the books."

I thought of the room in his basement where he had the case files of the children who'd been killed over the last decade. "You'd have to ask him about that."

"Would you say Tobin has a strong interest in sexual predators and missing children?"

"I'd say he has a strong interest in finding them both. What is this about?"

"How well do you know him?"

"Maria, what is this regarding?"

"Here's a man who has no family, hardly any close friendships. He lost his daughter eight years ago. The killer was never found."

"Yes. I know."

"He slips off for days at a time."

"He has reason to believe someone on the task force is dirty. He needs to be discreet."

"Do you know the circumstances regarding Adrienne's abduction and subsequent murder?"

"Look, cut to the chase here, Maria. What are you saying? That Tobin killed his daughter?"

She was quiet.

"That's insane."

"Over the years, he has shown—according to my source—an inordinate curiosity about certain cases involving the deaths of children in neighboring states."

"So now he's a serial killer too? He's just trying to find the people who're behind his daughter's death. If he hadn't been looking into things, we wouldn't be this close to the Final Territory."

She took another drag from her cigarette but said nothing.

"What do you have?" I asked her. "A man preoccupied with finding the people who molested and murdered his daughter and drove his wife to suicide—that's it. Is he obsessed with seeing justice done? Absolutely. Do I blame him for it? Not one bit."

"How much I blame him all depends." She dropped her cigarette butt and smothered it out beneath the toe of her high-heeled shoe.

"On what?"

"On what that Internal Affairs investigation turns up."

"I think we're done with this conversation."

"Just be careful," she said. "He might've been right that someone on the task force is behind all this."

"Him?"

"Yes. Him."

90

I took a seat between Christie and Jodie.

Tessa was also at the table.

Christie, who was eating dessert first, asked me if everything was okay.

"Yeah." But my thoughts were somewhere else, circling around the unsettling conversation I'd just had with Maria Aguirre.

Tobin is an expert on how child pornographers get away with their crimes. He knows the laws. He had the highest scores on his shooting range qualifications. He could have made the shot that killed Higgs.

No.

I couldn't believe what I was even thinking.

He was conveniently gone when Lily Keating was abducted. He lied to you about where he was.

He knows you're staying at Christie's place. He could have sent you the mask and hood this morning, and he—

"Did you solve my puzzle yet?" Tessa asked me.

"I'm sorry." I tried to redirect my thoughts. "What?"

"The logic problem. The Goomians."

"Oh. No. Not yet."

She must have been able to tell I was deep in thought, because she dropped it and started talking with her mom.

While they carried on their discussion beside me—
something about summer and Tessa's plans and how she
wanted to get a job so she could help out with money—
my mind was somewhere else entirely: Tobin and his possible involvement.

*He was so interested in your approach, in the geospatial
techniques.*

*What did he say while you were at the pool table? Every-
thing depends on how you wrap up the game. It's all about
planning your next shot before you take your current one.*

Is that what he's been doing?

*That room in his basement. All those files. Those pictures.
That might not be his research.*

That might be his scrapbook.

No!

Well, possibly, yes.

It didn't make sense that Tobin could be guilty.

*Send Lily Keating his picture. See if she can identify him
as Shane.*

No. I couldn't do it. It'd be a betrayal of his trust.

*It's not a betrayal, it's prudence. Send it. It'll settle this
once and for all.*

But what if he found out? I couldn't even imagine
how that would affect our friendship.

Think big-picture here. He'll understand.

Drawing out my phone as unobtrusively as I could, I
sent Tobin's photo to Lily Keating's email address.

++++

Francis was on the line with Angela Knight.

He hadn't had time to finish looking up who might
have sent him the threatening email signed graciousgirl4
earlier, and now he wondered if it might be okay to ask
Angela about it.

"What if a person was pretending to be someone else online and he threatened another user in a chat room?" he asked. "Would that be legal?"

"Well, it would depend on the nature of the threat."

"Oh. Okay."

"Why? Did someone threaten you, Mr. Edlemore?"

"It was . . . Well . . ." Then he told her what he had done and what'd happened when he found the man behind graciousgirl4's screen name. "If I forward his email to you, can you find out who sent it to me?"

"I'd need a good reason to."

"I'll send you his message. You can decide."

"Hang on, I think Lacey might have something for us."

++++

I didn't hear back from Lily.

But I did hear from Angela.

Her text informed me that she'd figured out what the file that'd been sent to Francis Edlemore would do:

> The algorithm in it is designed to disrupt hash values. It could affect all the files in the ICSC database. It'd be catastrophic.

I processed that.

The other day Mr. Edlemore had told me that the ICSC had categorized seven hundred million files of child pornography. Every digital photo and video file has, basically, a unique fingerprint. If you could change those, you could hide a file. So if someone disrupted those files it could set the ICSC back years in identifying and rescuing exploited children, making it that much more difficult for law enforcement to track down them or their molesters.

Sitting just to my left, Jodie checked her phone, then whispered to me, "Pat, something's up. Can we talk? It's sensitive."

This was getting to be my new routine.

"Go on," Christie told me, even before I could excuse myself.

"I just—"

"It's okay, Pat. Go do this."

Jodie left first. I waited a few moments before following so it wouldn't look suspicious.

When I met up with her outside the house, she said, "Okay, a couple things. DeYoung was able to get that warrant to pull Hearre Construction's files. They did a remodel on the home of one of the previous victims a month before the boy disappeared. We already know Wooford worked for them. Well, Higgs did too."

If they both worked in a seasonal construction job, then their home base would have shifted as their work location moved while they were traveling north or south with the construction jobs they were working.

The link is in the open houses and that construction company. Where they intersect we'll find what we're looking for. Maybe people doing home improvements before they're going to sell their homes? Could that be how the Final Territory finds out about the upcoming open houses?

Possibly.

"Also," she continued, "and here's the big thing: the computer techs managed to find out what was on the USB drive you found in Stewart's apartment. They just sent me a link. It's the one we've been looking for: Aurora's birthday."

"We need to watch that video."

"They warned me that we should be prepared. It's graphic."

We needed to go somewhere quiet and private where we wouldn't be interrupted, but I also wanted to be able to monitor Christie and Tessa.

I mentally reviewed the layout of the house from earlier when I was looking around.

"The library," I said. "C'mon. Follow me."

++++

The Piper saw a text from Shane that the video of Aurora's birthday had been discovered: "Things have to happen now, before it's too late."

Alright.

"Take them to the warehouse and get everything ready," the Piper replied. "We'll move up the time frame."

++++

We found our way to the library. I stood near the open window where I could see Christie's table. Jodie closed the door, locked it, and joined me.

Then she clicked on the link and brought up the video.

91

The footage started on a staircase.

Someone was descending it, carrying the camera or phone. The person's trousers and wingtip shoes were visible.

The walls—paneled.

The floor—shag carpeting. Light brown.

The person filming things entered a downstairs rec room with a black sheet hanging from one wall and studio photography lights near it. A large whiteboard stood on a tripod beside it.

Four people were standing in the room wearing blank white, expressionless masks identical to the one I'd been given. It was impossible to tell for sure, but based on posture, frame, and body size, the people all appeared to be men.

Two children—one boy, one girl—were playing with a set of blocks.

They looked about four or five.

I recognized the boy from the case files in Tobin's basement. "That's Ricky Aisely, one of the eighteen victims," I said softly, unsure if Jodie would know who he was. "His body was found fourteen months ago, eight weeks after he disappeared."

This is not good. This is not going to be good.

"Ricky and Aurora," one of the people said. I didn't recognize the voice. "Can you two stand up and look over here at the camera?"

There weren't any Auroras in the eighteen names Tobin had identified. She must have been a victim we weren't aware of.

The children did as requested.

"Why don't the two of you hold hands?"

They held hands.

"Good. Now, Ricky, she's your friend, isn't she?"

The boy nodded.

"Why don't you give her a hug, show her that you like her?"

He did.

"You're doing so good! Now, Aurora, do you see that candy on the stool over there? If you take off your shirt, I'll let you have some."

But rather than take her shirt off, the girl said, "When can I see my mommy?"

"Soon, honey. We're gonna take you back to your mommy in just a little while. But before we do that, we need to celebrate *your birthday!*"

Then one of the men wearing a mask wrote on the whiteboard "Aurora's birthday!"

Another one of them brought out a knife.

It went on from there.

Jodie and I watched it all the way to the end.

We had to.

When it was over, neither of us moved. Neither of us spoke.

Then, all at once, she hurried over to a wastebasket beside the wall and threw up.

Part of me was numb.

I tried to distance myself from my feelings of anger and revulsion. "We need to see if the carpet and paneling show up in any of the homes of the other victims. Also, find out if . . . Wait a minute."

Jodie returned to my side. "What is it?"

"I need to watch it again."

"I don't think I can, Pat."

"Let me see your phone."

I started the video and paused it when the person wrote the words "Aurora's birthday."

I knew that script, that handwriting.

It was the same as Randy's suicide note.

The man who wrote it used his right hand, but there was no tattoo on it.

I handed Jodie's phone back to her.

"What do you see?" she asked.

Eighteen months.

But Ricky was taken sixteen months ago.

Two years.

The LeBange . . . ?

That could explain why Stewart was killed. It could also explain why Randy McReynolds was looking for this.

"It's not him."

"What?"

"He didn't write it."

"What are you talking about?"

"The suicide note. It's not in Randy's handwriting."

"So whose handwriting is it?"

He could have been trying to expose his brother, or maybe to destroy it so his brother couldn't be found out . . .

"Do you know whose handwriting it is, Pat?"

"I think it might be his brother's."

Outside, the cellist stopped playing.

There was the clinking of glasses and then Marcus

Rockwell stepped up front and the chitchat and murmur of conversations faded into a silence inhabited only by the sound of distant traffic and nearby crickets.

"He's here," I said to Jodie. "Let's go find him."

++++

From her office in the FBI's Cyber Division, Angela Knight had Lacey working on locating the computer that'd been used to send Francis Edlemore the graciousgirl4 email.

Lacey came up with the address and Angela could hardly believe where the computer was.

She called Francis back. "It's at NYPD headquarters," she told him.

"What?"

"It belongs to Evan Madera. Does that name mean anything to you?"

++++

Francis had heard the name before —pedophiles sometimes quoted him—but he didn't know Madera personally.

"Do you know why the police have Madera's computer?" Angela asked.

"No."

"I want you to stay there at the ICSC, Mr. Edlemore. And whatever you do, don't download that file with the virus. I'm going to see if Lacey can come up with a patch for it."

++++

A podium was positioned near the garden and now Marcus Rockwell approached the microphone. "I'd like to welcome everyone here tonight. It's an honor to have you. In a moment I'm going to introduce the president of the International Child Safety Consortium, but first let me remind you that we are joined together tonight in a common effort to offer our financial support to their mission of protecting children worldwide from exploitation."

As he was speaking, Jodie and I arrived at the table where Billy had been, but he wasn't there.

When his wife saw our urgency, she looked worried. "He was called away. Is everything alright?"

"Where did he go?" Jodie asked, trying to keep her voice soft enough not to disturb the people nearby while Rockwell spoke.

"I don't know," Elle Lachman said. "He got a text, told me he had to leave and that he would see me later tonight."

"So he has his cell phone with him?" I said.

"Yes, I mean. Is he okay? Is something wrong?"

"We just need to ask him a few questions." Jodie handed her card to Ms. Lachman. "If he contacts you, I'm going to need you to let me know."

We stepped away.

"Call DeYoung," I said. "Get approval to track Billy's GPS signal from his phone or his car."

I tried Tobin.

No answer.

"You think Billy is the Piper?" Jodie asked me.

"I don't know, but he might've been the one to poison Randy. Pull his credit card statements, see if there's any indication that he purchased Tribaxil or ate at the LeBange on the night Randy died."

"If I go after him I might need to leave," Jodie told me.

"Go ahead. If I get called away, I'll have Maria stay with Christie and Tessa."

92

8:00 p.m.
1 hour left

The Piper assessed things.

The Russians had designed the virus to activate now, at eight o'clock, but according to the latest update, it still hadn't been downloaded.

As long as the file was opened, things would still work out, but the timing mattered if they were going to make their statement about the vulnerabilities of the ICSC now, during the event.

++++

While Jodie went to call DeYoung, as inconspicuously as I could I found Maria Aguirre and had her join me at Christie's table.

"This is a global problem," Marcus was saying into the mic, "and it requires a global solution—a solution that extends across borders, across nationalities, across religions. It has no ethnic or racial divides. It's a problem that touches people of all economic backgrounds and at every strata of society. And so we need a solution that protects every child no matter who they are or where they live."

I asked Maria if I could use her phone. "I need to check a couple things and my account is blocked."

After a slight hesitation, she passed her cell to me, and while Rockwell spoke, I went online to see who'd logged in to watch the grooming video Tobin had shown his team last week.

"Tonight the ICSC will be accepting donations of all kinds," Marcus announced, "and my hope and prayer is that many more countries will join their efforts. And now, if you would, please join me in giving a warm welcome to the president of the ICSC—Mr. Alejandro Gomez."

People applauded as Gomez took the platform.

The file came up.

Most of the officers had watched it over the weekend. Nearly all had.

Just two had not: Agent Aldéric Descartes and Officer Chip Hinchcliffe.

"Thank you, Marcus," Gomez said graciously. "I think I speak for all of us when I say that we couldn't have asked for a kinder, more generous host. Could we please give a round of applause for Marcus Rockwell for his hospitality tonight?"

People clapped again.

Maria said that all of the Bureau's task force members were on duty the day that Wooford died.

But what about—

"And of course," Gomez said, "my personal thanks go out to all of you for coming tonight. We have representatives from twenty-eight countries here. I would welcome you all in your own native languages, but since I'm not quite that multilingual, yet—I am an American after all—" Light laughter. "Let me just do it collectively by saying *cheers.*"

He raised his glass and those in attendance did as well.

Last week when I was at Stewart's apartment, I'd thought about how sometimes evidence isn't so much finding what is present, but what isn't present that should be.

Descartes? Hinchcliffe?

Why didn't they watch it?

That's the arena of motives—don't go there, Pat.

My own phone vibrated.

A text from an unidentified number: "It's time to take a ride, Dr. Bowers."

I hadn't been expecting to be called out anywhere until nine.

Quieting my voice, I told Maria, "It's happening now."

"What do you want me to do?"

"Stay with Christie and Tessa."

I texted back, "Where?"

Then waited.

Gomez went on, "The Internet has forever changed the way we live our lives, bringing together people from across the globe in ways that could never have been imagined just a few decades ago. But along with the many blessings and benefits that the Internet has afforded us has come an unprecedented opportunity for those who would abuse and exploit our children."

Jodie sent me a text: "Billy McReynolds has a prescription for Tribaxil. And he ate at the LeBange that night. The security footage shows both him and his brother."

My mind was spinning.

Was he Shane? Was he the Piper?

"Tonight," Gomez continued, "we come from different backgrounds, different religions, different continents, but no matter if you're a conservative or a liberal, whether you wear a baseball cap or a turban, whether you worship

God in a mosque or a temple or a cathedral, we share a common goal, a common passion—protecting our children from online threats and predators."

I received a reply to my text from a moment ago: "Get your car from the valet."

I whispered to Christie, "I need to go take care of something. Keep Tessa close."

Though I hadn't told her what was going on, she could obviously tell it was serious and said, "I'll be praying for you."

Right now I could use all the help I could get. "Thank you. Stick with Maria until you hear from me."

As surreptitiously as I could, I made my way to the circular drive in front of the house.

I kept Maria's phone with me.

Through the loudspeakers, I heard Gomez's voice carry across the lawn. "It's time for those who would exploit the children of the world to take notice. We are not going to accept it any longer. We are going to do everything within our power to protect our children from victimization, to thwart the efforts of those who would traffic in evil, and to prosecute, to the full extent of the law, those who would steal the innocence of the next generation."

I handed my return ticket to the valet.

"Just a moment, sir," he said. "We'll get your car right out for you."

++++

Tessa got a text from Cherise, one of the girls in her class at school: "Is that u?!"

Attached to it was a link to a video of that undercover police officer changing clothes in her bedroom, but it had Tessa's name on the file.

Oh.

Perfect.

Everyone was going to think it was her.

Just wait till word spread.

++++

On his way to the warehouse, Blake heard what they were planning with Bowers. He considered things carefully.

And came up with a plan of his own.

But it would require relocating his office.

++++

The attendant brought my car around.

"And now," Gomez concluded, "we're here tonight to join hands in a common cause. Let's make the Internet—and our world—a safer place for our children, a safer place for us all. I would like to let you know that Marcus Rockwell has agreed to match funds with whatever we raise tonight, up to fifty million dollars, and he has agreed to share Krazlc's proprietary search algorithms with us to help categorize and optimize our database. So, please, be generous and let's make a difference that will last a lifetime."

The valet parked.

Exited the car.

I checked my phone to see if there were further instructions, but none came up.

He handed my keys to me.

"Thanks."

Before taking a seat at the wheel, I scanned the grounds to see if I could locate anyone who might be watching or texting me.

Nothing.

No one.

I climbed into the driver's seat and, momentarily, a text came in: "Leave the estate. Park to the side of North Worthy Drive. We'll pick you up."

I pulled forward and headed toward the gate to the main road.

93

Jodie was speaking with the security personnel to find out if they knew anything about Billy McReynolds leaving when she heard from dispatch that they'd located his cell signal.

She hurried to get her car.

++++

Tessa didn't really want to monitor how many views her little video was getting, so she put her phone away.

Things would never be the same at school if that video went viral.

Maybe moving would be better after all? Get out of here? Get a fresh start?

However, then she had another thought: *It's not about what's best for you, it's about what's best for Mom. She needs to stay close to Patrick. It's the only way she'll be happy.*

Everything sifted through her mind, where they were at, where they needed to be.

She said to her mom, "I have an idea."

"What's that?"

"Agent Fleming is staying at Patrick's apartment?"

"For now. Yes. Why?"

"That might be the solution you've been looking for."

++++

I found a secluded section of road and pulled over, turned off the car, and retrieved the mask and the hood from the trunk.

++++

Francis's cell rang.

He checked the screen.

Skylar.

What?

Answer it.

No, don't! She's working with them!

The phone continued to ring.

But they're making her do it. That must be what's going on.

Francis answered. "What is it, Skylar?"

"I'm out front. You need to let me in."

"What? You're here?"

"Francis, please. They're after me."

"I don't—"

"Please! They'll hurt me."

Don't believe her.

I need to! I have to protect her!

"Alright," he said. "I'll be right there."

++++

I tried Tobin again.

He didn't pick up.

I processed what I knew, what was happening.

The LeBange.

Billy and Randy McReynolds.

Blake and his silent ladies.

Aurora's birthday.

The task force.

Tribaxil . . .

Hearre Construction . . .

I hadn't heard from Lily Keating about Tobin's photo.

Maria had told me that no one from the task force at the Bureau was off on the day Wooford died.

Descartes was looking through Romanoff's bank records.

Descartes, not Hinchcliffe.

I was missing something here.

Who went to the open houses? Who scouted them out?

Hinchcliffe had found out that someone using Shane's name had showed up at one of the open houses.

But who was Shane?

Could it be Hinchcliffe and maybe he mentioned Shane's name as a smokescreen?

It felt like I was circling around the clues but I couldn't quite pry open the truth from them. The top of the rug remained a mystery to me. The more data I had, the more elusive and complex the pattern seemed to become.

As I waited for more instructions to come through my phone, I found my thoughts returning to Tessa's logic problem about the Goomian boy trying to get to the store, and for a few moments I allowed them to pause there.

So, the river flows at five miles per hour and the boy needs to go fifteen miles. He swims at one mile per hour, which means—with the river's current—he's actually traveling at six miles per hour. So, in half an hour, he has gone three miles. Then he gets into a canoe that he can paddle at four miles per hour, plus the five of the current, so in the next half hour he travels four and a half more miles.

That's seven and a half total.

The war canoe goes ten miles per hour, but when you add in the five of the current, he's able to go seven and a half miles in the final thirty minutes. That's a total of fifteen miles.

Which is exactly where the store is.

But that's too easy. What are you missing? What are—?

Oh.

Then I had it.

Assumptions.

Yes.

They're so easy to make and so hard to step back from.

We naturally assume that south would be downstream.

But in her puzzle, the river flowed *north*.

The store was downstream. But the boy had headed south.

The wrong direction.

He never got to the store at all.

Assumptions.

Don't assume that—

A limo was coming my way. It slowed as it approached me.

Its windows were darkened so I couldn't see the driver.

When it stopped, no one got out.

A text: "Climb in. Then throw both of your phones out the window."

Okay. So whoever was behind this knew that I had a burner phone as well as my personal cell. But who knew that?

Only a handful of people.

Actually, anyone on the task force if they looked into things closely enough.

But I had an additional phone too: Maria's.

And she was the only one who knew about that.

Opening the limo's door, I saw that the backseat was empty, apart from a note written in the same script as the message that'd been in the box I was given at nine o'clock this morning.

As I climbed into the limo, I furtively turned off the ringer, dropped Maria's phone to the floor, and kicked it under the seat in front of me. Now there was a way for the team to track me.

I tossed the other two phones out the window as directed.

The note that'd been waiting for me on the seat read *Put on the mask and then the hood. We'll know if you don't.*

I put on the mask.

Slipped the hood on over the top of it.

The limousine pulled forward.

Without being able to see anything, my other senses sharpened. I noticed the smooth running purr of the motor and the soft hum of the air-conditioning that was blowing cool air across my hands.

I could smell the leather seats and the faint scent of smoke that still lingered in the air from someone who must have lit up while sitting in here.

++++

Francis approached the front doors of the ICSC. Outside the glass, Skylar stood alone, staring anxiously around.

He unlocked the door and opened it.

"I'm sorry, Francis," she muttered. "He made me do it. Please—"

"What?"

Ivan stepped out from behind the hedges alongside the building, aiming a gun at Skylar's chest. "Hello, Francis."

++++

I tried to keep track of the right and left turns, tried to gauge the time and the speed, but that soon proved impossible, and for all I knew they were taking an indirect route to wherever we were going just to confuse me.

The tattoo.

The overdose.

The note.

The two brothers at the restaurant.

Timing. Location . . .

They blind you, assumptions do.

The boy in the puzzle was going in the wrong direction from the start.

Just like you've been.

In a case like this, everything matters.

The Pied Piper was a man who led one hundred and thirty children away.

Wingtip shoes. The fifth person. The one filming everything.

Two people didn't watch the video last weekend that Tobin had shown: Hinchcliffe and Descartes.

And Tobin, of course, who'd obviously seen it before.

Yes.

Something that was so easy to miss. The answer was staring me right in the face.

Shane's identity.

And, if I was right, the Piper's.

94

Francis was seated at his desk. Skylar stood beside him. Ivan had the gun barrel pressed against the middle of her back.

"Download the file," he ordered Francis, "or this night is not going to have a happy ending for Miss Shapiro."

"Don't hurt her."

"I'll give you to the count of three."

Angela and Lacey had been working on a patch that might be able to stop the virus, but Francis hadn't heard back from them yet.

"One," Ivan said.

Francis pulled up the email message.

"Two."

He tried to figure out what to do, tried to decide—

"Th—"

"Wait!" Francis tapped quickly at the keys. "There."

"There what?"

"I logged out of my account."

"What?"

"I'm the only one who can get you back in there. Let Skylar go and I'll log in again. Then, when I'm done, you can kill me or do whatever you want with me. But she goes free."

"Francis, no! You—" Skylar began, but Ivan cut her off abruptly, cursing.

He raised the gun threateningly, as if he was going to hit her in the back of the head. "Log back in. Do it!"

"If you hurt her I swear I won't help you. You'll never get the file open."

Ivan scoffed. "You've got balls, I'll give you that." He removed his phone from his pocket, tapped at the screen, and then spoke to whoever he'd just called: "Alright. If I don't call you back in one minute exactly, I want you to take the kid at the hospital."

"No!" Francis said.

Ivan hung up. "Log in and download the file or you'll be responsible for both of their deaths."

Desperately, Francis tried to figure out what to do.

"Time is ticking." Ivan was staring at his watch.

Francis glanced around his desk for anything he could use as a weapon, anything at all, but all he could come up with was the St. Stephen's Hospital coffee mug.

Typing frantically, he pulled up the log-in box. "Let Skylar go and I'll type in my password."

Ivan nodded toward her and she scurried toward the door.

"Now do it," he demanded.

To save Derek, Francis entered his password.

Went to the email program.

Clicked on the file.

Just download it, don't open it. You'll be alright as long as you don't open it.

As the file began to download, Francis picked up the mug. "Call it in." He pretended to drink from it. "Tell them not to hurt Derek."

"Not until the file is opened."

You need to get him close.

Still holding the mug in one hand, Francis tilted the screen with the other so that only he could see it.

When Ivan reached over to straighten it out, Francis swung the mug as hard as he could, cracking it against the side of Ivan's head.

The force of impact caught him off guard. His head snapped around and it stunned him for a moment, but only for a moment. Then he shoved Francis roughly to the floor to get to the keyboard.

With the gun in one hand, he struggled to use the other to punch at the keys to open the file, but as he did, he suddenly cried out, straightened up, and reached around, back between his shoulder blades.

Skylar was standing behind him.

She'd driven a letter opener into his back. "That's for hitting me this morning."

Francis went for the gun, wrestling it from Ivan's hand. He aimed it at Ivan. "Get back!"

You don't know how to use this thing.

It's easy. Just squeeze the trigger.

Ivan didn't move.

Francis aimed just above the man's head and fired. The bullet punched a hole through the cubicle partition next to the desk.

"I said get back."

Ivan edged back, holding up his hands. "Careful with that, Francis."

"Call the hospital," Francis said. "Tell them not to hurt Derek or I'll shoot you in the knee and then work my way up."

Ivan gulped, then made the call.

"Get something to tie him up with," Francis told Skylar, who grabbed a USB cord from behind the printer on a nearby desk.

Francis's eyes were glued on Ivan, but as Skylar returned to his side, she gasped and stared at the computer screen. "It's too late, Francis. He opened the file."

++++

I could feel the limo decelerating.

We turned in a slow circle to the left and when we came to a stop, I honestly had no idea where we were.

Someone opened the driver's door, closed it, and a moment later opened the door beside me.

"Alright, we're here," a man said gruffly.

It was the same rough, gravelly voice of the behemoth who'd frisked me in the hallway outside Blake's office behind the pub.

He took my left elbow and led me away from the limo.

The cool air, the smell of the waterfront, and the slip-slap of waves close by told me that we were near the shore. We walked forty-one steps and the sound of the water disappeared.

Our footfalls echoed slightly.

We'd entered a building of some type.

A garage door closed noisily behind us.

Finally, the man leading me stopped. "That's good, right there."

Muffled cries came from the distance in two directions—both to my right and to my left.

He patted me down just as he had yesterday, took my SIG, but left my knife in my pocket.

I didn't know why he let me keep it, and for some reason I thought of what Blake had told me in his office: "Be careful who you trust, Agent Bowers. The truth that's right in front of you is often the hardest to see."

Be careful who you trust . . .

"You can remove the hood," the bouncer told me, "but keep the mask on."

I tugged off the hood and stared through the eyeholes of the mask.

95

9:00
The choice

Having been in the dark for so long, my eyes weren't used to the light, and at first I had to blink against the brightness.

I was in a warehouse.

The middle of it was lit from high fluorescents dangling from the ceiling, but the sides of the building were ruled by shadows.

The place must have served as a mannequin warehouse at one time because dust-covered body parts of mannequins were stacked on shelves nearby and dozens of bare mannequin bodies were positioned throughout the warehouse.

This is where Blake got his silent ladies.

Eight people in masks stood motionless and mute at various spots around me. One of them was setting up a video camera on a tripod. Two others, who were standing about five meters away from me, were aiming handguns at me. The big guy beside me wasn't wearing a mask, but it wouldn't have done much good at hiding his identity anyway, since he was twice the size of anyone else here.

On each end of the warehouse was a single wooden chair, and on each of the chairs, with a noose around their neck, and a taut rope stretching up to the ceiling, stood someone I knew.

Tobin on one chair.

Naomi Morgan, the Port Authority officer who'd impersonated Tessa, on the other.

Both had been gagged. Their hands were bound behind their backs.

A man in a mask stood beside each of their chairs.

Naomi? How did they find out about her?

The only one who knew about her was Tobin.

And DeYoung. You called him to let him know what you were doing—

Wait.

There was one other person on the task force who could've recognized her from the video. He—

One of the men stepped forward, and before he could speak, I said, "So this is why you left dinner early, Billy."

"Agent Bowers." Billy McReynolds's distinctive radio-voice resonated through the warehouse. "This isn't how we planned on having things play out, but you just wouldn't stop poking around, would you? Was it the video? Is that how you knew it was me?"

"The handwriting. It matched the suicide note I found on your brother. Also, the tattoo. You wouldn't have known about it if you saw him for the last time two years ago. But you saw him the night he died, met him at the LeBange, and that's when you slipped him the Tribaxil."

"Yes. His proverbial last supper. Poor, dear Randy."

"You wrote the suicide note and you put 'only' on the envelope—'open *only* in the case of my death.' Why would someone who was committing suicide phrase it like that? Since Randy would have recognized your handwriting on the front of the envelope, he probably thought it was your will or something. Is that what you told him?"

Billy was quiet.

"And then when he was dead, you came forward to identify it as *his* handwriting and made up the story about the sexual assault allegations. Very clever. It got us looking in the wrong direction from the start."

Jodie was going to try tracking Billy's phone and car. That should lead her here. Or maybe Maria's phone would.

Unless Billy was careful. Unless—

"You won't find the children, Agent Bowers," he told me. "And once this is over, you're going to have to live with the knowledge that you couldn't save them, that you were too late."

Keep him talking!

"Randy was innocent this whole time," I said. "He found out about the video of Aurora's birthday and you couldn't let him see you were on it, could you? Because he would have identified you. No, Randy didn't kill Stewart. And I'm guessing you didn't want to get your hands dirty, that's not what the Piper would do. So who did you send? Shane? It was messy. He's not quite as skilled with the knife as he is with a gun, I guess."

"You didn't do as Blake requested," Billy McReynolds said. "You didn't film Tessa Ellis changing. You chose to use Officer Morgan here." He pointed in her direction. "That was your first mistake."

"No, that's not what this is about. That can't be. It's the virus, right? At the ICSC."

"Oh, it's much more than that."

Why would they want to alter the hash values? It'd make the files untraceable, but—

Then it hit me.

"You mean to upload them." The weight of what I

was saying hit me hard. "No search engines will know to block them."

He held up a phone and checked the screen. "The file has been downloaded. Twelve minutes from now when I punch in the passcode, we'll change the landscape of the Internet forever. All available. All free. For all time. And there is no delete key on the World Wide Web."

That was almost the same phrase Lloyd had said to us in prison.

Maybe they were working together before he was arrested.

"In the meantime," Billy said, "I'm going to give you the chance to save one of them: Detective Cavanaugh or Officer Morgan. Who will it be? I'll leave that choice to you."

So what'll happen to the other one? They can't let us live. We know too much.

They can't—

"Good-bye, Agent Bowers. I have a few children to attend to."

I studied the room. Evaluated my options. The two men with the guns were too far away for me to disarm them. All I had was that knife.

Billy McReynolds left the warehouse.

Pat, you need to stop this!

"Take off your mask, Chip," I called. For a moment no one moved. "I know you're here. I know you're Shane."

The man closest to Tobin's chair removed his mask.

Officer Chip Hinchcliffe.

"And here I thought my mask was good enough."

"You didn't watch the video last weekend. Why not— was it because you helped produce it or simply because you'd seen it before?"

He shook his head. "There has to be more than that."

"None of the agents on the task force had time off on the day when Wooford was killed. It had to be someone from the NYPD. And you're the only other one besides Tobin who'd worked with Naomi, who could've identified her in the video I sent Blake. You also subscribed to the real estate mailing lists. What was it—researching more open houses?"

He's the one who attended them.

No—Tobin would have recognized him. So would they have sent someone else? Would they—

I was conflicted. I couldn't stall, because I needed to stop Billy, but I also needed to save Tobin and Naomi. I studied the distance between them. The ropes looked tight enough that if those men really did remove the chairs, Naomi and Tobin wouldn't drop far, so their necks wouldn't break, but they would choke to death. And it wouldn't take long.

By the time I got to one of them, it would be too late to save the other.

You need to save them both!

How?

Chip studied Tobin's face. "I have a friend in Internal Affairs. I know about the investigation. When you're dead, Detective, this case will die with you. I'll make sure of that—and I'm good at covering my tracks."

Hurry! You need to stop Billy. He's going to upload the files and kill the children.

"You know." Chip tapped a finger against Tobin's chest. "I remember taking Adrienne, standing there in your living room with my hand over her mouth so she wouldn't cry out while you rushed past us to follow Higgs in his sedan. You should have seen the look in her eyes. Yeah, I took her, I watched over her, and I killed her—all while I was working on the task force. It was quite a feeling, my friend. Nothing else like it."

Tobin's eyes became steel.

One of the men nearby went over and punched him in the gut. Tobin crumpled a little, but the rope around his neck kept him from buckling over.

"Why'd you do that?" Chip asked him harshly.

He spoke just loud enough for me to hear. "You'll have to forgive me. I get a little carried away some-times."

I stared at him.

That was precisely what I'd said to Blake when I was alone with him in his office.

Why would he give himself away like that?

His man left you with your knife . . .

"So, then," I said to him, "we have that in common."

He nodded.

"Alright, it's time," Chip called to the person beside Naomi's chair. "Kick it out." As the man did, Chip grabbed the chair that Tobin was standing on and slipped it out from under him.

Both Tobin and Naomi dropped, their feet dangling above the concrete floor.

Go!

Blake and his bouncer are closer to Tobin.

I whipped off the mask and bolted toward Naomi, flicking out my blade as I did.

The rope is weighted. It's stretched tight. It'll be easier to cut.

I heard gunshots behind me, but I kept running. Leaping over Naomi's upended chair, I slashed the blade against the rope, which frayed partway, but held. I had to swipe at it two more times before the rope severed.

I caught Naomi as she dropped, then loosened the rope around her throat and lowered her to the floor. "You're going to be alright."

After removing her gag, I cut her hands free.

She gasped for breath, then stared past me and pointed across the warehouse. "Pat, hurry!"

Spinning around, I saw that one of the Final Territory men was lying unmoving on his back. The rest of the men had scattered. The big guy was holding on to Tobin, bear-hugging him, supporting his weight so he wouldn't choke.

Blake had removed his mask and was crouched, aiming a gun at someone who was hiding behind a cluster of mannequins near the far wall. From his vantage point, I doubted Blake could see him, but I could. "Four from the left," I shouted as I raced across the warehouse to try to save Tobin. "Aim low."

Blake fired a volley of shots and there was a brief cry of pain, then a heavy thud.

Then silence.

He'd hit his mark.

When I arrived at Tobin's side, I realized someone had shot the man holding him. A widening stain of blood seeped from his side and he was cringing from the effort of keeping Tobin in the air.

I snatched up the chair, stood on it, and sliced through the rope.

The guy eased Tobin to the ground, then collapsed beside him.

While Blake went to put pressure on his man's gunshot wound, I leaned over Tobin. Quickly, I removed the rope from his neck, then took off the gag and freed his hands. "Relax," I said. "Just relax. It's over."

His breathing was coarse and choppy, but he managed to say, "Where?"

"Where?"

"Where'd Chip go?"

"Out the back," Blake told him. "By the waterfront. I shot him in the leg. He won't be far."

Tobin struggled to push himself to his feet.

"Just stay here," I said, but it did no good. His mind was made up. Half staggering, half running, he took off after the man who'd killed his daughter.

"Why are you helping us?" I asked Blake. "Why are you doing this?"

"Let's just say I've got my reasons." He was still holding his hand against the guy's bleeding side.

"Tell me where the children are."

"I don't know."

"Billy said he was going to take care of them. Where did he go?" I demanded.

"Agent Bowers, I don't know."

I dug the limo keys out of the bouncer's pocket, and as I did, it reminded me of the key he'd slipped into my own pocket yesterday. "Why'd you guys give me that key? What did you mean when you said it was the key to everything?"

"You're gonna need it to find the kids. That's all I know. That's all they told me."

The guy had taken my SIG when he frisked me. I retrieved it. "I'm going after Billy."

"We won't be here when you get back," Blake told me.

"I'll be coming for you."

"I'll be ready."

I rushed toward the door, still not sure how I was going to find McReynolds.

If he was telling the truth when he said he was going to upload the files in twelve minutes, I didn't have much time.

++++

Billy McReynolds parked the van, used his key, swung open the door, and descended the steps to where they kept the children.

96

I grabbed Maria's cell phone from under the seat in the back of the limo, and as I slipped behind the wheel, I called dispatch and told them to get units en route. They relayed that Jodie was already on her way.

I peeled out of the parking lot toward the city.

Where would the children be?

In his interview with Dr. Perrior, D'Nesh had said there were pillows on the walls of the place where they kept him, pillows that weren't pillows.

And he'd said they watched them through the windows.

Why did they bring you here to the warehouse?

They're moving the kids. Time is tight. They must be close.

I called DeYoung and he picked up almost immediately. "Pat, what is—?"

"The Hearre Construction records. Pull them up. Did they ever remodel BranchWide Studios?"

"Let me check."

It only took him a minute. "Yes. Four years ago. It looks like they put in four additional recording rooms."

"They're soundproof," I muttered. "They would be perfect."

Pillows that weren't pillows: sound baffles on the walls.

"It's the studio. Send backup."

I hit the brakes, screeched to a stop, spun around, and took off for the BranchWide Studios, which if I was right, would be close by, less than a mile away.

++++

Tobin Cavanaugh followed the spotty blood trail along the dock.

He was still having a hard time drawing in his breath and felt dizzy from the lack of oxygen while he'd been hanging from the rope, but he wasn't about to turn back now. He'd been waiting for this moment ever since the night his daughter was taken.

The months had come and gone. The years had come and gone. And he had not found justice, had not found relief, had not found peace.

Tonight he would find all three.

The blood trail ended in a thick wash of shadows behind a loading container near the edge of a pier that dropped off twenty feet to the black water of the bay. "I know you're in there, Chip."

Chip Hinchcliffe stepped out of the darkness holding a two-foot-long lead pipe that he must have found along the docks. "Hello, Tobin."

"Lay down the pipe, get on the ground, and put your hands behind your back. You're under arrest."

A slight headshake. "I'm afraid that's not the ending I had in mind here."

"I was hoping you'd say that."

Chip tightened his grip on the pipe. "I'm actually glad it turned out like this. Neither of us with our guns. Now I get to kill you like I did your daughter, up close and personal."

"Up close and personal works for me."

Tobin went at him, but Chip swung the pipe with blinding speed. Tobin swiveled sideways, but immediately Chip recovered, cocked the pipe back, and brought a crushing blow to the side of Tobin's leg that sent him crumpling to one knee.

As he was trying to rise to his feet again, Chip slammed the pipe against his back, knocking him to his hands and knees, and then again, flattening him to the ground.

Chip kicked him severely in the ribs and Tobin heard the sharp crack as at least one of his ribs snapped.

He drew in a tight, strangled breath and rolled over to face his attacker.

Chip stared down at him. "Adrienne used to cry in her room, asking for you and her mother. She never gave up hoping that you'd find her, until the very end when she realized no one was coming for her, no one was going to save her. But don't worry, I comforted her. Told her all the things a loving father would. Even as I squeezed the life breath out of her."

He raised the pipe high.

Tobin eyed the bloodstain on Chip's leg where Blake had shot him. Scooting closer, he kicked at it, connecting solidly. Chip staggered backward, losing his footing for a moment.

That was all Tobin needed.

Ignoring the pain, he sprang to his feet and rushed Chip, throwing his arms around him and driving him back off the pier toward the water.

He tightened his grip as they fell through the air.

Though the impact was jarring, Tobin held on.

The river swallowed them.

With the broken rib, Tobin wasn't able to get much of a breath before they went under.

Chip let go of the pipe and writhed desperately against

his grip. After a moment, he managed to free himself and kicked toward the surface, but Tobin grabbed his leg, dragging him back down.

This man killed Adrienne.

Chip kicked at Tobin's face with his free leg, but Tobin held on, working his hands up Chip's body to get to his neck.

He drove Misty to suicide.

Bubbles rose from his mouth as he ran out of air.

He took everything from you.

He got to Chip's neck and wrapped his arm around it, locking it in place with his other hand.

Chip struggled fiercely against him, but together they sank.

Tobin held on.

Even when Chip began to convulse.

Even when the last few dribbles of breath escaped from Tobin's mouth and his lungs were screaming for air.

Still, he held on.

Only when the convulsions stopped.

Only when Chip went limp did Tobin let go.

Up close and personal.

Yeah, that worked for him.

He strained for the surface and made it just long enough to snatch in one breath before the current grabbed him and his weakness overwhelmed him.

As he was sinking again, he heard someone calling his name.

There was a splash nearby.

Then, as the world grew dim, he felt an arm curl around his chest as somebody tugged him toward shore.

97

All the lights were off when I skidded to a stop outside the BranchWide Studios building.

No cars nearby.

Nothing.

I tried the front door, but it was locked and the key that Blake had told me was the key to everything didn't open it.

I gave the door a few swift kicks, but it was reinforced and the lock refused to give way.

Around the south side of the building I found a back door, but that one wouldn't open either.

Again the key didn't fit.

You were wrong. This isn't it!

They transported children back and forth from Romanoff's place in New Jersey. So they would've needed to load and unload the children, somewhere that wouldn't draw attention.

The recording studio is too conspicuous.

But then what about the remodeling work?

Billy said he was going to upload those files in twelve minutes.

You need to find him!

Where could they transfer the children without being seen?

Based on the floor plan of the building, I anticipated that any additional studio rooms would need to be located on a lower level.

If so, there might be another way in.

The garage next door, Lizzie's Auto Repair, was close.

Wait.

Skylar mentioned she'd "seen the garage."

D'Nesh had said he heard the people who took him mention the name Lizzie.

Billy McReynolds claimed Beth was the one who'd accused his brother of abusing her.

Beth could be short for Elizabeth.

So could Lizzie.

Lizzie's Auto Repair.

He was mocking us right from the start!

I ran to the door of the body shop.

Slid the key into the lock.

It clicked.

Gun ready, I eased the door open.

Three auto bays stretched back into the darkness.

A van stood in the middle of the garage.

I checked the driver's seat first.

Empty.

When I threw open the van's back doors, I found two children, both terrified, handcuffed to a chain that ran along the floor.

I recognized them from the case files: LeAnne Cordett and Andre Martin. She would have turned five by now. He was ten.

Maggie Rivers, who was eleven, was still missing.

"It's alright," I assured them. "I'm going to help you. Where's Maggie?"

Andre pointed across the garage. "Downstairs."

After tugging on the chain to try to free them, but

finding it secure, I put a finger to my lips. "Shh. Stay quiet now. I'll be right back."

I cleared the garage, then crossed the auto bay to a steel door beside the fuse box.

The door was ajar. When I pressed it open, I saw that it led to a staircase.

A dim lightbulb halfway down the steps was on.

SIG in a tactical position, I started down the stairs.

The paneling and carpeting were the same as in the video of Aurora's birthday.

The steps ended in the rec room where the two children had been. There were also toys and a side room with a bed and a shelf of knives.

A hallway led back underground, stretching westward and under the studio building. A stairwell at the far end would have led up into it.

Soundproof rooms on each side.

Each was reinforced with thick glass and had sound-absorbing baffles on the walls. It was chilling to think that they kept the children captive right under the recording studio where Billy hosted his daily radio program listened to by five million people.

In the dim light, I could make out mats on the floor of the rooms, as well as pillows and blankets. A scattering of books and dirty stuffed animals lay beside them. There was a drain in the corner of each room, perhaps for the children to use as a toilet. Near each mat, a thick chain was attached to the wall with an empty manacle where I imagined the children's ankles had been shackled.

Maggie Rivers was in the last room, unchained and crouching in the corner.

I opened her door. "It's okay, Maggie. I'm—"

But then I heard the van doors slam and the rough rattle of the garage door opening.

He's leaving. He's taking the other two children!

"Stay here," I told Maggie, then I sprinted through the hallway and back up the stairs.

Burst into the garage.

There was no one in the driver's seat.

He's here.

In the garage.

Scanning the auto bays, I saw no one, but there were plenty of shadows. "Billy?" I called. "It's over. Come on out."

Through the now-open garage door, I saw a car that hadn't been there earlier in front of the recording studio. A woman appeared in the darkening day and called to me in a concerned voice, "Agent Bowers?" It was Elle Lachman. "What's going on?"

I raised my gun at her. "Hands up."

She cried out in fear and put her hands up. "Don't shoot me! Please!"

"What are you doing here?"

"Billy called me, told me that he needed me. But I—"

"Stay right there."

I turned to inspect the garage, but movement in the corner of my eye caught my attention. By the time I spun around to face Elle again, Billy had stepped out of the darkness. He was aiming a Glock directly at his wife's head. "Drop your gun, Agent Bowers."

Elle gasped. "Billy, what are you doing?"

"Shut up." Then, as he led her into the garage, he called to me again, "Drop it or there's gonna be an awfully big mess to clean up in here."

I had my gun leveled at him. With Elle in the way, it reminded me of being in Romanoff's house last week when Higgs had the knife against Lily Keating's neck.

The distant sound of sirens came coursing through the night.

I didn't move, didn't get rid of my weapon. "Hear that, Billy? Put down your gun. Backup's on its way."

"Then I have nothing to lose, do I?" He cocked the gun.

"Billy," Elle pleaded, "put it down and—"

"Shut up!"

I didn't have a great look at Billy, but it might be all I was going to get. "It's over, Billy."

"It's far from over."

End this, Pat.

He's going to kill Elle.

Her life was in danger.

"Drop the gun!" I shouted.

He refused to lay down his weapon.

I didn't always follow protocol.

But now I did.

I let instinct direct me and I fired at Billy McReynolds until he was no longer a threat.

"No!" Elle shuddered and dropped to her knees beside her husband, then shook him. "Billy! Oh, please."

"Get back, Elle," I said.

She was draped over him, weeping.

"Back up," I repeated.

Trembling, Elle moved away from his body.

Keeping my gun on him, I approached Billy, kicked his Glock away, and knelt to check his pulse.

Nothing.

He was gone.

As I was patting down his pockets to find the phone that he was going to use to upload the files, I realized my mistake.

The renovations were done four years ago.
Billy has only been on the air for three.
Timing. Location.
Her name.
Elle.
He wasn't going to kill her.
He was never going to—
No, he didn't have his cell.
Not anymore.
The Piper had just taken it from him.

98

I began turning to face her. "Oh, you're good, Elle."

She stood about three meters from me and had just picked up the Glock I'd kicked away from her dead husband's hand. "I wish you hadn't said that. I was going to let you live."

Without hesitation she fired, hitting me in the right shoulder. The impact spun me sideways and when I was transferring my gun to my other hand so I could get a shot off at her, she came at me with surprising speed and kicked fiercely at my arm, hitting my radial nerve and jarring the gun free. With her foot, she sent it sliding to the other side of the garage.

"Uh-uh-uh, we can't have any of that, now."

Elle. Lizzie. Beth.

Elizabeth.

All the same person.

The one who was behind all this from the start.

"You knew you both couldn't escape," I said. "You convinced Billy to give up his life so you could get away."

"Now, who's going to believe nonsense like that? There aren't going to be any witnesses left. Apparently, before you could get here, Billy shot the three children. When the police officers find you dead, I'll tell them all about how you were valiantly trying to save me when Billy fired at you, right before you killed him. You'll be remembered as a hero. That should be of some comfort."

She hit a button on the wall to close the garage door and give herself some privacy for the four murders she was about to commit.

Backup won't know we're here. They won't get here until it's too late.

"You worked at the studio before Billy's show started," I said. "You're the one who had it renovated. When did you make the entrance to the basement from here in the garage? After he came on board or before?"

"I had it all done at once. Made it that much easier."

Children naturally trust women more than men. Maybe that's how she was able to get them to go with her. And she could've worn the slacks and wingtip shoes to make it look like a man was filming Aurora's birthday.

"You were the fifth person."

"The fifth person?"

"You filmed it."

"Sometimes. Yes."

"And Tobin would have recognized Chip, so are you the one who attended his open house?"

"Going after Adrienne was Chip's idea. It was bold. I give him credit for that." She tilted her head at me. "So, have you figured out why yet?"

"Why?"

"Why the ICSC?"

I thought of the people filming the scene of Randy's suicide last week.

People are curious. When there's a beheading video from the Middle East, it'll get hundreds of thousands of views within hours. Macabre curiosity is part of human nature.

"The best way to hide in a crowd," I said, "is to let

everyone wear a mask. When seven hundred million images and videos of child pornography are suddenly available for free and without any way for law enforcement to track them—well, millions of people will view and download them—just because they're curious, if nothing else. Law enforcement would have no way to know who the molesters and pornographers are and who the innocent people are."

"Based on people's viewing habits, my Russian colleagues and I are conservatively anticipating that twenty-five to thirty percent of smart phones and computers in the world will have child porn on them by the end of the week."

Keeping the gun on me, she started typing in the passcode on the phone.

Beyond her, at the top of the stairs, Maggie Rivers, who must have left the room in the basement, appeared.

No, no, no.

Don't let Elle see her!

Maggie looked at me, then at the fuse box beside her.

I nodded and she silently stepped toward it. I slid my left hand toward my pocket where I had the automatic knife.

"Look at me, Elle."

She peered at me. "Yes?"

"I'll need you to turn it off."

"I'm not turning anything off."

"All of them. When I tell you to."

She looked at me quizzically. "What are you talking about?"

Maggie reached for the fuse box.

I yelled to her, "Now, Maggie!"

"What?" Elle spun.

Maggie snapped off the fuses, drowning the garage in shadows. The children in the van cried out.

In the darkness I scrambled to my feet, snapping out the blade as I did.

It was all I had.

But it was enough.

Elle managed to get off one shot that whizzed past my face before I drove the knife into the side of her neck. A warm spray of blood splattered against my hand and cheek.

As the Piper dropped to the ground, I felt for the gun, tore it from her hands, and said to Maggie, "Leave the lights off. This isn't something you need to see."

99

Two days later
Friday, June 22
10:20 a.m.

"How's your coffee?" Christie asked me.

"Worth coming back for."

Yesterday, Francis Edlemore had told me about a coffeehouse and used bookstore I'd never been to called the Mystorium. Now, since it was on the way to the hospital where Tobin was recovering, I'd swung by with Christie and Tessa.

We had about ten minutes before we needed to leave.

My right arm was in a sling because of the GSW in my shoulder where Ellie shot me in the garage. It would slow down my workouts at the Hangout, but I'd dealt with injuries worse than this before.

It would heal.

I would recover.

And only a scar would remain.

Tessa wandered over to peruse some of the books in the half-off bin. Christie's phone rang and she stepped aside to take the call.

Tobin was doing well despite the punctured lung and

the two broken ribs he'd sustained in his fight with Chip Hinchcliffe. Thankfully, when Jodie had arrived at the warehouse and followed the blood trail, she'd found Tobin in the water in time and managed to get him to shore.

Ruined her evening gown.

The price you have to pay.

A lot had happened in the past two days.

After I'd left the warehouse Wednesday night, Naomi had tried to apprehend Blake and his bodyguard, but they overpowered her and got away.

Later, when SWAT went to the bar where Blake had been with his silent ladies, they found nothing. The room had been completely cleared out. He must have known earlier that he was going to be moving on.

I'd told him I was coming for him.

He'd said he would be ready.

Well, we'll see about that.

As for the Final Territory, we'd managed to stop the ICSC's files from being uploaded to the Internet, but, despite the patch Angela and Lacey had come up with, many of the files had still been infected when Ivan Romanoff managed to open the file containing the virus.

However, with Marcus Rockwell's offer to allow the ICSC to use Krazle's search algorithms, it looked like the files would be able to be reindexed. It would be a big job, but at least everything was still safely tucked away in their database.

Romanoff was in custody and was talking, trying to plea bargain. His confession, along with the information that Cyber was able to obtain from Elle Lachman's computer and Dr. Madera's mailing list, gave us enough to go after the known Final Territory members.

Yesterday, working with INTERPOL, we made arrests in fourteen countries, and it looked like nearly all of the fifty-two registered users had been identified, caught, or were being pursued.

Skylar turned herself in and was facing some serious charges for working with the Final Territory to extort Francis, but the last I heard he wasn't going to press charges and it looked like she was going to be given leniency from the state in exchange for her testimony.

Derek, the boy at St. Stephen's Research Hospital, was safe.

The three children we'd managed to rescue from the garage beside the BranchWide Studios were back with their parents.

At least the long and arduous healing process could begin for them. Dr. Perrior was going to work with the NYPD to make sure they received all the counseling they needed.

It would take time, but at least now that was something they actually had on their side.

Maria Aguirre put the paperwork through to expedite the internal review to clear me from the shooting last week, and though the Internal Affairs investigation involving Tobin was still ongoing, with all that we knew now, I imagined it wouldn't amount to anything.

Yesterday afternoon when I was visiting Tobin, he took off his wedding ring and set it beside his bed. "Misty would want me to move on," he explained to me softly. "The best way to remember her is to love her enough to finally do that. I guess I've known that for a long time. I just haven't been able to do it without, well, some sort of closure."

I told him about sending his photo to Lily Keating to see if she could identify him as Shane. "I'm sorry I ever doubted you," I said.

"You needed to be sure."

"No, I needed to trust you."

"You trusted where the facts were pointing. I'd rather you did that than trust me any day."

Last week he'd said to me that without hope the only thing that keeps us going is momentum or fear, that otherwise we'll see what a small role we play in "the sprawling script of the universe." All too often that leads to despair, and being chained to the past can be the most stifling thing of all.

But hope can break even the thickest chain. And I sensed that he had it again, or at least he was on the road to finding it. And that was probably worth the pain of all that he'd been through in the last couple days.

++++

Since Wednesday night Tessa had been dealing with the fallout from that woman cop impersonating her changing in her bedroom, and then the video of it being posted online.

But finally she'd realized that, when you stepped back to look at things, it wasn't really that huge of a deal, and the more she thought about it, the more she just found it ironic—here she was, popular on all these sites, getting all these comments, all this attention, and it wasn't even her.

Let 'em keep thinking it was her.

Idiots.

Leaving the half-off bin, she went to the front counter. The woman working there looked about four or five years older than her.

"Do you have any stuff by Poe?" Tessa asked.

"Sure. I mean, he tends more toward horror, but—"

"His Monsieur C. Auguste Dupin stories."

The woman seemed pleased. "Yes. I don't get that

many fans of Dupin in here. Let me see what I can find you." She typed at her computer to look up the books.

"He's way better than Holmes."

"Agreed." She tapped the screen triumphantly. "C'mon, I'll show you where they are." Then she extended her hand. "By the way, I'm Rebekah."

"Tessa."

"Good to meet you."

"You too."

++++

In Derek's room at St. Stephen's Research Hospital, Francis Edlemore handed over the bracelet that Skylar had made for him, the one he'd removed from his own wrist when he found out she wasn't to be trusted.

Derek admired it. "Will she be back? Miss Shapiro, I mean?"

"I'm not sure."

"She was nice."

"Yes. She was."

And she wasn't.

She was good.

She was bad.

She was both.

Just like you.

Just like everyone.

"I hope I see her again," Derek said.

"I hope so too."

Yesterday, Dr. Madera had sent the record of Francis's chats with graciousgirl4 to Claire, and honestly, Francis was glad that the truth was out there at last. Keeping secrets takes its toll.

Honesty is the best policy.

Yes, it is.

Francis wasn't sure he would be able to keep his job, but there were a lot of kids to help and someone needed to do it. Besides, now that the files had to be reorganized, they needed people there at the ICSC who knew what they were doing.

He hoped he could stay. It was his chance to do something right. To make a difference.

To do something good.

From what the NYPD had been able to discover from analyzing Dr. Madera's computer, he'd been spending a lot of time in chat rooms pretending to be a teenage girl. It wasn't illegal, but they were going to be keeping a closer eye on him.

Probably a good thing.

In light of all that had happened, Dr. Perrior had agreed to continue meeting with Francis if he wanted to, but Francis wasn't sure. Maybe he would try to move on without a counselor.

There was a lot to think about.

A lot to decide.

"Why wouldn't Miss Shapiro come back?" Derek asked.

"Well, she has some things to sort out, but I'm hoping she'll get a second chance to make them right." Then he told Derek about the tortoises in the Galápagos Islands getting a second chance. "There's a lot more of them now than there used to be."

"They live, like, a hundred and fifty years, right?"

"Some of them do, yes."

"That'd be cool."

"Yeah, it would."

Derek folded his arms grumpily. "I wish I was a tortoise."

"Why?"

"I heard the doctors talking to my mom. They didn't know I was listening. They said I wasn't gonna live very long."

Francis wanted to encourage Derek, but he didn't want to lie to him.

Honesty.

The best policy.

"Can I tell you a secret?" he said.

"Yeah."

"I was dead once. A long time ago. I died and the doctors brought me back to life."

"Really?"

"Yes. None of us knows how long we have. The secret is making each day count."

"Because it might be your last one?"

"And because wasting any of them would be a big mistake."

"Like blowing up a balloon?"

Francis looked at him curiously. "Blowing up a balloon?"

"Yeah. One day it's gonna pop, but you can make something cool out of it before it does."

"I like that. You're pretty smart, Derek."

"And you're pretty nice, Mr. Edlemore. For a blown up."

"Blown up? Oh, you mean grown up. Right? I mean— Oh. That was a joke."

Derek shook his head. But he was smiling.

"Here," Francis said, "let me tie that on your wrist for you." He leaned forward and took the two ends of the bracelet. "Then, we'll get started on making something cool."

++++

Christie finished up her call and Tessa went to check out. She seemed pretty excited about whatever book she'd found.

"Well," Christie said, joining me. "That was Jodie on the phone."

"Jodie?"

"Yeah. So, I need to tell you a couple things."

"Okay."

"First, regarding Omaha, I'm going to tell the firm there that I've decided to pursue another position."

"Here in the city?"

She nodded. "Yes."

"Excellent. This day is just getting better and better."

"The other night Tessa had a suggestion. I think we've come up with a plan. That's what I was talking with Jodie about."

"And that is?"

"She needs a place to stay and so do we. She's short on money and so are we. If we split expenses, and share a place, I think we can make it work."

"I like it," I said. "It's clever, simple, elegant." Then I had a thought. "Wait—your church is pretty conservative. What are the people there going to say when they find out you and your daughter are staying with a lesbian?"

"Time will tell."

Tessa came toward us carrying her book.

"So," I said. "What'd you get?"

"A collection of stories by Poe." She held it up proudly. "Please tell me you've heard of him."

"He wrote that poem 'The Raven.'"

"Um. Yeah. That would be him. But he wrote a bunch of other stuff too."

We passed outside into the daylight. "That would be a good nickname for you, by the way: Raven."

"Why's that?"

"Your black hair. Your spirit. And ravens are kind of mysterious in a tenebrous sort of way."

"Nice word. Tenebrous."

"Thanks. I've been saving it up for a special occasion."

"I guess I don't care if you call me that—Raven, I mean."

"So, in other words, you'd like it?"

"Someday those training wheels just might come off."

"I hope so."

"You know," she said, "you never did tell me the answer to my logic problem."

"Huh. I guess I didn't. The boy hadn't gone anywhere. He was right back in his own village because he'd headed in the wrong direction from the start."

"Yeah, well, you were too late on that one."

"It *was* pretty late," Christie agreed.

"Two against one," I said. "I guess you guys win."

"And it was double or nothing," Tessa reminded me helpfully. "Six weeks. That was the deal."

"Yeah, well, that first steak in August is gonna taste really good."

I took Christie's hand and I thought about what Tessa had told me the other night— that she would spend a year making up a puzzle if she needed to in order to keep her mom and me together.

It didn't look like that would be necessary, but it spoke to how much this girl loved her mother.

What about you?

Do you love Christie that much?

Honestly, I wasn't sure if I was ready to say that I loved her or not, but I *was* ready to start loving her.

And that was a good place to be.

Last week when I went to her apartment after leaving

the scene of Randy's suicide, I'd wondered if there was a grand scheme to things, a bigger plan at work.

Well, if there was, I couldn't think of anyone I'd rather uncover it with than this woman by my side.

"I thought of one," I said to her as we climbed into the car.

"A tongue twister?"

"In six weeks rich rare steaks."

Tessa groaned, Christie smiled and began to say it five times fast as we left to visit Tobin at the hospital.

100

Blake handed the glass of water to his bodyguard, Mannie, who was lying on the bed in the Bronx apartment where Blake had moved his things.

Wednesday night after they'd left the warehouse, he'd brought Mannie here and dug the two bullets out of his side with calipers, and then stitched the gunshot wounds back up with a sewing needle.

No sedative.

No anesthetic.

Mannie had only grimaced twice— once when Blake was digging around for the first bullet, and once when he was maneuvering the second one out and it scraped against one of his ribs.

"You're going to be alright," Blake told him. "We'll just give it a couple more days."

A quiet nod.

Then, while Mannie rested, Blake went into the other room where one of his silent ladies was holding his phone.

He removed it from her steady hand and put the call through to his contact at the Bureau, the person who'd gotten him access to the Federal Digital Database. They'd met in Los Angeles six years ago when he was still an undercover cop for the LAPD.

"Hello," the voice answered.

"Maria. It's Blake. We need to talk about Dr. Bowers."

"Go on. I'm listening."

No, the story wasn't over.

Not by a long shot.

One chapter had ended, but another, even bolder one, was about to begin.

SPECIAL THANKS TO

Brent Howard, Dr. John-Paul Abner, Brian Regli, Bob Hamer, Dr. D'Ovidio, Trinity and Eden Huhn, Pam Johnson, Ann and Steve Campbell, Dr. Todd Huhn, Liesl Huhn, J. J. Hensley, Dan Larsen, Andrew Young, Micah Haskins, Joe Taylor, Alan Rutledge, Dr. Rossmo, Justin Cockrell Amarilys and Carl Rassler